JANE BEL

The Last House on Halloween Street

When The Dead Come Knocking

Contents

One

Chapter 1: Fresh Start

arah pov

Sarah pov
The GPS died exactly three miles outside Hollow's End.

Sarah Brennan watched the screen flicker, pixels dissolving into static snow, then nothing. Just the gray-blue glow of a device that had given up. She tapped it twice—futile muscle memory from a life that had trained her to believe everything could be fixed with the right amount of persistence.

"Mom?" Lily's voice drifted from the backseat, edged with that particular pre-teen wariness that had become her default tone over the past six months. "Are we lost?"

"We're not lost, sweetheart. I know where we're going." Sarah kept her voice steady, performatively calm. The lie tasted familiar. She'd been telling versions of it since the divorce papers were finalized in July. *Everything's going to be fine. This is a fresh start. You'll love the new house.*

All lies built on the foundation of one truth: she had nowhere else to go.

Max pressed his face against the window, breath fogging the glass. At seven, he still possessed that unshakeable faith in maternal omniscience. "How much longer?"

"Ten minutes, baby."

The road narrowed as they descended into the valley. September had barely surrendered to October, yet the trees lining the route looked skeletal—branches reaching upward like exposed nerves, leaves absent or withered to brown husks that clung with stubborn desperation. Sarah's throat tightened. She'd researched Hollow's End obsessively after finding the listing: a historic coastal Massachusetts town, population 3,847, founded 1690, known for its preserved colonial architecture and picturesque autumn foliage.

The photographs had shown brilliant reds and golds, postcard-perfect New England autumn.

This looked like something had bled the color from the world.

"It's pretty," Lily said, in the tone of someone trying to convince herself. She was doing that a lot lately—manufacturing optimism to counterbalance Sarah's obvious desperation. Ten years old and already learning to parent her parent. The guilt was a familiar weight in Sarah's chest.

The town revealed itself gradually as they descended: white church steeple first, then clusters of colonial homes with dark shutters, a Main Street lined with brick storefronts. Quaint. Oppressively quaint. Jack-o'-lanterns already dotted porches even though October had barely begun, their carved grins too wide, too eager.

Sarah followed the hand-drawn map Robert Ashton had emailed—the realtor claimed his scanner was broken, which should have been the first red flag. The second was the price: a four-bedroom Victorian manor for less than her one-bedroom Boston apartment had cost annually. The third was how quickly he'd accepted her application, no credit check required, deposit waived.

But she'd been desperate. *Was* desperate. Past tense implied the desperation had ended.

They passed the town square where a bronze statue of colonial founders stood surrounded by dead grass. A banner stretched between two lampposts: HOLLOW'S END HARVEST MOON FESTIVAL - OCTOBER 31ST. Someone had already decorated the statue's base with cornstalks and pumpkins, though the pumpkins looked soft with rot, collapsing inward on themselves.

"Are we going to the Halloween festival?" Max's enthusiasm cut through Sarah's unease. At least one of them was still capable of joy.

"Maybe, sweetheart. We'll see."

She turned onto Maple Street, then Birch, following Ashton's directions. The neighborhoods grew sparser, houses set farther apart, the spaces between them filled with dense woods that seemed to lean inward. Then she saw the street sign, half-hidden behind overgrown branches:

HALLOWEEN STREET

Of course it was.

"Spooky name," Lily observed.

The street was a dead end—literally, terminating in a cul-de-sac bordered by forest so thick it looked impenetrable. Only five houses dotted the lane, each separated by acres of overgrown property. The asphalt was cracked and buckled, weeds pushing through in patterns that looked almost deliberate, almost like reaching fingers.

And the trees. God, the trees.

Every tree on Halloween Street was dead. Not autumn-bare, but genuinely dead—bark blackened as if by fire or disease, branches twisted into arthritic angles. No leaves clung to them, not even dead ones. They stood like sentinels marking a boundary into somewhere fundamentally *wrong*.

"Why are the trees like that?" Max's voice had gone small.

"Probably some kind of blight," Sarah said, hating how unconvincing she sounded. "A disease. They'll plant new ones."

The houses they passed were occupied—she could see curtains, cars in driveways, the detritus of human life—but something about them felt abandoned anyway. No children played in the yards. No one sat on their porches despite the mild afternoon. The jack-o'-lanterns on these porches weren't grinning. They were screaming.

Then she saw it: the last house on Halloween Street.

Sarah's breath caught despite herself.

The Victorian manor stood three stories tall, crowned with a widow's walk and a turret that jutted from the northeast corner like an accusing finger. White paint—or what had once been white—had weathered to the gray of old bone. The wraparound porch was supported by columns carved with symbols Sarah didn't recognize: geometric patterns that hurt to look at directly, like optical illusions designed to induce vertigo.

But it was *big*. Room for the kids to have separate bedrooms, space for a home office, a yard where Max could play. Everything they'd lost when David had kept the house in Newton, kept everything, really, except his court-mandated child support payments that barely covered groceries.

"It looks haunted," Lily said.

"It looks like it needs some paint," Sarah corrected, pulling into the gravel driveway. "And maybe some landscaping. But it's *ours*."

A black Mercedes sat parked near the porch—Robert Ashton's car. The realtor stood waiting, checking his watch with theatrical impatience. He was a soft man in an expensive suit, face flushed and perpetually damp, as if he were always either arriving from or departing toward somewhere more important.

Sarah killed the engine. The sudden silence felt dense, textured. She could hear wind moving through the dead trees, a sound like whispered warnings.

"Remember," she said, turning to face her children, "this is our adventure. Our fresh start. I know things have been hard, but this is going to be good. I promise."

Lily's expression said she'd heard that promise before and stopped believing it. Max just nodded, trusting.

They climbed out. The air smelled wrong—not quite rot, not quite chemical, but something in between. Like meat left too long in a refrigerator, or flowers decaying in a vase of stagnant water.

"Mrs. Brennan!" Robert Ashton's voice was too loud, too jovial. He descended the porch steps with aggressive cheer, hand extended. "Right on time! Well, nearly on time. I was beginning to worry—cell service can be spotty out here. And GPS has a tendency to—" He made a vague gesture, as if technology's failure was both expected and mildly amusing.

Sarah shook his hand. His palm was slick with sweat. "We found it fine."

"Wonderful, wonderful!" He was already moving back toward the house, keys jangling. "Let me show you around. I know you saw the photos, but pictures really don't do the place justice. Built in 1892 by the Kane family— very prominent locally, very wealthy. The craftsmanship is extraordinary.

Original hardwood, original fixtures, most of the original furniture included in the sale..."

He was talking too fast, words tumbling over each other. Sarah followed him up the porch steps, Lily and Max flanking her like uncertain sentries. The porch boards creaked under their weight—not the healthy groan of old wood, but something that sounded almost pained.

Ashton fumbled with the lock. "Key sticks a bit. Just needs some WD-40, nothing serious..."

The door swung inward on hinges that shrieked.

The interior was dim despite the afternoon sun—high ceilings and dark wood absorbed light rather than reflecting it. The entryway opened into a grand foyer with a sweeping staircase that curved upward into shadow. To the left, a parlor with furniture draped in white sheets, ghostly shapes in the gloom. To the right, a formal dining room with a table set for twelve, china gathering dust, as if the Kane family had simply stood and walked away mid-meal.

"How long has it been empty?" Sarah asked.

"Three years," Ashton said quickly. "Previous tenants had to relocate for work. Very sudden. They left most of their belongings, as you can see. Saves you the trouble of furnishing!"

He was lying. Sarah had spent enough time in courtrooms watching David's lawyer lie to recognize the tells: the quick blink, the slight uptick in pitch, the way Ashton's hand went to his collar as if his tie was too tight.

Max had already broken away, drawn to the parlor. "Mom, look at the fireplace!"

It was indeed impressive—a marble monstrosity carved with more of those geometric symbols, the hearth large enough to stand in. Above it hung a portrait: a Victorian family in formal dress. A stern-faced man with dark eyes and a severe expression. A beautiful woman with haunted eyes and a rigid smile. Between them, a young boy, perhaps six, staring directly at the viewer with unsettling intensity.

"The Kane family," Ashton said, appearing at Sarah's elbow. "Previous owners felt it would be disrespectful to remove it. Part of the house's history."

The boy in the portrait looked eerily like Max. Same dark curls, same delicate features, same wide eyes. Sarah's skin prickled.

"Let me show you the kitchen!" Ashton was already moving, desperate to keep the tour momentum going.

The kitchen was massive—restaurant-grade appliances from the 1960s, butcher-block counters, a breakfast nook with windows overlooking the backyard. Which was a tangle of dead rosebushes surrounding a stone birdbath filled with black water.

"Needs some gardening," Ashton admitted, "but the bones are good!"

He rushed them through the first floor: a library with floor-to-ceiling bookshelves and leather furniture, a sunroom where no sun seemed to reach, a bathroom with a clawfoot tub and fixtures that looked like tarnished surgical instruments.

"And here's the basement access—" Ashton gestured to a door beneath the staircase, then immediately pivoted. "But let's see the bedrooms first, shall we? The second floor is really where this house shines."

Sarah noticed he didn't open the basement door.

Upstairs, the hallway stretched longer than physics should allow, doors lining both sides. Ashton showed them the master bedroom first—enormous, with a four-poster bed that could sleep four, an adjoining bathroom, and windows that looked out over Halloween Street's dead trees.

"Lily, Max, pick your rooms!" Ashton's enthusiasm sounded increasingly forced.

The children disappeared down the hallway, doors opening and closing. Sarah heard Lily's gasp of delight—probably the room with the window seat. Max's excited shout suggested he'd found something equally appealing.

Sarah turned to Ashton. "Why is it so cheap?"

His smile faltered. "I'm sorry?"

"This house. This neighborhood. Why is the rent a third of market value?"

"Well." He tugged his collar. "Hollow's End isn't exactly a hot market. Limited job opportunities, aging population, young people moving to Boston—"

"Mr. Ashton."

He met her eyes, and for just a moment, she saw something flicker in his expression. Guilt? Fear?

"Mrs. Brennan, I'm not going to lie to you—"

"That would be refreshing."

"—the house has a... reputation. Locally. You know how small towns are, ghost stories, folklore. The Kane family died here in the 1960s under tragic circumstances. Some people are superstitious." He shrugged, attempting dismissive. "But that's all it is. Superstition. The house is structurally sound, mechanically updated, perfectly safe. You seem like a practical woman. I didn't think ghost stories would bother you."

"They don't," Sarah said. "I don't believe in ghosts."

"Good. Excellent. Then we're all set!" He pulled the keys from his pocket, pressed them into her hand. His fingers were ice-cold despite the warmth of the day. "One month free rent while you settle in, first payment November first. I've emailed you all the documentation. If you need anything—anything at all—call me. Anytime."

He was already moving toward the stairs.

"Mr. Ashton—"

He paused halfway down, not turning. "Yes?"

"Is there anything else I should know?"

For a long moment, he stood frozen. Sarah heard her children's voices from down the hall, Lily explaining to Max which room would be whose. Normal sounds. Safe sounds.

When Ashton spoke, his voice had dropped to barely above a whisper:

"Don't answer the door after sunset on Halloween night."

Sarah blinked. "What?"

He turned then, smile fixed back in place, professional mask restored. "Just a local tradition! Halloween in Hollow's End can get a bit... enthusiastic. Teenagers playing pranks, that sort of thing. Better to keep the lights off, avoid encouraging them. Have a wonderful first night, Mrs. Brennan!"

He practically fled down the stairs. Sarah heard the front door open, close, the Mercedes engine roar to life. Gravel crunched as he drove away too fast.

She stood alone in the hallway of her new house, keys cutting into her palm.

"Mom! Come see my room!" Max's joy was untainted, pure.

Sarah moved down the hallway, forcing a smile. Max had chosen the room at the end—bright despite the afternoon waning, with built-in shelves and a window overlooking the backyard. He was already planning where his toys would go, which shelf for his books, could he paint the walls blue?

Lily's room was across the hall, larger, with the window seat Sarah had predicted. "It's perfect," Lily said, and almost meant it.

They spent the next hour unloading the car—not much, Sarah had sold most of their furniture to cover deposits and moving costs. Suitcases and boxes, the detritus of a collapsed life compressed into a dozen containers.

By the time they finished, sunset was bleeding across the horizon, turning the sky the color of a healing bruise. Sarah ordered pizza—the delivery driver refused to come to the door, leaving it at the end of the driveway with a mumbled excuse about his car acting up.

They ate in the kitchen, Max chattering about his new room, Lily quieter but engaged. Normal. This could be normal.

After dinner, Sarah helped them settle into bed—Max in his new room with his favorite stuffed dinosaur, Lily with her book and reading lamp. She kissed them both, promised tomorrow they'd explore the town, find the good playground, the library.

Then she returned to the master bedroom to unpack her own things.

The room was darker now, shadows pooling in corners. Sarah turned on the overhead light—a crystal chandelier that provided surprising little illumination—and began hanging clothes in the massive wardrobe.

She was reaching for another dress when she noticed it.

The bedroom door had a lock.

But the lock was on the *outside*.

Sarah stood frozen, hand still extended toward the wardrobe. She stared at the door, at the heavy iron bolt mounted on the exterior frame, at the keyhole beneath it.

Not a bathroom door child-lock. Not a privacy latch. A *bolt*. The kind meant to keep something in.

Or someone.

Her rational mind scrambled for explanations: historic houses had different conventions, maybe it was original to the home, maybe the Kanes had repurposed a different kind of room—

But her hindbrain, the part that still remembered being prey, whispered the truth: this room was designed to be a cell.

From somewhere deep in the house—the basement, she thought, though sound traveled strangely here—she heard it:

Three distinct knocks.

Deliberate. Patient. Waiting.

Sarah's breath caught. She stood perfectly still, listening.

Silence.

Then, so faint she might have imagined it, a sound like children singing. A nursery rhyme she almost recognized, the melody distorted, the words swallowed by distance and time.

Don't answer the door after sunset on Halloween night.

It was October first.

Thirty days until Halloween.

Sarah turned off the light and climbed into the enormous bed, pulling the covers to her chin like armor against the dark.

From outside, wind moved through the dead trees of Halloween Street, and in that wind, she could almost hear laughter.

Childish. Delighted. Wrong.

She closed her eyes and told herself, one more time:

Everything is going to be fine.

But even Sarah Brennan, professional liar to herself, had stopped believing it.

Two

Chapter 2: The House Remembers

arah pov

S The house settled around them like a living thing finding its preferred position.

Sarah told herself that's all it was—old wood contracting in the October chill, foundation stones shifting after decades of weight, the natural sounds of a Victorian manor adjusting to new occupants. She'd read about this online during the frantic week of packing: historic homes had personalities, the real estate blogs promised. Character. Charm. *Quirks that became endearing once you understood them.*

None of those cheerful articles mentioned how a house could sound like it was *breathing*.

She stood in the kitchen—her kitchen now, though the word felt presumptuous—unpacking boxes by the yellow glow of a single overhead bulb. The other fixtures didn't work yet. Tucker Davis, the handyman Robert Ashton had recommended, wasn't available until tomorrow. Something about not working after dark. She'd thought it was a joke about overtime rates.

Now, listening to the house exhale through gaps in the floorboards, she wondered.

"Mom?" Lily appeared in the doorway, her ten-year-old face pale in the insufficient light. "Max says he hears singing."

Sarah set down the stack of plates she'd been unwrapping. "Singing?"

"From the basement." Lily's voice carried that particular tone Sarah had learned to recognize over the past six months—the one that meant her daughter was trying very hard to sound braver than she felt. "He says it's a lady singing a lullaby."

The basement. Sarah had only glanced down there during Robert's rushed tour—stone steps descending into darkness, a smell of damp earth and something else. Something that reminded her of the funeral home where her mother's viewing had been held. Flowers trying to mask decay.

She found Max in his new bedroom, sitting cross-legged on his race car bedspread, head tilted like a dog hearing a distant whistle.

"Hey, buddy." Sarah kept her voice light, casual. "Lily says you're hearing music?"

Max didn't look at her. His seven-year-old face held an expression she'd never seen before—not quite afraid, but listening with such intensity that it frightened her more than tears would have.

"It's coming from the water," he said. "The singing. She's down in the water and she wants someone to hear her."

Sarah's mouth went dry. "Max, there's no water in the basement."

"Yes, there is." Now he looked at her, his brown eyes too knowing, too certain. "There's a well. And she's down there. She's been down there for a really long time, Mom. She's so tired of singing."

"Who told you about a well?"

"Ben did."

"Who's Ben?"

For the first time, Max smiled. It didn't reach his eyes. "My new friend. He lives here too. He says we're going to be best friends because we look the same."

Sarah felt ice crystallize in her chest. "Max, there's no one else in this house."

"I know." Max returned his attention to the wall, head tilting again. "Ben's not *in* the house. He *is* the house. He's been waiting for me."

11

After settling Max into bed—a process that took three stories, two glasses of water, and a promise to leave the hallway light on—Sarah found Lily in the second-floor corridor. Her daughter stood before a door Sarah hadn't noticed during the tour. How was that possible? The hallway only had four doors: master bedroom, Max's room, Lily's room, bathroom. This door made five.

"It was locked before," Lily said without preamble. "I tried it this afternoon. But now..."

The door stood slightly ajar. Not open, but no longer latched. As if something inside had pushed from within.

"Lily, go to your room."

"Mom—"

"Now."

Her daughter obeyed, but Sarah felt those eyes on her back as she approached the door. The brass knob was cold enough to sting her palm. She pushed.

The door swung open on silent hinges—too silent, too smooth for a house this old—and revealed a nursery frozen in time.

Powder blue walls. White furniture with delicate scrollwork. A mobile of hand-carved wooden animals hanging motionless above a crib. Shelves lined with toys that should have looked cheerful but instead seemed watchful: a rocking horse with black glass eyes, tin soldiers in neat rows, a porcelain doll with golden ringlets and a smile that didn't match the expression in its painted face.

Everything was pristine. No dust. No cobwebs. As if someone had cleaned this room yesterday. As if someone still cared for it.

A record player sat on a small table, its brass horn catching the hallway light. Sarah stepped closer, fighting the urge to turn and run. The record on the turntable looked vintage—a black vinyl disc with a faded label she couldn't quite read in the dimness.

Her hand moved of its own accord, fingers finding the crank.

Don't, something whispered in her mind. *Don't wind it. Don't make it sing.*

She wound it anyway. Three full turns.

The mechanism engaged with a series of clicks. The turntable began to spin. The brass horn trembled.

Then: music. Thin and wavering, like a voice filtered through water and decades. A woman singing a lullaby Sarah almost recognized, the words just slightly wrong, the melody half a step off from familiar.

Hush little baby, don't you cry
Mama's going to sing you a lullaby
And if that lullaby won't soothe
Mama's going to hide you where he can't choose
And if that hiding place ain't deep
Mama's going to send you off to sleep
So sleep, my darling, sleep down low
Where the water's dark and the roses grow

The song ended. The record continued spinning in silence.

Then, from behind her, a child's voice: "That's my mommy singing."

Sarah spun. The doorway was empty. The hallway beyond stood vacant, but she could have sworn—

A boy. Just for a second. Standing in the shadows where light couldn't quite reach. About Max's age, Max's height, wearing clothes from another era. She'd seen him. She'd *seen* him.

The record player emitted a sharp crack. The vinyl had split down the middle, rendering it useless.

Sarah ran from the room.

She found the attic access at midnight.

Sleep was impossible. Every time she closed her eyes, she heard that lullaby with its wrong words, its drowning melody. Max was right—there *was* singing from somewhere in the house. Or the house was making her remember singing. Or she was losing her mind after six months of divorce proceedings and shame and starting over in a town where she knew no one.

The pull-down ladder creaked as she climbed. Her phone's flashlight carved a weak cone through the darkness above.

The attic smelled of mothballs and old paper and that same funeral home sweetness. Boxes crowded the sloped space, stacked with archaeological precision. Sarah made her way between them, hunched under the low ceiling, until her light caught something that made her stop.

Photographs. Dozens of them, in ornate frames, arranged on a cedar chest like a shrine.

She knelt, phone trembling in her grip.

The first photo showed a family of three posed on the front porch. A man with severe features and cold eyes. A woman whose beauty was undermined by the terror barely hidden in her smile. And a boy—maybe six years old— who looked exactly like Max. The same cowlick. The same slight gap between his front teeth. The same spattering of freckles across his nose.

Sarah's fingers found the frame's backing. A label in faded ink: *Kane Family, October 1962. Victor, Eleanor, Benjamin.*

Benjamin Kane. The boy who lived here before. The boy Max called Ben.

She forced herself to examine more photographs. Benjamin on a tricycle. Benjamin with a birthday cake. Benjamin in the backyard, standing beside dead rose bushes, his smile not quite reaching his eyes.

Benjamin floating face-down in dark water, his small hands spread like starfish, his hair drifting—

Sarah gasped and dropped the photo. It clattered against the floor. When she picked it up again, hands shaking, the image showed Benjamin in a Halloween costume. Just a little boy dressed as a ghost.

She'd imagined the drowning photo. Stress. Exhaustion. The power of suggestion after Max's comment about water.

But when she tilted the frame, she could see the image underneath the costume photo. A darker photograph, hidden beneath. She could make out the edge of what looked like a well, and small fingers gripping its stone rim.

He's been waiting for me, Max had said.

Sarah shoved the photographs back onto the chest and retreated toward the ladder, her breath coming in shallow gasps. The attic suddenly felt smaller, the shadows between boxes deeper and more deliberate. As if something was rearranging itself in the darkness just beyond her phone's reach.

As if the house was deciding how much to show her.

14

How much she could handle on the first night.

The digital clock on her nightstand read 3:32 AM when Sarah finally surrendered to exhaustion. She'd checked on both children three times. Max slept deeply, unnaturally still. Lily tossed and murmured, drawing invisible pictures in her sleep.

The house had gone quiet. Even the breathing sounds had stopped. Sarah took it as a good sign.

She was wrong.

At 3:33 AM exactly, every clock in the house stopped.

Sarah woke to absolute silence—the kind that pressed against eardrums, that felt like being underwater. She fumbled for her phone. Dead. The nightstand clock's display was dark. Her watch had stopped, hands frozen at 3:33.

Then: *knock knock knock.*

Three deliberate raps. Not from the hallway. Not from the window.

From inside her room.

Sarah's breath caught. She'd locked the bedroom door. She'd checked it twice, still paranoid from the divorce, from the months of David letting himself into their house whenever he wanted, taking what he claimed was his, disrupting the fragile peace she'd tried to build for the children.

The lock was on the outside of the door.

She'd noticed it during Robert's tour, thought it strange but didn't question it. Old houses had odd modifications. Maybe a previous owner had a sleepwalking problem. Maybe—

Knock knock knock.

Closer this time. On the door itself. From the inside of the room.

Sarah's hand found the lamp, switching it on. Nothing happened. The bulb was dead, or the power was out, or the house had decided she should face this in darkness.

She grabbed her phone—still dead, impossible—and held it like a weapon. "Who's there?" Her voice cracked. "Lily? Max?"

Knock knock knock.

Right behind her.

Sarah whirled. The door stood closed, locked from outside. The windows were shut. She was alone in the room.

Except she wasn't.

The temperature dropped so suddenly she could see her breath. The darkness seemed to thicken, to take on texture and weight. And standing in the corner where shadow pooled deepest, where moonlight from the window somehow couldn't reach—

A woman in a white nightgown, hair long and dark and wet, face obscured by the angle and the darkness and perhaps by mercy.

The woman raised one hand. Pointed at the door.

Then she opened her mouth, and Sarah saw the black thread. Crude stitches running through the woman's lips, sealing them shut, the flesh around them swollen and discolored even after—how many years? How many decades of trying to scream warnings through a sewn mouth?

The woman in white pointed at the door again. More insistent.

Sarah understood. *Get out. Take your children. Leave before—*

The figure vanished.

The lights blazed back to life.

Sarah's phone chirped, powering on, showing 3:34 AM.

The bedroom door's lock clicked open from the outside.

She sat there in the sudden brightness, shaking, as the house resumed its breathing. In the hallway, she heard Lily's door creak open.

"Mom?" Her daughter's voice, small and frightened. "Mom, I had a bad dream. I saw a lady in a white dress and her mouth was—"

Sarah was already moving, gathering Lily, checking on Max, her mind racing through logistics. They'd leave in the morning. First light. Pack what they could, abandon the rest. Drive to Melissa's in Connecticut. Figure it out later.

But when she tried Melissa's number, it went straight to voicemail.

When she tried her mother's old friend in town, no answer.

When she called the Hollow's End Police Department, a recorded message informed her the office opened at 8 AM.

16

She pulled up directions to the nearest hotel. Her phone's GPS couldn't locate Halloween Street. The map showed their address as a blank space, a gap in the grid where the house should be but somehow wasn't.

Sarah checked the front door. Locked from inside, but when she tried to unlock it, the mechanism wouldn't budge. The key turned uselessly in the old lock.

She tried the back door. The same.

The windows in the parlor. They'd open three inches and no further, as if painted shut, though she could see no paint.

They were locked in.

The house had shown her a warning. The house had let her see just enough to be afraid.

And now the house wasn't letting them leave.

Sarah gathered both children into the master bedroom, pushed furniture against the door, and waited for morning. Lily fell asleep against her shoulder. Max stared at the wall with that too-knowing expression, humming a tune Sarah didn't recognize at first.

Then she did.

The lullaby from the nursery. The one about hiding where he can't choose. The one about sleeping down low where the water's dark.

"Max, honey, where did you learn that song?"

"Ben taught me." Max smiled without looking at her. "He says tomorrow I get to see the well. He says it's really deep and really dark and Eleanor's still down there. He says if I'm very good, very quiet, I can hear her singing even without the record player."

"Who's Eleanor?"

"Ben's mommy." Max's eyes finally shifted to meet hers, and in them Sarah saw something that didn't belong in a seven-year-old's gaze. Knowledge. History. Tragedy that had soaked into the walls and floorboards and was now seeping into her son like water into dry earth.

"She tried to save him," Max whispered. "But the daddy wouldn't let her. So the daddy put her in the water and put Ben in the water and then the daddy went away too. And now they're all here forever, Mom. All of them. Waiting."

17

"Waiting for what?"

Max's smile widened. "For us. They've been waiting for a family that looks like them. Lily looks like Eleanor. I look like Ben. And you…"

He paused, tilting his head, listening to something Sarah couldn't hear.

"The daddy says you look like someone who'll understand. Someone who knows what it's like when you can't protect your babies. Someone who's already lost everything once and will do *anything* not to lose it again."

"Max, stop it. You're scaring me."

"I'm not trying to scare you, Mom." His voice was his own again, small and confused. "I'm just telling you what Ben tells me. He says we're home now. He says we're exactly where we're supposed to be."

He yawned, curling against her other side.

"He says it'll all make sense on Halloween. When the dead come knocking."

Outside, the October wind picked up, rattling windows, sending dead leaves scraping across the porch like fingernails testing for weaknesses.

Three blocks away, Hannah Winters stood in her darkened kitchen, staring toward the house at the end of Halloween Street. The lights were on in the master bedroom. The new family was awake.

She picked up her phone. Put it down. Picked it up again.

She should warn them. Tell them what happens when you stay past the first week. Explain about the knocking, the well, the ritual. Give them the choice Eleanor never had.

But if she warned them and they left, the house would need another family. And another. And eventually, one of those families would have a daughter who looked like Hannah's own daughter. Gone now. Taken by the well in 1987 when Hannah made the mistake of refusing.

The Collectors had promised her that participating just once would end it. They'd lied.

Hannah put the phone away.

"I'm sorry," she whispered to the darkness, to the house at the end of the street, to the mother who'd just realized her new home was a trap. "I'm so sorry. But better you than me. Better your children than my memories."

She drew the curtains and tried not to listen for the singing that would start soon.

It always started on the second night.

When the house decided you were worth keeping.

Three

Chapter 3: The Neighbor

⤜᪣⤝

S *arah pov*

 The knock came at precisely ten o'clock in the morning, three sharp raps that seemed to echo through the house longer than they should have. Sarah paused in the middle of unpacking kitchen boxes, her hands buried in crumpled newspaper, and felt an inexplicable chill crawl up her spine.

It was just a knock. Neighbors did this. Brought casseroles, introduced themselves, welcomed newcomers to the street. Normal, mundane, utterly unremarkable.

So why did her heart rate spike?

"I'll get it!" Lily called from somewhere upstairs, her footsteps thundering toward the staircase.

"No—wait, I've got it," Sarah said, wiping her hands on her jeans and moving quickly toward the foyer. She didn't know why she felt the sudden, urgent need to reach the door first, to position herself between her children and whoever stood on the other side. Maternal instinct, maybe. Or something deeper, some animal awareness that had awakened the moment they'd crossed the threshold of this house two days ago.

The woman on the porch was perhaps sixty, with steel-gray hair pulled into a neat bun and a face that might have been kind if not for the calculating sharpness in her pale blue eyes. She wore a cardigan despite the unseasonable warmth of early October, and she held a casserole dish wrapped in a checkered kitchen towel like an offering.

"Sarah Brennan?" The woman's smile didn't quite reach her eyes. "I'm Hannah Winters. I live three houses down—the yellow colonial with the black shutters. Thought I'd bring you something for dinner. Moving is exhausting, especially with little ones."

"That's very kind of you." Sarah accepted the dish, heavy and still warm, and stepped back. "Would you like to come in? I'm afraid the place is still a disaster, but I can make coffee—"

"I'd love to." Hannah was already crossing the threshold before Sarah finished the sentence, moving with a strange familiarity, as if she'd walked through this door many times before. Her gaze swept the foyer, the partially unpacked boxes, the furniture still draped in moving blankets, and something flickered across her face. Relief? Disappointment? It vanished too quickly to identify.

Sarah led her toward the kitchen, hyper-aware of the older woman's presence behind her, the soft click of her sensible shoes on the hardwood floors. The house felt different with Hannah inside it—smaller, somehow, as if the walls were contracting.

"It's a beautiful home," Hannah said, but her voice carried no conviction. "You got quite a deal on it, I imagine. Robert Ashton can be very... motivated when he has the right property."

Sarah set the casserole on the counter and turned to face her guest. "He did mention it had been empty for a while. Three years, I think he said?"

"Three years, two months, and sixteen days." Hannah's precision was unsettling. "Not that anyone's counting."

The kitchen window framed a view of the backyard—the tangle of dead rosebushes, the ancient oak tree with its motionless swing, the fence line where the property dissolved into shadow even in daylight. Hannah's gaze drifted toward it, and her expression hardened into something unreadable.

"Mom!" Max barreled into the kitchen, Superman cape flying behind him, and skidded to a stop when he saw Hannah. His smile faltered. "Oh. Hi."

"And you must be Max." Hannah's warmth seemed genuine now, though something about it felt performative, like an actress hitting her mark. "My goodness, what a handsome boy. How old are you, sweetheart?"

"Seven." Max edged closer to Sarah, his small hand finding hers. "We just moved here. From the city."

"I know, darling. We all know." Hannah's eyes never left Max's face, studying him with an intensity that made Sarah's protective instincts flare. "You look so much like—" She stopped abruptly, lips pressing together as if physically restraining the words.

"Like who?" Sarah asked, her voice sharper than intended.

"No one. Just a thought." Hannah's smile was apologetic, dismissive. "Old age makes you see resemblances everywhere. Ghosts of the past in every face." She laughed, but the sound was hollow.

Lily appeared in the doorway, her sketchbook clutched to her chest, dark hair falling across her face. She'd been quiet since the move, spending hours drawing in the corners of rooms, speaking in monosyllables. The divorce had hit her harder than Max, who bounced back with the resilience of the very young.

"Lily, honey, this is Mrs. Winters. She's our neighbor."

Lily raised her eyes, assessing Hannah with the brutal honesty of a ten-year-old. "You don't like this house."

Hannah's composure cracked, just for an instant. "What makes you say that, dear?"

"Your hands are shaking." Lily gestured with her pencil. "And you keep looking at the basement door like something's going to come out of it."

Sarah followed her daughter's gaze. Hannah had indeed been staring at the basement door—that heavy oak barrier they'd found locked with a padlock the first day, the one Tucker Davis would be coming to open later this week. Hannah's knuckles were white where she gripped the edge of the counter.

"Lily, that's rude—"

"No, no, she's perceptive." Hannah released the counter, flexing her fingers. "You're right, sweetie. This house and I have... history. Not good history. But that doesn't mean it can't be different for you. Fresh start, clean slate. That's what your mother wants, isn't it?"

The way she said it made Sarah's skin prickle. How much did this woman know about her life? About the divorce, the reasons they'd fled Boston, the desperate need for somewhere—anywhere—affordable and far from her ex-husband's lawyers?

"Coffee?" Sarah offered again, needing something to do with her hands.

"Please."

As Sarah busied herself with the ancient coffeemaker—one of the few appliances the previous owners had left behind—Hannah wandered toward the kitchen table where Lily had spread out her drawings. Sarah watched from the corner of her eye as the older woman studied them, her face growing progressively paler.

"You're very talented, Lily." Hannah's voice had thinned, gone reedy. "These are quite... detailed."

Lily shrugged. "I draw what I see."

"What you see?" Hannah picked up one of the sketches—the one Lily had drawn last night, the one Sarah had found disturbing enough to hide in a drawer before unpacking it again this morning. "You saw this?"

It was a family portrait of sorts: a man, a woman, and a small boy. But they were underwater, bubbles streaming from their open mouths, hair floating upward, eyes wide and glassy. The detail was extraordinary—the way the woman's dress billowed, the boy's outstretched hand, the man's face twisted in something between rage and despair.

"In my dream," Lily said matter-of-factly. "They live here. In the walls, maybe. Or under the floor. They're very sad."

Hannah set the drawing down with trembling hands. When she looked at Sarah, her eyes were bright with unshed tears. "How long have you been having these dreams?"

"Since we moved in. The first night."

"Mrs. Winters," Sarah interrupted, abandoning the coffee to stand between Hannah and her daughter, "if there's something we should know about this house—"

23

"There's always something to know about old houses." Hannah's composure was rebuilding itself, brick by brick. "History. Memories. The past doesn't leave quietly, especially not in Hollow's End. This town holds onto things. Sometimes too tightly."

"That's not an answer."

"No. It's a warning." Hannah moved toward the foyer, her earlier friendliness evaporating. "Keep salt lines at your doorways. Don't leave windows open at night. And—" She paused at the basement door, placing one hand flat against it. The gesture was almost reverent, or perhaps fearful. "Don't go down there after dark. The basement… it has a way of keeping what goes into it."

"What does that mean?" Sarah followed her, frustration building. "Mrs. Winters, if you know something—"

"I know that every family who's lived here has left. Quickly. Quietly. Except the ones who didn't leave at all." Hannah's hand dropped from the door as if burned. "I know that this street has a reputation. That Halloween Street isn't just a name—it's a description. A warning. A promise."

"A promise of what?"

"That the veil is thinnest here. Always has been. Even in July, even in March, there are… thin places in this house. Places where the dead get closer than they should." Hannah was moving faster now, heading for the front door with the single-minded determination of someone fleeing. "But in October? As we get closer to All Hallows' Eve? The house wakes up. It remembers."

Sarah grabbed her arm, forcing Hannah to stop. "Remembers what?"

"What it's owed."

The words hung in the air between them, incomprehensible and terrifying. Outside, the afternoon sun was beginning its descent, shadows lengthening across the overgrown lawn. Hannah glanced at the grandfather clock in the hallway—stopped at 3:33 like every other clock in the house—and genuine fear crossed her face.

"I have to go. Before sunset." She pulled free of Sarah's grasp. "Listen to me, Sarah. I don't know you, and you have no reason to trust me, but I'm going to say this anyway: Get your children out of this house. Sell it, abandon it, burn it down if you have to. But don't stay here through Halloween."

"Why? What happens on Halloween?"

Hannah was at the door now, hand on the knob. She looked back, and in the fading light, she looked ancient, haunted, carrying the weight of terrible knowledge.

"The dead come knocking," she whispered. "And if you answer... if you let them in... they don't leave. They never leave."

She was gone before Sarah could respond, the door slamming shut with a finality that felt like punctuation. Through the window, Sarah watched Hannah practically run to her car, a silver Honda parked at the curb. The woman didn't look back, didn't slow down, just climbed into the driver's seat and pulled away with the urgency of someone escaping a burning building.

"She was scared," Lily said from the kitchen doorway.

Sarah turned to find both children watching her, their young faces serious, absorbing the adult anxiety they weren't supposed to notice. She forced a smile that felt like it might crack her face.

"She was just... eccentric. Old people get strange ideas about things." Even as she said it, Sarah didn't believe it. Hannah Winters hadn't been eccentric. She'd been terrified.

"Mom?" Max's voice was small. "Why did she say the dead come knocking?"

"It's just a Halloween thing, buddy. You know, ghosts and goblins and—"

"But it's only October third," Lily interrupted. "Halloween is almost a month away. Why would she warn us now if it's just about Halloween?"

Because it's not just about Halloween, Sarah thought but didn't say. Because something is very, very wrong with this house, and I just spent our last dollar on the down payment, and we have nowhere else to go.

"I'm sure it's nothing," she lied.

But that night, after the children were asleep, Sarah stood in the kitchen and stared at the basement door. In the darkness, she could almost convince herself she heard something from beyond it—not quite knocking, not quite scratching, but something rhythmic and deliberate. Something that wanted out.

Or wanted in.

She thought about Hannah's white-knuckled grip on the counter, the way she'd touched the basement door like it might bite her, the tears in her eyes when she'd seen Lily's drawing. The family underwater. Drowning.

Sarah pulled out her phone and googled "Halloween Street Hollow's End Massachusetts history."

The results were sparse. A few real estate listings. Some historical society mentions of the street's construction in 1890. And then, buried three pages deep, a newspaper article from 1963:

TRAGEDY ON HALLOWEEN STREET: LOCAL FAMILY FOUND DEAD

The accompanying photo showed the house. Her house. The same Victorian facade, the same wraparound porch, the same turret windows. But in the black-and-white image, it looked different somehow—more alive, perhaps, or more malevolent. The caption read: *Kane family residence, where Victor Kane, 42, was found dead from a self-inflicted gunshot wound. His son, Benjamin, 7, drowned in the basement well. Wife Eleanor, 38, remains missing.*

Benjamin, seven years old. The same age as Max.

Who looked just like him, according to Hannah's unfinished sentence.

Sarah's hand shook as she enlarged the photo, trying to see into the windows, as if the house might reveal its secrets across sixty years of separation. But the windows were dark, reflecting nothing but the photographer's flash.

From upstairs came a soft thump, then Lily's voice, muffled but audible: "It's okay, Ben. She didn't mean to scare you. My mom's nice. You'll see."

Sarah took the stairs two at a time, her heart hammering. Lily's door was cracked open, a sliver of hallway light falling across her daughter's bed. Lily was sitting up, eyes open but glassy, staring at the corner of the room.

"Lily?" Sarah pushed the door open wider. "Who are you talking to?"

"Ben. He says he's sorry about earlier. About the knocking. He just wanted to say hello." Lily's voice had the dreamy quality of sleep-talking, but her eyes were fixed on something Sarah couldn't see. "He's been alone for so long. He's happy we're here. He's happy Max looks like him. It makes him feel less lonely."

"Lily, wake up." Sarah shook her daughter gently, then more firmly. "Lily!"

Lily blinked, focus returning to her eyes. She looked up at Sarah, confused. "What's wrong?"

"You were talking in your sleep. About someone named Ben."

"Oh." Lily lay back down, pulling the covers to her chin. "He's not scary, Mom. He's just sad. He wants his mother back, but she's in the water. Under the ground. He can hear her crying sometimes."

Sarah's blood turned to ice. "Honey, there's no one here. It was just a dream."

"Maybe." Lily's eyes were already closing, sleep reclaiming her. "But he says to tell you that Mrs. Winters is right. Don't answer the door on Halloween. No matter what you hear. No matter whose voice it is. Because the people who knock aren't always the people they used to be."

Sarah sat on the edge of the bed until Lily's breathing deepened into genuine sleep, then she walked to the corner where Lily had been staring. There was nothing there—just wallpaper and baseboard and the junction of two walls.

But the air was cold. Colder than the rest of the room. And when Sarah's breath misted in front of her face, she could have sworn she smelled water. Not clean water, but the thick, mineral smell of a well left too long untended.

She backed out of the room and stood in the hallway, listening to the house settle around her. Every creak sounded like footsteps. Every sigh of old wood sounded like breathing.

From the kitchen, three floors below, came the sound she'd been dreading: three deliberate knocks, evenly spaced, impossibly loud.

But there was no one at the door.

The knocking was coming from inside the basement.

Sarah stood frozen at the top of the stairs, her phone clutched in one hand, Hannah Winters' warning echoing in her mind: *Don't go down there after dark. The basement has a way of keeping what goes into it.*

The knocking came again. Three beats. A pause. Three beats.

Like something asking for permission.

Like something wanting to be let out.

Or in.

Sarah didn't go down. She locked her bedroom door, checked on both

27

children twice more, and lay awake until dawn, listening to the house knock, and knock, and knock.

And wondering what would happen when she finally answered.

Four

Chapter 4: Settling In

❧

*S*arah pov

The laptop screen cast a blue glow across the kitchen table, turning the October afternoon outside the window into something distant and unreal. Sarah positioned herself so Melissa wouldn't see the peeling wallpaper behind her or the water stain on the ceiling that looked disturbingly like a handprint.

"You look exhausted," Melissa said, her face pixelated for a moment before resolving into crisp concern. Her sister's Boston apartment was visible behind her—clean, modern, *safe*. Everything Sarah's new life wasn't.

"Moving is exhausting." Sarah forced brightness into her voice. "The kids are adjusting great. Lily loves her new room, and Max has already made a friend."

"A friend? You just got there three days ago."

Sarah's smile faltered. She glanced toward the living room where Max sat on the floor, arranging toy cars in careful circles, whispering to empty air. "A neighbor kid, I think. He keeps talking about someone named Ben."

Melissa's expression shifted—something flickered across her face that Sarah couldn't quite read. Her sister reached for something off-screen, and papers rustled. "Sarah, I need to tell you something. I've been researching Hollow's

End."

"Melissa—"

"Just listen. I know you think I'm being paranoid, but I went through the town's digital newspaper archives last night. There are *gaps*."

Sarah's chest tightened. "Gaps?"

"Whole weeks missing. October 1963—nothing. October 1984—nothing. October 1999, October 2006, October 2021—all blank. No papers digitized, no explanation." Melissa leaned closer to her camera, her voice dropping. "And when I tried to find property records for your address, half the documents were sealed by court order."

The kitchen suddenly felt colder. Sarah pulled her cardigan tighter. "That doesn't necessarily mean—"

"Sarah, the last family who lived in that house? I found an obituary. Mother and two daughters, died three years ago. No cause of death listed, no funeral home mentioned. Just… died. All three of them. In that house."

The words hit like ice water. Sarah's mouth went dry. She thought of Hannah's warning, Robert Ashton's nervous energy, the way townspeople stared when she drove past.

"Why are you telling me this?" Sarah's voice came out smaller than she intended.

"Because I'm worried about you. Because you moved there so *fast*, and I know you were desperate to get away from David and start over, but—" Melissa's eyes glistened. "What if this was a mistake? What if you should come stay with me until you find somewhere else?"

Sarah looked around the kitchen—at the vintage charm she'd convinced herself to love, the original cabinets she'd thought were quaint, the basement door that even now stood slightly ajar despite her locking it twice already that morning. The late afternoon sun slanted through the window at a strange angle, creating shadows that seemed too long, too dark.

"I can't afford to move again," Sarah said quietly. "The deposit, the moving costs, breaking the lease… Mel, I'm barely keeping my head above water as it is."

"Then let me help—"

"No." The word came out sharper than she meant. Sarah softened her tone. "I appreciate it, really. But I need to do this myself. For the kids. They need stability, not their mom running scared from internet conspiracy theories."

Melissa opened her mouth to argue, but a crash from upstairs made Sarah jump. "I have to go. One of the kids probably knocked something over."

"Sarah—"

"I'll call you tomorrow. Love you."

She closed the laptop before Melissa could protest, her heart hammering. The house settled around her with a groan of old wood, and for just a moment, Sarah could swear she heard humming—a woman's voice, distant and mournful, coming from somewhere deep in the walls.

"Mom! Max is being weird again!"

Sarah found Lily in the hallway outside Max's room, arms crossed, her expression caught between annoyance and something else. Something that looked like unease.

"What's wrong, honey?"

"He's talking to himself. And he keeps saying things he shouldn't know."

Sarah pushed open Max's door. Her seven-year-old son sat cross-legged on the floor surrounded by his toys, but he'd arranged them in an odd pattern— all the cars pointing toward his closet, the action figures standing in a circle as if guarding something.

"Max? Everything okay, buddy?"

He looked up at her with those wide brown eyes, so much like his father's, and smiled. "Ben was just telling me about the house. Did you know there used to be a swing in the backyard? Right where the dead rosebushes are?"

Sarah's blood turned to ice. She hadn't mentioned the rosebushes to the kids. She'd specifically avoided taking them into the backyard because the twisted, blackened canes looked like skeletal fingers clawing from the earth.

"Who's Ben, sweetheart?"

"My friend. He lived here a long time ago. He's seven, like me." Max returned his attention to his toys, moving a small car closer to the closet. "He says his daddy used to take him down to the basement to look at the well.

31

Ben didn't like the well. The water was always so cold."

Sarah knelt beside him, trying to keep her voice steady. "Max, is Ben here right now?"

"Uh-huh. He's standing right behind you."

Sarah spun around. The doorway was empty except for Lily, who had gone pale.

"He says you have pretty hair like his mommy did," Max continued, oblivious to the terror crawling up Sarah's spine. "But his mommy went away. She went into the ground with the roses, and his daddy told him never to tell anyone."

"Max, stop it." Sarah's voice cracked. She grabbed his shoulders, forcing him to look at her. "This isn't funny."

His expression crumpled with confusion. "I'm not being funny. Ben's my friend. He's trying to help us."

"Help us with what?"

"He won't say. He just keeps crying and pointing at the basement door."

Lily made a small noise of fear. Sarah pulled Max into a hug, her mind racing. Imaginary friends were normal. Kids his age had vivid imaginations. This didn't mean anything. It *couldn't* mean anything.

But even as she thought it, she felt the temperature in the room drop, and in the mirror above Max's dresser, just for a second, she saw a flicker of movement—a small boy in old-fashioned clothes, watching them with dark, sorrowful eyes.

When she whipped around to look, there was nothing there.

Tucker Davis arrived at four o'clock in a pickup truck that had seen better decades. He was a weathered man in his sixties with calloused hands and the kind of face that had spent too much time squinting into the sun. Sarah liked him immediately—he had an honest quality that seemed rare in Hollow's End.

"Appreciate the work," he said, toolbox in hand as Sarah led him inside. "Been slow this month. Folks around here tend to do their own repairs."

"The basement door won't stay shut," Sarah explained, leading him through the kitchen. "I've locked it twice today, and it keeps swinging open. I think the frame might be warped."

Tucker examined the door, running his fingers along the old wood. "Frame looks solid to me. Lock's engaged proper." He frowned. "You sure you're locking it?"

"Positive. I even—" Sarah stopped. She'd almost said *I even heard something trying to get out*, but that sounded insane. "I even tried wedging a chair under the handle. Found the chair kicked halfway across the kitchen this morning."

Something flickered in Tucker's eyes. Recognition, maybe. Or fear. "Mind if I take a look down there? Might be something with the hinges on the other side."

Sarah nodded, though every instinct screamed at her not to let him go down there, not to follow him, to take the kids and run. But she was being ridiculous. It was just a basement.

The stairs creaked under their weight. The air grew noticeably colder with each step, carrying that same smell of damp earth and something else—something sweet and rotten, like flowers left too long in stagnant water.

Tucker pulled a flashlight from his belt. The basement stretched before them, larger than Sarah remembered, filled with shadows that seemed to move independently of the light. Old furniture hulked in corners. Paint cans rusted on sagging shelves. And at the far end, barely visible in the gloom, was a door she hadn't noticed before.

"What's that?" Sarah whispered.

Tucker's jaw tightened. "Storm cellar, probably. Old houses like this always have them." But he didn't sound convinced.

They approached slowly. The door was heavy oak, bound with iron straps that had oxidized to a deep rust-red. The metal handle was shaped like a twisted root, and when Tucker's flashlight beam hit it, Sarah saw something that made her stomach turn: scratch marks on the wood, deep gouges that looked like fingernails had clawed at it from the inside.

"Jesus," Tucker breathed.

He pulled on the handle. The door didn't budge. He pulled harder, muscles straining, and suddenly it flew open with a groan of protesting metal.

The smell that billowed out was overwhelming—earth and decay and the wet-stone scent of deep places that had never seen sun. Tucker's flashlight beam penetrated the darkness, revealing stone walls descending into blackness, and at the bottom, the dull gleam of water.

No—not water. A well.

It was easily six feet across, lined with ancient stones that looked hand-carved. An iron grate covered the opening, secured with a padlock that looked far newer than the well itself. But the padlock hung open, and the grate had been pushed aside several inches, just enough for something to slip through.

"That shouldn't be open," Tucker said, his voice barely audible. "That should be sealed. Filled in. Christ, this has to be from the original foundation, and nobody builds wells inside anymore. This is—this is all wrong."

Sarah took a step closer. She could hear it now—a sound rising from the well's depths. Not wind. Not water. Something else. Something that sounded like children singing nursery rhymes in harmony, the words too distorted to make out but the melody unmistakable and utterly wrong.

"Do you hear that?" she whispered.

Tucker went rigid. "We need to leave. Now."

"But the door—"

"*Now*, Ms. Brennan."

The singing grew louder. The water in the well began to ripple, though nothing had disturbed it. And then, rising from the darkness, came a smell Sarah recognized from her worst nights in the hospital when Max was born and they thought he wouldn't make it—the smell of death, clinical and absolute.

Tucker grabbed her arm and pulled her toward the stairs. Sarah stumbled after him, unable to tear her eyes from the well until they reached the basement door. Tucker slammed it shut and threw the lock, then wedged his toolbox against it for good measure.

His hands were shaking. His face had gone gray.

"I can't work here," he said. "I'm sorry, Ms. Brennan. I don't care what you pay me. I'm not going back down there."

"What is it? What's wrong with the well?"

34

Tucker's eyes met hers, and in them, Sarah saw genuine terror. "Three years ago, I had to do some work for the police. They found the last family who lived here. Mother and two little girls." He swallowed hard. "They were in the basement. All three of them. Floating face-down in that well, even though it's supposed to be sealed and bone-dry. Medical examiner couldn't explain how they got in there, or how there was water when the well's been capped for sixty years."

Sarah's knees went weak. She gripped the counter for support.

"That well shouldn't have water in it," Tucker continued, backing toward the front door. "It shouldn't be open. And there sure as hell shouldn't be anything *singing* down there. You seem like a nice lady, and those are good kids. Get them out of this house. Tonight if you can. Some places are just wrong, and this is one of them."

"I can't—I don't have anywhere—"

But Tucker was already out the door, practically running to his truck.

Sarah stood alone in her kitchen, listening to the basement door rattle softly against its lock, and wondered what kind of fresh start involved children singing from impossible depths and wells that held drowned bodies.

Night fell with unsettling speed.

Sarah made dinner on autopilot—mac and cheese, the kids' favorite, though Lily barely touched hers and Max kept staring at the basement door. She tried to act normal, tried to pretend Tucker's reaction hadn't confirmed every creeping fear she'd been suppressing.

"Can Ben come to dinner?" Max asked.

"No, honey. Imaginary friends don't eat."

"He's not imaginary. He's right there." Max pointed at the empty chair across from him. "He says he used to sit in that chair. His mommy made pot roast on Tuesdays."

Sarah's appetite vanished. "That's nice, Max. Eat your dinner."

After the kids were in bed—after she'd checked their rooms three times, made sure the windows were locked, and left the hallway light burning bright—Sarah sat on the couch with a glass of wine she didn't want and tried to think rationally.

There had to be an explanation. Gas leaks could cause hallucinations. Carbon monoxide could make people see things, hear things. She'd call someone tomorrow to check the furnace, the pipes. There was a logical reason for all of this.

The basement door creaked.

Sarah's head snapped toward it. The door stood open—not just unlocked, but wide open, revealing the stairs descending into darkness.

She'd locked it. She'd watched Tucker wedge his toolbox against it. The toolbox now sat five feet away, as if gently moved aside.

Sarah stood on shaking legs and approached. Cold air breathed up from below, carrying that smell of wet earth and rotted flowers. And underneath it, something else. Perfume. Old-fashioned perfume, the kind her grandmother used to wear.

"Hello?" Her voice sounded small and foolish.

No answer. Just the house settling, the October wind rattling windows, the furnace clicking on with a rattle that sounded almost like bones.

Sarah grabbed the door to slam it shut—and froze.

Muddy footprints led from the basement stairs across the kitchen floor. Small footprints, child-sized, the tread pattern old-fashioned and strange. They tracked through the kitchen, into the hallway, and up the stairs.

Toward the children's rooms.

Terror turned her blood to ice. Sarah took the stairs two at a time, her heart hammering so hard she thought it might burst. The footprints continued down the hallway, wet and dark against the hardwood, leaving puddles that smelled like well water.

They led to Lily's door.

Sarah burst inside to find Lily asleep, peaceful, undisturbed. But at the foot of her bed, in the moonlight streaming through the window, Sarah saw them clearly: small, muddy footprints in a circle around her daughter's bed, as if someone had been walking around and around, watching her sleep.

And on Lily's nightstand, placed with careful precision, was something that hadn't been there when Sarah tucked her in.

A child's toy car. Rusted and ancient, the paint faded, the wheels caked with mud and something darker. Something that looked like dried blood.

Sarah picked it up with trembling hands. On the bottom, scratched in uneven letters, was a name:

BENJAMIN

From somewhere deep in the house, from the basement or the walls or the very foundation itself, came the sound of a child laughing.

Sarah clutched the toy car and stared at the muddy footprints circling her daughter's bed, and finally—*finally*—admitted to herself that whatever was wrong with this house had nothing to do with gas leaks or carbon monoxide.

Something lived here. Something that knew her children's names. Something that left gifts and warnings and walked from the basement well to their bedrooms while they slept.

And whatever it was, it had been here long before the Brennan family arrived.

Sarah sat on the floor beside Lily's bed, watching the door, clutching the toy car, and waited for dawn—knowing sleep would be impossible, knowing that even if she wanted to leave, the house wouldn't let them.

Not until it got what it wanted.

Outside, the October wind picked up, carrying with it the sound of distant singing—children's voices, cheerful and bright, coming from the direction of the backyard where dead rosebushes grew.

Ring around the rosie, pocket full of posies...

Sarah closed her eyes and began to pray.

Five

Chapter 5: The Town Knows

arah pov

SThe morning of October 7th arrived with a fog so thick it pressed against the windows like something alive. Sarah stood in the kitchen of the Last House on Halloween Street, watching the gray murk swallow the dead trees in the backyard, and tried to convince herself that everything would feel more normal once they got out of the house for a while.

She was wrong, of course. But she didn't know that yet.

"Can we get pumpkins?" Max asked, dragging his dinosaur backpack across the scuffed hardwood floor. His voice had that hollow quality it had carried since the sleepwalking incident two nights ago—the one where she'd caught him at the top of the basement stairs, whispering about swimming with Ben.

"Maybe," Sarah said, forcing brightness into her tone. "Let's see what the store has."

Lily appeared in the doorway, already dressed, her sketchbook tucked under her arm like a shield. She'd been drawing obsessively since they arrived—page after page of drowning figures, faceless men, and that woman in the white dress who appeared in every composition like a ghost already haunting the margins of their lives.

"I don't want to go," Lily said quietly.

"We need groceries, sweetie. And it'll be good to see the town in daylight." Sarah heard the false cheer in her own voice and hated it. When had she become this person? This woman who pretended everything was fine while muddy footprints appeared in hallways and all the clocks stopped at 3:33 AM?

Since the divorce, probably. Or maybe since she'd signed the papers on this house without asking enough questions.

Lily's dark eyes—too old for ten, Sarah thought with a pang—fixed on her mother. "The town already knows about us."

"What do you mean?"

But Lily just shook her head and followed Max toward the front door, her thin shoulders hunched like she was walking into winter instead of a grocery run.

Hollow's End in early October should have been picturesque. The kind of postcard New England town that autumn tourists would pay good money to photograph—white church steeples rising above forests ablaze with color, colonial-era buildings with their weathered charm, that crisp apple-cider sharpness to the air that promised hayrides and harvest festivals.

Should have been.

Instead, as Sarah drove the winding road from Halloween Street into the town proper, everything looked slightly *wrong*. The trees weren't displaying fall colors so much as dying in shades of rust and rot. Jack-o'-lanterns on front porches were carved with expressions that looked more anguished than festive, their toothy grins twisted into silent screams. Halloween decorations hung from lamposts and storefront windows—witches and skeletons and black cats—but they felt less like celebration and more like warning.

Or warding.

The main street was called, with zero irony, Gallows Road. Sarah had learned this from the GPS, which had taken three tries to find a signal this morning, as if even the satellites were reluctant to acknowledge Hollow's End's existence.

She found parking in front of a place called Pearl's Diner, its windows fogged with breakfast steam. A few people sat at the counter inside, and when Sarah turned off the ignition, every single one of them turned to stare.

Not curious glances. Not friendly small-town acknowledgment.

Staring. The kind of fixed, unblinking attention that made the hair on the back of Sarah's neck stand up.

"Mom?" Max's voice was small from the backseat. "Why are those people looking at us?"

"They're not, honey. They're just—" But Sarah's voice died as she made eye contact with a middle-aged man in a flannel shirt. His expression wasn't hostile exactly. It was worse. It was *pitying*, the way you might look at someone walking unknowingly toward a cliff edge.

Sarah grabbed her purse with more force than necessary. "Come on. Library first, then groceries."

The Hollow's End Public Library occupied a brick building that had probably been grand in 1790 but now looked exhausted, its facade stained with centuries of weather and neglect. The windows were tall and narrow, like reproachful eyes. A historical marker out front proclaimed it had served as a meeting house during the witch trial era, which explained absolutely nothing and everything at once.

Inside smelled like old paper, lemon furniture polish, and something else Sarah couldn't identify—something organic and faintly sweet, like flowers left too long in a vase.

The circulation desk was empty, but Sarah could hear movement deeper in the stacks. "Hello?"

A woman emerged from between the shelves, and Sarah felt some of the tension leave her shoulders. Here, at last, was a normal, friendly face—round and warm, with laugh lines around her eyes and graying hair pulled back in a practical bun. She wore a cardigan with embroidered autumn leaves and a name tag that read MARGARET WU - HEAD LIBRARIAN.

"Oh!" Margaret's expression flickered through several emotions too quickly to read—surprise, concern, something that might have been fear. But she recovered with a smile that didn't quite reach her eyes. "You must be the new family. At the—" She stopped herself. "I heard someone had moved into the house at the end of Halloween Street."

"Sarah Brennan." Sarah extended her hand. "And these are my kids, Lily and Max."

Margaret's handshake was warm but brief, and Sarah noticed she was careful not to make eye contact with the children. "Welcome to Hollow's End. Can I help you find something?"

"Actually, I was hoping to learn a bit about the town's history. And maybe..." Sarah lowered her voice, glancing at where Lily and Max had drifted toward the children's section. "Maybe about the house we're renting. The Victorian at the end of Halloween Street."

The temperature in the library seemed to drop ten degrees.

Margaret Wu's smile evaporated. Her hands went to the collar of her cardigan, clutching it closed like she'd suddenly felt a draft. "The Kane house."

"Is that what it's called?"

"Was." Margaret moved behind the circulation desk, putting the barrier between them. "I'm not sure what you're hoping to find, Mrs. Brennan, but I'd suggest... well, I'd suggest letting sleeping dogs lie."

The phrase—the same one Hannah Winters had used—sent ice down Sarah's spine. "What does that mean? What sleeping dogs?"

"Nothing. I just mean—" Margaret's eyes darted toward the children, then back to Sarah. Her voice dropped to barely above a whisper. "Has anything... happened? In the house?"

Sarah thought about the knocking. The stopped clocks. The muddy footprints. Max's sleepwalking. Lily's drawings. The nursery that looked preserved from another era. The basement door that wouldn't stay closed.

"No," she lied. "Why would you ask that?"

Margaret's expression said she knew Sarah was lying, and that she understood why. "My grandmother worked for the Kane family. Back in the '60s. She was there when..." The librarian trailed off, shaking her head. "I shouldn't. It's not my place to frighten you with old stories."

"Please." Sarah leaned across the desk, desperation leaking into her voice. "Something is wrong with that house. I need to know what happened there."

For a long moment, Margaret Wu just looked at her, and Sarah saw something terrible in the older woman's eyes: the look of someone watching history repeat itself, powerless to stop it.

"The newspaper archives are in the basement," Margaret finally said, her voice barely audible. "October 1963. But Mrs. Brennan? Some things are better left buried."

Before Sarah could respond, the library's front door opened with a pneumatic hiss. An elderly man in a dark suit entered, moving with the careful precision of someone whose bones hurt. He had the look of retired clergy—that particular brand of severe kindness—and when his eyes landed on Sarah, they widened with recognition.

No. Not recognition. *Realization.*

Margaret moved quickly, intercepting him before he could speak. "Father Gabriel, your books came in—"

"Is that her?" The old priest's voice was soft but carried in the library's hush. "Is that the new mother?"

The way he said "mother"—with such weight, such significance—made Sarah's stomach turn over.

"Father, please—" Margaret tried to guide him away, but Father Gabriel Cross shook her off gently, his eyes never leaving Sarah's face.

"How many children?" he asked.

"I—what?" Sarah glanced back at Lily and Max, who had frozen in the children's section, watching the exchange with wide eyes.

"How many children did you bring to that house?"

"Two," Sarah heard herself say. "Why does that matter?"

Something passed over Father Gabriel's face—grief, or maybe resignation. "Because it always starts with two. The last family had two daughters. The family before that, a boy and a girl. Before that—" He stopped himself, seemed to reach some internal decision. "Mrs. Brennan, I'm going to give you my card. When things begin to happen—and they will—you'll need spiritual guidance."

"I don't need—"

"Not yet," Father Gabriel agreed. "But you will."

Margaret looked like she wanted to physically remove the priest from the library, but Sarah found herself taking the business card he extended. It was simple, traditional: FATHER GABRIEL CROSS, ST. MICHAEL'S PARISH, with a phone number below.

The priest held her gaze for a beat longer than comfortable. "I've been watching that house for forty years, Mrs. Brennan. Waiting for someone to finally break its hold. I don't know if you're the one. But if you are..." He paused. "God be with you. Because you're going to need Him."

Then he turned and walked out, leaving Sarah standing in the library with his card burning in her hand and Margaret Wu looking like she might be sick.

"I'm sorry," Margaret whispered. "He's not usually... He's been watching the house ever since the last family. Since they—" She cut herself off again. "Please, Mrs. Brennan. Be careful. Watch your children. And if you hear knocking—"

"What?" Sarah's voice came out sharper than she intended. "If I hear knocking, what?"

But Margaret just shook her head and fled to the back office, leaving Sarah alone with her children and a terrible, growing certainty that she'd made a catastrophic mistake moving here.

The grocery store was worse.

Hollow's End Market occupied a squat building on the corner of Gallows Road and Cemetery Lane—because of course there was a street called Cemetery Lane. The automatic doors opened with a cheerful chime that felt obscene given the atmosphere, and Sarah felt every eye in the store turn toward them.

It wasn't paranoia. The other shoppers—a handful of women with canvas tote bags, an elderly couple comparing prices on canned goods, a teenager stocking shelves—all stopped what they were doing to stare at Sarah and her children.

And unlike the library, there was no warmth in their expressions. No curiosity. Just that same awful pity, mixed now with something else.

Guilt, Sarah realized. They looked *guilty*.

"Mom, I don't like it here," Max whispered, pressing close to her leg.

"It's fine, baby. Let's just get what we need and go." Sarah grabbed a shopping cart, the metal cold under her fingers, and started down the first aisle. Lily trailed behind, her sketchbook clutched to her chest like armor.

They were in the produce section—Sarah mechanically selecting apples that all seemed slightly bruised, slightly wrong—when the woman approached.

She was ancient, probably in her late eighties, dressed in a wool coat despite the relatively mild October weather. Her hands were gnarled with arthritis, spotted with age, and when she reached out to grab Sarah's arm, her grip was surprisingly strong.

"You need to leave," the old woman hissed, her breath smelling of peppermint and decay. "You need to get those babies out of that house."

Sarah tried to pull away, but the woman's fingers dug deeper, hard enough to bruise. "Excuse me—"

"I know what you're thinking. You're thinking it's just an old house, just old stories. You're thinking you can fix it, make it a home." The woman's eyes were rheumy but fierce, boring into Sarah's with desperate intensity. "You can't. That house has been hungry since before you were born, and it will eat those children if you let it."

"Let go of me." Sarah's voice came out steady despite the fear crawling up her throat.

"Did they tell you about the last family? About what happened to those little girls?" The woman's voice was rising, drawing more attention. "Did they tell you about the knocking?"

"Ma'am, please—"

"Three knocks. Always three. That's how you know they're coming for—"

"Mrs. Ashwood, that's enough."

The voice was calm, authoritative, and deeply kind. Sarah looked up to see Father Gabriel Cross standing at the end of the aisle, though she hadn't heard him enter the store. Behind him, Officer Ryan Beck—his name tag visible on his police uniform—looked uncomfortable but ready to intervene.

The old woman—Mrs. Ashwood—released Sarah's arm immediately, shrinking back like a chastised child. "I was just trying to warn her, Gabriel."

"I know, Constance. But scaring people in the grocery store isn't the way."

Father Gabriel moved closer, and Sarah was struck by the sadness in his eyes. "Go on home now. Officer Beck will give you a ride."

"She needs to know," Mrs. Ashwood insisted, even as Beck gently took her elbow. "She needs to know about the ritual. About what happens on Halloween. About—"

"That's enough." Beck's voice was firmer now, and he guided the elderly woman away, but not before she threw one last desperate look at Sarah.

"Save them," she mouthed silently. "Before midnight on Halloween. Save them."

Then she was gone, leaving Sarah shaking in the produce section with Lily and Max pressed against her sides and Father Gabriel Cross watching her with that terrible, knowing compassion.

"I apologize for Mrs. Ashwood," the priest said quietly. "She lost her grandson twenty years ago. He lived in your house with his mother. After they... well. She's never been quite the same."

Sarah's mouth was dry. "What happened to them?"

Father Gabriel was silent for a long moment, his weathered face unreadable. Then he reached into his jacket and pulled out a business card—the same one he'd given her at the library. This time, he turned it over and wrote something on the back in careful script.

When he handed it to her, Sarah saw the handwritten note:

When you need me—and you will

"I can't tell you what to do, Mrs. Brennan," Father Gabriel said softly. "But I can tell you this: that house has stood for over a century, and in that time, it's seen more tragedy than any building should hold. Some of that tragedy was..." He paused, choosing his words carefully. "Human in origin. Murder. Suicide. Terrible choices made by terrible people."

"And some of it wasn't human?" Sarah heard herself ask.

The priest's expression didn't change, but something flickered in his eyes— acknowledgment, maybe, or warning. "I'm a man of God, Mrs. Brennan. I believe in evil. Both the kind that lives in human hearts and the kind that... lingers. In places. In objects. In land that's been soaked with too much blood and tears."

He took a step closer, and Sarah could smell incense and old books clinging to his clothes.

"Watch your children," he said. "Every moment. Don't let them go into the basement. Don't answer if you hear knocking after dark. And if they start talking about someone named Ben..." He trailed off, shaking his head. "Call me immediately."

Sarah's blood turned to ice. "How do you know about Ben?"

"Because there's always a Ben." Father Gabriel's voice was infinitely sad. "Or a Sarah, or an Elizabeth. There's always a child's voice calling from the dark, trying to lure the living down to where the dead are waiting."

He started to turn away, then stopped. "One more thing. Halloween is in twenty-four days. I don't know what you believe about the supernatural, Mrs. Brennan, but I'm telling you as someone who's witnessed things I can't explain: that night is when the veil between worlds is thinnest. And that house..." He looked at her with such profound sorrow that Sarah felt tears prick her eyes. "That house has been waiting for Halloween for a very long time."

Then he walked away, his footsteps echoing in the too-quiet store, leaving Sarah with her half-filled cart and her terrified children and a growing certainty that she'd brought her babies into something far worse than a bad divorce or a fresh start.

She'd brought them to a place that had been hungry for decades.

And it had been waiting specifically for them.

Sarah abandoned the shopping cart in the middle of the store. She grabbed Lily's hand, scooped Max onto her hip despite him being too old for it, and walked out into the gray October afternoon with her heart hammering and Father Gabriel's card clutched in her free hand.

The drive back to Halloween Street felt longer than it should have, the fog thickening as they left the town center, swallowing the road in increments until Sarah was driving blind, following only the faint yellow line and her own terrified instinct.

When they finally pulled into the driveway of the Last House on Halloween Street, the Victorian loomed out of the mist like something from a nightmare—all those dark windows and peaked roofs and that wraparound porch with its rocking chair moving slowly back and forth despite the windless air.

Sarah sat in the car with the engine running, watching the house watch them back.

"Mom?" Lily's voice was very small. "What did that old lady mean? About the knocking?"

Sarah looked at her daughter in the rearview mirror—this brave, brilliant ten-year-old girl who drew pictures of drowning people and somehow knew more than she should—and tried to find words that wouldn't terrify her.

She failed.

"I don't know, baby," Sarah whispered. "But we're going to find out."

In the back seat, Max had fallen asleep, his head lolling against the window. And as Sarah watched, his lips moved, forming silent words.

She couldn't hear him through the glass.

But she could read his lips well enough.

Ben says we can't leave. Ben says it's almost time.

Sarah closed her eyes and pressed Father Gabriel's card against her chest, right over her racing heart, and prayed to a God she wasn't sure she believed in anymore.

Because the town knew.

The town had always known.

And now, so did she.

The house was waiting for Halloween.

And it was waiting for her children.

The question was: what would Sarah do when the knocking finally came?

47

Six

Chapter 6: The First Manifestation

arah pov

The drawings started appearing on October 7th.

Sarah found the first one on the kitchen table during breakfast, partially hidden beneath Max's cereal bowl. She'd been pouring coffee, trying to ignore the way the house seemed colder than it had any right to be despite the furnace running constantly, when the edge of construction paper caught her eye.

She pulled it free, and her hand froze mid-reach for the sugar.

The image was rendered in Lily's careful ten-year-old hand, but there was nothing childlike about the subject matter. A family—stick figures with detailed faces—stood in what appeared to be a room filled with water. The water line came up to their necks, drawn in layers of blue crayon so thick it had torn through the paper in places. Above the water, their mouths were open in perfect O's. Below the surface, their hands reached upward.

Drowning.

Her daughter had drawn a family drowning.

"Lily?" Sarah's voice came out steadier than she felt. "Sweetie, can you come here for a second?"

Lily appeared in the kitchen doorway, still in her pajamas, her dark hair sleep-mussed and tangled. She looked so small framed by the oversized Victorian doorframe, so vulnerable. Sarah's heart clenched.

"Yes, Mom?"

Sarah held up the drawing, keeping her expression neutral. "Can you tell me about this picture?"

Lily glanced at it, then shrugged with the casual indifference only a child could muster when confronted with their own disturbing art. "It's just a drawing."

"I can see that. But what made you want to draw... this?"

Another shrug. Lily moved to the refrigerator, pulling out the orange juice. "I don't know. I just saw it."

The words sent ice down Sarah's spine. "Saw it? Saw it where?"

"In my head, I guess." Lily poured juice with careful concentration, tongue poking out between her teeth. "Ben says the water comes up really fast. You don't have time to scream."

The juice carton slipped from Sarah's fingers, splashing across the counter in a bright orange flood.

"Ben told you that?" Sarah heard herself ask, her voice very far away. "Your imaginary friend Ben?"

Lily looked up at her mother with those wide, innocent eyes—so brown, so clear, so absolutely certain. "He's not imaginary, Mom. He lives in the basement. He says he's been waiting for us."

By noon, Sarah had found six more drawings.

One showed a man with no face standing in a doorway, his silhouette filled with solid black crayon. Another depicted a woman in a long dress, her hair covering her face, standing in what looked like a garden of dead flowers. A third showed the house itself—their house—with every window filled with staring eyes.

Sarah had gathered them all, hands shaking, and shoved them into a folder she then buried at the bottom of her desk drawer. Out of sight. As if that would somehow undo what Lily had put on paper.

The October afternoon pressed against the windows, the light already failing though it wasn't even three o'clock. Outside, Halloween Street was deserted as always, the neighboring houses quiet and watchful. Dead leaves skittered across the asphalt in patterns that looked almost deliberate, almost like words Sarah couldn't quite read.

She found herself standing at the kitchen window, coffee mug clenched between her hands, staring at the backyard. The garden was a tangle of dead rosebushes and weeds, the grass brown and crispy despite the recent rain. Nothing grew properly back there. Even the weeds looked sick.

Behind her, Max played with his toy cars in the living room, making quiet engine noises. Lily was upstairs in her room, probably drawing more nightmares to pin to Sarah's growing catalog of reasons to panic.

This is fine, Sarah told herself firmly. *Children have vivid imaginations. Lily's processing the divorce, the move, all the changes. Max is feeding off her anxiety. It's perfectly normal.*

The lie tasted bitter.

The truth was that nothing about this house felt normal. Nothing about the past week had felt normal. The clocks stopping at 3:33. The knocking from inside her locked bedroom. Tucker Davis's refusal to come back after hearing voices from the well. Hannah Winters's terrified flight at sunset.

The footprints. Those goddamned muddy footprints that appeared no matter how many times Sarah mopped the floors, always child-sized, always leading from the basement to the children's rooms.

Sarah pressed her forehead against the cool glass, closing her eyes. Six days. They'd been here six days, and already the house felt like it was trying to swallow them whole.

"Mommy?"

Sarah's eyes snapped open. Max stood in the kitchen doorway, clutching his favorite toy car—the red one he'd named Lightning. His face was pale, his eyes too wide.

"What's wrong, baby?"

"I don't like it when the singing starts."

Sarah's blood turned to slush. "What singing?"

"The kids singing. In the walls." Max looked around the kitchen as if

50

searching for the source. "Don't you hear them?"

Sarah listened. The house was silent except for the ancient pipes groaning somewhere in the walls and the whisper of wind around the eaves. No singing. No voices at all.

"There's no one singing, Max. It's just the house settling."

"No." He shook his head firmly. "It's the kids. Ben and the others. They sing the nursery rhymes. Ben says they sang them when the water came up." His voice dropped to a whisper. "He says it helped. A little."

Sarah crossed the kitchen and knelt in front of her son, gripping his small shoulders. "Max, listen to me. Ben isn't real. There are no children in the walls. It's just your imagination—"

"He's in the basement!" Max's voice rose, sharp with frustration. "He *lives* there! He showed me where the water comes from!" He pointed at the floor, toward the basement stairs just beyond the kitchen. "There's a big hole in the ground and it's full of dead people and Ben says when Halloween comes, they all wake up!"

"Max—"

"He says I have to come swim with him! He says it's almost time! He says the water's getting higher and Daddy can't save us because Daddy doesn't live here anymore and the water knows and—"

"ENOUGH!"

Sarah's shout echoed through the kitchen, bouncing off the vintage tile and high ceilings. Max flinched, tears springing to his eyes. Immediately, Sarah's anger drained away, replaced by crushing guilt.

"I'm sorry," she whispered, pulling him into a fierce hug. "I'm so sorry, baby. Mommy didn't mean to yell. It's just... there's no one in the basement. I promise you. We're safe here."

But as she held her seven-year-old son and felt him tremble against her, Sarah realized she didn't believe her own words. And worse—she didn't think Max believed them either.

The nightmare came at 2:47 AM.

Sarah woke to screaming—high, piercing, the sound of absolute terror. She was out of bed and running before her mind fully caught up with her body, her bare feet slapping against the cold hardwood floors.

Max's room. The screaming was coming from Max's room.

She burst through his door to find him sitting bolt upright in bed, eyes open but unseeing, mouth stretched wide in a continuous shriek. The moonlight streaming through his window painted everything in shades of silver and black, turning his small room into something from a nightmare.

"Max! Max, baby, wake up!" Sarah grabbed his shoulders, shaking gently. "It's just a dream! You're safe!"

But Max kept screaming, staring at something Sarah couldn't see. His hands clawed at his throat as if trying to pull something away.

"The water!" he gasped between screams. "It's coming up! It's in my mouth! I can't breathe! Mommy, I can't breathe!"

"There's no water, sweetheart! Look at me! You're in bed! You're dry! There's no—"

Max's eyes suddenly focused on her face, and what she saw there made her breath catch. Not her son's innocent confusion. Something older. Something that knew things no seven-year-old should know.

"He's pulling me down," Max whispered in a voice that wasn't quite his own. "Father's holding me under. Mother's screaming but her mouth is full of water. The room is full and we're all going to drown and—"

He blinked, and suddenly he was Max again, just Max, her baby boy, confused and terrified and sobbing.

"Mommy?"

Sarah crushed him against her chest, rocking him like she had when he was an infant. "It's okay, it's okay, it was just a bad dream, you're safe, Mommy's got you."

Behind her, Lily appeared in the doorway, her silhouette backlit by the hallway nightlight. "Is Max okay?"

"He's fine, honey. Just a nightmare. Go back to bed."

But Lily didn't move. "Did he dream about the water again?"

Sarah's rocking faltered. "*Again?*"

"He dreams about it every night," Lily said matter-of-factly. "Ben dreams

52

about it too. It's how he died. The water came up in the basement and he couldn't get out and his daddy watched and—"

"Stop it." Sarah's voice was sharp. "Both of you, stop talking about Ben. There is no Ben. There are no dead children. There is no—"

A sound from downstairs cut her off. A creak. A footstep. The distinct sound of someone—some*thing*—moving through the first floor.

All three of them froze.

Another creak. Closer to the stairs now. The sound of small feet on hardwood, moving with purpose.

"He's awake," Max whispered against Sarah's shoulder. "Ben's awake."

Sarah's heart hammered against her ribs. She wanted to dismiss it, to rationalize it as the house settling or the wind or her imagination. But she could hear it clearly now—footsteps. Definitely footsteps. Moving through the parlor, into the hall, approaching the base of the stairs.

"Stay here," Sarah breathed, placing Max carefully back in his bed. "Both of you, stay right here. Don't move."

"Mom, don't—" Lily started.

But Sarah was already moving, her maternal instinct overriding her terror. If someone had broken into her house, if someone was threatening her children, she would end them.

She grabbed the baseball bat Max kept by his door—a gift from his father, unused since the divorce—and crept into the hallway. The house was dark except for the small nightlights she'd installed in every outlet, casting pools of weak yellow light that did nothing to dispel the shadows.

The footsteps had stopped.

Sarah stood at the top of the stairs, bat raised, listening. The silence was absolute. Not even the usual groaning of the pipes or settling of old wood. Just... nothing.

"Hello?" Her voice sounded pathetically small in the vast darkness. "I know you're there. I've called the police. They're on their way."

She hadn't, of course. Her phone was charging on her nightstand. But the intruder didn't need to know that.

No response. No movement.

Sarah descended one step. Two. Three. The stairs creaked under her weight, each sound impossibly loud in the stillness. Four steps. Five.

She was halfway down when she saw it.

A small figure standing at the base of the stairs, barely visible in the shadows. Child-sized. Motionless.

Sarah's breath stopped.

"Max?" she whispered, though she knew—*knew*—Max was still in his room. She'd left him there thirty seconds ago. "Lily?"

The figure didn't respond. Didn't move. Just stood there in the darkness, watching.

Sarah's hands tightened on the bat. "Who are you?"

And then, in a voice like wind through dead leaves, like water bubbling up from deep places:

"Ben says it's time to swim."

Sarah's scream caught in her throat as the figure moved—not toward her, but toward the kitchen. Toward the basement door.

She ran down the remaining stairs, bat raised, ready to—what? Hit a child? Even if that child shouldn't exist, was in her locked house at three in the morning, speaking with her son's voice?

She reached the kitchen just in time to see the basement door swing slowly closed.

Sarah stood in the kitchen doorway, chest heaving, bat trembling in her hands. The basement door was shut tight, the old brass knob gleaming dully in the moonlight from the windows.

She hadn't imagined it. She *couldn't* have imagined it.

"Mom?"

Sarah spun to find Lily at the top of the stairs, Max clutched against her side.

"I told you to stay in the room!"

"Max was sleepwalking again," Lily said quietly. "I tried to stop him but he's too strong."

Sarah's stomach dropped. "What do you mean, again?"

"He sleepwalks every night now. He always goes to the basement. I have to keep bringing him back to bed."

Sarah looked at her daughter's serious face, at her son pressed against her side, and felt the foundations of her reality crack a little further.

"How long has this been happening?"

"Since the first night." Lily paused. "I didn't want to worry you."

Sarah crossed the kitchen on numb legs and gathered both children in her arms. They felt solid, real, warm. Alive. Not like the cold figure she'd seen at the base of the stairs. Not like the voice that had used Max's words.

"We're sleeping in my room tonight," she announced, her voice brooking no argument. "All of us. Together."

She ushered them upstairs, locked her bedroom door (though she knew locks meant nothing in this house), and tucked them both into her king-sized bed. They fell asleep almost instantly, exhausted by terror.

Sarah sat in the chair by the window, bat across her lap, and watched them breathe.

Outside, the October moon painted Halloween Street in shades of bone and shadow. The houses across the street were dark, their windows like empty eye sockets. The trees were skeletal silhouettes against the sky.

Sarah's gaze drifted to the backyard, to the tangle of dead roses and—

She froze.

There was someone standing in the garden.

A woman in a long Victorian dress, her hair hanging loose around her shoulders, stood among the dead rosebushes as if she'd grown there. She was perfectly still, face tilted up toward Sarah's window.

Sarah couldn't breathe. Couldn't move. Could only stare as the figure stood motionless in the moonlight, impossibly present, impossibly there.

The woman wore white—a nightgown, Sarah realized distantly. A nightgown stained dark around the hem, around the sleeves. The stains looked black in the moonlight, but Sarah knew with absolute certainty they would be red in daylight.

Blood.

The woman raised one hand—slowly, deliberately—and pointed directly at Sarah's window. At Sarah. Her mouth moved, forming words Sarah couldn't hear through the glass.

Sarah wanted to look away, to close her eyes, to pretend this wasn't happening. But she was paralyzed, trapped in the woman's gaze, forced to witness.

Then the woman's mouth opened wider, impossibly wide, and even through the glass Sarah heard the sound that emerged:

A scream. Water-choked and desperate. The sound of someone drowning. Sarah blinked—

—and the woman was gone.

The garden was empty. Just dead roses and brown grass and shadows. Nothing else.

But scattered across the porch below, clearly visible in the moonlight, were dozens of white roses. Fresh roses. Dead roses. The same roses from the garden, torn from their thorny stems and arranged in a pattern Sarah recognized from one of Lily's drawings.

The pattern of a body. A woman's body, laid out in flowers.

And in the center, where the heart would be, a single black rose.

Sarah's hands shook as she finally tore her gaze away from the window. She looked at her children, sleeping peacefully in her bed, unaware of what stood watch in the garden below.

Eleanor Kane, she thought, though she didn't know how she knew. *That was Eleanor Kane. Victor's wife. The one who disappeared. The one who was never found.*

Sarah pulled her knees to her chest, wrapped her arms around them, and waited for dawn. The bat stayed across her lap. Her eyes stayed on the window. And in the reflection of the dark glass, she could swear she saw a woman in white standing just behind her chair.

But when she turned to look, there was nothing there.

Just the house. Just the shadows. Just the growing certainty that October 7th had changed everything, and whatever had been watching them since they arrived was done with subtlety.

The dead were making themselves known.

And they wanted her children.

Seven

Chapter 7: Detective Murphy Investigates

⸎

S arah pov

The police station smelled like burnt coffee and old paperwork, a reassuring mundanity that made Sarah want to weep with relief. Outside, October sunlight filtered through the maple trees lining Main Street, their leaves a riot of orange and crimson that should have felt beautiful but instead reminded her of blood and fire. She'd left Lily and Max with Hannah Winters—a decision that had twisted her stomach with anxiety, but she couldn't bring the children here, couldn't let them hear her describe what was happening in their home.

Detective James Murphy looked exactly like central casting's idea of a small-town cop: mid-forties, graying at the temples, tired eyes that had seen enough to be skeptical of everything. He sat across from her in the interview room, a yellow legal pad in front of him, pen poised with professional patience.

"Ms. Brennan," he began, his voice carefully neutral. "You reported break-ins. Plural. Can you walk me through each incident?"

Sarah's hands trembled as she folded them in her lap. Where did she even start? The footprints? The knocking? Max nearly walking into the basement in his sleep? She'd rehearsed this on the drive over, determined to sound rational, competent, not like a hysterical divorced woman cracking under pressure.

"Someone has been entering my house," she said, forcing her voice steady. "Multiple times. At night. I've heard footsteps, found doors open that I know I locked, and there are... there are muddy footprints."

Murphy's pen scratched against paper. "Muddy footprints. Where?"

"In the upstairs hallway. Leading from the basement to my daughter's bedroom." Sarah swallowed hard. "Small footprints. Child-sized."

The detective's expression didn't change, but something flickered in his eyes. Recognition? Concern? "Any signs of forced entry? Broken windows, damaged locks?"

"No. That's what's so—" She stopped herself before saying *impossible*. "That's what I can't explain. Every door and window is locked from the inside when I check, but the footprints are there. Fresh. Wet mud, like someone just walked through the backyard."

"And your backyard is muddy?"

"The rose garden is. The soil there never seems to dry out, even though we haven't had rain in a week." She didn't mention that nothing grew in that garden except dead, blackened stems. Didn't mention the dreams where she saw hands clawing up through that mud. "Detective Murphy, my son is seven years old. He's been having nightmares, talking to someone who isn't there, and three nights ago I found him sleepwalking toward the basement. When I woke him, he said... he said his friend Ben told him it was time to swim."

Murphy's pen stopped moving. The silence stretched between them, heavy with unspoken things.

"There's no pool in the house," Sarah continued, her voice barely above a whisper. "No bathtub in the basement. Just an old sealed well that the previous owners covered. But Max has never seen it. I haven't let the children down there since the handyman refused to keep working."

"Tucker Davis?"

"Yes. He said he heard voices. Children singing." Sarah met Murphy's eyes, desperation bleeding through her carefully maintained composure. "I know how this sounds. I know. But I'm not imagining this. Something is wrong with that house."

The detective set down his pen and leaned back in his chair, studying her with an expression she couldn't quite read. Outside the interview room, phones rang and officers traded shift-change small talk. Normal sounds from a normal world that felt impossibly distant from the Victorian nightmare at the end of Halloween Street.

"Ms. Brennan," Murphy said carefully, "I'm going to come out to your property and document everything. But I need you to understand that what you're describing—no forced entry, no evidence of an intruder—makes it very difficult to pursue this as a breaking and entering case."

"I'm not crazy," Sarah said, hating the defensive edge in her voice.

"I didn't say you were." Murphy's tone gentled slightly. "I said it's difficult. Not impossible. Let me come take a look."

The drive back to Halloween Street felt longer than it should have, Murphy's patrol car following her sedan like a tether to sanity. Sarah's hands gripped the steering wheel too tight, knuckles white, as the October afternoon light slanted through the trees in golden shafts that looked too beautiful for the dread coiling in her chest.

Hannah's car was still in the driveway when they arrived—thank God. Sarah had texted her from the station, asking her to stay until she returned. Hannah had responded immediately: *Of course. The children are safe with me. Take your time.*

Safe. Such a simple word. Such an impossible promise.

Murphy parked and emerged from his vehicle with a practiced economy of movement, eyes already scanning the property. Sarah noticed his gaze linger on the dead rose garden, the skeletal trees that seemed to lean inward toward the house, the way the shadows pooled too dark beneath the wraparound porch even in afternoon sunlight.

"Interesting architecture," he said, which wasn't a compliment.

The front door opened before Sarah could fish out her keys. Hannah stood in the threshold, her smile warm but her eyes worried. "Sarah, you're back. The children are in the kitchen having a snack. They've been perfect angels."

"Thank you so much, Hannah." Sarah introduced Murphy, watching how

Hannah's expression shifted—something cautious sliding behind her friendly demeanor.

"Detective," Hannah said, nodding. "I hope everything's all right."

"Just following up on Ms. Brennan's report. I'll need to look around, if that's acceptable."

"Of course." But Hannah didn't move from the doorway immediately. Her gaze flicked to Sarah, something urgent and unspoken passing between them. "Sarah, if I could have a word before I go?"

Murphy gestured for them to proceed. "I'll start with the exterior, work my way in."

Sarah followed Hannah to the porch's far corner, out of earshot. The older woman's fingers were cold when they grasped Sarah's wrist.

"You called the police," Hannah whispered, not quite accusatory but close.

"Someone is getting into my house, Hannah. Someone is terrorizing my children."

"It's not a *someone*." Hannah's eyes were wide, almost frantic. "Sarah, please. The police can't help you with this. They'll find nothing, document nothing, and then you'll be alone with it again, except now you'll have involved outsiders. The house doesn't like that."

"The house doesn't—" Sarah pulled her wrist free, anger flaring hot and bright. "Hannah, I appreciate your concern, but I need help. Real help. Not cryptic warnings and salt circles."

Hannah's face crumpled. "I'm trying to protect you. Those children—"

"Mom?" Lily appeared in the doorway, Max behind her, both clutching granola bars. "Is everything okay?"

Sarah forced a smile. "Everything's fine, sweetie. Detective Murphy is just going to look around. Why don't you and Max finish your snack upstairs? I'll be right in."

The children retreated, but Lily's eyes—too knowing, too worried for a ten-year-old—lingered on Hannah before she turned away.

"I should go," Hannah said quietly. "But Sarah, please. Be careful what you invite in. Questions have a way of opening doors that should stay closed."

She left before Sarah could respond, hurrying to her car with an urgency that set Sarah's nerves jangling. Through the kitchen window, Sarah watched Murphy circling the house, photographing the dead rose garden, the cracked foundation, the windows with their original wavy glass that seemed to distort everything viewed through them.

He was thorough, she'd give him that. He spent twenty minutes examining the exterior before requesting entry, and then methodically worked through the first floor—checking locks, testing windows, documenting everything in his notebook with the kind of professional detachment that should have been comforting but instead made Sarah feel foolish.

"Ms. Brennan," he called from the back hallway. "Can you come here, please?"

She found him crouched near the basement door, which stood slightly ajar despite Sarah's certainty that she'd locked it that morning. Murphy was photographing something on the hardwood floor.

Muddy footprints.

Small. Child-sized. Leading from the basement stairs into the hallway, then disappearing halfway to the kitchen as if whoever made them had simply evaporated.

"These what you've been seeing?" Murphy asked, his voice carefully controlled.

"Yes." Sarah's throat felt tight. "Exactly like that."

Murphy took multiple photos from different angles, then used a gloved hand to touch the nearest footprint. His finger came away wet with dark, silty mud. He smelled it, frowning.

"This mud is fresh. Recently tracked in." He stood, looking at the basement door. "You said there's a well down there?"

"Yes. Sealed. Tucker Davis saw it and refused to keep working."

"Mind if I take a look?"

Sarah did mind, actually. The thought of going down into that basement in the growing dark of late afternoon made her skin crawl. But Murphy was already opening the door, clicking on his flashlight, and she couldn't very well refuse.

The basement stairs creaked under their weight, each step an accusation.

The air grew colder as they descended, carrying that mineral smell of deep earth and standing water. Murphy's flashlight beam swept across the stone foundation, the cobwebbed corners, the ancient furnace crouched in the shadows like a sleeping beast.

And there, in the center of the far wall: the well.

It was exactly as Tucker had described—a circular stone structure about four feet across, sealed with an iron grate that looked Victorian in origin. Rust stained the metal in patterns that resembled dried blood. Sarah hung back on the stairs while Murphy approached it, his footsteps echoing in the confined space.

"This grate been opened recently?" he asked.

"Not by me. It was sealed when we moved in."

Murphy crouched, examining the edges. Sarah saw his shoulders tense.

"Ms. Brennan, this grate has been moved. Recently. See these scrape marks on the stone? Fresh. And the rust is disturbed here, and here." He looked back at her, his professional mask slipping for just a moment. "Someone has been opening this."

"From which side?" The question came out before Sarah could stop it.

Murphy's silence was answer enough.

The scrape marks, Sarah could see now, curved outward. Away from the well. As if something had pushed the grate up from below.

"Let's go back upstairs," Murphy said, standing quickly. Too quickly.

They climbed in silence, but at the top of the stairs, Murphy paused. His flashlight beam had caught something on the wall—scratches in the old plaster. Fresh scratches. They formed words, carved in a childish hand:

BEN IS LONELY BEN WANTS TO PLAY BEN WANTS LILY

Sarah's vision swam. She grabbed the doorframe to steady herself.

"When did this appear?" Murphy's voice was sharp.

"I don't know. I haven't been down here in days. I told the children not to go in the basement."

Murphy photographed the words, his jaw tight. Then he shut the basement door firmly and tested the lock. It engaged with a solid click.

They sat in the kitchen while Murphy filled out his report. Through the window, Sarah could see the sun sinking toward the horizon, bleeding orange and red across the October sky. Halloween was creeping closer. Twenty-four days away. The thought made her stomach turn.

"Ms. Brennan," Murphy said finally, setting down his pen. "I'm going to be honest with you, and I need you to listen carefully."

Sarah nodded, wrapping her hands around a mug of coffee she hadn't touched.

"I've found evidence of... disturbances. The muddy footprints are real. The well grate has been tampered with. Those words in the basement are real. But I haven't found evidence of forced entry, which means either someone has a key to your house, or—"

"Or what?"

Murphy met her eyes. "Or something else is happening here."

"Something else," Sarah repeated flatly.

The detective was quiet for a long moment. Outside, a murder of crows settled in the skeletal trees, their caws harsh and mocking. Murphy's gaze drifted to the window, then back to Sarah.

"This is off the record," he said quietly. "Not in my report. But you're the fourth family to live in this house in the past twenty years. The other three... they all left. Quickly. In the middle of their leases or mortgages, losing deposits, taking financial hits they couldn't afford. And they all reported the same things you're reporting. Footprints. Knocking. Children's voices. Sleepwalking."

Sarah's coffee mug rattled against the table as she set it down. "And you're just telling me this now?"

"There's nothing to tell, officially. No crimes were committed. No evidence of breaking and entering. No suspects. Just... families who got spooked and left." Murphy's fingers drummed against his notebook. "The family before you, the Hendersons—they had two daughters. Eight and twelve. They lasted six weeks. Mrs. Henderson called us seventeen times in those six weeks. Same reports as yours. We investigated every time. Found nothing."

"What happened to them?"

"They left town. Didn't even come back for their belongings. The bank foreclosed, the estate sale company cleared out the house, and the property sat empty for three years before your real estate agent got involved." Murphy's expression was grim. "And before the Hendersons, there was a single woman, a writer, who lasted two months. And before her, an elderly couple who made it eight weeks before the husband had a heart attack and the wife refused to spend another night here."

"Jesus Christ." Sarah pressed her palms against her eyes. "Why didn't anyone tell me? Why didn't Robert Ashton—"

"Legally, he didn't have to disclose. No deaths occurred on the property itself—the elderly man died at the hospital. No crimes. Just… unfortunate turnover." Murphy leaned forward. "Ms. Brennan, I'm going to file this report. I'm going to log the evidence I found. But I'm also going to tell you what I told Mrs. Henderson three years ago: document everything. Keep a detailed record—dates, times, what you see and hear. And seriously consider whether staying here is worth it."

"I can't leave." The words came out harder than Sarah intended. "I can't afford to break my lease. I can't afford another security deposit, first and last month's rent, all of it again. I'm barely making ends meet as it is. My ex-husband is fighting me on child support, and I used everything I had to get us out of our old situation and into this house. This terrible, impossible, haunted fucking house."

She was crying now, hot tears of frustration and fear tracking down her face. Murphy had the grace to look away, giving her a moment to compose herself.

"Then document everything," he said again. "And call me if anything escalates. I can't investigate what I can't see, but I believe you. I want that on record. I believe something is happening in this house."

"But you can't help me."

"I'll do what I can within the law. But Ms. Brennan—Sarah—if it were my kids?" Murphy stood, gathering his paperwork. "I'd get them out. Legal consequences, financial ruin, whatever it took. I'd get them out."

He left her sitting at the kitchen table as afternoon bled into evening, the house settling around her with creaks and groans that sounded almost like whispers. Upstairs, she could hear Lily and Max playing, their innocent laughter a jarring counterpoint to the dread pooling in her chest.

Sarah pulled out her phone and opened a new note. Titled it: *Documentation.* Started typing.

October 7th, 4:47 PM. Detective Murphy found muddy footprints in hallway. Well grate has been moved from inside. Words scratched in basement wall: "Ben is lonely. Ben wants to play. Ben wants Lily."

Murphy says three families before us reported same phenomena. All left within weeks.

Twenty-four days until Halloween.

She stared at that last line, something cold and certain settling in her bones. Twenty-four days. The house seemed to breathe around her, patient and hungry.

Sarah saved the note and called upstairs to the children. "Lily! Max! Come down for dinner!"

Their footsteps thundered overhead, running toward the stairs. But beneath their noise, Sarah heard something else. Softer. Slower. A third set of footsteps, keeping pace.

Child-sized.

Coming from the basement.

She didn't go check. She couldn't. Instead, she went to the front door and tested the lock—secure. Tested the windows—latched. Drew the curtains against the gathering October dark.

Outside, the first trick-or-treaters of the season were already appearing on neighboring lawns, testing costumes, laughing in the autumn dusk. Their joy felt like a mockery. Halloween was coming, Sarah thought, and the house was waiting.

In the basement, something knocked three times against the iron grate.

Then three times more.

Then three times again.

Sarah turned up the radio to drown out the sound and called her children to dinner, pretending everything was fine, pretending they were safe.

But she'd started the documentation now, and some part of her knew:

Detective Murphy's visit hadn't solved anything. It had only confirmed that she was trapped in a nightmare with no clear escape.

And the dead, it seemed, were getting impatient.

Eight

Chapter 8: The Well

❧

S arah pov

The basement door was open.

Sarah stood at the top of the stairs, one hand frozen on the doorknob, her heart performing acrobatics in her chest. She'd locked it that morning. She was *certain* she'd locked it—had tested the handle twice, her palm sweating against the old brass, before going into the kitchen to make the children breakfast.

Now it gaped like a mouth, exhaling air that tasted of wet stone and something older, something that made her sinuses ache with the memory of graveyards and standing water.

"Lily?" Her voice echoed down into darkness. "Max?"

No answer. But she could hear them—the shuffle of small feet on concrete, a whisper that might have been her daughter's voice or might have been the house settling in ways houses shouldn't settle.

Sarah descended.

The basement stairs were narrow and steep, each step groaning under her weight as if offended by her presence. The October afternoon sunlight reached only the first three steps before giving up entirely, surrendering to a darkness that seemed too thick for a simple absence of light. It had texture, this darkness—she could almost feel it brushing against her skin as she moved deeper, like cobwebs or the trailing fingers of something that had learned to wait very, very patiently.

Tucker Davis had left his work lamp in the corner where he'd abandoned his tools three days ago. Sarah fumbled for it, her hands shaking. When the light blazed to life, she almost wished she'd left it off.

The basement was exactly as wrong as she remembered.

It was too large for the house's footprint, stretching back into impossible distance, the walls constructed from stones that predated the Victorian structure above by centuries. Someone had carved symbols into the rock—not the neat, geometric designs of decoration, but frantic, desperate scratches that looked like warnings. Or wards. The kind of marks you'd leave if you were trying to keep something in.

Or out.

"Mom?"

Sarah spun toward Lily's voice, the work lamp's beam cutting wild arcs through the dark. Her daughter stood in the far corner—*too far*, the basement shouldn't extend that deep—her small frame silhouetted against a darkness that seemed to pulse with its own rhythm.

Max was beside her, kneeling.

"Oh, thank God." Sarah's relief lasted exactly as long as it took her to reach them and see what they were kneeling beside.

The well.

Tucker had mentioned it—had refused to touch it, in fact, his weathered face going gray when Sarah asked why. She'd thought it was just an old cistern, the kind of historical artifact that made this house so cheap. She'd planned to have it professionally sealed, maybe turned into a wine cellar or cold storage.

She hadn't planned to let her children anywhere near it.

The well was circular, perhaps four feet in diameter, ringed with stones so old they'd gone smooth and black with age. An iron grate covered the opening, its bars thick as a man's thumb and forged in a pattern that hurt to look at—interlocking shapes that seemed to shift and reform when you weren't looking directly at them. Rust had claimed most of the metal, creating a lacework of orange decay.

But that wasn't what made Sarah's breath catch in her throat.

Max had his face pressed against the grate, his cheek flattened against the iron bars, his eyes closed. One small hand gripped the metal, knuckles white with pressure. His lips were moving—not speaking, but mouthing words Sarah couldn't hear, like he was responding to someone.

"Max!" Sarah grabbed his shoulder, trying to pull him back.

He didn't budge. It was like trying to move a statue. His seven-year-old body had become impossibly heavy, rooted to the floor by something that had nothing to do with normal physics.

"Max, let go. Let go *right now.*"

"He can't hear you." Lily's voice was small, frightened. Her daughter stood a careful three feet from the well, her arms wrapped around herself, her face pale in the work lamp's harsh light. "He's been like that for five minutes. I tried to pull him away but he—Mom, he's so strong. He shouldn't be that strong."

Sarah wedged her fingers under Max's hand, trying to pry his grip from the grate. His skin was ice cold, his pulse rabbiting beneath her touch. "Max, baby, please. Come back to Mommy."

Nothing. Just those moving lips, forming soundless words, and a expression on his face that she'd never seen before—a kind of hungry fascination, the look of a child discovering something wonderful and terrible all at once.

Then she heard it.

Singing.

It drifted up from the well's depths, thin and sweet and utterly wrong. A child's voice, maybe, or something pretending to be a child's voice, the way a parrot might mimic human speech without understanding the words. The melody was old—she recognized it from somewhere deep in her own childhood, a nursery rhyme her grandmother used to sing. But the words were wrong, inverted, turned inside out into something that made her teeth ache.

Ring around the rosie Pocket full of posies Ashes, ashes We all fall...

The voice didn't say "down." It said something else, a word in a language Sarah didn't know but understood anyway, felt in her bones and the base of her skull. A word that meant *drowning* and *joining* and *coming home*.

Max's lips shaped that word.

"No." Sarah hooked both arms around her son's chest and *pulled*, putting all her weight into it, her feet scrabbling for purchase on the damp floor. "No, you don't get him. You don't get my baby—"

Max tore free.

The separation was so sudden that Sarah fell backward, landing hard on the concrete with Max in her lap. He gasped—a huge, drowning gulp of air—and started crying. Real crying, the kind that came with hiccups and snot and the full-body shudders of a terrified child.

"Mama," he sobbed into her shoulder. "Mama, I'm sorry, I'm sorry, he said— he said if I listened he'd show me where the toys are, the good toys, the ones that still work even though they're old, and I just—I just wanted to see—"

"Shh, baby, it's okay." Sarah held him tight, her own heart hammering. Over his head, she looked at Lily. "How did you two get down here? I locked the door."

Lily's eyes were too wide, too dark. "It opened. We were playing in the hallway and it just… opened. And Max said he heard someone calling his name." She swallowed hard. "I told him not to go down, but he said Ben needed him."

"Ben?"

"His imaginary friend. The one he talks to at night."

Sarah's blood went cold. Benjamin Kane. The boy who drowned. The boy whose nursery was perfectly preserved upstairs, whose toys still sat in neat circles, whose *something* was still in this house, waiting.

"Both of you, listen to me." Sarah struggled to her feet, Max still clinging to her like a barnacle. "Neither of you come down here again. Ever. Do you understand? This basement is off-limits. The door stays locked, and if you even *think* about opening it—"

"Mom." Lily's voice was barely a whisper. "The well."

Sarah turned.

70

The singing had stopped. But now she could hear something else—a voice, definitely a woman's voice, ragged and desperate and muffled, as if speaking through layers of cloth. Or through a mouth sewn shut with black thread.

"Please," the voice whispered, echoing up from impossible depths. "Please, someone help me. He put me down here. He said I couldn't tell. He said if I screamed he'd take Benjamin next and I couldn't—I couldn't let him—please, God, please, I've been down here so long and it's so *dark*—"

Eleanor Kane.

The name slammed into Sarah's mind with the force of revelation. Eleanor Kane, whose body was never found. Eleanor, who vanished the same night her husband died and her son drowned.

Eleanor, who might still be down there, at the bottom of the well, in whatever passed for "down there" in this impossible depth.

"Please," the voice begged. "Please don't leave me here. Not again. Not in the dark. The water's rising and I can't—I can't hold my breath much longer—"

Lily made a small, wounded sound. "We have to help her."

"No." Sarah grabbed her daughter's arm before she could move toward the well. "No, we're leaving. Right now."

"But she's—"

"Not real." Sarah pulled both children toward the stairs, her skin crawling with the certainty of being watched. "She's not real, baby. It's just the house. It's just..."

But even as she said it, she knew it was a lie. The house wasn't *just* anything. The house was a throat, and they were living in its mouth, and sooner or later it was going to swallow.

They climbed the stairs, Sarah herding the children ahead of her, the work lamp's beam dancing crazily across stone walls. Behind them, the woman's voice followed, growing fainter but never quite stopping:

"Please... please... the water... I can't... Benjamin, baby, Mama's sorry... Mama's so sorry..."

Sarah slammed the basement door and locked it, tested it twice, then dragged the hall table in front of it for good measure. Her hands were shaking so badly she could barely manage the task.

"Mom?" Max's voice was very small. "Is Mrs. Kane really down there?"

Sarah knelt in front of her children, taking their faces in her hands. Max's cheeks were still wet with tears. Lily's eyes held a knowledge no ten-year-old should possess.

"I don't know," Sarah said honestly, because what else could she say? That ghosts weren't real? That dead women didn't whisper from wells? That houses were just wood and stone and couldn't possibly want anything?

She'd tried those lies already. The house had proven her wrong.

"What I *do* know," she continued, "is that neither of you go near that door again. Not today, not tomorrow, not ever. Promise me."

They promised. Sarah wanted to believe them.

The rest of the day passed in a haze of forced normalcy. Sarah made grilled cheese sandwiches that no one ate. She put on a movie the children usually loved—they sat stone-faced and silent, barely blinking. When Melissa called for their daily check-in, Sarah lied with a brightness that hurt her throat: "Everything's fine! Just settling in. The kids love it here!"

She couldn't say the truth. Couldn't say *I think there's a dead woman at the bottom of the well in my basement. I think she's been there since 1963. I think she's begging for help and I don't know if she's a ghost or a memory or something worse.*

Couldn't say *My son was possessed by something for five minutes today and I don't know if I got all of it out of him.*

So she lied. And hated herself for it.

By eight PM, both children were in bed, exhausted by terror. Sarah sat in the hallway between their rooms, a baseball bat across her knees (as if that would help against whatever lived in this house), and tried to think.

She could leave. Should leave. Pack the kids in the car tonight and just drive until Halloween Street was nothing but an unpleasant memory.

Except they'd tried the doors yesterday and they wouldn't open. Tried the windows and the glass wouldn't break. And even if she could get out, where would they go? She'd spent every penny on this place. Melissa's apartment was tiny. The divorce had left her broke and broken, and this house—this

72

cursed house—was all she had.

The trap had closed and she hadn't even noticed the teeth.

At 9:47 PM, Sarah dozed off sitting upright, the bat still in her grip.

At 11:33 PM, a sound woke her.

Stone scraping against stone.

It came from below, from the basement, a grinding rasp like something impossibly heavy being dragged across concrete. Or like iron bars being moved. Bent. Opened.

Sarah stood on legs that had gone numb from sitting, the bat gripped in white-knuckled hands. She crept down the stairs, each step careful, avoiding the creaky boards she'd already memorized.

The hall table she'd pushed against the basement door sat exactly where she'd left it.

The door, however, was open.

Not thrown wide—just cracked, maybe six inches, enough for darkness to leak out like oil. The lock hung loose, screws pulled halfway from the wood as if something had pushed from the other side with immense, patient pressure.

The scraping sound came again, echoing up from below.

Sarah stood frozen, every instinct screaming at her to run upstairs, to grab the children and—and what? The house wouldn't let them leave. She knew that with the same bone-deep certainty she knew her own name.

She pushed the door open wider.

The basement stairs descended into darkness, the work lamp long since dead or removed. But there was light down there—a faint, sickly phosphorescence that seemed to emanate from the stones themselves, the same color as old bones and deep-sea creatures.

Sarah descended, the bat raised, her breath coming in short, panicked gasps.

The well waited for her.

The iron grate lay on the floor beside the opening, its bars bent and twisted like taffy, the metal still smoking as if superheated from within. The interlocking pattern that had hurt to look at was broken, its protection shattered.

The well itself yawned open, a perfect circle of darkness that seemed to extend down forever and ever and ever, deeper than basements should go, deeper than the earth itself.

Something moved in that darkness.

Sarah watched, hypnotized by horror, as pale fingers crept over the well's stone lip. They were a woman's fingers, elegant and long, but the nails were black and broken, the skin waterlogged and peeling. They scrabbled for purchase, finding it, pulling.

An arm followed. A shoulder. A head emerging from the depths, hair plastered to a skull, water streaming from empty eye sockets.

Eleanor Kane crawled out of the well.

She moved with the jerky, unnatural motion of something that had forgotten how bodies worked, limbs bending at wrong angles, joints popping with sounds like gunshots in the confined space. Her dress—once fine, now rotting—clung to a frame that was more skeleton than flesh. And her mouth—

Her mouth was sewn shut with black thread, the stitches pulling at dead skin, creating a grotesque pucker where lips should be. But the stitches were old, rotting, and they were breaking.

As Sarah watched, paralyzed, Eleanor's mouth tore open.

The scream that emerged wasn't sound—it was pressure, a wave of grief and rage and sixty-two years of drowning that slammed into Sarah like a physical thing. She fell backward, the bat clattering from nerveless fingers.

And Eleanor Kane kept crawling, kept pulling herself from the well, her ruined throat working, her torn mouth forming words Sarah could finally, horribly hear:

"Where is my son? Where is my Benjamin? He took my baby and I couldn't scream and I couldn't tell and the water rose and rose and I NEED MY BABY—"

Sarah scrambled backward on her hands and feet, too terrified to stand, too shocked to run. Eleanor reached for her with those terrible fingers—

The lights came on.

All of them, simultaneously, blazing with enough force that bulbs shattered in their fixtures. And in that harsh, sudden illumination, Eleanor Kane was gone.

74

Just gone. No fade, no dramatic dissolution—there one moment, absent the next, as if she'd never been there at all.

Except the grate was still bent. Still ruined.

And Sarah could hear water dripping somewhere in the darkness, slow and steady, like the tick of a clock counting down to something inevitable.

She ran.

Up the stairs, slamming the basement door behind her, throwing every lock, dragging furniture until a barricade four feet high blocked the entrance. Her hands bled from splinters. She didn't care.

The well was open.

The well was open and Eleanor was out and Sarah didn't know what that meant but she knew, with the certainty of prey recognizing a predator's roar, that everything had just gotten so much worse.

She checked on the children—still sleeping, thank God, still safe in their beds.

Then she stood in the hallway, bleeding and shaking, and admitted the truth she'd been avoiding since that first night:

They were trapped in this house with something that wanted them.

And Halloween was still three weeks away.

Outside, the October wind picked up, rattling windows, and somewhere in the distance, a child's voice sang a nursery rhyme about falling down, down, down into the dark.

Sarah didn't sleep that night.

She sat between her children's rooms and waited for dawn, the bent and broken grate's image burned into her mind—metal that strong didn't just bend. It took force. It took purpose.

It took something that had been down in that well for sixty-two years, growing stronger on rage and grief and unanswered questions, waiting for someone stupid enough to buy the last house on Halloween Street.

Waiting for someone weak enough to bring children.

And when dawn finally came, gray and cold through windows that wouldn't open, Sarah made a decision:

She was going to find out exactly what happened in this house in 1963.

Because if she was going to survive Halloween with her children intact, she needed to know what Eleanor Kane wanted.

And whether giving it to her would save them.

Or damn them.

Nine

CHAPTER 9: *"The Collectors"*

S arah pov

The grandfather clock in the hallway struck two in the morning, its chime discordant and wrong, like someone had tuned it to a frequency meant to unsettle rather than mark time. Sarah sat curled in the wingback chair in what she'd begun calling the library—though it was really just a dusty room lined with bookshelves that smelled of mildew and something sweeter, more organic. Rot, maybe. Or very old flowers left too long in a vase.

Eleanor Kane's diary lay open in her lap.

The leather cover was soft with age, the pages brittle and yellowed at the edges, covered in a careful, feminine script that slanted slightly to the right. Pressed between several pages were dried flowers—roses, Sarah thought, though they'd faded to the color of old blood. She'd found a few petals scattered on the floor beneath where the diary had been hidden, as if Eleanor had carried them with her even in her final moments.

Margaret Wu had pressed the journal into Sarah's hands that afternoon with trembling fingers, her voice dropping to barely a whisper: "My grandmother cleaned for the Kanes. She found this hidden in the nursery, sewn into the lining of Benjamin's toy chest. She kept it all these years, afraid to destroy it but more afraid of what would happen if anyone knew she had it. When she died, she left it to me with one instruction: give it to whoever lives in that house next. Give them the truth."

Sarah had wanted to read it immediately, but Lily and Max had been with her at the library, and something about the weight of the diary in her hands told her this wasn't meant for daylight or young eyes.

So she'd waited until now. Until the house was as quiet as it ever got—which was to say, not quiet at all. The walls still creaked. The pipes still groaned. And every so often, from somewhere deep below, came the sound of water dripping, each drop distinct and deliberate, like Morse code tapped out by the dead.

The lamp beside her flickered, and Sarah's breath caught before the light steadied. The bulb was new. She'd replaced it just that morning after finding the old one shattered in its socket, the filament twisted into a shape that looked disturbingly like a noose.

She pulled the crocheted throw tighter around her shoulders and began to read.

March 3rd, 1963

Today Victor told me about The Collectors. We've been married for twelve years, and he's never once mentioned them. I thought I knew my husband. I thought I understood the source of his family's wealth, their influence in Hollow's End. I was a fool.

It happened after dinner. Benjamin was in bed, and I was embroidering in the parlor when Victor poured himself a scotch—his third—and said, "Eleanor, there's something you need to know about this house. About what's required of us."

At first, I thought he was going to confess to an affair. How I wish that had been it.

He told me about a society formed in 1897 by the seven wealthiest families in Hollow's End: the Kanes, the Ashtons, the Hargroves, the Prescotts, the Winthropes, the Townsends, and the Becketts. These men—and they were all men then, though their wives participated in their own ways—discovered something beneath the land where they'd built their homes.

Halloween Street, Victor said, was constructed atop a mass grave. Criminals hanged in the colonial era. Witches accused and condemned. Sinners buried without benefit of holy ground. Hundreds of them, maybe more, their bones stacked like cordwood beneath the earth.

The founding families noticed strange occurrences shortly after the street was completed. Children falling ill with no cause. Wives waking with bruises shaped like handprints. Men driven to violence by voices only they could hear. One family's infant daughter was found drowned in a locked nursery, though there was no water anywhere in the room.

That's when they brought in the medium—a woman from New Orleans whose name Victor wouldn't speak. She told them the dead beneath the street were restless. Angry. That they'd been denied peace and now they would deny peace to the living. The hauntings would continue, escalating, until the entire street was consumed.

Unless they made a bargain.

Sarah's hands had gone numb. She set the diary down for a moment, pressing her palms against her eyes until she saw stars. In the hallway, floorboards creaked—the distinctive pattern of someone climbing the stairs. But both children were asleep upstairs. She'd checked on them twenty minutes ago, kissing their foreheads, tucking blankets around their small bodies.

The creaking stopped at the top of the landing.

Sarah forced herself to breathe. To pick up the diary again. To keep reading, because now she had to know. She had to understand what she'd brought her children into.

March 10th, 1963

I haven't been able to write. Every time I try, my hand shakes so badly the words become illegible. But I must document this. Someone must know.

The bargain the medium proposed was this: a ritual, performed every seven years on Halloween night when the veil between the living and the dead is thinnest. Each founding family would offer something precious to the burial ground. A sacrifice, she called it, though she dressed it up in prettier language.

79

The sacrifice had to be blood. Had to be willing. Had to be a child of the family line.

I can barely write those words. A child. They wanted the families to murder their own children to appease the dead.

Victor insisted it wasn't murder. The medium had been very specific about the ritual's requirements. The child had to go willingly into the earth. Had to accept their fate as an offering. The families would gather at midnight in the cellar of whichever house was designated that year, and the chosen child would be led to a prepared grave—Victor described it as a "resting chamber"—where they would be given a sleeping draught and laid to rest while prayers were spoken.

The euphemisms made me ill. Sleeping draught. Resting chamber. As if there were any gentleness in what they were describing.

I asked Victor if he'd ever witnessed this ritual. If he'd ever seen it performed.

He wouldn't answer directly. He only said, "It's been going on for sixty-six years, Eleanor. Nine cycles. Nine sacrifices. And Hollow's End has prospered beyond measure. No child has died of illness in three generations. Our businesses thrive while others fail. We've been protected."

"Protected," I echoed. "By murdering children."

"By honoring the dead," he corrected. "By maintaining the balance."

That's when I understood. The ritual wasn't coming. It had already happened. Nine times. Nine children had died in this house, in the Ashton house, in all the houses on Halloween Street. And their families had covered it up, had called it illness or accident or simply never spoken of it at all.

I asked about the children. Where they were buried. What happened to them.

Victor's face went cold. "They're honored," he said. "They're remembered by those who matter. And they serve a greater purpose."

I didn't sleep that night. Or any night since.

The lamp flickered again, and this time when it steadied, the light seemed dimmer, as if something were draining the electricity from the bulb. Sarah glanced toward the doorway—still empty, but she could feel eyes on her. The sensation of being watched had become so constant in this house that she'd almost stopped noticing it. Almost.

In Lily's room upstairs, something thumped against the floor. Once. Twice.

Then silence.

Sarah wanted to go check on her daughter, but her body felt leaden, anchored to the chair by dread and the terrible magnetism of Eleanor's words. She turned the page, and a photograph slipped out, falling onto her lap.

It showed seven families gathered in front of the Kane house—must have been taken in the early 1950s, based on the clothing and the quality of the image. The adults stood in a formal line, faces solemn, hands clasped in front of them. But it was the children that made Sarah's breath catch.

Seven children, ranging in age from about five to thirteen, stood in front of their parents. Seven children, each one holding a white lily.

The funeral flower.

Sarah's vision swam. She turned the photograph over and found names written in faded ink: *Susannah Ashton, 1904. Thomas Hargrove, 1911. Caroline Prescott, 1918. James Winthrop, 1925. Dorothy Townsend, 1932. Michael Beckett, 1939. Grace Kane, 1946.*

Grace Kane. Victor's younger sister.

One more name would complete the cycle of nine. One more child would have been sacrificed in…

1953.

Sarah did the math in her head, ice crawling up her spine. Seven years after Grace. Then 1960 would have been scheduled for the eighth sacrifice. And 1967 would have been the ninth.

But according to the newspaper articles Margaret had shown her, Victor had died in 1963. Four years before the next ritual was due.

What had happened? What had changed?

October 15th, 1963

Victor told me tonight. He was drunk—drunker than I've ever seen him—and the words spilled out of him like poison from a wound.

Benjamin is the chosen one. For the 1967 ritual.

They selected him three years ago at a Collectors' meeting. The families take turns, Victor explained, and it's been eighteen years since a Kane child was offered. Grace died for our prosperity. Now Benjamin must do the same.

I wanted to scream. I wanted to kill him. Instead, I asked, very calmly, "And you agreed to this?"

"I didn't have a choice," Victor said. "If we refuse, the covenant is broken. The protection ends. The dead will come for all of us, not just our family but every family on this street. They'll drag us into the earth, Eleanor. All of us. I've seen what happens when the dead are denied what they're owed."

I asked him what he meant. What he'd seen.

He told me about the Hargrove family. In 1946, Charles Hargrove had second thoughts after his daughter Caroline's death in the 1918 ritual. When the 1953 ritual came due and his youngest son was chosen, Charles refused. He took his boy and tried to run.

They made it as far as the edge of town. Their car went off the road—no explanation, just veered straight into a tree at midnight. Charles, his wife, his son, and his two daughters all died on impact. The Collectors ruled it an accident. But Victor had been there when they pulled the bodies from the wreckage.

"Every single one of them had soil in their mouths," Victor whispered. "Not regular soil. Black earth, the kind you find in very old graves. And their eyes... Eleanor, their eyes were sewn shut with black thread, even the baby. The dead had claimed them for breaking the covenant."

I felt something break inside me then. Some fundamental understanding of who my husband was—or who he'd become, living in this house, breathing in its secrets.

I told him I would never let him sacrifice our son.

He looked at me with something like pity. "You think you have a choice, Eleanor. You don't. None of us do. The ritual is in four years. You'll come to understand by then. You'll see it's merciful. Benjamin won't suffer. He'll sleep, and he'll never wake, and he'll save us all."

"He's seven years old," I said.

"Grace was nine," Victor replied. "And she was brave. She understood what was required of her."

That's when I knew I had to get Benjamin out of this house. Out of Hollow's End. I don't care if the dead come for me. I don't care if I break some hellish covenant. My son will not die to appease corpses in the ground.

I've been planning. Saving money from the household accounts. I have a cousin

in Portland who knows nothing of The Collectors or Hollow's End. She'll take us in,
no questions asked, if I can just get Benjamin there.

We leave in two weeks. On October 31st, while Victor is at the Collectors' meeting
preparing for the ritual four years hence, Benjamin and I will disappear.

Let the dead come. I'll face them before I let them have my son.

Sarah's heart was hammering so hard she could feel it in her throat, in her
temples, behind her eyes. She turned the page with shaking hands, knowing
what was coming but needing to see it anyway.

The handwriting changed in the next entry. It was rushed, frantic, the
letters digging into the paper.

October 30th, 1963

He knows. God help me, Victor knows.

I don't know how he found out. I was so careful. But tonight, after dinner, he
locked the doors. All of them. I heard the bolts slide into place, one after another,
like a countdown.

When I tried the front door, I found he'd removed the keys. The windows are
nailed shut—I discovered that when I attempted to open one in the kitchen. The
heads of the nails have been filed smooth. I can't get any purchase to pull them out.

Benjamin is in his room. He doesn't understand why we can't go to his friend's
Halloween party tomorrow. I told him his father wants a quiet family evening. I
lied to my son, and he believed me because he still trusts the world.

Victor won't speak to me. He's in his study, drinking, listening to records. The
same song over and over—some terrible thing with children singing in French. The
melody carries through the house like a funeral dirge.

I tried to reason with him an hour ago. Begged him to let us leave, promising I'd
never speak of The Collectors, never reveal what I knew. He looked at me like I was
already dead.

"The covenant cannot be broken," he said. "If you run, you condemn everyone on
this street. Thirty-seven souls, Eleanor. Can you live with that? Can Benjamin?"

I told him I'd rather save my son and damn the world.

He smiled—actually smiled—and said, "Then you understand how the dead feel.
They were damned, and now they'll take their due."

I don't know what he's planning. But I've hidden this diary in Benjamin's toy chest, sewn it into the lining where Victor would never think to look. If something happens to me—

If something happens to us—

Someone needs to know the truth about Halloween Street. About The Collectors. About what these families have done in the name of protection.

They're not honoring the dead. They're feeding them. Perpetuating a cycle of murder disguised as ritual. And I won't—I can't—

Sarah turned the page. This was it. The final entry. The words that came just before whatever horror had unfolded on October 31st, 1963.

October 31st, 1963 — 11:47 PM

He's going to kill us.

Victor came to my room an hour ago. He had a rope in his hands and something in his pocket—I couldn't see what, but it clicked when he moved, like scissors or shears.

He said the covenant had been amended. That he'd spoken with the other Collectors, and they'd agreed to an emergency ritual. Benjamin would be sacrificed tonight instead of waiting until 1967. The dead were restless, Victor claimed. They knew I'd tried to run. They were demanding payment immediately.

"Better this way," he told me, so calmly, as if discussing what to have for breakfast. "Benjamin won't know. I'll give him the sleeping draught in warm milk. He'll drift off in his bed and never wake. Painless. Merciful."

I fought him. Scratched his face until I drew blood. Screamed for Benjamin to run. But Victor is stronger, and he locked me in this room before I could reach our son.

I can hear Benjamin crying in the nursery. He's calling for me. "Mama, where are you? Mama, I'm scared."

Victor is in the hallway. I hear his footsteps, slow and deliberate. He's humming that song—the one with the children singing. It's getting closer.

Oh God. He's at Benjamin's door. I can hear it opening.

The children are singing again. Not on the record—from somewhere below us. From the basement. They're singing in unison, dozens of voices, maybe hundreds, and they're getting louder.

Benjamin is crying. He's saying, "I don't want to swim. I don't want to go in the water, Papa."

There's a well in the basement. Victor had it sealed years ago, said it was dangerous, but I can hear water down there sometimes, moving against stone.

He's taking Benjamin to the well.

No. No no no no—

I have to get out. Have to—

The door. He's coming up the stairs. He's coming for me next.

Benjamin isn't crying anymore. I can't hear him. Why can't I hear him?

The children are still singing. Their voices are—

He's outside my door. The lock is turning.

God forgive me, I should never have—

The entry ended mid-sentence, the final word smeared, as if Eleanor's hand had been jerked away from the page.

Sarah sat frozen, the diary trembling in her hands. In the house around her, something fundamental had shifted. The temperature had dropped so suddenly her breath misted in the air. And from somewhere below—from the basement, from behind that door that never stayed locked—came the sound of children singing.

The same melody. The same words, though Sarah couldn't understand them. French, maybe, like Eleanor had written. A lullaby that sounded like a requiem.

And beneath the singing, barely audible but unmistakable: the sound of water. Rising. Rushing. Calling.

Sarah looked down at the diary one last time, at Eleanor's desperate final words, and understood with perfect, terrible clarity:

Victor had killed his wife and son that night to fulfill the covenant. Had murdered them both rather than break The Collectors' pact with the dead. And the ritual had been incomplete—interrupted, corrupted, wrong.

Which meant the dead beneath Halloween Street had been waiting sixty years for what they were owed.

Waiting for another mother. Another child.

Waiting for Lily.

The lamp went out. In the sudden darkness, Sarah heard footsteps on the stairs—small footsteps, child-sized, ascending from the basement.

And a voice, young and hollow, echoing through the walls:

"Mama's in the water. Papa put her there. Now it's time for your little girl to swim."

Sarah ran.

Ten

Chapter 10: The Collectors

Sarah pov

The diary's leather cover felt wrong in Sarah's hands—too cold, too smooth, like touching dead skin. She sat at the kitchen table at 2:47 AM, unable to sleep, unable to stop thinking about Eleanor Kane's missing body and Benjamin's drowned corpse and the sealed well that kept trying to open itself from the inside.

Margaret Wu's warning echoed in her mind: *My grandmother said Eleanor was terrified those last weeks. Said she kept whispering about collections and payments and debts to the dead.*

Sarah opened the diary.

The first entry was dated January 3rd, 1963, written in elegant cursive that belonged to another era:

Victor presented me with this journal as a New Year's gift. He says I should document our life together, preserve our family's legacy for Benjamin. I wonder if he knows how carefully I must choose my words. How much I cannot say, even here, even to paper that no one else should read.

The house is so cold this winter. No matter how high we turn the furnace, I cannot seem to get warm. Benjamin complains of voices in the walls. Victor tells him to stop being foolish, but I have heard them too. Singing. Always singing.

Sarah's throat tightened. She glanced toward the darkened hallway where Lily and Max slept—where Max had claimed to hear singing from the basement just days ago. The same house. The same voices. Sixty-two years apart.

She kept reading.

January 15th, 1963

Victor held a dinner party last night for what he calls his "associates." I am forbidden from using their real name, even in private, but I will write it here because I must tell someone, even if that someone is only paper: The Collectors.

Twelve families. Twelve men who sit in our parlor drinking my husband's cognac and speaking in euphemisms about "maintaining balance" and "honoring the covenant" and "the price of prosperity."

They do not know I listen from the top of the stairs. They do not know I have learned to move through this house like a ghost myself, silent and unseen.

Last night, they spoke about the next collection. It falls on Halloween. October 31st, 1963. Seven years since the last.

I did not understand at first. I thought they meant collecting debts or taxes or some other business matter. But then Thomas Ashton (Robert's grandfather—God, he looked just like his grandson, same weak chin, same nervous hands) spoke about his daughter Mary and how "unfortunate" it was that she would be "of age" this year.

Victor squeezed his glass so hard I thought it would shatter. He said, "That won't be necessary for us. Benjamin is only eight. Far too young."

And Gerald Winters (Hannah's father, I realize now) laughed. Laughed. He said, "Victor, the covenant doesn't care about age. Only about blood. You know the rules. Every family, every seven years. No exceptions."

I nearly fell down the stairs. I had to press my hand against my mouth to keep from screaming.

Sarah's hands trembled. She set the diary down, walked to the sink, and splashed cold water on her face. The kitchen clock read 3:03 AM. Upstairs, something creaked—footsteps that weren't footsteps, movement that wasn't quite movement.

She returned to the table and forced herself to continue.

February 8th, 1963

I have been researching. Our library has old newspapers, records, death certificates. I have been so careful. I tell the librarian I'm writing a local history project.

The pattern is clear once you know to look for it:

1897 - Halloween. Five children dead. Drowning, they said. A terrible accident at the autumn festival.

1904 - Halloween. Seven dead. A fire at the orphanage. Such a tragedy, they said.

1911 - Halloween. Four dead. Influenza, they claimed. Only the sick were the children of The Collectors' families, and they all died on the same night.

Every seven years. Always children. Always blood relatives of the twelve families.

I found something else in the archives—a map from 1890 showing what stood here before they built Halloween Street. It was labeled "Gallows Ground - Colonial Cemetery - Condemned 1710 - DO NOT DISTURB."

They built this street, these beautiful houses, directly on top of a mass grave. Criminals, witches, the accused—anyone Hollow's End wanted to forget. Hundreds of bodies buried without prayer, without sanctity.

And now their descendants live here. Dwell here. Prosper here.

But at what cost?

Sarah felt ice crystallize in her stomach. The room seemed to tilt, the shadows in the corners deepening, reaching. She thought of Lily and Max sleeping upstairs, thought of the muddy footprints that led from the basement to their rooms, thought of Max whispering *Ben says it's time to swim.*

The house groaned around her, wood settling or something walking through walls.

She read faster now, skimming through months of entries where Eleanor's elegant handwriting became increasingly frantic, letters slanting, ink blotted with what might have been tears.

June 12th, 1963

I confronted Victor last night. I could not keep silent any longer.

I told him I knew about The Collectors. I knew about the covenant. I knew what they planned to do on Halloween.

He did not deny it. He simply looked at me with such cold eyes—eyes I had never seen before, like he was a stranger wearing my husband's face—and said, "It has always been this way, Eleanor. Since the street was built. It is the price we pay for everything we have. The businesses that never fail. The crops that always flourish. The sicknesses that pass us by. The dead demand their due."

I said, "You're talking about murdering our son."

He said, "I'm talking about sacrifice. There is a difference."

He explained it all then. How in 1897, the founding families of Halloween Street began experiencing terrible luck. Their children died. Their businesses failed. They saw apparitions—hanging victims, drowned corpses, burned witches—crawling from the earth beneath their homes.

A traveling medium came to Hollow's End. She told them the land was cursed because the dead had never been properly laid to rest. She said the only way to appease them was blood sacrifice. Not animals. Not strangers. Blood relatives. "Willing" offerings to the mass grave.

The families were desperate. So they chose the oldest, the sickest, the "least essential" children and performed the ritual that first Halloween. And it worked. The hauntings stopped. Prosperity returned.

They've done it every seven years since. Twelve families. One sacrifice each. Always children. Always on Halloween when the veil is thinnest.

Victor said, "We won't choose Benjamin. I swear to you. We'll select the next youngest instead—"

I struck him. I struck my husband across the face and told him if he touched our son, if he even THOUGHT about harming Benjamin, I would tell the police everything.

He grabbed my wrist. He said, "No one will believe you. The police are paid to look away. The medical examiner is one of us. The town council protects The Collectors. You are alone in this, Eleanor."

But I am not alone. I have Benjamin. And I will save him, even if it means burning this entire street to the ground.

Sarah's heart hammered against her ribs. She stood abruptly, pacing the kitchen, trying to process the enormity of what she was reading. A murder cult. Generational conspiracy. Ritual sacrifice disguised as accidents, illnesses, tragedies.

And they had sold her this house. Robert Ashton, grandson of one of the original Collectors, had handed her the keys with that nervous smile and ridiculous warning about not answering doors on Halloween.

They knew. The town council knew. The police knew. Everyone knew, or they were complicit, or they were too afraid to speak.

She was utterly alone.

Just like Eleanor.

Sarah returned to the diary, her hands shaking so badly she could barely turn the pages.

August 30th, 1963

I have made arrangements. A cousin in Vermont has agreed to take us in, no questions asked. On October 15th, I will tell Victor I'm taking Benjamin to visit my mother in Boston. Instead, we will drive north and never come back.

I have packed a bag. Hidden it in the attic. I have saved what money I could without Victor noticing.

Two more months. Just two more months and we will be free.

Benjamin asked me yesterday why I cry so much now. I told him it was allergies. He is so sweet, so innocent. He cannot know. He must never know what his father planned for him.

I hear the singing more often now. It comes from the well in the basement. Victor had it sealed years ago, said it was "unstable," but I know the truth. That well goes down into the burial ground. That well is where they dispose of the bodies after the rituals.

Sometimes I dream of hands reaching up from the water. Small hands. Children's hands. Pulling me down into darkness.

I wake up screaming, and Victor tells me I'm hysterical. He's started locking the bedroom door from the outside "for my own protection." He says I'm not well. He says I'm imagining things.

But I'm not. I'm the only one seeing clearly.

October 12th, 1963

Three days. Three days until we leave.

Victor is suspicious. He watches me constantly. He's forbidden me from leaving the house without him. He's taken my car keys, my money, everything I had hidden.

But I found the spare keys. I know where he keeps the cash. On October 15th at 2 AM when he's in his deepest sleep, Benjamin and I will run.

The house knows. I can feel it watching me, listening. The walls breathe. The floorboards creak with weight that isn't there. Last night, I saw a woman in a white dress standing in Benjamin's room. When I turned on the light, she was gone, but the smell remained—earth and rot and something ancient.

I don't care. Let the dead watch. Let them know I refuse. I will not give them my son.

October 14th, 1963

Tomorrow. Tomorrow we leave.

Victor held a Collectors meeting here tonight. I heard everything through the heating vent.

They know I plan to run. Someone told them. Who? The cousin I contacted? The bank teller I spoke to? It doesn't matter now.

Gerald Winters suggested they take Benjamin early "to ensure compliance." Victor refused. He said he would "handle his wife."

After they left, Victor came upstairs. He didn't speak to me. He just stood in the doorway of our bedroom for the longest time, watching me pretend to sleep.

Then he whispered: "I'm sorry, Eleanor. I truly am. But the covenant must be kept."

He locked the door from the outside.

I am trapped. Benjamin is in the nursery down the hall, also locked in.

I've been prying at the door frame with a letter opener for two hours. The wood is old. I think I can break it free. I MUST break it free.

Tomorrow is October 15th. The collection is in sixteen days.

I will not let them have my son.

I will not.

I will—

The next entry was dated October 29th, 1963. Two weeks had passed. The handwriting had changed—shakier, more frantic, ink smeared as if written in terrible haste.

October 29th, 1963

He caught us.

We made it to the car. We were in the driveway, Benjamin in the back seat with his little stuffed bear, and I was starting the engine. I could taste freedom. I could feel the weight lifting.

Then Victor appeared in the headlights. Not walking. Not running. Just THERE. As if he'd materialized from shadows.

He yanked open my door. He pulled me from the car by my hair. Benjamin was screaming. I was screaming. The neighbors' lights came on, but no one helped. No one even opened their doors.

They knew. Of course they knew. The entire street is Collectors' families.

Victor dragged me back into the house. He locked Benjamin in the nursery—I heard my baby crying, heard him pounding on the door, calling for me.

Victor took me to the basement. To the well.

He unsealed it. The smell that rose up—God, the SMELL—decay and standing water and something worse, something that made my brain scream that I was smelling death itself, concentrated death, centuries of it.

He showed me the bottom. Held a lantern over the edge. I saw bones down there. Small bones. Children's skulls arranged in circles.

He said, "This is what happens to those who refuse the covenant. The dead take them anyway, but they take them slowly. Painfully. You cannot outrun this, Eleanor. You can only obey."

I spat in his face.

He struck me. Tied my hands. Left me in the basement with the well unsealed.

I can hear them singing down there. The children The Collectors murdered. Sixty-six years of sacrifices. Singing and singing and singing.

Tomorrow is October 30th. The collection is in two days.

Benjamin will not die. I will find a way. I must find a way.

October 30th, 1963 - Morning

Victor left for work. Gerald Winters is watching the house, stationed in his parlor across the street.

I've been working at the ropes for hours. My wrists are bleeding, but the knots are loosening.

Benjamin is still locked in the nursery. I can hear him talking to someone—probably his imaginary friend. He's always been such a sensitive child. Sometimes I think he sees things I cannot.

If I can free myself, I can break down his door. The back door is unwatched. We can run through the woods to the main road. We can—

Victor is home. Early. He's coming down the stairs.

He knows I've been trying to escape. I can hear it in his footsteps.

I must hide this diary. Must hide the truth. If I die—

October 30th, 1963 - Evening

He knows I tried to loosen the ropes. He's tied me differently now. Tighter. I cannot feel my hands anymore.

He says he's sorry. He keeps saying it over and over like a prayer. "I'm sorry Eleanor. I'm sorry. But it's for the family. For our future. For the prosperity of everyone on this street."

I told him we have no future if we murder our son.

He said, "We'll have other children."

As if Benjamin is replaceable. As if our boy is just livestock to be offered.

I tried to reason with him one last time. I begged. I told him we could expose The Collectors, tell the authorities, stop this cycle of horror.

He laughed. Laughed. He said, "The authorities are us, Eleanor. The mayor is a Collector. The sheriff is a Collector. The judge, the doctor, the newspaper editor—all of us. Hollow's End belongs to us. It always has."

Then he did something I will never forgive.

He brought Benjamin down to the basement. Made him look into the well. Made our eight-year-old son see the bones of the children who came before.

He said, "This is your duty, Benjamin. Tomorrow night, you will go to the well willingly and join them. You will make our family proud."

Benjamin looked at the bones. Then he looked at Victor. And my sweet, innocent boy said, "No, Father. I won't."

Victor's face went white. Then red. Then something else—something hollow and terrible.

He hit Benjamin. Hit our son so hard the boy fell.

I screamed through the gag he'd placed in my mouth. I thrashed against the ropes until my wrists bled freely.

Victor picked Benjamin up and locked him in the nursery again.

He returned and stood over me. He said, "Tomorrow at midnight, the collection will be completed. Whether Benjamin goes willingly or not. Whether you approve or not. The covenant MUST be kept."

I can feel the house listening. I can feel the dead beneath us, patient, waiting.

Tomorrow is Halloween.

October 31st, 1963 - 3:33 AM

I broke free.

The blood from my wrists made the ropes slippery. I pulled and pulled and PULLED until my hands slipped through.

Victor is asleep upstairs. The house is silent except for the singing from the well.

I'm going to get Benjamin. I'm going to save my son.

And then I'm going to burn this godforsaken house to the ground with Victor in it.

October 31st, 1963 - 4:15 AM

Benjamin is free. We're going to run.

The front door is locked with a key I cannot find. The windows won't open—Victor must have nailed them shut.

The back door. We'll try the back door.

We have to be quiet. So quiet. The floorboards creak, and every sound is like a gunshot.

Benjamin is holding my hand. He's trembling. He whispers, "Mama, the children *in the well are calling my name."*

I tell him to ignore them. I tell him we're leaving, we're going to be safe, we're—

A noise upstairs. Victor's bedroom door opening.

He knows.

We're running for the back door. Benjamin is so small, so light. I can carry him if I must. I will carry him to the ends of the earth.

The back door is opening. The night air is—

October 31st, 1963 - 6:47 AM

He caught us.

We were in the backyard, almost to the woods, almost FREE. Then Victor was there. With Gerald Winters. With Thomas Ashton. With all of them. The Collectors.

They surrounded us. Benjamin was crying. I was screaming for help, but no one came. The neighbors stayed in their houses. The street was silent except for my voice and Benjamin's sobs.

Victor looked at me with such sadness. Such SADNESS. As if I was the one who had done wrong. As if I was the betrayer.

He said, "You've made this so much harder than it needed to be."

They dragged us back inside. Back to the basement. Back to that awful well with its chorus of murdered children.

The Collectors held me while Victor took Benjamin to the well's edge.

My son looked at me. Eight years old. Still clutching his stuffed bear. His eyes so wide, so trusting, so confused.

He said, "Mama? What's happening?"

Victor pushed him in.

I heard the splash. I heard Benjamin scream. I heard him call for me—"MAMA! MAMA HELP ME! I CAN'T SWIM! MAMA THE WATER IS RISING! MAMA PLEASE!"

And I couldn't reach him. They held me back. I fought. God how I fought. I bit and clawed and screamed until my throat bled.

Benjamin's cries became gurgles. Then silence.

The Collectors released me. I crawled to the well, but Gerald Winters sealed it before I could look inside. I clawed at the grate until my fingernails tore off.

Victor said, "The covenant is satisfied."

I looked at him—the man I had married, the man I had loved, the father who had just murdered our son—and I said, "I will destroy you. If it takes me a hundred years. If I have to come back from death itself. I will destroy you and everyone who helped you."

Victor's expression didn't change. He said, "You're hysterical. You need rest."

They're locking me in the bedroom. I can hear them discussing what to do with me.

Thomas Ashton says I'm "a liability." Gerald Winters agrees. They're debating whether to say I had a breakdown and committed suicide, or perhaps an accident—

Victor is arguing for keeping me alive. He says he loves me. He says we can move past this.

Move past murdering our son.

I will never move past this.

I would rather die than spend another day in this house of horrors.

October 31st, 1963 - 7:13 PM

The sun is setting. Soon it will be dark.

They think I've calmed down. They unlocked the bedroom door. Victor brought me dinner on a tray, like I'm an invalid.

He sat on the edge of the bed and took my hand. He said, "Eleanor, I know you're angry. But you'll understand eventually. This is how it's always been. This is how it must be."

I nodded. I let him think I'd accepted it.

I let him kiss my forehead.

I let him leave the room.

And then I took the knife I'd hidden from the dinner tray.

I am going to kill my husband. I am going to expose The Collectors. I am going to make sure everyone knows what happened to Benjamin.

I don't care if they kill me afterward. I don't care if I hang for murder.

Justice for my son is all that matters now.

I can hear them downstairs. The Collectors have gathered for some kind of celebration. Celebrating the successful completion of the ritual. Celebrating the murder of twelve children.

I am going down there.

I am going to—

The entry ended mid-sentence, the pen trailing off the page in a long, jagged line as if Eleanor had been interrupted—or attacked.

The next page was blank.

And the next.

Sarah flipped frantically through the rest of the diary, but the remaining pages were empty. No more entries. No explanation of what happened.

Just Eleanor's voice, silenced mid-word.

Sarah sat frozen at the kitchen table, the diary open before her, her breath coming in short, sharp gasps.

The kitchen clock read 3:33 AM.

A floorboard creaked behind her.

Sarah spun in her chair.

A woman stood in the doorway. Pale. Victorian dress soaked with dark water. Hair tangled with pond weeds. Her mouth was sewn shut with black thread, the stitches crude and terrible, pulling her lips into a permanent silent scream.

Eleanor Kane.

The ghost raised one dripping hand and pointed at Sarah. Then she pointed up—toward the second floor where Lily and Max slept.

Her meaning was crystal clear: *They're coming for your children, just like they came for mine.*

Sarah's scream caught in her throat.

And from the basement, from the sealed well that would not stay sealed, came the sound of children singing:

"*Ring around the rosie Pocket full of posies Ashes, ashes We all fall DOWN—*"

The lights went out.

In the darkness, Sarah heard three deliberate knocks on the basement door.

The dead were waking.

And Halloween was twenty-one days away.

Eleven

Chapter 11: Dr. Rhodes

Sarah pov

The waiting room of Dr. Amelia Rhodes' practice smelled like lavender and lies. Sarah sat between Lily and Max on a too-soft couch, her hands clasped so tightly her knuckles had gone white. Through the frosted glass door, she could hear the murmur of the current session ending—a normal family, probably, with normal problems. A child who wouldn't sleep in their own bed. A teenager acting out. Problems that could be solved with behavioral charts and communication strategies.

Not children who drew drowning scenes in anatomically perfect detail. Not a seven-year-old who spoke in his sleep about mothers trapped in dark water.

Sarah had found three more of Lily's drawings that morning, hidden beneath her daughter's mattress like contraband. Each one more disturbing than the last: skeletal hands reaching up from a stone well, a woman's face beneath black water with her mouth sewn shut, a faceless man standing in a doorway with something dark dripping from his hands.

The door opened. A mother emerged with a young boy, both smiling. The normalcy of it made Sarah's chest ache.

"Mrs. Brennan?" Dr. Rhodes appeared in the doorway—a woman in her early forties with kind eyes and silver-streaked dark hair pulled into a professional bun. She wore a cardigan despite the October chill being kept at bay by the office heating. "Please, come in. All three of you."

The office was designed to be comforting: soft lighting, plush chairs, shelves lined with books on child development and family therapy. A desk sat in the corner, surface clear except for a laptop and a Mason jar full of colored pencils. Toys were arranged in careful groupings—a dollhouse, building blocks, art supplies on a low table.

Everything calculated to put children at ease, to encourage them to play, to express.

Sarah wondered if Dr. Rhodes had ever encountered children who drew things they shouldn't know how to draw.

"Thank you for seeing us on such short notice," Sarah said, her voice steadier than she felt. Melissa had recommended Dr. Rhodes after finding her online—the only child psychologist in Hollow's End with availability. In retrospect, Sarah should have found that suspicious.

"Of course." Dr. Rhodes gestured to the seating area—a couch for Sarah, smaller chairs for the children, her own wingback positioned to observe them all. "I understand you've recently moved to the area. Big transitions can be difficult for children, especially after..." She glanced at the intake form Sarah had filled out. "A divorce. That's a significant loss for a family unit."

"Mom didn't want the divorce," Max said immediately, settling into his chair with uncharacteristic stillness. "Dad did. He said Mom was too sad all the time and he needed to find happiness."

Sarah's face burned. "Max—"

"It's all right." Dr. Rhodes' voice was gentle. "Max, it sounds like you're very aware of what was happening. That must have been confusing."

"Not confusing." Max swung his legs, heels thumping against the chair. "Adults leave when things get hard. That's what they do."

The matter-of-fact tone in his seven-year-old voice broke something in Sarah's chest.

Dr. Rhodes made a note on her tablet, then turned her attention to Lily, who had been silent since entering. "Lily, your mother mentioned you enjoy drawing. I have supplies here if you'd like to use them while we talk."

Lily's gaze flickered to Sarah, then to the art table. After a long moment, she slid from the couch and moved to the supplies with the wariness of a wild animal approaching a trap.

"Mrs. Brennan," Dr. Rhodes said, "why don't you tell me what's been concerning you?"

Where to begin? The knocking at 3:33 AM? The way Max spoke to invisible friends? The footprints that appeared from nowhere? Sarah had rehearsed this on the drive over, practicing how to sound worried-but-rational, concerned-but-not-crazy.

"The move has been harder than I expected," she started carefully. "The house is old, and it makes sounds at night. The children have been having nightmares. Lily's been drawing disturbing images, and Max has been talking to an imaginary friend named Ben who tells him things about the house that Max shouldn't know."

Dr. Rhodes nodded, her expression professionally neutral. "Imaginary friends are quite common at Max's age, especially during times of stress. And Lily's at a developmental stage where processing emotions through art is very healthy. Have you noticed any other behavioral changes? Aggression? Withdrawal? Sleep disturbances?"

"Max tried to drown himself in the bathtub four days ago."

The words came out flat, toneless. Sarah heard them as if someone else had spoken.

Dr. Rhodes' pen stilled. "Tried to drown himself?"

"I found him with his head underwater. When I pulled him out, he said he had to 'go to Ben,' that he'd promised." Sarah's voice cracked. "He had no memory of it afterward. He was confused about why he was soaking wet."

The temperature in the room seemed to drop. Dr. Rhodes set down her tablet with careful deliberation.

"And Lily? Has she exhibited any dangerous behaviors?"

"Sleepwalking. She heads toward the basement in the middle of the night. Last week I found her standing at the top of the basement stairs with her eyes open, but she wasn't... there. She was somewhere else."

101

At the art table, Lily had selected black and red pencils. She was drawing with focused intensity, her small hand moving in confident strokes that seemed too practiced, too sure.

Dr. Rhodes leaned forward slightly. "Mrs. Brennan, I need to ask you something, and I need you to answer honestly. Have you or the children experienced anything in the house that you can't explain rationally? Things moving on their own? Voices? Apparitions?"

Sarah's breath caught. This wasn't a question a normal child psychologist asked.

"Why would you ask that?"

"Because I need to understand the full scope of what we're dealing with." Dr. Rhodes' professional mask had slipped, revealing something underneath—not skepticism, but recognition. Knowledge. "You're living in the Kane house, aren't you? The Last House on Halloween Street."

The confirmation sat between them like a body.

"You know the house," Sarah whispered.

"I've studied it for seven years." Dr. Rhodes rose and moved to a filing cabinet, extracting a thick folder. "I'm not just a child psychologist, Mrs. Brennan. I have a doctorate in parapsychology from Duke University. I came to Hollow's End specifically because of that house."

She opened the folder, spreading documents across her desk. Sarah recognized photographs of her house from different eras—1890s, 1920s, 1963, 2003. In each photo, a family stood on the porch. In each photo, they looked terrified.

"Seventeen families have lived in that house since it was built in 1890," Dr. Rhodes said. "Twelve of those families experienced what you're experiencing. Of those twelve, seven families lost members to unexplained deaths. Three families simply vanished—missing persons cases that were never solved. The remaining two..." She paused. "The remaining two completed the ritual."

Sarah's mouth had gone dry. "What ritual?"

Before Dr. Rhodes could answer, Lily spoke from the art table, her voice dreamy and distant: "The collection. Every seven years when the veil is thin. Blood for the hollow ground."

Both women turned to stare at her.

Lily continued drawing, seemingly unaware she'd spoken.

"Lily," Sarah said carefully, "what did you just say?"

"That's what Ben tells Max. That's what the singing says." Lily didn't look up from her drawing. "The children in the walls sing it at night. Don't you hear them, Mama?"

Dr. Rhodes moved to the art table, and Sarah followed on trembling legs.

The drawing was nearly complete. Lily had rendered the well in the basement with disturbing accuracy—the stone walls, the iron grate, the darkness below. But rising from that darkness were hands. Dozens of them. Skeletal, yes, but drawn with such anatomical precision that Sarah could identify individual carpals and metacarpals, the delicate phalanges reaching upward.

"Lily," Dr. Rhodes said softly, "where did you learn to draw bones like this?"

"Mrs. Kane showed me. She visits sometimes." Lily added more shading to the water. "She can't talk because her mouth is sewn shut, but she shows me things. She's very sad. She's been in the water for a long time."

Sarah's vision tunneled. Eleanor Kane. The missing wife from 1963.

"Max," Dr. Rhodes said, not taking her eyes off Lily's drawing, "can you tell me about your friend Ben?"

Max had been unusually quiet, sitting perfectly still in his chair, staring at nothing. When he spoke, his voice was different—flatter, older, with an odd cadence that made the hair on Sarah's neck stand up.

"Mother's in the water. Father put her there. I watched."

Sarah grabbed the edge of the table. "Max?"

"He sewed her mouth shut first so she couldn't scream. She tried to run away with me, but Father caught us at the back gate. He said she was going to ruin everything. He said the collection had to happen or the dead would come." Max's eyes remained unfocused, staring at something only he could see. "He held my head under the water until the burning stopped. It didn't take very long. Then he put me in the well with Mother."

"Jesus Christ," Sarah breathed.

"Max." Dr. Rhodes moved to kneel in front of him, her professional

103

composure cracking. "Max, is Ben speaking right now?"

"Ben is always speaking. Ben never stops speaking." Max's head turned with mechanical precision to look directly at Dr. Rhodes. "He says you know. He says you've been watching the house for years, waiting to see if this family would be the one. He says you're too late. The harvest moon is coming, and Father is getting stronger."

Dr. Rhodes rocked back on her heels. "How does he know I've been watching?"

"The dead see everything." Max's voice carried no emotion, no inflection. "They see the living like the living see ghosts—faint, translucent, barely there. But when the veil thins, we become solid. And when we're solid, we can touch."

Sarah grabbed Max by the shoulders. "Max, baby, come back. Come back to me right now—"

"She can't help you." Max's eyes finally focused, looking directly at Sarah with an expression no seven-year-old should have—ancient, pitying, knowing. "Mother tried to refuse too. Father killed her. Then he killed me. Then he killed himself, but the ritual was already broken. Now we're all stuck here, waiting for someone to finish what was started. Waiting for the collection."

"Max!" Sarah shook him, terrified. "Maxwell Brennan, you stop this right now—"

"He can't hear you." Dr. Rhodes' hand closed over Sarah's wrist, gentle but firm. "Don't shake him. You'll only traumatize him more when he comes back."

"When he comes *back*? What the hell is happening to my son?"

"He's being used as a conduit. The spirit—Benjamin Kane—is speaking through him." Dr. Rhodes stood, moving quickly to her desk. She pulled out a thick leather journal, flipping through pages covered in dense handwriting. "The knocking you've been hearing. Three knocks at 3:33 AM. Always three knocks."

"How did you—"

"Because it happens to every family. The knocking is a summoning. In folklore, spirits of the dead cannot cross thresholds without permission. They knock three times—a trinity, a request, an invitation. Most people ignore it. Some answer."

Sarah felt sick. "I haven't answered."

"Haven't you?" Dr. Rhodes looked up from her journal. "Have you said 'come in' when you heard knocking? Have you opened a door? Have you invited anyone—*anything*—inside?"

The first night. Sarah had been half-asleep when she heard the knocking. She'd assumed it was one of the kids needing her. She'd called out groggily: *Come in.*

The door had never opened. But something had changed after that night. The cold spots had appeared. The footprints had started.

"Oh God," Sarah whispered.

"Once you invite them in, they can anchor themselves to the living. Children are easiest—their boundaries between reality and imagination are already thin. The spirits use them as vessels to communicate, to move through the house, to prepare for the ritual."

"What ritual?" Sarah demanded. "Everyone keeps talking about a ritual but no one will tell me what it actually is."

Dr. Rhodes closed her journal, her expression grave. "The house sits on a burial ground—a colonial hanging site where condemned prisoners were buried without consecration. The ground is cursed, saturated with the anguish of the executed. In 1890, when the house was built, a secret society called The Collectors formed among Hollow's End's wealthy families. They believed that to prevent the dead from rising, they needed to offer appeasement every seven years on Halloween night when the veil between worlds is thinnest."

"Appeasement," Sarah repeated. "You mean sacrifice."

"A blood relative. A child, traditionally, though some families offered elderly members they considered burdens." Dr. Rhodes' voice was clinical, detached, but Sarah could see the horror in her eyes. "The sacrifice was brought to the well in the basement—which connects directly to the burial ground below. They were killed there and offered to the earth. The families believed this kept their own members safe from supernatural harm."

Lily was adding more hands to her drawing. The page was becoming crowded with skeletal fingers.

"But Victor Kane refused," Sarah said, pieces clicking together. "That's what Eleanor's diary said. He wouldn't sacrifice Benjamin."

"And his refusal broke the covenant. Without the sacrifice in 1963, the ritual was left incomplete. The dead didn't receive their offering. So they took Victor, Eleanor, and Benjamin anyway—but it wasn't the same. It wasn't willing. The curse wasn't satisfied."

"So now what? They want us to finish what Victor started?" Sarah's voice rose. "They want me to sacrifice my children?"

"They want one child. The ritual requires one blood sacrifice from the family living in the house." Dr. Rhodes met Sarah's eyes. "That's what the summoning is for. That's what Benjamin is preparing Max for. That's what Eleanor is showing Lily. They're being conditioned to accept their deaths as inevitable."

The room tilted. Sarah grabbed the edge of the desk.

"No. No, absolutely not. I'm not—we're leaving. Right now. We're getting in the car and driving away and never coming back."

"You can't."

"Watch me—"

"Mrs. Brennan." Dr. Rhodes' voice cut through Sarah's panic. "I've interviewed survivors from two of the families who escaped that house. Both described the same thing: once the summoning begins, once you've given permission for the dead to enter, the house won't let you leave. Doors seal. Cars won't start. Roads lead in circles. The house holds you until Halloween night. Until the ritual can be completed."

Sarah thought of Father Gabriel's warning: *Leave. Tonight.* She thought of the way every exit had seemed to resist her when she'd tried to leave after the bathtub incident. How her car keys had mysteriously vanished for three hours. How she'd tried to call a locksmith only to find her phone had no signal despite showing full bars.

"There has to be another way."

"There is." Dr. Rhodes pulled out another document—a photocopy of a handwritten letter dated October 1897. "The first family to face this ritual found a loophole. They tried to destroy the well itself, severing the connection to the burial ground. But the explosion they set triggered a supernatural backlash that killed one family member anyway. The curse demands blood. If it doesn't receive the ritual sacrifice, it takes payment in other ways."

At the art table, Lily had stopped drawing. She sat perfectly still, pencil hovering over the paper, her small body rigid.

"Lily?" Sarah moved toward her daughter.

"They're listening now," Lily whispered. "I can feel them listening."

The temperature plummeted. Sarah could see her breath. The lights flickered.

Max spoke again in that wrong, flat voice: "Seven days until the harvest moon. Seven days until the veil falls. Seven days until the collection. Father is waiting. Mother is waiting. I am waiting. We are all waiting for the girl."

"The girl?" Dr. Rhodes stepped forward. "Why the girl specifically?"

Max's head rotated to face Lily with mechanical precision. "Because she looks like Mother. Because she has Mother's soul. Because she's the one who tried to save me before. She'll try to save him again." His gaze shifted to Sarah. "And that's when Father will take her."

"No," Sarah said, her voice breaking. "You can't have her. You can't have either of them."

"We don't want the boy." Max's—no, Benjamin's—voice was almost sympathetic. "We never wanted him. He isn't part of the bloodline. Father doesn't care about him. But the girl... the girl is special. The girl is chosen."

The implications hit Sarah like a physical blow. Max was from her ex-husband, not her bloodline. But Lily—Lily carried Sarah's family blood. Sarah's mother, Sarah's grandmother, all the way back.

"What bloodline?" Sarah demanded. "I'm not from Hollow's End. I have no connection to this place."

Benjamin's laugh through Max's mouth was chilling. "Ask Mother about the Hales. Ask her about Constance. Ask her why she really moved here."

The lights went out completely.

In the darkness, Sarah heard Dr. Rhodes fumbling for her phone flashlight.

When the beam cut through the black, Max was slumped in his chair, breathing normally, his eyes closed. Lily remained frozen at the art table.

"Max?" Sarah shook him gently. "Baby, wake up."

His eyes fluttered open—his own eyes now, confused and frightened. "Mom? Why is it dark? Why am I so cold?"

Sarah pulled him into her arms, feeling him shiver against her. Over his head, she looked at Dr. Rhodes, who was staring at her with an expression of dawning horror.

"The Hales," Dr. Rhodes whispered. "Constance Hale is the town historian. She's lived in Hollow's End her entire life. Her family has been here since the colonial era." She pulled up something on her tablet, fingers flying over the screen. "Sarah Brennan. Maiden name?"

"Hale," Sarah said numbly. "Sarah Hale."

"Jesus." Dr. Rhodes turned the tablet around. On the screen was a genealogy chart. Sarah saw her mother's name, her grandmother's name, reaching back and back through generations. At the root: *Constance Hale, b. 1678, executed 1692 for witchcraft.*

Not the town historian Constance. The original Constance.

"The Woman in White," Dr. Rhodes said. "The first spirit to haunt Halloween Street. She was hanged for refusing to reveal where she'd hidden her daughter from the witch hunters. She buried the child alive to save her from execution. The daughter suffocated. The Woman has been haunting that land ever since, waiting for..." She looked at Lily. "Waiting for her daughter's bloodline to return."

Sarah's legs gave out. She sank to the floor, still holding Max.

"The house didn't choose us randomly," she whispered. "It was waiting for us. Waiting for Lily."

"The ritual has never been about appeasing the dead," Dr. Rhodes said. "It's been about feeding the Woman in White. She's been collecting Hale descendants for three hundred years, trying to replace the daughter she killed. And now she has one trapped in her house."

At the art table, Lily finally moved. She set down her pencil and turned to face them. Her eyes were distant, unfocused, looking through them rather than at them.

When she spoke, it was in two voices layered over each other—her own and something older, something that had been screaming beneath Halloween Street for centuries.

"Seven days, daughter-of-my-daughter's-daughter. Seven days until you come home to me. Seven days until we're together forever in the dark, in the water, in the earth where children belong."

Then Lily blinked, and she was herself again, looking around in confusion. "Mama? Why are you on the floor? Why are you crying?"

Sarah couldn't answer. She could only hold her children and stare at the drawing Lily had made.

The skeletal hands reaching up from the well.

Waiting.

Always waiting.

And at the bottom of the well, barely visible in Lily's careful shading, a woman's face with empty eye sockets and a sewn-shut mouth.

Waiting for her daughter to come home.

Dr. Rhodes walked them to the car, the October afternoon sun doing nothing to warm Sarah's ice-cold skin. Before Sarah could open the door, Dr. Rhodes grabbed her arm.

"There's something else you need to know. The families who survived—they had something in common. They didn't fight the spirits. They didn't try to negotiate. They broke the connection between the living and the dead by destroying the anchor point."

"The well."

"The well. But more specifically, what's in the well. The bones of every sacrifice going back to 1897. The bones are what hold the curse. They're what the Woman in White uses to anchor herself to this world." Dr. Rhodes pressed a business card into Sarah's hand. "I have contacts—paranormal researchers, people who've dealt with this before. We have six days before Halloween. Six days to figure out how to end this without losing Lily."

Sarah looked at the card. At the bottom, handwritten: *Isaac Stone -*

Paranormal Investigation - 24/7 Emergency Line.

"And if we can't figure it out in six days?"

Dr. Rhodes' expression was answer enough.

Sarah loaded her children into the car, both of them exhausted, neither remembering what they'd said or done in the office. As she pulled away from the curb, she glanced in the rearview mirror.

Dr. Rhodes stood on the sidewalk, watching them go, and for just a moment, Sarah saw another figure standing behind her.

A woman in a white colonial dress, her mouth sewn shut with black thread, her empty eyes fixed on the car.

Fixed on Lily.

Sarah drove faster, but the woman's image followed in the mirror, never getting closer, never getting farther away.

Just watching.

Waiting.

Counting down the days until the harvest moon would rise and the veil would fall and the collection would finally be complete.

Sarah's phone buzzed. A text from an unknown number:

The well must be destroyed. Everything else is a lie. But destroying it will cost you something. Everything requires payment. Are you willing to pay?

Sarah didn't answer. She didn't know what the right answer was.

She only knew she had six days to decide if she was willing to sacrifice everything to save her daughter.

Or if she'd let the Woman in White have what she'd been waiting three centuries to claim.

Twelve

Chapter 12: The Possession

❧⟨ೱ⟩❧

S *arah pov*

The wrongness started at breakfast.

Sarah noticed it in the way Max held his fork—delicately, precisely, like someone unaccustomed to modern utensils. He cut his pancakes into perfect geometric squares, arranging them on his plate in a pattern that looked almost ritualistic. When Lily reached for the syrup, he pulled it away with a sharp, adult gesture.

"Ladies should wait to be served," he said, his seven-year-old voice carrying an inflection that didn't belong to him. "It's only proper."

Sarah's hand froze halfway to her coffee mug. "Max, honey, what did you say?"

He looked up, and for just a moment—a fraction of a heartbeat—his eyes weren't quite right. Too focused. Too old. Then he blinked, and he was her little boy again, confused by her reaction.

"Can Lily have the syrup?" he asked in his normal voice, the one that still had traces of his lisp. "I was just being silly."

Lily kicked Sarah under the table, her eyes wide with unspoken warning. Sarah forced a smile, but her appetite had vanished. Outside the kitchen

window, October 15th was gray and cold, the skeletal trees of Halloween
Street rattling in wind that sounded too much like whispers.

That was the first moment. There would be more.

By midmorning, Max had retreated to the parlor, sitting perfectly still in
the wingback chair that had belonged to Victor Kane. Sarah watched him
from the doorway, her stomach tight with dread. He wasn't playing, wasn't
fidgeting, wasn't doing any of the things a seven-year-old boy should be doing
on a Tuesday morning.

He was simply sitting, hands folded in his lap, staring at the portrait of the
Kane family above the mantle.

"Max?" Sarah stepped into the room. The temperature dropped noticeably,
her breath misting in the air. "Sweetie, are you okay?"

"Father kept his important papers in the study," Max said without looking
at her. His voice had that strange quality again—too formal, too measured.
"Behind the bookshelf. Third panel from the left. Mother tried to find them
once, but she didn't know about the spring mechanism."

Sarah's blood turned to ice. "What did you say?"

Max turned to face her, and this time his eyes were definitely wrong. Darker.
Ancient. "He hid the covenant documents there. The ones that prove what
he did. What they all did." He tilted his head, studying her with unsettling
intensity. "Don't you want to know the truth, Mrs. Brennan? Or are you
content to remain ignorant until Halloween night?"

"Who are you?" The words came out as barely a whisper.

Max blinked, and the wrongness drained from his face. He looked around,
confused, tears instantly springing to his eyes. "Mommy? Why are you scared
of me?"

Sarah's maternal instinct overrode her terror. She crossed the room in
three strides and pulled him into her arms, feeling his small body shake with
sobs. He was warm, solid, *real*—her baby boy, not whatever had been speaking
through him.

"I'm not scared of you," she lied, holding him tighter. "I'm never scared of
you."

But her eyes drifted to the portrait of Victor Kane, and she could swear his painted smile had widened.

The study was on the second floor, a room Sarah had barely entered since moving in. Dark wood paneling absorbed what little light filtered through the heavy curtains. Built-in bookshelves lined three walls, filled with leather-bound volumes that smelled of mildew and secrets.

Sarah counted to the third panel from the left, her hands trembling. This was insane. There was no way Max could know about hidden compartments. He was seven years old. He'd never been in this room.

But his voice—*that other voice*—had been so certain.

She ran her fingers along the wood, searching for the spring mechanism. Nothing. Maybe she'd imagined the whole thing. Maybe Max had just been playing pretend, and she was so sleep-deprived and terrified that she was—

Click.

A section of the panel swung inward, revealing a hollow space behind the books. Sarah's breath caught. Inside was a leather folder, edges brittle with age, and a small wooden box.

With shaking hands, she pulled out the folder. The documents inside were yellowed, dated 1897, written in elaborate script. She recognized some of the names: Kane, Cromwell, Winters, Ashton. The founding families of Hollow's End.

The Covenant of the Collectors, the title read. *Being an Agreement for the Preservation of Prosperity through Blood Tithe and Ritual Sacrifice.*

Sarah's vision blurred. It was all real. Every impossible thing Eleanor's diary had described, every nightmare Hannah had hinted at—it was documented here in careful, legal language. Seven-year cycles. Family bloodlines. The "appeasement of entities bound to the hanging ground of Halloween Street."

A schedule of sacrifices dated back over a century. The last entry was 1963: *Victor Kane—designated offering: Benjamin Kane (male child, age 6). Status: INCOMPLETE. Consequences: Unknown.*

Sarah opened the wooden box. Inside was a lock of child's hair, a small milk tooth, and a photograph. Benjamin Kane, smiling at the camera, holding a toy boat. On the back, written in a woman's desperate scrawl: *If we're found, please know I tried to save him. I tried to save us all. —Eleanor*

"Did you find it?"

Sarah spun around. Max stood in the doorway, but his posture was all wrong—too straight, too rigid. When he spoke, that other voice came through more clearly now, layered beneath his own like a palimpsest.

"She hid that box before Father caught her. She was always hiding things. Secrets in the walls, hope in the floorboards." Max walked forward with measured steps that didn't match his small stride. "But Father found her anyway. He always did."

"Stop it." Sarah's voice cracked. "Whatever you are, get out of my son."

"I'm trying to help you, Mrs. Brennan." Max's face was expressionless, eerie in its blankness. "Father is still here. He's in the walls, in the foundation, in the very bones of this house. And he wants what he was denied." Those too-old eyes fixed on her. "He wants to complete the ritual. He wants Lily."

"No." Sarah grabbed Max's shoulders, trying to shake the wrongness out of him. "You leave her alone. You leave both of them alone!"

Max smiled, and it was Victor Kane's smile. "You can't stop what's already begun. The knocking will continue. The veil grows thinner. And when Halloween night comes…" He leaned closer, his child's voice dropping to a whisper that sounded like wind through a tomb. "…the door will open, whether you will it or not."

Then he collapsed. Sarah caught him before he hit the floor, his small body suddenly boneless and exhausted. He blinked up at her with his normal eyes—confused, frightened, completely unaware of what had just happened.

"Mommy? Did I fall asleep again?"

Sarah clutched him to her chest, tears streaming down her face. "It's okay, baby. It's okay."

But it wasn't okay. Nothing was okay.

She looked down at the documents scattered across the floor, at the proof of a century of ritualized murder, and felt the last threads of her rational world unravel. The house groaned around them, satisfied, as if it had been waiting for this exact moment of understanding.

The rest of the day passed in a haze of hypervigilance. Sarah watched Max constantly, searching for signs of the presence that had spoken through him. He seemed normal—playing with toy cars, arguing with Lily over the TV remote, eating dinner with his usual messy enthusiasm.

But Sarah couldn't forget that voice. That ancient, knowing voice.

She called Dr. Rhodes three times, leaving increasingly frantic voicemails. She tried to reach Father Gabriel, but he was still in the hospital. She even attempted to contact Detective Murphy, but what could she say? *My son is being possessed by the ghost of a murdered child who's giving me information about secret compartments in the walls?*

By 7 PM, exhaustion had settled into her bones. Melissa had taken Lily to her room to read, giving Sarah a break from maintaining the pretense that everything was fine. Max was in the bathtub, singing one of his nonsense songs, the sound of splashing water oddly comforting in its normalcy.

Sarah sat on the hallway floor outside the bathroom, head in her hands, trying to think. They needed to leave. Tonight. Somehow, they'd find a way to break through whatever supernatural barrier kept the doors locked. They'd take an axe to the walls if they had to.

The singing stopped.

Sarah's head snapped up. "Max? You okay in there?"

Silence.

She was on her feet in an instant, hand on the bathroom door. "Max, answer me."

The sound of water sloshing. Then, soft and distant, a child's voice: "I have to go to Ben. I promised."

Sarah slammed the door open.

Max was underwater, sitting at the bottom of the tub with his eyes open, staring up at her through the rippling surface. He wasn't struggling. Wasn't trying to rise. Just sitting there, lungs full of water, peaceful as a drowned boy in a photograph.

"MAX!"

She plunged her hands into the water, grabbing him under the arms and hauling him up. He came easily, limply, water streaming from his hair and mouth. For one horrifying second, Sarah thought he was dead—his lips were blue, his skin pale, his eyes glassy.

Then he coughed, water spurting from his mouth, and sucked in a desperate breath.

"Mommy?" His voice was tiny, confused, terrified. "Why am I wet?"

Sarah pulled him from the tub, wrapping him in a towel, her whole body shaking. "You went underwater, baby. Do you remember?"

Max's face crumpled. "I was just singing. I was singing the boat song. And then…" His eyes widened with sudden, terrible memory. "Ben was there. In the water. He said we could swim together. He said it doesn't hurt after the first minute. He said Mother is waiting at the bottom of the well and we should go visit her."

"Oh, God." Sarah held him so tight she was afraid she might break him. "You don't go anywhere Ben tells you. Do you understand? Nowhere."

"But he's my friend," Max whispered, and he was crying now, big tears rolling down his cheeks. "He's lonely, Mommy. He says Father made him stay in the water and he's been there for so, so long. He just wants a friend."

"I know, baby. I know." Sarah rocked him back and forth, her own tears falling into his wet hair. "But you can't go with him. You have to stay with me."

Max nodded against her shoulder, but his voice was small and sad when he spoke again: "He says Halloween is coming. He says he doesn't want to be alone when the door opens. He says if I don't come to him, he'll have to come get me."

Sarah's blood froze. "What door, Max? What door is opening?"

But Max had gone limp in her arms, exhausted, possibly in shock. His breathing evened out into the deep rhythm of sleep—or something like it.

Sarah carried him to her bedroom, refusing to let him out of her sight. She laid him on the bed and sat beside him, one hand on his chest to feel it rise and fall, proof that he was breathing, that he was alive, that she hadn't lost him to the bathtub or the well or whatever hungry darkness lived in this house.

Melissa appeared in the doorway, took one look at Sarah's face, and went pale. "What happened?"

"He tried to drown himself." Sarah's voice was flat, emotionless. She'd gone beyond terror into a strange, numb place. "Or something tried to drown him. I don't know anymore. I don't know anything except that we're going to die in this house if we don't find a way out."

"We'll leave tonight," Melissa said firmly. "I don't care what it takes. We'll break every window, tear down every door—"

"We've tried. You know we've tried." Sarah looked at her sister with hollow eyes. "The house won't let us go. It has us. It has *him*." She gestured to Max, so small and vulnerable in the too-large bed. "And it's going to use him to get to Lily."

Thunder rumbled outside, though the afternoon had been clear. The lights flickered. Somewhere in the house, a clock began to chime—three times, though it was only 8 PM.

On the nightstand, Sarah's phone buzzed with a text from an unknown number: *The boy knows the way down. The boy will show her where Mother waits. Only 16 days until the door opens. Only 16 days until the collection is complete.* —*V.K.*

Sarah deleted the message with shaking hands, but it didn't matter. Victor Kane's words were burned into her mind.

She looked at her son, sleeping fitfully, murmuring words in a language he didn't know. She thought of the documents in the study, the proof of a century of murdered children. She thought of Eleanor's desperate attempt to save Benjamin, and how it had ended with both of them dead or worse.

History was trying to repeat itself. The house demanded its sacrifice. And Sarah was running out of time to figure out how to break a curse that had been fed with blood for over a hundred years.

Outside, the October wind picked up, rattling the windows like skeletal fingers seeking entry. In the basement, something heavy dragged across the floor. In the nursery upstairs, a music box began to play—a lullaby Sarah recognized from her own childhood, the melody distorted and wrong.

Max stirred, opened his eyes, and looked directly at her. For just a moment, his pupils were completely black, reflecting nothing.

"She's still down there," he whispered in that terrible, layered voice.

"Waiting. Under the roses. Father said she'd stay there until someone came to join her. Lily looks just like her. Did you know that? Lily has Mother's eyes."

Then he closed his eyes and was asleep again, his breathing deep and peaceful, as if he'd said nothing at all.

Sarah sat in the darkness, her hand on her son's chest, and felt the last of her hope drain away. The possession wasn't just influencing Max. It was using him as a messenger, a tool, a weapon aimed directly at Lily.

And Halloween was sixteen days away.

Sixteen days until the door opened.

Sixteen days until the dead came knocking.

Sixteen days to find a way to save her children from a curse that had been hungry for sixty-two years.

Thunder cracked directly overhead, and in the flash of lightning, Sarah saw them: dozens of faces pressed against the bedroom window. Colonial dead, their mouths moving in silent screams, their hands leaving fog prints on the glass.

They were waiting.

They'd been waiting for a very long time.

And they were done being patient.

Thirteen

Chapter 13: Calling Father Gabriel

Sarah pov

The water in the bathtub was still draining when I made the call, my hands shaking so badly I could barely hold my phone. Max sat wrapped in three towels on the bathroom floor, lips blue, eyes vacant, while Melissa tried to get him to drink warm tea. He kept whispering the same words over and over: "Ben needs me. I promised. The water's not cold when you stop fighting."

My son had tried to drown himself.

My seven-year-old baby had held his own head underwater with a strength that shouldn't have been possible, and when I'd dragged him out—his small body rigid, fighting me—he'd smiled. Actually smiled, water pouring from his mouth, and said in a voice that wasn't quite his own: "Mother's waiting for us at the bottom."

Father Gabriel Cross answered on the second ring.

"The Last House," I said, my voice breaking. "You were right. Please. My son—something's in him. Something's in all of us."

Silence stretched across the line, broken only by my ragged breathing. Then: "I'll be there in twenty minutes. Lock your children in a room with you. Don't let them out of your sight. And Sarah?" His voice dropped. "Don't answer if you hear knocking."

He hung up before I could ask what he meant.

Melissa helped me get the kids into my bedroom—the master suite with its exterior lock that I now understood wasn't meant to keep people out, but to keep something *in*. Max was still barely responsive, wrapped in blankets, staring at nothing. Lily sat cross-legged on the bed, drawing with crayons she'd brought from her room. I didn't want to look at what she was creating, but I couldn't help myself.

Three figures at the bottom of a well. A woman with black thread across her mouth. A child with water pouring from his eyes. And standing at the edge, looking down—Lily had drawn herself.

"Sweetheart," I said carefully, "what is that?"

"Benjamin showed me," she answered without looking up. "This is what happened to them. This is what happens to everyone." She added more black crayon to the woman's sewn mouth. "Mrs. Kane tried to scream but she couldn't. Mr. Kane made sure. He didn't want anyone to hear what they were doing wrong."

"Lily—"

"The water's not really water, Mom." She finally looked at me, and her eyes were too old, too knowing. "It's all the sadness of everyone who died scared. That's why it's so cold. That's why Max wanted to go in. The sadness pulls you down."

Melissa grabbed my arm. "Jesus Christ, Sarah, we need to get them out of this house. Tonight. Right now. I don't care if we have to break every window—"

Three knocks echoed through the bedroom door.

We all froze.

Three more knocks. Slow. Deliberate. Patient.

"Don't answer it," I whispered, pulling both children closer. "Nobody answers."

Knock. Knock. Knock.

Max's head lifted. His pupils were dilated, black swallowing the blue. "That's Ben. He wants to come in. We should let him in."

"No, baby. No, we—"

"He says his daddy's angry." Max's voice was distant, dreamy. "He says his daddy's going to make you understand. He says you can't keep us out forever."

The knocking stopped.

The temperature in the room plummeted so fast I could see my breath. Frost began spreading across the window like clutching fingers.

Then we heard the sirens.

Father Gabriel Cross arrived with his nephew Nathan in a decades-old station wagon that looked like it had survived multiple apocalypses. The priest was in his late sixties, silver-haired and stern-faced, with the kind of weathered hands that came from a lifetime of hard prayer. Nathan was younger—maybe thirty—with kind eyes and a nervous energy that immediately put me on edge.

They came prepared.

Two leather cases of implements: vials of holy water, blessed salt in mason jars, crucifixes of varying sizes, a Bible so worn the spine was held together with tape, rosary beads, candles, and small bottles of anointing oil. Gabriel handled each item with reverent care as he laid them out on the dining room table.

"The house resisted me on the phone," Gabriel said without preamble. "I felt it push back when you called. That means whatever's here is strong. Organized. Intelligent." He looked at me with eyes that had seen too much. "How long have the manifestations been occurring?"

"Two weeks. But they're getting worse. Tonight Max—" My voice caught. "He tried to drown himself. He said someone named Ben told him to."

Gabriel and Nathan exchanged a look.

"Benjamin Kane," Nathan said quietly. "The son who drowned in the basement well in 1963. We researched the house after our first meeting, Mrs. Brennan. The archives are... extensive."

"Why didn't you warn me more clearly?" The anger felt good, hot and clean against the cold fear. "You left me a business card and a cryptic note. My children are in danger—"

"Because we've tried before." Gabriel's voice was granite. "Three times in the past twenty years, we've attempted to help families in this house. Twice, we were forbidden entry. The third time, I made it as far as the parlor before something threw me through the front door. Cracked three ribs." He touched his side unconsciously. "The house chooses who enters and when. The fact that it's allowing us in now means it wants something."

"Or it's confident we can't stop it," Nathan added, then wilted under his uncle's glare.

Melissa had stayed upstairs with the children. I could hear her reading to them, her voice steady and soothing, a lifeline of normalcy in this nightmare.

"What do we do?" I asked.

Gabriel began filling his pockets with vials and salt. "We perform an exorcism. Not of a person—of the house itself. We'll start in the nursery, where Benjamin's spirit seems strongest, and work our way down to the basement. The goal is to break whatever's binding these spirits to the physical location and release them."

"Release them where?"

"To whatever judgment awaits them." He met my eyes. "I won't lie to you, Sarah. This is dangerous. For all of us. Whatever's in this house has had decades to grow strong, to feed on fear and tragedy. It may not want to leave."

"What happens if it doesn't work?"

Nathan answered before Gabriel could stop him: "Then we get you and your children out, seal the house, and let the Church handle it."

"And if it won't let us leave?"

Silence.

"Then we fight," Gabriel said simply.

The nursery was worse than I remembered.

In the two weeks since we'd discovered it, the room had transformed. The toys weren't just arranged in circles anymore—they formed intricate patterns, spirals within spirals, like something was trying to communicate in a language

122

of wooden blocks and tin soldiers. The rocking horse moved slightly, though no one was near it. The windows were covered in condensation despite the cold, and when I looked closer, I realized the moisture formed words: MOTHER MOTHER MOTHER repeated endlessly across the glass.

Benjamin's bed was made with military precision, the covers pulled so tight they looked painted on. On the pillow sat a photograph I'd never seen before: Victor, Eleanor, and Benjamin Kane, posed in front of this very house. Someone had scratched out Eleanor's face with something sharp.

"This is the epicenter," Gabriel said, his voice barely above a whisper. "The heart of the haunting. Whatever happened to Benjamin Kane, this is where his spirit is anchored strongest."

Nathan began arranging candles in a circle while Gabriel opened his Bible to marked pages. I stood near the door, every instinct screaming at me to run, to grab my children and flee, but where would we go? The house had already proven it could trap us, could seal us in whenever it wanted.

"Sarah," Gabriel said, gesturing me into the circle. "Stand here. Don't step outside the salt line for any reason. No matter what you see or hear."

"What am I going to see?"

"The truth," he said. "And the truth in places like this is rarely kind."

He began to pray in Latin, his voice strong and commanding. Nathan joined in, their words creating a rhythm, a cadence that seemed to press against the walls themselves. Gabriel sprinkled holy water in the cardinal directions, and for a moment—just a moment—I felt hope.

Then the lights went out.

Not gradually. Not flickering. Just instant, complete darkness so absolute I couldn't see my own hands.

"Keep praying!" Gabriel commanded, and I heard him strike a match.

The candles lit, but their flames burned *wrong*—too bright, casting shadows that moved independently of their sources. The temperature continued to drop. My breath came out in clouds so thick I could barely see through them.

Gabriel raised a crucifix toward the bed. "In the name of the Father, the Son, and the Holy Spirit, I command you to release this place! By the authority of the Church and the power of Christ, I—"

The holy water began to boil.

Not metaphorically. The vials in Gabriel's pockets started hissing and bubbling, steam rising through the glass. He yanked them out, but the glass was already turning black, the blessed water inside transforming into something thick and oil-dark.

"Uncle—" Nathan's voice was terrified.

The crucifixes were melting.

Silver and brass ran like wax, dripping onto the floor with sounds like hissing snakes. The rosary beads in Nathan's hands shattered, spraying across the hardwood. The Bible in Gabriel's hands grew hot—I could see his hands reddening, blistering, but he held on.

"I said RELEASE THIS PLACE!" Gabriel roared.

The rocking horse exploded.

Wood and metal erupted outward with the force of a bomb, and I screamed, throwing my arms up, but the shrapnel stopped at the salt circle's edge, hanging in midair for one impossible moment before dropping to the floor.

Then the toys began to move.

All of them. Simultaneously. The blocks stacked themselves into towers. The tin soldiers marched in formation. The stuffed animals turned their heads toward us with movements that were too smooth, too fluid. And from somewhere in the walls came the sound of a child singing:

"Ring around the rosie, Pocket full of posies, Ashes, ashes, We all fall down."

"It's not Benjamin," Nathan whispered, backing toward the door. "Uncle Gabriel, that's not the boy. That's something else using his voice."

Gabriel kept praying, but I could hear the strain in his voice now, the fear creeping in. The walls themselves seemed to pulse, breathing in and out, and the wallpaper began to peel, revealing older wallpaper beneath, and older still, layers upon layers, like the house was shedding skin.

The singing grew louder:

"Mother tried to save me, Father wouldn't let her, Down into the water, Down down down forever."

"That's not the nursery rhyme," I said. "That's not how it goes."

"It's what happened," a small voice said from behind us.

We all spun around.

Max stood in the doorway, still wrapped in towels, his hair plastered to his head. But his eyes—God, his eyes were solid black, no whites visible at all.

"Benjamin wants to show you," Max said in that terrible wrong voice. "He wants you to understand what Daddy did."

"Max, baby, come here—"

"I'm not Max right now." He tilted his head at an angle that was too far, too wrong. "I'm Ben. I've been Ben since the first night. Max is sleeping. He's dreaming about swimming. He likes swimming now."

Gabriel stepped forward, raising what remained of his crucifix. "Release the boy, spirit. In the name of—"

The windows shattered.

All of them, simultaneously, glass exploding inward with the force of a hurricane. But again, the shards stopped at the salt circle's edge, creating a wall of frozen glass around us. Through the broken windows, I could see the backyard, and standing beneath the dead rose bushes was a figure in a white dress.

Eleanor Kane.

Her mouth was sewn shut with black thread. Her hands reached toward us. Her eyes pleaded.

"She's trying to warn you," Max/Benjamin said. "She tried to warn everyone. But Daddy made sure she couldn't talk."

The floor began to crack.

Fissures spread from the center of the room, and I could see something beneath the hardwood—something dark and wet. Water began seeping up through the breaks, cold and black and smelling of decay.

"The well," Nathan gasped. "It's coming up from the basement."

Gabriel grabbed my arm. "We need to leave. Now. This isn't an exorcism— it's an invitation. We're not casting anything out. We're being pulled in."

But when we turned to the door, Max was gone.

And in his place stood a man I recognized from the photographs.

Victor Kane.

He wore a suit covered in blood and gunpowder residue. Half his face was missing, blown away by the self-inflicted gunshot wound that had killed him in 1963. But his remaining eye was very much alive, and very, very angry.

"You don't leave," he said in a voice like grinding gravel, "until someone pays the debt."

He pointed at Gabriel.

The priest flew backward as if yanked by invisible ropes. His body slammed into the wall, then the ceiling, then crashed down onto the floor outside the salt circle. I heard the sickening crack of breaking bone.

"Uncle!" Nathan lunged forward, breaking the protective circle.

Immediately, the toys attacked.

Tin soldiers became missiles, blocks became bludgeons, stuffed animals sprouted teeth and claws. Nathan screamed, trying to shield his face as the nursery's contents descended on him like a swarm. Gabriel tried to stand, but his leg was bent at an impossible angle, white bone visible through torn fabric.

I ran.

I'm not proud of it, but I ran. Through the doorway, past Max's empty shell standing motionless in the hall, toward the master bedroom where Melissa and Lily were screaming questions I couldn't answer.

Behind me, I heard Victor Kane's spirit laugh.

It sounded like drowning.

The ambulance arrived seventeen minutes later. The EMTs found Gabriel at the bottom of the main staircase, his leg shattered, multiple lacerations, going into shock. Nathan had two broken ribs and more cuts than they could count. Both men were conscious enough to insist they'd fallen, that it was an accident, that the old house had dangerous stairs.

They were lying to protect us. Or to protect themselves. I couldn't tell which.

As they loaded Gabriel onto the stretcher, he grabbed my wrist with shocking strength. His eyes were fever-bright, desperate.

"It's not demons," he whispered, blood flecking his lips. "It's older. The land itself is cursed. The house is just... just a mouth. A way in." His grip tightened painfully. "Leave. Tonight. Don't wait. Don't pack. Don't think. Take your children and leave before—"

"Before what?"

"Before it decides it's ready." He was crying now, tears cutting tracks through the dust and blood on his face. "Before Halloween. Before the ritual night. Before whatever happened in 1963 happens again. Sarah, please. I've seen what this house does to families. I've seen what's left when it's finished. Please."

The EMTs pulled him away, loading him into the ambulance. Nathan went with him, still clutching his uncle's hand.

I stood on the porch as the ambulance drove away, its red lights disappearing into the October night. The house loomed behind me, and I swear I could feel it watching, waiting, pleased with itself.

Hannah Winters stood in her yard across the street, illuminated by her porch light. She wasn't smiling anymore.

Melissa appeared at my shoulder. "I packed bags. For all of us. We're leaving. Right now."

"Where will we go?"

"I don't care. Anywhere. A hotel. My apartment. A homeless shelter. Anywhere but here."

I turned to look at the house. The nursery window—now broken—reflected the moon. For just a moment, I saw Benjamin Kane's face in the glass, and his mouth moved, forming words:

Too late. Too late. Too late.

"Get the kids," I said.

But when we tried the front door, it wouldn't open.

And when we tried the back door, it wouldn't budge.

And when Melissa picked up a chair to break a window, the chair froze in midair, held by invisible hands.

The locks clicked.

All of them.

Every door. Every window. Every exit.

One by one, from the top of the house to the bottom, I heard them lock.

Click. Click. Click.

And from the basement, three slow knocks.

Then three more.

Then three more.

The dead were knocking.

And we couldn't leave.

Max was still standing in the hallway when I found him, but his eyes were his own again—terrified, confused, not remembering anything after the bathtub. I held him and tried not to cry, tried not to scream, tried not to let him see that his mother had just realized the truth:

Father Gabriel's exorcism hadn't failed because we weren't faithful enough.

It had failed because this house was never haunted.

It was alive.

And it was hungry.

Fourteen

Chapter 14: Trapped

arah pov

S The sound of Father Gabriel's screams still echoed in Sarah's ears three hours after the ambulance took him away. She stood in the foyer, staring at the dark smear of blood on the hardwood where he'd landed after the invisible force hurled him down the stairs. The paramedics had looked at her with barely concealed suspicion, as if she'd been the one to push an elderly priest hard enough to shatter his femur.

Leave. Tonight.

His final words burned in her mind like a brand.

"Mom?" Lily's voice drifted down from upstairs, small and frightened. "Is Father Gabriel going to be okay?"

Sarah didn't answer. She was already moving, her decision crystallizing with the cold clarity of absolute terror. They were leaving. Right now. She didn't care that it was nearly ten o'clock at night, didn't care that she had nowhere to go, didn't care about the money she'd lose or the explanation she'd have to give Melissa.

Nothing mattered except getting her children out of this house.

"Lily, Max!" Sarah took the stairs two at a time, her heart hammering. "Pack a bag. Now. Only what you can carry. We're leaving."

"Leaving?" Max appeared in the nursery doorway, his Spider-Man pajamas hanging loose on his thin frame. He'd lost weight in the two weeks they'd been here. They all had. "But it's nighttime."

"I don't care. We'll drive to Aunt Melissa's. We'll go to a hotel. We'll sleep in the car if we have to." Sarah was already in Lily's room, yanking clothes from drawers and stuffing them into a duffel bag. Her hands shook so badly she could barely grip the fabric. "Get dressed. Both of you. Right now."

Lily stood frozen by her bed, clutching the worn stuffed rabbit she'd had since she was three. "Mom, you're scaring me."

"Good." Sarah's voice cracked. "You *should* be scared. We all should be. This house—" She stopped, swallowing the hysteria rising in her throat. She had to hold it together. Had to be strong. Had to get them out. "Just pack. Please, baby. Trust me."

The children moved then, sensing the genuine panic in their mother's voice. Sarah raced to her own room, throwing toiletries and documents into her overnight bag. Birth certificates. Social security cards. The divorce papers. Her laptop. Everything else could be replaced.

Eleanor's diary.

She grabbed it from her nightstand, the leather-bound journal that had belonged to a woman who'd died trying to save her son from this house. From the ritual. From the curse that Sarah now understood was absolutely, horrifyingly real.

She shoved it into her bag and zipped it closed with trembling fingers.

Ten minutes. That's all it took to pack their lives into three bags and a backpack. Sarah herded Lily and Max down the stairs, moving fast, trying not to look at the portraits of the Kane family that lined the walls. Victor's painted eyes seemed to follow them, and Sarah could swear his expression had changed—his mouth curved into something that might have been a smile.

"Get in the car," Sarah ordered, juggling bags while fishing in her jacket pocket for keys. "Buckle up. Don't—"

Her fingers closed on empty fabric.

The keys. Her car keys. She'd put them in this pocket an hour ago when she came back from checking the mail. She *knew* she had.

"Mom?" Lily clutched her rabbit tighter. "What's wrong?"

"Nothing. Just—wait here." Sarah dropped the bags and ran back upstairs, checking the nightstand, the dresser, the bathroom counter. Nothing. She tore through the master bedroom, throwing aside pillows, checking under the bed, her breathing coming faster and faster.

Gone.

They're not gone. You misplaced them. You're panicking. Just think.

She forced herself to retrace her steps. Mail. She'd gotten the mail. Walked back to the house. Put the keys... where? Kitchen counter. She'd put them on the kitchen counter while she sorted through the bills.

Sarah ran downstairs, nearly tripping over Max's backpack. The kitchen was dark, illuminated only by the sickly yellow glow of the overhead light that had been flickering since day three. She slapped the light switch, but nothing changed—the bulb continued its erratic pulse, casting the room in alternating brightness and shadow.

The counter was empty.

"No, no, no..." Sarah pulled out drawers, checked the fruit bowl, even opened the refrigerator as if the keys might have somehow ended up inside. Her chest felt tight, lungs struggling to pull in air. "Where are they? Where the *fuck* are they?"

"Mom!" Lily's shocked voice reminded Sarah that she never swore in front of the kids.

"Sorry. Sorry, I just—" Sarah pressed her palms against the counter, trying to steady herself. "My keys are missing."

"Maybe they fell?" Max suggested helpfully. He got down on his hands and knees, peering under the cabinets. "I'll help look."

They searched for twenty minutes. Every drawer, every cabinet, every possible surface. Sarah even checked the basement door, wondering with sick dread if the keys had somehow ended up down there with whatever lived in the well.

The basement door was locked from the outside, the padlock she'd installed after Max's sleepwalking incident still firmly in place.

"Okay." Sarah straightened up, forcing herself to think past the panic. "Okay.

It's fine. We'll call a cab. Or Uber. Or—" She pulled out her phone.

The screen was black.

"No." She pressed the power button. Nothing. Held it down. Still nothing. "No, no, I just charged you. You were at ninety-three percent."

She plugged it into the wall charger. The screen remained dark, the device completely unresponsive, as if it had never worked at all.

"Lily, honey, can I see your iPad?" Sarah's voice sounded strange to her own ears, too high, too strained.

Lily retrieved it from her backpack. The screen showed a full battery charge, but when Sarah tried to open it, the device powered down instantly. Dead. Completely dead.

"What about the landline?" Max asked.

Sarah hadn't even thought of that. The house had come with an old rotary phone in the kitchen, a avocado-green relic that she'd meant to have disconnected. She grabbed the receiver and held it to her ear.

Silence. Not even a dial tone. Just dead air.

She checked the cord. It was plugged in. The connection looked fine. But the line was completely dead.

"Mom, you're shaking." Lily's small hand touched Sarah's arm.

She was. Her whole body trembled as the realization settled over her like a suffocating blanket. No keys. No phones. No landline. But that didn't mean—

"Come on." Sarah grabbed both children's hands. "We're walking. The Winters house is right next door. We'll go there, call someone from Hannah's phone—"

She pulled them toward the front door. The old brass knob felt ice-cold under her palm, cold enough to burn. She turned it.

Nothing happened.

Sarah yanked harder. The knob turned freely in her hand, the mechanism clicking, but the door didn't budge. It felt solid, immovable, as if the wood had fused directly into the frame.

"Move back." Sarah's voice came out as a growl. She braced her shoulder against the door and *shoved*. Pain shot through her joint but the door didn't move a millimeter. She tried again, throwing all her weight against it. Again. Again.

"Maybe it's stuck?" Max offered. "Old houses get stuck sometimes."

"It's not stuck." Sarah stepped back, chest heaving. Her shoulder throbbed. "It's locked. From the inside."

"But we're on the inside," Lily said slowly. "How can it be locked from the inside?"

Sarah didn't answer. She was already moving to the window beside the door, fumbling with the latch. It opened easily—too easily, as if the house were mocking her. She pushed up on the lower sash.

It didn't move.

She pushed harder, muscles straining. The window was ancient, the wood swollen with age and moisture. Maybe it really was just stuck. Sarah grabbed a letter opener from the hall table and tried to wedge it into the crack between the sashes.

The letter opener snapped in half.

"Kitchen," Sarah muttered. "Kitchen windows."

She ran, the children following, their footsteps echoing too loudly in the old house. The kitchen window over the sink faced the backyard. Sarah cranked the handle, heard the satisfying click of the lock disengaging, and pushed.

Nothing.

She pushed harder. Grabbed a spatula and tried to pry it open. The spatula bent but the window didn't budge.

"Dining room." Her voice had taken on a manic edge. "Living room. There are six windows on the first floor. One of them has to—"

But she knew. Even as she ran from room to room, testing windows that looked perfectly normal, that opened an inch or two before stopping as if meeting invisible resistance, she knew.

The house wasn't letting them leave.

"Mom, this is scary." Max's voice wavered. "I don't like this."

Sarah grabbed a heavy brass candlestick from the mantel. "Stand back."

"Mom, what are you—"

She swung the candlestick at the living room window with all her strength.

It should have shattered. Safety glass, regular glass, it didn't matter—she'd put every ounce of fear and fury into that swing. The candlestick connected with a solid *thunk*, and for a split second Sarah felt triumph.

Then the candlestick rebounded, the force of impact traveling up her arm, and the window remained perfectly intact. Not even a crack. Not even a chip in the glass.

"No." Sarah swung again. And again. The impacts echoed through the house like gunshots, but the window held. She swung until her arms burned, until sweat poured down her face, until sobs tore from her throat.

The glass didn't even scratch.

The candlestick fell from her nerveless fingers and rolled across the floor.

Lily was crying now, silent tears streaming down her face. Max stood frozen, his face pale and shocked. They'd never seen their mother like this— wild, desperate, breaking.

"It's okay." Sarah dropped to her knees, pulling them both into a fierce hug. "It's okay, babies. We're okay. I'll figure this out. I promise. I'll get us out."

But even as she said it, she felt the lie in her bones.

A soft knock came from the front door.

All three of them froze.

Three gentle taps. Knuckles on wood. Patient. Deliberate.

"Don't answer it," Lily whispered.

Sarah rose slowly, positioning herself between the children and the door. Through the frosted glass panel, she could make out a figure standing on the porch. Familiar height. Familiar shape.

"Hannah?" Sarah's voice cracked. "Hannah, is that you?"

The figure moved closer to the glass. Sarah could see her face now, distorted by the frosted panes but unmistakably Hannah Winters. Her neighbor. The woman who'd brought casseroles and warnings.

Hannah raised one hand and pressed it against the glass. Her mouth moved, forming words Sarah couldn't hear through the door.

"What?" Sarah stepped closer, ignoring Lily's frightened whimper. "I can't hear you!"

Hannah's lips moved again, slowly, carefully. Sarah watched, reading the words.

You. Can't. Leave.

"Help us!" Sarah pounded on the door from her side, the wood solid and unyielding under her fists. "Hannah, call the police! Call someone! The doors won't open!"

Hannah's expression didn't change. She kept speaking, her mouth forming words with careful precision.

Until. It's. Finished.

"What does that mean?" Sarah screamed. "Finished? What has to be finished?"

But Hannah just shook her head slowly. Her hand slid down the glass, leaving a streak of condensation. Then she stepped back, her form growing dimmer in the porch light, and Sarah realized something that made her stomach turn to ice.

Hannah wasn't concerned. She wasn't panicked. She wasn't even surprised. She'd *expected* this.

"Hannah!" Sarah hammered on the door. "HANNAH!"

But the figure on the porch was already retreating, walking calmly down the steps, across the lawn, disappearing into the October darkness.

Sarah slumped against the door, forehead pressed to the cold wood. Behind her, she could hear Max's frightened breathing and Lily's quiet crying.

"What do we do?" Lily asked. "Mom, what do we do?"

Sarah didn't have an answer. She turned around slowly, taking in the foyer—the blood-stained floor, the portraits on the walls, the grandfather clock that had stopped at 3:33 AM and never started again.

The house settled around them with a groan that sounded almost satisfied. Somewhere upstairs, a door closed softly.

Then the lights began to flicker.

Not randomly. Sarah watched, her horror mounting, as the overhead fixture pulsed in a pattern. The bulb would glow bright for a long moment, then dim, then bright again. Three long pulses. Then darkness. Three short pulses of light. Then three long again.

Three long, three short, three long.

"What is that?" Max whispered.

Sarah's mouth went dry. She'd learned morse code in summer camp, a lifetime ago when she was twelve and the world still made sense.

Three long. Three short. Three long.

SOS.

The universal distress signal.

But it was backwards. The short signals came in the wrong place, as if the message were being sent in reverse. Or as if whoever was sending it was on the other side of something, their signal distorted, inverted.

The other side.

The lights continued their pattern. SOS. SOS. SOS. Growing faster now, more frantic. The bulb blazed bright enough to hurt Sarah's eyes, then plunged them into darkness so complete she couldn't see the children standing right beside her.

"Mom!" Lily grabbed her hand.

The lights stopped flickering and went out entirely. The house plunged into absolute darkness.

Sarah fumbled for her phone out of habit before remembering it was dead. "Stay close to me. Both of you. Don't let go of my hand."

"I can't see anything," Max's voice trembled on the edge of tears.

Sarah's eyes slowly adjusted to the darkness. Moonlight filtered weakly through the frosted glass panel in the door, providing just enough illumination to make out shapes. The stairs rising into deeper shadow. The hallway stretching toward the kitchen. The basement door at the end of the hall, a rectangle of absolute black.

And standing at the top of the stairs, barely visible in the gloom, a figure.

Too tall to be Max. Too still to be Lily. Too *there* to be anything natural.

Sarah's breath stopped. She couldn't move, couldn't think, could only stare at the silhouette watching them from the landing.

Then the figure took a step down. The old wood didn't creak under its weight.

Another step.

"Don't look," Sarah whispered, pulling the children toward her. "Don't look at it. Just close your eyes."

But she couldn't look away. The figure descended slowly, deliberately, one step at a time. As it moved into the weak moonlight, Sarah could make out more details. A suit. Dark, old-fashioned. A man's shape.

Victor Kane was coming down the stairs.

His face was mostly shadow, but Sarah could see the hollow darkness where his eyes should be, and the terrible stillness of his expression. He reached the bottom of the stairs and stopped, standing in the foyer, head tilted as if listening to something only he could hear.

Then he turned toward them.

Sarah grabbed both children and backed away, her spine hitting the unyielding front door. Victor took a step forward. Then another.

"Leave us alone!" Sarah's voice came out as a hoarse scream. "Get away from my children!"

Victor stopped. His mouth moved, and when he spoke, his voice came from everywhere at once—from upstairs and downstairs, from inside the walls, from inside Sarah's own skull.

"Your children?" The words dripped with dark amusement. "You think you own them? You think your fear, your love, your desperation gives you any claim?"

"They're MINE!" Sarah pushed Lily and Max behind her, making herself a barrier. "You can't have them!"

"Can't I?" Victor's form flickered like a bad television signal. "You're in my house. You sleep in my bed. You walk on my floors. You breathe my air. Everything here belongs to me. Including you."

He raised one translucent hand, pointing at the children cowering behind Sarah.

"The ritual requires a child. It's been sixty-two years. I tried to refuse and look what it cost me. My son. My wife. My life. Everything." His voice dropped to a whisper that nonetheless filled every corner of the house. "I won't refuse again. One way or another, the debt will be paid."

"No." Sarah's voice was steel. "No. You can't have them. I don't care what ritual you need, what debt you owe. I don't care if this whole house comes down around us. You can't have my children."

Victor stared at her for a long moment. Then he began to laugh—a hollow, mirthless sound that raised every hair on Sarah's body.

"You think you have a choice?" He gestured to the sealed doors, the unbreakable windows. "You're already mine. This house has claimed you. It claimed you the moment you signed those papers, the moment you carried your children across the threshold. You invited yourselves in."

He took another step closer.

"And now you can't leave until it's finished."

The lights blazed back to life with a pop that made Sarah flinch. But when her eyes adjusted, Victor was gone. The foyer was empty except for her, Lily, and Max, all of them pressed against the door, trembling.

Max was the first to speak. "Mom? Was that... was that Mr. Kane?"

Sarah couldn't answer. Her throat had closed up, her mind reeling. She slid down the door until she was sitting on the floor, Lily and Max tucked against her sides.

From somewhere deep in the house—maybe the basement, maybe everywhere at once—came the sound of children singing. A nursery rhyme, the words too distorted to make out, but the melody clear and sweet and utterly wrong.

The house groaned around them like a living thing settling into comfort.

They were trapped. Truly, completely trapped, in a house that wanted blood.

Sarah pulled her children closer and tried not to think about how many days remained until Halloween.

Seven.

They had seven days to figure out how to escape, how to break the curse, how to survive.

Or seven days until one of them had to die.

The singing continued, floating up from the depths of the house, and outside the window, Sarah could swear she saw Hannah—Julia—standing on her lawn, watching the house with an expression that might have been pity.

Or satisfaction.

Fifteen

Chapter 15: The Séance

⚜

S arah pov

The card appeared on the morning of October 17th, slipped beneath the front door that hadn't opened in two days.

Sarah found it when she came downstairs, her body aching from another sleepless night spent watching over Max. The boy had finally fallen into an exhausted sleep around dawn, muttering about cold water and Benjamin's promises. Lily was curled in the armchair beside his bed, refusing to leave her brother alone. The sight of them—her children, huddled together against terrors they shouldn't have to face—made Sarah want to scream until her throat bled.

The business card was cream-colored, elegant, with raised lettering that caught the weak October light filtering through the grime-covered windows:

ISAAC STONE *Paranormal Investigation & Spiritual Consultation* "I Find What Hides in the Dark"

On the back, handwritten in precise script: *I can help. The parlor. Tonight at midnight. Bring only those you trust with your children's lives.*

Sarah's hands trembled as she held it. The front door was still sealed— she'd checked it obsessively every hour. The windows remained unbreakable, mocking her with views of freedom just beyond the glass. When she'd tried to smash the parlor window with a fireplace poker yesterday, the glass hadn't even trembled. The iron had bent instead, twisted into a shape that looked disturbingly like reaching fingers.

And yet this card had appeared.

"Mom?"

Sarah spun to find Lily on the stairs, still wearing yesterday's clothes. Her daughter looked years older than ten—her eyes shadowed with knowledge no child should possess, her small frame rigid with tension.

"Who's Isaac Stone?" Lily asked, descending with careful steps, as if the house might punish sudden movements.

"I don't know." Sarah pocketed the card quickly, but Lily had already seen it.

"We should do it," Lily said quietly. "The séance. We need to know what they want."

"We know what they want." Sarah's voice cracked. She couldn't say it aloud, couldn't give voice to the thing that stalked her nightmares: her daughter's blood soaking into cursed earth, her daughter's small body dragged into that black well, her daughter's eyes going glassy and empty like Benjamin's must have when the water closed over his head.

"We need to know *why*." Lily moved to the parlor doorway, staring at the room where Victorian furniture sat arranged like a stage set. "And maybe… maybe we can negotiate."

"You can't negotiate with the dead, Lily."

"Maybe that's been everyone's mistake." Her daughter's voice carried an eerie calm. "Maybe everyone was so scared they never tried *asking*."

Sarah wanted to argue, to forbid it, to lock Lily in her room and barricade the door. But what good would it do? The house went where it wanted. Doors opened and sealed according to rules Sarah didn't understand. Max had been taken from his locked bedroom in the middle of the day.

There was no safety here. Only choices between terrible options.

"If we do this," Sarah said slowly, "I need someone else here. Not just this Isaac Stone. Someone I trust."

"Dr. Rhodes," Lily suggested immediately. "She knows about this stuff. And she actually believes us."

Dr. Amelia Rhodes arrived at 11:47 PM, during one of the house's brief windows of permeability. Sarah had called her that afternoon on a phone that worked sporadically, catching three minutes of connection before the line dissolved into static and children's laughter.

"I came as quickly as I could," Amelia said, stepping into the foyer with a leather bag slung over her shoulder. She wore jeans and a thick sweater instead of her usual professional attire, her gray-streaked hair pulled back severely. "The house let me in. That's... not a good sign."

"Why?" Sarah locked the door behind her—a useless gesture, but one that made her feel slightly less helpless.

"It means whatever's here wants me present." Amelia's gaze swept the foyer, landing on the staircase where shadows pooled thicker than they should. "The spirits are getting stronger. I can feel them. It's like the air is *crowded*."

Sarah felt it too—that sense of invisible pressure, of the house holding its breath. The walls seemed to lean inward, listening. The temperature had dropped steadily since sunset, until Sarah could see her breath misting in the parlor.

"The children?" Amelia asked.

"Max is sleeping. Melissa's with him." Sarah's sister had refused to leave after the bathtub incident, setting up camp in Max's room with a baseball bat and grim determination. "Lily insisted on being part of this."

"No." Amelia's voice was sharp. "Sarah, absolutely not. Whatever we contact tonight—"

"I'm already part of it." Lily appeared at the top of the stairs, backlit by the hallway's flickering lights. She descended with unnatural grace, one hand trailing along the bannister. "They want me. Pretending they don't won't change anything."

Amelia and Sarah exchanged glances. There was no arguing with the truth in those words.

At 11:58 PM, a knock echoed through the house.

Not the usual three knocks that plagued Sarah's nights. This was different—

a single, measured rap against wood that seemed to come from everywhere and nowhere.

Sarah opened the front door to find a man standing on the porch.

Isaac Stone was tall and lean, somewhere in his fifties, with a lined face that suggested he'd seen things that aged the soul. He wore a long black coat over dark clothing, and his eyes—pale gray, almost colorless—held an intensity that made Sarah want to step back.

"Mrs. Brennan." His voice was low, cultured, with the faint trace of an accent Sarah couldn't place. "Thank you for trusting me."

"I don't trust you," Sarah said flatly. "But I'm out of options."

"Fair enough." He stepped inside, carrying a worn leather case. His gaze moved past Sarah to Amelia. "Dr. Rhodes. I've read your work on parasitic hauntings. Brilliant thesis on trauma-sustained manifestations."

"Mr. Stone." Amelia's tone was guarded. "Your reputation precedes you. Not all of it reassuring."

"I don't traffic in reassurance." Isaac's attention shifted to Lily, and something flickered in his expression—recognition, or perhaps pity. "You must be Lily. The one they've chosen."

Lily nodded, not flinching from his stare. "How did you know to come?"

"The house called me." Isaac set his case down and began removing items: candles, salt, bundles of dried herbs Sarah didn't recognize. "Or rather, someone trapped inside it did. I received a message three days ago—coordinates and a desperate plea. When I researched the location, I knew immediately what I'd find."

"The Kane house," Sarah whispered.

"One of seven houses I've been tracking for the past thirty years." Isaac's hands moved with practiced efficiency, arranging items on the parlor's central table. "Houses built on ground so saturated with death that the boundary between worlds has worn thin. Halloween Street isn't just haunted, Mrs. Brennan. It's a *threshold*. And this house is the door."

Sarah's stomach twisted. "You said someone inside called you. Who?"

"I don't know yet. But we're going to find out." He glanced at the grandfather clock in the corner—its hands frozen at 3:33, like every other clock in the house. "It's midnight. Time to see who's been waiting for us."

A woman appeared in the parlor doorway.

Sarah jumped, hand flying to her chest. She hadn't heard anyone approach, hadn't heard the front door open again.

The woman was perhaps forty, with wild auburn curls and a round, friendly face that seemed at odds with the gravity in her dark eyes. She wore layers of flowing fabric—scarves, shawls, a long skirt—and crystal pendants that caught the light.

"Sorry I'm late," she said breathlessly. "The house fought me. Took me twenty minutes to get through the front door, and I was standing right in front of it." Her gaze found Isaac. "You started without me?"

"Claire." Isaac's voice held warmth for the first time. "Everyone, this is Claire Donovan. She's the most powerful medium I've ever worked with. If anyone can make contact tonight, it's her."

Claire Donovan moved into the room with surprising grace for someone so substantially built, her scarves trailing like wings. She stopped suddenly in the center of the parlor, head tilting as if hearing distant music.

"Oh," she breathed. "Oh, there are so many of them."

"How many?" Amelia asked sharply, pulling out a notebook.

"Dozens. Maybe hundreds." Claire's eyes had gone unfocused, staring at something the rest of them couldn't see. "Layer upon layer. Colonial dead. Victorian dead. Modern dead. They're *stacked*, like sediment. This house is built on grief."

Sarah felt Lily press closer to her side. She wrapped an arm around her daughter, holding tight.

"Can you identify any of them specifically?" Isaac was lighting candles now, placing them at the cardinal points around the table. "The Kane family?"

"They're here. Victor. Eleanor. The boy—Benjamin." Claire's voice had gone distant, dreamy. "But there's something else. Something older. Something that was here *first*." Her eyes suddenly focused on Lily with alarming intensity. "She sees you, little one. She's been waiting for you."

"Who?" Sarah demanded, stepping protectively in front of her daughter. "Who sees her?"

"The Woman in White."

The candles all flickered simultaneously, though there was no breeze.

Isaac moved quickly, completing his preparations. He sprinkled salt in a circle around the table, then arranged the herbs—sage, rosemary, something that looked like dried flowers—in specific patterns. From his case, he withdrew a small silver bell and an old leather journal.

"Everyone sit," he instructed. "Keep your hands on the table, touching. Do not break the circle, no matter what happens. Do not invite anything in. Do not make promises. Do not give permission for anything. Understood?"

Sarah nodded, numb with dread. This was insane. They were actively reaching out to the things that had been tormenting her family. But what choice did they have? At least this way, they might get answers.

Lily took her seat calmly, too calmly, and placed her small hands palm-down on the dark wood. Sarah sat beside her, then Amelia, then Isaac. Claire completed the circle, sitting across from Lily.

"Before we begin," Amelia said quietly, "I need to state for the record that this is an extremely dangerous procedure. Séances can open doorways that are difficult to close. Whatever we contact—"

"Will tell us the truth," Lily interrupted. "That's what we need. The truth."

Claire reached across and took Lily's hand. "You're very brave, sweetheart. But Isaac's right—don't make any deals. The dead are excellent at twisting words."

"I won't," Lily promised.

Isaac rang the silver bell once. The sound hung in the air impossibly long, echoing from corners that shouldn't produce echoes.

"We call upon the spirits who dwell within these walls," Isaac began, his voice taking on a formal cadence. "We seek communion with those who have passed beyond the veil. We come in peace and with respect. We ask that you make yourselves known."

Silence. Heavy, expectant silence.

Then the temperature plummeted.

Sarah's breath came out in white clouds. Frost spread across the windows in delicate, lace-like patterns. The candles guttered but didn't go out, their flames bending at impossible angles.

"Someone's here," Claire whispered. Her eyes had rolled back, showing only whites. "Multiple presences. They're... arguing. Fighting for dominance. They all want to speak."

"Who has the strongest claim?" Isaac asked calmly, as if this were a perfectly normal conversation. "Who has been here longest?"

"The woman. The first woman. The one they hanged." Claire's voice was changing, deepening, taking on an accent. "She says... she says she was innocent. She says they all were. Thirty-seven souls buried in unhallowed ground, denied peace, denied justice. She says the town built over their graves and called it progress."

"When?" Amelia was scribbling notes frantically. "When did this happen?"

"1692." Claire's head lolled, neck loose. "The same year as Salem, but no one remembers. No one wrote it down. Hollow's End erased its sins."

Sarah's heart hammered. 1692. More than three hundred years of rage, simmering beneath Halloween Street.

"What do you want?" Sarah couldn't stop herself from asking. "What do all of you want?"

Claire's head snapped toward her, movements jerky and unnatural. When she spoke, it wasn't her voice—it was higher, older, filled with centuries of fury:

"Justice. Remembrance. Blood."

The last word came out as a hiss that made Sarah's skin crawl.

"The Kanes," Isaac pressed, keeping his tone even. "Victor, Eleanor, Benjamin. Are they among you?"

"The man is here. The murderer. He screams and screams but no one hears him. Good." Claire smiled, and it was a terrible expression. *"The woman is here. She tried to save the boy. We liked her. We wanted to help her. But she died before we could."*

"And Benjamin?" Lily's voice was small but steady. "Is Ben here?"

Claire's head turned slowly toward the little girl. The movement was too smooth, too controlled. Whatever was looking through Claire's eyes wasn't human.

"The boy-child lingers. He doesn't understand he's dead. He thinks he's still waiting for his mother to come save him." A pause. *"Much like another child in this house."*

"Don't," Sarah warned, squeezing Lily's hand. "Don't talk about my daughter."

"Your daughter." The thing inside Claire laughed—a sound like breaking glass. *"No. She was never yours. She was always ours. We've been waiting for her. Three hundred thirty-three years, we've been waiting."*

"What does that mean?" Amelia demanded. "Why Lily specifically?"

Claire's body went rigid. Her back arched until Sarah heard vertebrae pop, her mouth opening impossibly wide. When she spoke, multiple voices emerged—layered, discordant, speaking in rounds:

"She has the look. Eleanor's eyes. Eleanor's face. Eleanor's soul, perhaps, returned."

"That's impossible," Sarah said, but her voice shook. She remembered the photographs in the attic—Eleanor Kane's portrait with its haunting, knowing gaze. And she remembered looking at it and thinking, inexplicably: *She looks like Lily in twenty years.*

"Nothing is impossible when the veil is thin." Claire's fingers splayed on the table, pressing down so hard the wood groaned. *"Every seven years, we grow stronger. Every seven years, the boundary weakens. This year—this Halloween—the veil will tear entirely. And we will be free."*

"Free to do what?" Isaac's voice had gone sharp.

"To take what was taken from us. To consume what buried us. To drag this cursed town into the ground where it belongs."

The candles flared suddenly, flames shooting up a foot high. Shadows danced on the walls, taking shapes—human shapes, hanging shapes, writhing in eternal agony.

"The ritual," Lily said quietly. "The blood ritual. That's supposed to stop you, isn't it? That's why the Collectors started it."

"The Collectors." The voices inside Claire spat the word. *"Murderers playing dress-up. They thought they could appease us with their pathetic offerings. But there is no appeasement. There is only debt."*

147

"Then why do you want Lily's blood?" Sarah's voice rose despite her attempts at control. "If the ritual doesn't work, why do you want her?"

The silence that followed was somehow worse than the voices.

Then Claire's head turned fully toward Lily, her neck twisting at an angle that should have broken it. Her eyes opened—and they were completely white, no iris, no pupil, just blank white orbs that wept blood.

When she spoke, it was a single voice now. Female. Ancient. Filled with a hatred so pure it felt like a physical force:

"Because she looks like the one who tried to defy the cycle. Because she carries the resonance of a mother's love strong enough to challenge death itself. Because if we consume her—her innocence, her light, her potential—we can use that power to tear the veil completely. Not just on Halloween Street. Everywhere. The dead will rise. The boundary will fall. And the world will finally understand what it means to be buried alive."

"No," Sarah breathed.

"Yes." The thing wearing Claire smiled with bloody teeth. *"The ritual doesn't appease us, foolish woman. It feeds us. Every sacrifice strengthened us. Every child's death saturated the ground with trauma. Victor Kane tried to stop the cycle—tried to deny us—and look what it cost him. His wife. His son. His soul."*

"You're lying," Amelia said sharply. "Spirits lie. You're trying to manipulate us—"

Claire's hand shot out faster than humanly possible, grabbing Amelia's wrist. The psychologist screamed as frost spread from the point of contact, ice crystals forming on her skin.

"We do not lie. We have no need for lies. The truth is horrible enough."

Isaac rang the bell again, sharp and commanding. "Release her. You were invited to speak, not to harm."

"Harm?" The entity laughed. *"We haven't even begun to show you harm. But we will. Midnight, October 31st. When the Harvest Moon rises full and red. When the veil reaches its thinnest. That is when the girl-child must come to the well, must spill her blood on the stones, must sink into the water that drowned the boy. That is when we claim what was promised."*

"Nothing was promised!" Sarah slammed her free hand on the table. "I

148

never agreed to anything! Lily never agreed to anything!"

"The house agreed. The land agreed. The moment you crossed the threshold, the moment you signed your name to the deed, the moment you chose to stay despite every warning—you agreed. The contract was made in 1890 when they built these cursed homes on our graves. Every family who lives here pays the debt. Your payment comes due on Halloween."

Lily spoke, her voice cutting through the chaos with surprising strength: "And if I refuse? If I don't come to the well? What then?"

The entity turned its full attention to her. Blood streamed from Claire's eyes like tears, dripping onto the table and pooling in dark rivulets.

"Then everyone dies. Not just you. Not just your brother, your mother, your aunt. Everyone on Halloween Street. Forty-seven souls. We will drag them all down into the earth. We will pull this entire street into the grave and feast on their terror for the next three hundred years. Forty-seven for one. That is the exchange. That is the price of your defiance."

"You're bluffing," Isaac said, but his voice lacked conviction.

"Are we?" Claire's body convulsed violently. *"Ask the families who lived here before. Oh wait—you can't. They're all DEAD."*

The last word echoed, distorting, becoming a chorus of screams. The candles exploded, wax spraying across the table. The windows cracked simultaneously, spiderwebs of broken glass spreading across every pane.

Claire began to seize, her body jerking with unnatural force. Her eyes—still bleeding, still white—found Lily one last time.

"We'll be waiting, little Eleanor. At the well. At midnight. Don't be late. We've been so terribly lonely."

Then Claire collapsed forward, her head hitting the table with a sickening crack. Blood poured from her nose, her ears, her eyes, soaking into the wood.

"Claire!" Isaac lunged forward, breaking the circle. "Someone call 911!"

"The phones don't work!" Sarah was already moving, grabbing napkins from the sideboard, trying to stop the bleeding. "Jesus, there's so much blood—"

"It's not all hers," Amelia said, her voice shaking as she examined Claire's face. "Some of it is... it's old blood. It's manifestation blood. The entity marked her."

Claire's eyes fluttered open—brown again, human again, confused and terrified.

"What happened?" she mumbled, then screamed as she saw her own blood-soaked hands. "What happened to me?!"

"You were possessed," Isaac said grimly, supporting her head. "By something very old and very angry. The Woman in White."

"I don't remember. I don't remember anything after we started." Claire was crying, her tears mixing with the blood on her face. "Did I hurt anyone? Did I say something terrible?"

Sarah looked at Lily, who sat frozen in her chair, face pale as death.

"You told us the truth," Sarah said quietly. "That's all."

But it wasn't all. It wasn't even close to all.

Because now they knew: Lily had three weeks to live. Three weeks until Halloween. Three weeks until the choice between one death or forty-seven.

And somewhere in the walls, something laughed—high and cold and patient.

The Woman in White had delivered her message. Now she would wait for her answer.

They managed to stop the bleeding, but Claire couldn't stand without support. Isaac and Amelia half-carried her to the couch while Sarah cleaned up the parlor, trying not to think about the blood that had already soaked into the wood, staining it darker.

Lily sat motionless at the table, staring at the space where the entity had manifested through Claire.

"Mom," she said finally, voice barely above a whisper. "She called me Eleanor."

Sarah's hands stilled on the bloody napkins. "She was confused. Trying to scare you."

"Was she?" Lily turned to look at her mother, and the expression in her ten-year-old eyes was far too old. "What if I am Eleanor? What if I'm her, come back? What if that's why they want me?"

"You're not." Sarah crossed to her daughter, kneeling so they were eye-level. "You're Lily Anne Brennan. You're my daughter. You're your own person. Whatever that thing said—"

"Felt true," Lily finished. "It felt true, Mom. When she looked at me, I felt... I felt like I'd been here before. Like I'd stood in this parlor and watched someone die and I couldn't stop it."

Sarah pulled Lily into her arms, holding tight. Her daughter felt so small, so fragile. How could anyone—anything—look at this child and demand her blood?

From the couch, Claire spoke weakly: "I'm sorry. I'm so sorry. I should have been stronger. Should have kept it out—"

"You have nothing to apologize for," Isaac said firmly. "That entity is one of the most powerful I've ever encountered. The fact that you made contact at all is remarkable."

"But now we know what we're facing," Amelia added, her scientific mind clearly trying to process the impossible. "An entity—multiple entities—that have been growing stronger for over three centuries. Fed by trauma, anchored to this specific location, and laser-focused on Lily as a... what? A power source?"

"A key," Isaac corrected. "She's the key that opens the final door. The entity—The Woman in White—she's been trapped here for 333 years. She wants to use Lily's death as a catalyst to break free completely."

"Then we make sure she doesn't get what she wants," Sarah said flatly. "We find another way."

"There may not be another way." Isaac's tone was gentle but honest. "Mrs. Brennan, in thirty years of investigating paranormal phenomena, I've never encountered a case this advanced. The house is completely compromised. The spirits have had decades—centuries—to establish dominance. Usually, I'd recommend immediate evacuation, but—"

"But we can't leave," Sarah finished bitterly. "We're trapped. The house won't let us go."

"Which means it's confident," Amelia said slowly. "It believes it's already won."

Lily pulled away from Sarah's embrace, wiping her eyes. When she spoke, her voice was steady:

"Then we need to prove it wrong."

They stayed together in the parlor as night deepened toward dawn, no one willing to scatter into the house's dark corners. Claire dozed fitfully on the couch, occasionally whimpering in her sleep. Isaac pored over his journal, cross-referencing notes. Amelia typed on her laptop until the battery died, documenting everything.

Sarah held Lily close and tried not to think about the deadline ticking down.

Fourteen days until Halloween.

Fourteen days to find a solution to a problem that had been building for 333 years.

Fourteen days to save her daughter from a curse that had already claimed so many others.

Outside, the wind picked up, rattling the cracked windows. Somewhere in the distance, Sarah heard children singing—that same nursery rhyme Max had been humming, the one that made her skin crawl:

Ring around the rosie Pocket full of posies Ashes, ashes We all fall down

But the voices carried new words now, words that definitely weren't part of the original:

Eleanor tried to run away Benjamin died the very same day Victor's gun went bang bang bang Now it's time for the blood exchange

Sarah closed her eyes and held her daughter tighter, as if she could protect Lily through sheer force of will.

But deep down, in the part of her mind she tried to ignore, she knew the terrible truth:

The Woman in White was right. A choice was coming. One death or forty-seven.

And Sarah had no idea which option she could live with.

If she chose to live at all.

Sixteen

Chapter 16: Hannah's Truth

~~⸰⸰⸰~~

Sarah pov

The house breathed around them.

Sarah felt it in the walls—a rhythmic expansion and contraction like lungs filling with stale air. The temperature had dropped ten degrees since Isaac Stone and Claire Donovan had fled three hours ago, Claire still bleeding from her eyes, mumbling incoherently about drowning children and roots growing through ribcages. The medium's blood had left a trail down the front steps, black in the moonlight, and hadn't dried.

It was October 22nd. Nine days until Halloween.

Nine days until midnight.

Sarah stood in the parlor, arms wrapped around herself, staring at the three portraits of the Kane family that hung above the mantle. In the wavering candlelight—the electricity had died permanently at sunset—Victor Kane's painted eyes seemed to track her movements. Eleanor's mouth curved in what might have been a smile or a scream. And little Benjamin, no more than seven years old in the portrait, looked exactly like Max.

Too much like Max.

Upstairs, Lily and Max were barricaded in Lily's room, the door reinforced with furniture Sarah had dragged up the stairs while her arms screamed in protest. Melissa had driven back to Boston two hours ago to gather supplies—salt, iron filings, anything that might help—though Sarah suspected her sister simply needed to escape the suffocating wrongness of the house for a few hours. She didn't blame her.

The knocking had stopped at 3:33 AM, as it did every night. But the silence that followed was worse. In the silence, Sarah could hear *them*—whispers in the walls, footsteps in empty rooms, the wet sound of something dragging itself across the attic floor.

She'd tried to leave again an hour ago. Every door remained sealed, every window refusing to break no matter how hard she struck them. Even the second-story windows wouldn't shatter. Sarah had thrown a chair through Lily's bedroom window and watched it bounce off the glass as if hitting rubber.

They were trapped.

The house wanted them here for Halloween. The house would keep them here.

Sarah turned toward the kitchen, thinking she might make tea—something normal, something human, something to anchor herself to reality—when three sharp knocks echoed through the front door.

She froze.

The knocking wasn't supposed to start again until tomorrow night. The pattern was consistent, had been consistent for weeks: 3:33 AM, three knocks, then silence until the next night. This was different.

Three more knocks. Deliberate. Patient.

Then a voice, muffled through the heavy oak door: "Sarah? It's Hannah. Please, let me in."

Sarah's hands clenched into fists. Hannah Winters. The neighbor who'd brought casseroles and sympathy. The woman who'd warned her about salt lines and closing windows. The woman who'd stared at the basement door with naked terror and fled every evening before sunset.

The woman who'd known. Who'd always known.

"The doors are sealed," Sarah called out, her voice cracking. "I can't open them even if I wanted to."

Silence. Then: "Try. Please. I need to talk to you before it's too late."

Something in Hannah's voice—a rawness, a desperation—made Sarah approach the door despite every instinct screaming at her to run. She grasped the brass handle, expecting the familiar resistance, the supernatural lock that had kept them prisoner for days.

The handle turned smoothly.

The door opened.

Hannah Winters stood on the porch, backlit by the sickly yellow glow of the streetlamp at the end of Halloween Street. But she looked different. Older, somehow. The warm, grandmotherly figure had been replaced by something harder, more angular. Her eyes were red-rimmed, her grey hair wild around her face, and she clutched a worn leather journal to her chest like a shield.

"Thank you," Hannah whispered. She stepped across the threshold before Sarah could reconsider.

The moment Hannah entered, the door slammed shut behind her with a sound like a coffin closing.

Sarah stumbled backward. "What—"

"The house let me in because I'm family," Hannah said quietly. She moved past Sarah into the parlor, her eyes roaming over the portraits, the furniture, the bloodstain on the floor where Claire had collapsed. "Because I'm a Kane. Or I was, a very long time ago."

The words hung in the air like smoke.

Sarah's mind raced. "You're... you said your name was Hannah Winters."

"It is now." The older woman turned, and in the candlelight, Sarah saw the resemblance—the sharp cheekbones, the deep-set eyes, the aristocratic nose that matched Victor Kane's portrait exactly. "I was born Julia Margaret Kane. Victor was my uncle. I was thirteen years old in 1963, the night he murdered Eleanor and Benjamin. The night the ritual was supposed to happen."

The parlor seemed to contract around them. Sarah felt the walls lean in, listening.

"You're Julia Kane," Sarah breathed. "You were *there*."

"I was there." Julia—not Hannah, never Hannah—set the journal on the side table with shaking hands. "I've been watching this house for sixty-two years. Waiting. I've lived in Hollow's End my entire life, taken a new name, a new identity, because I couldn't leave. The curse won't let me leave. And every seven years, when the ritual comes due again, I watch new families move in. I watch them discover the truth. I watch them try to escape."

"You *knew*," Sarah hissed, rage building in her chest like a fire. "You knew what this place was, and you let us move in anyway. You let me bring my *children* here—"

"I had no choice!" Julia's voice cracked. "Don't you understand? The house chooses its victims. The town council, the real estate agent, they all help guide the right families here. Single mothers. Vulnerable women with children. Those who won't be believed if they speak about what happens. But the house itself makes the final selection. It *called* to you, Sarah. It wanted Lily the moment you drove past Halloween Street."

Sarah thought of that first day, the way she'd felt an inexplicable pull toward the Victorian manor. The way Lily had pressed her face against the car window and whispered, *That one, Mommy. That's our house.*

"Why?" Sarah demanded. "Why does it want her?"

Julia's face crumpled. "Because she looks like Eleanor. Same eyes. Same soul, maybe. I don't know. But I've seen the pattern. Every seven years since 1963, a girl who resembles Eleanor moves into this house. And every seven years, the ritual demands completion."

"The ritual that your uncle started."

"No." Julia shook her head violently. "The ritual that The Collectors started in 1897. My uncle was just one participant in a cycle that had been running for decades. Every seven years, each family gives a sacrifice—usually a child, always a blood relative—to appease the spirits buried beneath Halloween Street. To keep them from rising and consuming the entire town."

Sarah's stomach churned. "That's insane. That's murder."

"It's survival," Julia said flatly. "The town was built on a mass grave, Sarah. Hanged criminals, accused witches, unbaptized children—all buried in unconsecrated ground. Their anger seeped into the land. The first families who built here started dying within a year. Disease. Accidents.

156

Madness. Until someone—some traveling spiritualist or con artist, no one remembers—taught them the appeasement ritual. Blood for peace. Children for prosperity."

The portraits seemed to watch them, Victor's painted face stern and unyielding.

"Your uncle refused," Sarah said slowly. "Eleanor's diary said he refused to sacrifice Benjamin."

"He did." Julia's hands twisted together. "My mother—Victor's younger sister Elizabeth—begged him to complete the ritual. She said if he didn't, the curse would spread beyond his family, that we'd all be punished. Victor told her he'd rather die than harm his son. That he'd face whatever consequences came."

"So he killed them instead," Sarah whispered. "He murdered Eleanor and Benjamin himself."

"To spare them." Julia's eyes glistened. "That's what he wrote in his suicide note. He couldn't complete the ritual—couldn't hand his son over to those *things* in the well. But he knew they'd suffer if the spirits took them. So he made it quick. He drowned Benjamin in the well, shot Eleanor in the backyard, then put the gun in his own mouth."

The house groaned around them, timbers settling with sounds like breaking bones.

"The ritual was interrupted," Julia continued, her voice monotone now, reciting facts like a historian. "Victor's death invalidated the sacrifice—it had to be willing, had to be ritualized properly. So the curse focused itself on this house, on the Kane bloodline. Every seven years, it tries to complete what Victor started. It pulls in families, manifests the Kane ghosts, and demands what it was denied: a child's willing sacrifice before midnight on Halloween."

Sarah's hands trembled. "Lily."

"Lily," Julia confirmed. "But it's not just about her resemblance to Eleanor. The curse is intelligent, Sarah. It's learned. It knows that a mother's love is the strongest force in the world—and the easiest to manipulate. If you sacrifice Lily, you complete the ritual Victor broke. The curse ends. The town is safe for another seven years."

"No." The word came out strangled. "Absolutely not."

"Then everyone on Halloween Street dies at midnight on October 31st." Julia's voice was hard now, practical. "The entire street will sink into the burial ground. Forty-seven people, Sarah. Men, women, children. All dead because you refused."

"You can't ask me to—" Sarah's voice broke. "She's my daughter. She's *ten years old.*"

"My brother was nine."

The words fell like stones.

Sarah stared at Julia—at this woman who'd played at being a friendly neighbor while hiding six decades of trauma behind casseroles and cryptic warnings.

"What?" Sarah breathed.

Julia's face was carved from marble. "My mother completed the ritual in 1963. After Victor's death disrupted everything, after the spirits began manifesting throughout the town, attacking anyone with Collector blood. The council convened an emergency meeting. They said one of the original families had to finish what Victor started. My mother... she chose my little brother, David. He was nine years old. He had blonde hair and my father's laugh. He loved trains."

Sarah felt sick.

"She took him to the well on November 1st, 1963—one day after the deadline—and she offered him to the spirits. He went willingly because she told him it would save everyone. That he'd be a hero." Julia's voice was empty, hollowed out. "I watched from the stairs. I saw her bind his hands with black thread. I saw her lower him into the well. I heard him calling for her as the water rose. Calling for Mommy to pull him up. Mommy to save him."

Tears streamed down Julia's weathered face, but her expression remained fixed.

"She sewed his mouth shut first," Julia whispered. "So the neighbors wouldn't hear him scream."

The candles flickered. Somewhere above them, a door opened and closed softly.

Sarah wanted to vomit. She wanted to run. She wanted to grab her children and smash through the walls if necessary, consequences be damned.

"Your mother was a monster," Sarah said hoarsely.

"My mother saved forty-seven people," Julia countered. "And because of her sacrifice, because David's blood completed a ritual, the curse was appeased for seven more years. Then fourteen. Then twenty-one. It gave the town time. Time to grow, to prosper, to forget what we'd paid for that prosperity."

"At the cost of murdering a child!"

"Yes!" Julia's composure finally cracked. "Yes, at that cost! And I've lived with it every day for sixty-two years! I've watched the house take family after family, trying to complete Victor's interrupted ritual. I've seen mothers go mad trying to protect their daughters. I've seen children drown in that well. I've seen the spirits tear families apart piece by piece when they refuse the ritual."

She stepped closer, her eyes wild.

"I've watched, Sarah, because I deserve to watch. Because I said nothing that night when my mother took David to the basement. Because I was too afraid, too young, too *broken* to stop her. So I stayed. I became Hannah Winters. I bought the house next door. And every seven years, I witness what my family's sin created."

"Then help me stop it," Sarah pleaded. "Help me break this cycle—"

"There is no breaking it!" Julia's voice rose to a shriek. "Don't you understand? I've tried! For sixty-two years, I've researched, consulted mediums, brought in priests and paranormal investigators and anyone who might know a way to end this curse without blood. There *is* no other way. The land demands payment. The dead demand justice. And the only currency they accept is what they were denied: a child's life."

Sarah shook her head, backing toward the stairs. "No. I won't. I *can't*."

"You think Eleanor didn't say the same thing?" Julia followed her, relentless. "You think she didn't beg Victor to find another way? He tried, Sarah. He spent months researching, performing counter-rituals, attempting to negotiate with the spirits. Nothing worked. And when he finally accepted that the

159

only choices were to sacrifice his son or let the curse spread, he chose a third option: murder-suicide. Quick deaths. Merciful deaths."

"That's not mercy," Sarah spat. "That's cowardice."

"Maybe." Julia's voice dropped to a whisper. "But tell me, Sarah—when midnight comes on Halloween, when the spirits manifest in their full power, when they start tearing Max apart in front of you because the ritual wasn't completed—will you still call it cowardice? When Lily is possessed and forced to drown her own brother? When the house collapses into the grave and forty-seven people die screaming? Will you still say you made the right choice?"

Sarah's back hit the staircase banister. Upstairs, she could hear Lily singing softly to Max—a lullaby their grandmother used to sing, sweet and innocent.

"There has to be another way," Sarah said desperately.

"There isn't." Julia pulled a knife from her coat pocket—old, ritualistic, the handle wrapped in black thread. "I brought this. It belonged to my mother. She used it to… to make the sacrifice quick. Painless. If you want, I can help you. I can guide you through the ritual. Lily won't suffer. I promise you, she won't suffer."

The knife glinted in the candlelight. Sarah saw rust-colored stains on the blade.

David's blood. Still there after sixty-two years.

Something snapped in Sarah's chest—not breaking, but hardening. Calcifying into fury.

"Get out."

Julia blinked. "Sarah—"

"Get out of my house." Sarah's voice was steel. "You come here, tell me you've watched families die for six decades, that you've done *nothing* to help them, and then you offer me a knife to murder my daughter? You think because your mother was a monster, I should become one too?"

"I'm trying to save you—"

"You're trying to absolve yourself!" Sarah screamed. The house shuddered around them, paintings rattling against walls. "You want me to kill Lily so you can tell yourself that you were right, that there was no choice, that what your mother did to David was *justified*. Well I won't give you that absolution. I won't complete your sick ritual."

Julia's face hardened. "You'll regret this."

"Maybe. But I'll regret it as a mother who tried to save her child, not one who murdered her."

For a moment, they stood frozen in the parlor—two women, two mothers, separated by an impossible choice made sixty-two years apart.

Then the front door swung open.

Both women turned, shocked. The door had been sealed for days, immovable, but now it gaped wide, revealing the dark maw of Halloween Street beyond. Cold October wind rushed in, extinguishing half the candles.

"The house is letting me leave," Sarah said slowly. "It's giving me a choice."

Julia looked at the open door with something like despair. "It's letting you eject me. The curse recognizes what I am—a Kane who broke the covenant. I'm as much an enemy to it as the spirits below."

Sarah didn't hesitate. She grabbed Julia's arm and dragged her toward the door. The older woman didn't resist, her body limp, the knife clattering to the floor.

At the threshold, Sarah shoved Julia onto the porch. The woman stumbled, catching herself on the railing, her face illuminated by the diseased streetlight.

"Sarah, please," Julia begged. "I'm trying to help you understand—"

"Understand what? That I should give up? That I should kill my daughter to save myself from guilt?" Sarah's hands gripped the doorframe. "You think you're the first mother to face this choice? Eleanor tried to refuse. Look what happened to her."

Julia's face went white. "Those were my words. How did you—"

"Because I know what happened, Julia." Sarah's voice was cold. "Victor murdered Eleanor because she refused to sacrifice Benjamin. She tried to run, tried to save her son, and her husband shot her for it. You've spent sixty-two years telling yourself that completing the ritual is the merciful choice. But Eleanor knew the truth. Victor knew it too, at the end. There is no mercy in this. There's only horror."

"Then you'll die," Julia said flatly. "All of you. And I'll watch it happen again."

"Then watch," Sarah said. "But you'll watch me *fight*, not surrender."

She slammed the door in Julia's face.

The locks engaged with a series of heavy clicks—one, two, three—like coffin nails being driven home. Through the door's small window, Sarah saw Julia standing on the porch, shoulders slumped, the knife still clutched in one hand.

Then Julia looked up, and her eyes met Sarah's through the glass.

"You think you're the first mother to face this choice?" Julia called through the door, her voice carrying despite the barrier. "Eleanor tried to refuse. Look what happened to her."

The same words. Exactly the same.

Sarah's blood ran cold.

Julia continued, her voice rising: "They're not just offering you a choice, Sarah. They're showing you the consequences of refusal. Eleanor tried to save Benjamin, so Victor killed them both. If you refuse the ritual, if you force the spirits to take what they're owed, they won't make it quick. They won't make it merciful. They'll tear your children apart slowly, make you watch every moment, and then they'll take you too."

"I don't care," Sarah shouted through the door. "I won't be the one who hurts them!"

Julia's laugh was bitter, broken. "You think the spirits care who wields the knife? You think it matters whether you sacrifice Lily willingly or they force you to do it through possession? Either way, she dies. Either way, you'll be the one who kills her. The only difference is whether it's your choice or theirs."

Sarah pressed her forehead against the door, tears streaming down her face.

"My mother made her choice," Julia continued relentlessly. "She decided it was better to control how David died than to let the spirits torture him. She decided mercy was a quick blade and her own hands, not claws from the dark and hours of screaming. Was she wrong? Maybe. But at least David's last words were 'I love you, Mommy,' not 'Why won't you help me?'"

"Stop," Sarah whispered.

"Nine days, Sarah. Nine days until Halloween. Think about what you're choosing. Think about whether your pride is worth your daughter's suffering."

Sarah lifted her head. Through the window, she watched Julia turn and walk down the porch steps, her figure receding into the darkness of Halloween Street. The streetlamp flickered once, twice, then died completely.

Julia's voice drifted back, barely audible: "I'll be here on Halloween night. When you change your mind—and you will change your mind—I'll be waiting with the knife. My mother's knife. The mercy blade."

Then she was gone, swallowed by the October darkness.

Sarah stood alone in the parlor, surrounded by portraits of the dead and the ghost of choices she couldn't take back. The house settled around her with sounds like satisfaction.

From upstairs, Lily called out: "Mom? Is everything okay?"

Sarah wiped her eyes, steadied her voice. "Everything's fine, sweetheart. Go back to sleep."

She looked at the knife Julia had dropped—still lying on the floor, blade pointed toward the basement door like a compass needle finding north.

Nine days.

Nine days to find another way, or nine days to decide if Julia was right. If mercy was a mother's hands and a quick blade. If some choices were so terrible that even the wrong decision was better than letting fate decide.

Sarah picked up the knife. The handle was cold despite the black thread wrapping. She could feel the weight of it, the history. David's death. How many others? How many children had died on this blade in the name of mercy?

She walked to the kitchen and threw the knife into the sink, covering it with dish soap and water. She wouldn't touch it again. She wouldn't even look at it.

But as she turned away, she glimpsed her reflection in the darkened window—and saw Eleanor Kane standing behind her, mouth sewn shut with black thread, eyes wide with warning.

Sarah spun around.

The kitchen was empty.

But on the counter, written in condensed moisture, were three words in Eleanor's handwriting (she recognized it from the diary):

DON'T TRUST JULIA

Sarah's breath caught. "Eleanor?"

The words dripped, letters dissolving into water, running down the cabinet like tears.

Below them, a new message formed:

SHE WANTS LILY DEAD

NOT TO SAVE ANYONE

TO FEED HER GUILT

Sarah stared at the messages as they too dissolved, leaving only clean countertop behind.

Upstairs, the floorboards creaked—three times, deliberately, a rhythm she now recognized.

Three knocks. Always three.

The house was trying to tell her something. Eleanor was trying to warn her.

Julia Kane wasn't trying to help. She was trying to complete a ritual she'd failed to stop sixty-two years ago. She was trying to make Sarah into her mother, to create another woman who'd chosen the knife over defiance.

To prove that there had never been a choice at all.

Sarah climbed the stairs slowly, each step an act of will. At the top, she paused outside Lily's room and pressed her ear to the door. Inside, she heard her daughter reading to Max—something about brave knights and rescued princesses and happily ever afters.

Stories where the mother saved her children.

Stories where love was stronger than curses.

Sarah made her decision then, standing in the hallway of a house built on bones and watered with blood. She didn't know how she'd do it. Didn't know if it was even possible. But she knew, with the certainty of marrow and sinew, that she would not pick up that knife.

Not for Julia's absolution.

Not for the town's safety.

Not even for mercy.

Some choices, once made, could never be unmade. Some horrors, once committed, haunted forever—not as ghosts but as the living dead, women like Julia who'd survived their children and spent decades trying to justify what survival had cost.

Sarah would not become that woman.

She would find another way, or she would die trying.

Behind her, from the darkness at the end of the hallway, came the sound of wet breathing and the scrape of fingernails on wood. Victor Kane's ghost, perhaps. Or Benjamin's. Or Eleanor's.

It didn't matter.

They were all dead already.

Sarah was still alive. And so were her children.

For nine more days, she would keep them that way.

Whatever came next—she would face it standing.

Not kneeling with a blade.

Not ever.

Seventeen

CHAPTER 17: "Melissa's Arrival"

S arah pov

The headlights cut through the October darkness at 2:47 AM, and for one irrational moment, Sarah thought it might be help—real help, the kind that came with authority and solutions and the power to make nightmare houses behave like normal buildings made of wood and nails.

Then she recognized Melissa's silver Subaru.

Sarah stood on the porch of the Last House on Halloween Street, wrapped in a cardigan that did nothing against the cold that came from *inside* the walls rather than the autumn air. Behind her, the house breathed—she'd stopped pretending it didn't. The floors creaked with footsteps that belonged to no one. The walls occasionally sweated condensation that smelled like standing water and decay. And every surface seemed to be watching her with the patient malevolence of something that had all the time in the world.

Melissa emerged from the car looking like she'd aged five years in the three weeks since Sarah had last seen her. Her auburn hair, usually meticulously styled, was pulled into a messy ponytail. Her face was makeup-free and haggard in the porch light. She wore yoga pants and a Boston College sweatshirt—Melissa, who never left the house without full armor of professionalism.

"Jesus Christ, Sarah." Melissa's voice cracked as she climbed the porch steps. "Your voicemail. I've been calling for six hours. Six *hours*. Your phone goes straight to voicemail, and I—"

She stopped mid-sentence, finally looking at her younger sister. Really looking.

Sarah knew what she saw. A woman who'd lost twelve pounds in three weeks. Eyes ringed with the kind of exhaustion that came from sleeping in ninety-minute increments, always jerking awake at 3:33 AM to phantom knocking. Hair unwashed for three days because the upstairs shower had started running black water, and the thought of standing naked and vulnerable under it made Sarah's skin crawl.

"You look like hell," Melissa whispered.

"The house killed my phone." Sarah heard how insane it sounded even as she said it. "It kills everything electronic eventually. Batteries drain. Screens crack for no reason. Tucker's power drill died mid-charge, and he said the battery was *melted* inside."

Melissa's expression cycled through concern, disbelief, and something that looked uncomfortably like pity. "Sarah, honey, I think you need to—"

"Don't." Sarah's voice came out sharper than intended. "Don't tell me I need rest, or perspective, or a therapist. I need you to believe me. That's why you're here, isn't it? Because some part of you heard that voicemail and knew I wasn't making it up."

The voicemail Sarah barely remembered leaving, sobbing into the phone at 11 PM while Lily and Max slept drugged on children's Benadryl—the only way Sarah could ensure a few hours without Max sleepwalking toward the basement or Lily drawing skeletal hands reaching from wells.

Melissa, something's wrong with the house. Not wrong like foundation issues. Wrong like it's ALIVE. It won't let us leave. The doors seal themselves. Max tried to drown himself. There are ghosts—real ghosts—and they want Lily, and I don't know what to do, and I'm so scared, Mel. I'm so fucking scared, and I can't protect them, and I need you.

Melissa's face softened with the kind of fear that came from recognizing truth in madness. "Let me see the kids."

They stood in the doorway of Max's room—Sarah had moved both children into the same bedroom on the second floor after the bathtub incident. Safety in numbers, even if the numbers were a traumatized ten-year-old and her seven-year-old brother who spoke to ghosts.

Max slept curled around his stuffed dinosaur, but even unconscious, his face was tight with anxiety. His lips moved soundlessly, forming words Sarah didn't want to understand. Lily lay in the twin bed across from him, her sketchbook clutched to her chest like a shield. Even in sleep, her hand moved, fingers twitching as if still drawing.

"They look..." Melissa began, then stopped.

"Haunted," Sarah finished. "They look haunted. Because they are."

She led Melissa downstairs, moving through the house with the paranoid awareness of someone navigating enemy territory. The parlor was "safe"—or as safe as any room could be in a house that periodically bled from the wallpaper. Sarah had learned the geography of relative danger: the basement was forbidden territory where the well sat like a throat waiting to swallow. The nursery on the second floor was a locus of activity where Benjamin Kane's ghost was strongest. The master bedroom was manageable during daylight, a nightmare after dark. The kitchen existed in an uneasy truce, functional but hostile.

The parlor, with its salt lines refreshed daily and iron nails driven into the doorframe by Tucker Davis before he'd fled for the last time, was the closest thing to sanctuary the house allowed.

Sarah had set up camp there: a laptop (battery perpetually dying), stacks of library books and photocopied newspaper articles, Eleanor Kane's diary, and a corkboard covered in red thread connecting dates, names, and events like a detective hunting a serial killer.

Because that's what Victor Kane had been, Sarah now understood. Just a killer who'd hidden behind ritual and curse.

Melissa studied the corkboard, her face growing paler with each connection she traced. "The Collectors. A secret society. Blood sacrifice every seven years." She turned to Sarah. "This is... this is insane."

"Read the diary." Sarah thrust the leather-bound journal into her sister's hands. "Eleanor Kane lived in this house. She was married to Victor. He was going to kill their son for some fucked-up ritual, and when she tried to stop him, he killed them both. Her body was never found, Mel. The police reports say she 'disappeared,' but I *know* she's here. I can feel her."

Melissa sank onto the Victorian sofa—the only piece of original furniture Sarah hadn't dragged to the curb. The velvet upholstery was moth-eaten and smelled like must, but it was structurally sound, and Sarah had learned not to question small mercies.

For thirty minutes, Melissa read while Sarah paced. The house settled around them with creaks and groans that could be old wood or could be something else. The grandfather clock in the hallway ticked steadily until it didn't, stopping dead at 3:33 before resuming five minutes later. Normal. Everything was *so normal.*

When Melissa finally looked up, her eyes were wet.

"The last entry. October 30th, 1963. 'He's coming up the stairs. The children are singing again. Benjamin is crying. I should never have—'" Melissa's voice broke. "It just ends. Mid-sentence."

"Because Victor killed her before she could finish." Sarah collapsed onto the sofa beside her sister. The proximity of another adult, someone who shared her blood and history and memories of a childhood that didn't include supernatural horror, made something in Sarah's chest unclench slightly. "Dr. Rhodes—the parapsychologist—thinks Eleanor's trapped here. Her death was traumatic and sudden. She died trying to protect her child. That kind of thing... it leaves an imprint."

"Sarah." Melissa gripped her hand. "We need to leave. Tonight. Right now. Pack the kids in my car and just go. You can stay with me as long as you need. We'll figure out the house later, the money later, all of it later. But you can't stay here."

Sarah had known this was coming. Had anticipated it, even wanted it, because part of her still believed in the simple logic of fleeing danger. But she'd tried. God, she'd *tried.*

"The house won't let us." Sarah pulled her hand away and walked to the parlor window. Outside, Halloween Street stretched into darkness, the streetlights creating pools of sickly yellow illumination that seemed to make the shadows deeper rather than dispelling them. "Three days ago, I packed everything. Had the kids dressed and ready. We made it to the front door, Mel. I had my hand on the doorknob."

"And?"

"The door wouldn't open. Not locked—the knob turned fine. But the door wouldn't *budge*. Like it was welded to the frame. I tried the back door, same thing. Every window in the house. Max found a crowbar in the garage, and I broke every window on the first floor. The glass shattered, but there was something *behind* it. Like... invisible wall. I could feel it. Cold and solid and absolutely impassable."

Melissa's face had gone the color of old bone. "That's not possible."

"None of this is possible!" Sarah's voice rose dangerously, and she forced herself to breathe, to maintain the precarious control that was all that stood between functional and catatonic. "But it's happening anyway. We're trapped here until Halloween. Five more days. The ritual—this sacrifice Victor was supposed to do—it happens on Halloween at midnight. And the house is waiting."

"Waiting for what?"

Sarah met her sister's eyes. "For me to give it Lily."

The words hung in the air like poison. Saying them aloud made them more real, gave shape to the amorphous dread that had been building since the first 3:33 AM knocking.

Melissa stood abruptly. "No. Absolutely not. We'll call the police, the FBI, someone. This is illegal detention, or—or—"

"Detective Murphy already knows. The whole town knows. They've been feeding families to this house for *decades*, Mel. It's not a secret. It's a *system*."

Before Melissa could respond, the temperature dropped twenty degrees in an instant. Their breath became visible, crystallizing in the air. The parlor lights dimmed, then flickered, then steadied at half-brightness—just enough to see, not enough to feel safe.

"Sarah." Melissa's voice had gone very small. "What's happening?"

"It knows you're here." Sarah grabbed her sister's arm. "It always knows. Stay close to me, don't go anywhere alone, and whatever you do—*whatever you do*—don't answer if you hear knocking."

The cold intensified. Frost began forming on the windows in patterns that looked disturbingly like grasping hands. And from somewhere deep in the house—the basement, probably, always the fucking basement—came the sound of a child singing a nursery rhyme Sarah didn't recognize.

"Three little children in a row, Down to the water they must go, Mother begs and father lies, Down they go with open eyes—"

"That's Max," Melissa whispered. "That's Max's voice, but he's asleep, I saw him—"

"It's not Max." Sarah pulled her toward the hallway. "It's Benjamin. The boy who drowned. He uses Max's voice sometimes. To fuck with us. To remind us what happens to children in this house."

They took the stairs two at a time, Sarah's heart hammering against her ribs. The children's room was at the end of the hall, and the distance had never seemed longer. The walls seemed to breathe, expanding and contracting like lungs. The portraits of long-dead Hollow's End families that lined the stairwell seemed to turn, following their progress with painted eyes.

Sarah threw open the children's bedroom door.

Max and Lily were exactly where they'd left them. Asleep. Safe. Undisturbed.

But Max's mouth was open, and the singing was coming from him—coming *through* him—even though his eyes were closed and his chest rose and fell with the steady rhythm of deep sleep.

"—Mother's in the garden under roses red, Father sewed her mouth so she can't wake the dead, Three little children, count them if you can, One, two, three—find mother if you can."

The singing stopped. Max's mouth closed. The room's temperature returned to normal with a sudden snap that made Sarah's ears pop.

Melissa stood frozen in the doorway, her face a mask of horror. "What the *fuck* was that?"

Sarah didn't answer. Because she'd heard it. The last line. The one that hadn't been there before.

Find mother if you can.

Eleanor Kane. Her body never found. And now a ghost—or the house, or something worse—was giving them directions disguised as a children's rhyme.

Mother's in the garden under roses red.

They waited until dawn. Sarah didn't trust the darkness anymore, didn't trust the house's ability to trap them or turn them around or make hallways longer than physically possible. She'd learned these lessons the hard way.

At 6:47 AM, with weak October sunlight filtering through the frost-damaged windows, Sarah and Melissa stood in the backyard staring at the dead rose bushes.

The garden had been beautiful once. Sarah had seen it in old photographs from the Kane family estate sale—Eleanor's pride and joy, full of prize-winning roses in white and red and pink. Now it was a tangle of thorny vines gone wild, blackened leaves, and soil that looked almost gray in the morning light. Nothing grew here. Nothing had grown here for sixty-two years.

"Under roses red," Melissa repeated, her breath misting in the cold. She'd borrowed Sarah's winter coat, but both of them trembled from something that had nothing to do with temperature.

Sarah had brought a shovel from the garage. It felt heavy in her hands, weighted with terrible purpose. "She has to be here. Victor killed her, and he'd need to hide the body quickly. The police searched the house but never really searched the property. Not thoroughly."

"Sarah, if there's a body, we need to call—"

"And tell them what? That a ghost told us where to dig?" Sarah drove the shovel into the earth beneath the largest cluster of dead rose bushes. The ground resisted, then gave way. The soil smelled wrong—not like clean earth, but like something had been rotting beneath it for decades, the decay never quite completing. "Help me or don't, but I'm doing this."

Melissa grabbed the second shovel Sarah had brought. "You're insane."

"I'm haunted. There's a difference."

They dug in silence, the only sounds the scrape of metal on soil and their labored breathing. The work was harder than Sarah expected. The earth was compacted, dense, as if it had settled under weight and time. Her muscles, already weakened from three weeks of poor sleep and worse appetite, screamed in protest.

Twenty minutes in, Melissa's shovel hit something solid with a dull *thunk.* Both sisters froze.

"Maybe it's a rock," Melissa said. Neither of them believed it.

Sarah dropped to her knees and brushed soil away with her bare hands. The cold earth caked under her fingernails, dark and wormy. Her fingers touched something smooth and hard.

Bone.

She recoiled, scrambling backwards, her breath coming in short gasps.

"Oh God," Melissa whispered. "Oh God, oh God—"

But Sarah was already digging again, more carefully now, excavating around the bone with the delicacy of an archaeologist. Because she needed to see. Needed to *know.*

The skeleton emerged in pieces: first a femur, then pelvic bone, then the curve of a rib cage. The bones were brown with age, still held together by desiccated ligaments and scraps of fabric—a dress, Sarah realized, a white dress gone the color of old teeth.

But it was the skull that made Sarah's stomach lurch.

The jaw was wired shut.

Not just shut. *Sealed.* Heavy gauge wire wrapped around the mandible and maxilla, threading through where the lips would have been, pulled tight and twisted at the back. And the mouth itself—

Sarah leaned closer, her hand trembling as she brushed soil from the skull. The mouth had been sewn shut with thick black thread that had somehow resisted decay. The stitches were small, precise, pulled tight enough that they'd torn through the soft tissue in places. There were dozens of them, crisscrossing the jaw, ensuring that even in death, Eleanor Kane couldn't scream.

"He sewed her mouth shut," Sarah breathed. "He murdered her, and before he buried her, he sewed her fucking mouth *shut*."

Melissa made a choked sound and turned away, vomiting into the dead roses.

Sarah couldn't look away. The skeleton's hands were positioned at its chest, wrists crossed, and as she carefully brushed more soil away, she saw the glint of metal: handcuffs. Old-fashioned police handcuffs, rusted but intact, binding Eleanor's wrists together.

He'd restrained her. Made sure she couldn't escape even if by some miracle she'd survived the initial attack. Then he'd silenced her, sewn her mouth shut so she couldn't scream for help, couldn't tell anyone what he'd done, couldn't warn the next family or the next or the next.

And then he'd buried her in her own garden, under the roses she'd loved, and let everyone believe she'd simply disappeared.

Sarah sat back on her heels, soil-covered hands shaking. The morning sun had fully risen now, but it felt cold and distant. The house loomed behind them, its windows like blank eyes, watching.

"He silenced her," Sarah said quietly. "That's why she can't speak. Why her ghost just mouths words. Eleanor's trying to warn people, but Victor made sure she never could. Even in death."

Melissa wiped her mouth with the back of her hand, her face green. "The thread. You said there's black thread in the house."

The realization hit Sarah like a physical blow. "On the pillows. On Lily's pillows, on Max's, on mine. I kept finding bits of black thread, thick thread like upholstery thread, and I thought maybe it was from the furniture or—" She pressed her hands to her mouth. "Oh God. It's the same thread. He's been leaving it for us. Victor's ghost. He's *telling* us what he's going to do."

"What he's going to do?"

Sarah's eyes drifted to the house, to the second-floor window where Lily's room was. In the glass, she could see a reflection that didn't match reality: a man's silhouette, tall and broad-shouldered, watching them. Watching her.

Victor Kane.

"When the ritual happens," Sarah whispered, "he's going to make sure Lily can't scream either."

They called Detective Murphy from Melissa's phone—the only device that still worked, probably because it hadn't spent enough time in the house yet. He arrived within an hour, face grim, accompanied by Officer Beck and a crime scene team.

The forensics photographer documented everything while Sarah and Melissa sat on the porch steps, wrapped in blankets, giving statements that felt surreal in the daylight. A skeleton in the rose garden. Handcuffs. A sewn mouth. Evidence of a sixty-two-year-old murder finally coming to light.

"Victor Kane was never prosecuted for his wife's disappearance," Murphy said, flipping through a notepad. "He died the same night—self-inflicted gunshot wound to the head in his study. The investigation concluded murder-suicide, but without Eleanor's body..." He trailed off, looking at the garden where his team was carefully excavating the remains. "This changes things."

"Does it?" Sarah heard the bitterness in her own voice. "She's been dead for sixty-two years. He's been dead for sixty-two years. What does any of this change?"

Murphy's expression softened with something that might have been pity. "It means you were right. About the house, about the history, about—" He stopped, glancing at his officers. "About everything. I'm going to recommend the house be condemned pending further investigation."

"You can recommend whatever you want." Sarah stood, shrugging off the blanket. "The house won't let us leave. We're stuck here until Halloween. Until midnight. Until whatever Victor started sixty-two years ago finally finishes."

She walked back inside, leaving Murphy and Melissa on the porch, their voices fading behind her.

The house was quiet in that predatory way it had, like a cat waiting for a mouse to move. Sarah stood in the foyer, looking at the grand staircase, the crystal chandelier, the beautiful crown molding that hid rot and rage.

"I found her," Sarah said to the empty air. "I found Eleanor. I know what you did to her, Victor. I know you silenced her."

The temperature dropped slightly. The house's acknowledgment.

"But I'm not Eleanor. And Lily isn't Benjamin." Sarah's voice grew stronger. "You're not going to sew my daughter's mouth shut. You're not going to make her scream in silence. I will burn this fucking house down before I let you touch her."

From upstairs came the sound of a door slowly creaking open.

Then a child's laughter—high and bright and utterly wrong.

And from the basement, from the depths where the well waited like a hungry mouth, came three deliberate knocks.

Knock.

Knock.

Knock.

The dead were getting impatient.

Sarah had five days to figure out how to save her children from a curse that had already claimed too many lives.

Five days until Halloween.

Five days until midnight.

The house creaked around her, settling into itself, and Sarah could swear it sounded satisfied.

Eighteen

CHAPTER 18: THE TOWN'S COMPLICITY

Sarah pov

The rain began the moment Sarah pulled into the parking lot of Ashton Realty, which felt less like coincidence and more like the universe punctuating her fury with weather. Fat drops hammered the windshield, turning the world beyond into a watercolor blur of dying October browns and sickly yellows. Beside her, Melissa gripped the door handle so tightly her knuckles had gone bone-white.

"Are you sure about this?" Melissa asked, though her voice carried no real hope of dissuasion. They were far past caution now.

Sarah killed the engine. "He sold us that house knowing what would happen. He *knew*."

The past three hours had been a descent into clarity so sharp it felt like swallowing glass. Eleanor's skeleton in the backyard. The black thread through her jaw. The realization—crystalline and terrible—that nothing about their arrival in Hollow's End had been accidental. Someone had *placed* them in that house. Someone had looked at her divorce papers, her two children, her desperation, and had seen opportunity.

Someone had fed them to whatever waited at the end of Halloween Street.

"Let me do the talking," Sarah said, opening the car door. Cold rain immediately found her skin, soaking through her jacket in seconds. "If this goes badly—"

"It's already bad," Melissa interrupted, following her out. "It's been bad since the first night. We're just finally asking the right questions."

The real estate office occupied a converted Victorian on Main Street, its cheerful yellow paint and white trim an obscene contrast to Sarah's mood. A plastic jack-o'-lantern grinned from the window display, surrounded by fake autumn leaves and a sign promising "PERFECT HOMES FOR FALL MOVES!" Sarah wanted to put her fist through the glass.

The door chimed as they entered—a bright, welcoming sound that made her teeth ache.

Robert Ashton sat at his desk, phone pressed to his ear, and the moment his eyes landed on Sarah, his face transformed. Color drained from his features like water down a sink. The phone slipped from his fingers, clattering onto the desk's surface.

"I'll call you back," he said to no one—the line had already gone dead from the fall.

"Hello, Robert." Sarah crossed the small office in three strides, planting her hands on his desk. She was dimly aware of Melissa locking the front door behind them, flipping the "OPEN" sign to "CLOSED." "We need to have a conversation about that house you sold me."

"Mrs. Brennan, I—" He half-rose from his chair, then seemed to think better of it and sank back down. "I can explain—"

"You sold me a death trap," Sarah said, her voice knife-quiet. "You sold me a house where people die every seven years. You looked at my children and you put them in that place knowing what would happen to them."

"It's not—it's not like that—"

"Then what is it like?" Melissa's voice cut from behind, sharp as breaking ice. "Because from where we're standing, it looks an awful lot like conspiracy to commit murder."

Ashton's face crumpled. For a moment, Sarah thought he might cry, and the pathetic quality of his fear sparked something vicious in her chest. This man had smiled when he'd handed her the keys. Had shaken her hand. Had wished her family well.

"I didn't have a choice," he whispered.

"There's always a choice," Sarah said. "You *chose* to sell that house to a single mother with two young children. You *chose* not to warn me. So start talking, Robert. Why?"

He stared at his desk, at his hands, at anything but her face. Outside, thunder rumbled—a long, low sound like the earth clearing its throat. The rain intensified, turning the windows into rivers.

"The town council," he finally said. "They... they pay me. Every seven years, when the house becomes available again, they pay me to find a family."

Sarah's stomach dropped. "Find a family? You make it sound like shopping."

"That's exactly what it is." The words burst from him in a rush now, as if a dam had broken. "They give me criteria. Single mothers, preferably. Divorced or widowed. With children, ideally two or more. Someone vulnerable. Someone who won't be believed if they start talking about... about what happens in that house."

The office suddenly felt too small, the air too thick. Sarah was aware of her heartbeat in her throat, in her ears, drowning out the rain.

"How long has this been going on?" Melissa asked.

"Since 1897," Ashton said miserably. "My great-great-grandfather started the practice. It's been passed down through my family, along with the agency. We're the... the suppliers, I suppose you'd call it."

"Suppliers." Sarah tasted bile. "We're not products, Robert. We're people. My children are *people*."

"I know that!" He looked up, and his eyes were red-rimmed, desperate. "God, don't you think I know that? But if I refuse—if I break the contract—"

"What contract?" Melissa moved closer, her phone out now, recording. "Explain."

Ashton's laugh was broken glass. "The real one. Not the mortgage paperwork. The one my ancestor signed with The Collectors in 1897. If an Ashton refuses to supply the house, if we break the chain, then *we* become the offering instead. My entire family. My wife. My daughter." His voice

179

cracked. "So I choose you. God help me, I choose strangers."

Sarah felt the words land like physical blows. The casual arithmetic of it—his child weighed against hers, and hers found wanting simply because he'd known her name first.

"The previous family," Sarah said, forcing the words through clenched teeth. "Tell me about them."

Ashton flinched. "Three years ago. October 2022. Rebecca Chen and her two daughters—Amy and Jessica. Seven and nine years old."

The same ages as Max and Lily.

"What happened to them?"

"They answered the door on Halloween night." Ashton's voice had gone hollow, mechanical. "The knocking came just after sunset, and Rebecca thought it was trick-or-treaters. The neighbors heard screaming around eight PM, but by the time anyone got inside, it was over."

Sarah's hands trembled against the desk. "Over how?"

"Their mouths and eyes were sewn shut." The words fell like stones into still water. "Black thread, the kind you'd use for mourning clothes in the Victorian era. The coroner said they died of asphyxiation—the thread sealed their airways. But that's impossible. You can't sew a living person's mouth shut without them fighting, and there were no defensive wounds. No signs of struggle."

"What was the official ruling?" Melissa asked, though Sarah could hear the tremor beneath her sister's professional tone.

"Murder-suicide. They said Rebecca had a psychotic break, killed her daughters, then herself. It was the only explanation that made sense to people who don't know about the house." Ashton rubbed his face. "But I knew. We all knew. She'd refused the ritual. Refused to choose. So the house chose for her."

The ritual. Sarah's vision tunneled. "What ritual?"

"I don't know the specifics—only The Collectors' inner circle knows that. But it happens at midnight on Halloween. Some kind of offering to the land beneath the house. If you refuse…" He gestured helplessly. "The Chen family is what happens when you refuse."

Thunder cracked directly overhead, so loud the windows rattled. The lights flickered, and in that stuttering darkness, Sarah saw it with terrible clarity: her own children's faces, frozen in death, black thread through their precious skin.

"Who's on the town council?" Melissa demanded. "Give me names."

"Mayor Cromwell chairs it, but the real power is the founding families. The descendants of The Collectors." Ashton pulled open a desk drawer with shaking hands, withdrew a folder. "I'm not supposed to have this. I copied it years ago, insurance policy if they ever came for my family. Names, addresses, family trees going back to 1897."

He slid the folder across the desk. Sarah opened it, scanning pages of genealogical records, council meeting minutes, financial transactions. Her eyes snagged on a list of names:

Cromwell. Hayes. Wellington. Tucker. Rhodes. Wu. Cross.

The families that ran Hollow's End. The doctor, the librarian, the handyman, the priest—they all had ancestors on this list.

"They're all complicit," Sarah whispered. "The entire town."

"Not everyone knows," Ashton said quickly. "Most people just think Halloween Street is unlucky, haunted. They don't know about the ritual, the cycle. But the families who matter? The ones with money and power? Yes. They know. They've always known."

Sarah felt something crack inside her chest—not breaking, but hardening. Crystallizing into something sharp and furious.

"Why are you telling us this?" Melissa asked. "If you're so afraid of them, why give us ammunition?"

Ashton's smile was ghastly. "Because you're going to die anyway. The pattern never breaks. Every family either completes the ritual or dies trying to escape. I've sold that house twelve times in my career. *Twelve times.* Not one family has survived Halloween night."

"Then why the folder?" Sarah pressed. "Why keep records if you think we're doomed?"

He met her eyes for the first time since they'd entered, and what Sarah saw there wasn't quite hope—more like desperate, threadbare fantasy.

181

"Because maybe—*maybe*—you'll be different. Maybe you'll be the one who breaks the pattern. And if you do..." He swallowed hard. "If you do, I want them to burn for what they've made me do. Every name in that folder, every transaction, every death they've orchestrated. I want it exposed."

Sarah closed the folder, tucked it under her arm. "Where are the town hall archives?"

"Basement level, restricted access. But I have keys." Ashton pulled a ring from his drawer, worked two brass keys free. "One for the building's side entrance—it's alarmed, but it goes straight to the archives stairwell. The other for the vault where they keep the original Collectors' documents."

"Why do you have access to restricted archives?" Melissa asked suspiciously.

"Because sometimes families need to be reminded of their obligations. Sometimes they get ideas about leaving, about refusing. The council sends me down there to pull records, show them what happened to the last person who said no." His hands shook as he held out the keys. "The archives have everything. Every ritual, every sacrifice, every family that's died in that house. Three hundred and twenty-seven years of murder."

Sarah took the keys. They were cold and heavy, marked with rust spots that looked disturbingly like old blood.

"If you're lying to us," she said softly, "if this is some kind of trap, I will make sure you're the first one who pays."

"I'm not lying." Ashton slumped in his chair, suddenly looking decades older. "I'm a coward and a murderer-by-proxy, but I'm not a liar. Not about this." He paused. "There's one more thing you should know."

"What?"

"The ritual isn't random. The Collectors don't just want any children. They're looking for specific traits, specific... resonances with the past." He glanced at the folder in Sarah's hands. "Your daughter, Lily. She looks just like Eleanor Kane. Same eyes, same face shape. That's why you were chosen. The house wanted her specifically."

The rain hammered harder, as if trying to break through the roof. Sarah felt Melissa's hand on her shoulder, grounding her before she could launch herself across the desk at this pathetic, complicit man.

182

"October twenty-third," Ashton continued. "Three years ago, the Chen family moved in on October first. They died on October thirty-first. You moved in October first this year. Do you see the pattern?"

"One month," Sarah whispered. "They give us one month."

"One month to discover the truth. One month to prepare. One month to make your choice." Ashton's voice dropped to barely audible. "Or one month to say goodbye."

Sarah turned toward the door, then stopped. One final question burned in her throat.

"The Chens. Where are they buried?"

"Hollow's End Cemetery, but not in the main section. There's a corner in the back, past the old stone wall. That's where they put the families from the house. Unconsecrated ground. Suicides aren't allowed in hallowed earth, you see."

Of course. Even in death, the town's conspiracy held. Victims blamed, their memories tainted, their graves segregated from the respectable dead.

"Thank you for your honesty," Sarah said, though the words tasted like poison. "Even if it came thirty days too late."

She and Melissa left him there, a broken man in a cheerful office, surrounded by photos of happy families moving into homes that probably weren't death traps. The door chimed again as they exited—that same bright, welcoming sound.

Outside, the rain had become a deluge. Sarah and Melissa ran for the car, the folder clutched against Sarah's chest like a shield. They threw themselves into the front seats, slamming doors against the weather.

For a moment, neither spoke. The only sound was rain drumming the roof, a rhythm like urgent knocking.

"He's been doing this for his entire career," Melissa finally said, her voice hollow. "Twelve families. How many children is that?"

"Don't." Sarah's hands white-knuckled the steering wheel. "Don't make me think about the numbers."

"We have to think about the numbers. Because we're number twelve. And he said no one survives."

Sarah started the engine. Through the rain-blurred windshield, she could see Ashton still sitting at his desk, head in his hands.

"Then we'll be the first," she said.

They drove through Hollow's End's rain-soaked streets toward the town hall, and Sarah felt the weight of the folder on her lap like a stone. Three hundred and twenty-seven years of secrets. Three hundred and twenty-seven years of murder dressed up as ritual, as necessity, as sacrifice.

The town hall was a granite monstrosity at the end of Main Street, built in the Georgian style with columns and a bell tower. Even in daylight—or what passed for it under these apocalyptic clouds—the building exuded cold authority. The kind of place where official decisions were made, recorded, and filed away forever.

The kind of place where conspiracies were documented.

Sarah parked in the empty lot behind the building. It was three-thirty on a Wednesday afternoon; the offices would be closing soon for the day, but they didn't have time to wait for darkness. Every hour that passed was an hour closer to Halloween.

Eight days left.

"Side entrance," Sarah said, checking Ashton's directions against the building's layout. "Should be around back, past the dumpsters."

They found it exactly where he'd said: a unmarked metal door with a cipher lock. Sarah used the first key, and the lock clicked open with a sound like breaking bones. No alarm sounded.

Inside was a concrete stairwell descending into darkness. The air smelled of mildew and old paper and something else—something organic and rotten, like meat left too long in a warm place.

"This is a terrible idea," Melissa whispered, but she was already following Sarah down.

The stairs seemed to go on forever, down and down into the building's bowels. Sarah counted thirty-two steps before they reached the bottom and a second door, this one marked with a simple placard: **RESTRICTED ACCESS - AUTHORIZED PERSONNEL ONLY**.

The second key turned smoothly. The door opened onto darkness.

Sarah found a light switch inside the frame. Fluorescent bulbs flickered to life, revealing a vast space filled with floor-to-ceiling shelves, all groaning under the weight of files, boxes, and leather-bound volumes. The air was thick enough to taste—centuries of secrets sealed in a concrete tomb.

"Jesus," Melissa breathed. "How are we supposed to find anything in here?"

But Sarah was already moving, drawn by some instinct she didn't fully understand. Her feet carried her past rows of modern file boxes, past shelves of bound newspaper archives, toward the back of the room where the oldest materials lived.

There, behind a cage of wrought iron, she found it: a vault door with a brass plate reading **FOUNDING FAMILIES ARCHIVE - 1692-PRESENT**.

The vault wasn't locked. The door swung open at her touch, as if it had been waiting.

Inside were twelve leather-bound ledgers, each one thick as a Bible. Sarah pulled the first from the shelf, opened it to a random page, and began to read by the anemic light filtering through the cage.

The handwriting was Victorian-era script, elegant and precise:

October 31st, 1897

The ritual was completed at midnight in the home of Jonathan Blackwood, 13 Halloween Street. The offering was Mary Blackwood, age seven, first-born daughter. The child was brought to the well at 11:47 PM, sedated with laudanum to prevent distress. At midnight, Jonathan Blackwood fulfilled his covenant with the Collectors. The sacrifice was accepted.

The following harvest was record-breaking. Blackwood's shipping business prospered beyond all expectations. The pattern holds. Blood for prosperity. Children for fortune.

Next ritual scheduled: October 31st, 1904

Assigned family: Wellington

Sarah's hands trembled so badly she nearly dropped the ledger. Page after page documented the same horror: names, dates, ages. Children offered to whatever hungered beneath Halloween Street. And after each entry, a note about the family's subsequent prosperity.

"Sarah." Melissa's voice was strange, strangled. "Sarah, look at this."

She held another ledger, this one more recent. Sarah took it, found the page Melissa had marked.

October 31st, 1963

Victor Kane has refused the covenant. Despite all persuasion, despite the threat of sanctions, he will not offer his son Benjamin Kane (age six) to fulfill his family's obligation. Eleanor Kane has attempted to flee with the child. She has been intercepted.

Emergency council meeting convened October 30th. Decision reached: if Kane will not honor the covenant voluntarily, it will be honored involuntarily. The ritual must proceed.

October 31st, UPDATE: Victor Kane found deceased, apparent self-inflicted gunshot wound. Eleanor Kane missing, presumed fled. Benjamin Kane found drowned in the property well, approximately 3:17 AM, November 1st. Cause of death consistent with ritual requirements. Covenant satisfied, though irregularly.

Note: House remains unstable due to improper ritual completion. Recommend seven-year monitoring cycle. Next offering due: October 31st, 1970.

"They killed them," Sarah whispered. "The Collectors killed the entire Kane family because Victor wouldn't sacrifice his son."

"Keep reading," Melissa said grimly.

Sarah's eyes tracked down the page to a final notation, added in different ink:

Addendum: Eleanor Kane's remains located November 15th, 1963, buried in property rear garden. Evidence suggests she was silenced before she could reveal covenant details to authorities. Thread work consistent with traditional binding ritual. Disposal appropriate.

The ledger slipped from Sarah's fingers, hit the concrete floor with a sound like a judge's gavel.

"They murdered her," Sarah said. The words came from somewhere far away, as if someone else was speaking through her mouth. "They murdered her and covered it up and sewed her mouth shut so she couldn't tell anyone, and then they ruled it a family tragedy."

"And then they did it again," Melissa said, pulling more ledgers. "And again. And again."

She spread them across a table: 1970, 1977, 1984, 1991, 1998, 2005, 2012, 2019, 2022. Each ledger contained the same story. A family moved in. A family was given thirty days. A family either complied or died.

Not one had survived refusal.

Not one.

Sarah found her own name in the most recent ledger, dated October 1st, 2025:

Sarah Brennan and children (Lily, age 10; Max, age 7) placed at 13 Halloween Street as per seven-year cycle. Profile matches requirements: vulnerable, isolated, appropriate ages for ritual consideration. Lily Brennan shows strong resemblance to Eleanor Kane—potential for enhanced ritual effectiveness.

Offering due: October 31st, 2025, midnight

Assigned overseer: Julia Kane (Hannah Winters)

Expected outcome: Compliance or elimination

Next cycle: October 31st, 2032

Sarah's vision grayed at the edges. They'd planned this. Every moment since she'd seen the house listing online had been orchestrated. Her desperation after the divorce, her need for a fresh start, the impossibly low price—all of it calculated to lead her children to slaughter.

"We need to leave," Melissa said, already gathering ledgers, stuffing them into her bag. "We take these to the state police, to the FBI, to anyone who'll listen—"

"No one will believe us." Sarah's voice sounded dead even to her own ears. "A house that demands child sacrifice? A three-hundred-year conspiracy? We sound insane."

"Then what do we do?"

Sarah looked at the ledgers, at the meticulous records of centuries of murder, and felt something cold and furious crystallize in her chest.

"We document everything," she said. "We photograph every page. We make copies. And then—"

The lights went out.

The sudden darkness was absolute, pressing against Sarah's eyes like physical weight. Melissa's gasp echoed off concrete walls.

"Sarah—"

"Don't move." Sarah fumbled for her phone, activated the flashlight. The beam cut through blackness, illuminating dust motes and the rows of shelves stretching away into nothing.

Footsteps echoed from the stairwell. Multiple sets. Coming down.

"They know we're here," Melissa whispered.

Sarah grabbed as many ledgers as she could carry, shoving them into her jacket, under her arms. Melissa did the same. They couldn't take them all—there were decades of records—but they could take enough. Enough to prove. Enough to expose.

The footsteps reached the bottom of the stairs. The door opened.

Flashlight beams swept the archive room, and Sarah recognized Mayor Cromwell's voice: "Check the vault. They came for the ledgers, I guarantee it."

Sarah and Melissa pressed themselves against the shelving, trying to become shadows. Through gaps in the metal racks, Sarah could see four figures spreading through the room. Mayor Cromwell, Sheriff Garrett, and two others she didn't recognize.

"Mrs. Brennan," Cromwell called out, his voice echoing. "I know you're here. Robert called me right after you left. Poor man was quite upset."

Sarah's hand found Melissa's in the dark. Her sister's palm was slick with sweat.

"We don't want trouble," Cromwell continued, moving deeper into the archive. "We just want the ledgers back. You don't understand what you're interfering with. This is bigger than you. Bigger than your children."

Nothing is bigger than my children, Sarah thought with volcanic fury.

"The covenant protects this entire town," Cromwell said. He was close now, maybe fifteen feet away, separated only by a row of shelving. "Do you know why Hollow's End prospers when so many New England towns are dying? Why our businesses thrive, our children succeed, our people live long, healthy lives? The sacrifice of the few for the good of the many. That's how civilization has always worked."

Sarah's hand tightened on her phone. She had one chance at this.

She hurled the device as hard as she could toward the far end of the archive. It clattered against metal shelving, the flashlight beam spinning wild patterns across the ceiling.

"There!" one of the men shouted, and all four figures rushed toward the sound.

Sarah and Melissa ran for the exit, their footsteps masked by the commotion. They burst through the door and took the stairs three at a time, lungs burning, arms full of stolen history.

Behind them, Cromwell's voice echoed up the stairwell: "You can't run from this, Mrs. Brennan! The covenant will be honored! One way or another, it always is!"

They exploded out the side entrance into the rain, which had somehow intensified—a biblical deluge that soaked them instantly. Sarah couldn't see five feet ahead. They ran for the car, threw themselves inside, and Sarah gunned the engine.

She didn't look back as they fishtailed out of the parking lot, didn't slow down until they'd cleared Main Street and were heading back toward Halloween Street, toward the house that wanted to eat her children.

The ledgers sat between them on the console, water-damaged but intact. Proof. Evidence. Three centuries of murder documented in elegant handwriting.

"They'll come for us," Melissa said, shivering. "You know that, right? They can't let us live with this knowledge."

"I know." Sarah's hands ached from gripping the wheel. "But we have eight days. Eight days to find a way to break this."

Thunder cracked overhead, and in the flash of lightning, Sarah saw their reflection in the windshield—two women clutching stolen secrets, racing toward the house that waited at the end of Halloween Street.

The house that wanted Lily.

The house that had taken twelve families before them.

The house that had never, not once in three hundred and twenty-seven years, failed to claim what it was owed.

Sarah pressed the accelerator harder, as if speed could outrun the truth now burning in her chest like poison:

They weren't just haunted.

They were *marked*.

And the entire town—everyone who smiled and waved and pretended to be normal—was in on it.

The rain fell like judgment, and somewhere in the distance, Sarah thought she could hear laughter. Or maybe it was just the wind.

Or maybe it was the sound of Halloween Street, waiting.

Always waiting.

Nineteen

CHAPTER 19: THE ARCHIVES

S arah pov
  The town hall loomed against the October sky like a mausoleum, its colonial brick facade the color of dried blood in the moonlight. Sarah's hands trembled as she fitted Robert Ashton's key into the side entrance lock, the metal cold enough to burn. Beside her, Melissa kept watch, her breath forming ghost-shapes in the freezing air that had no business being this cold in mid-October.

"If we get caught—" Melissa whispered.

"We're already dead," Sarah finished. The words hung between them, more literal than metaphorical. Three days had passed since they'd found Eleanor Kane's skeleton in the backyard, three days of the house growing hungrier, more aggressive. This morning, she'd found Lily standing at the basement door, hand on the knob, eyes glazed. When Sarah had grabbed her, Lily had turned and smiled with someone else's face. "Mother's waiting," she'd said in Eleanor's voice. "Mother's in the water, and she's so very cold."

The lock clicked. Sarah pushed the door open into absolute darkness that seemed to *resist* their entry, as if the building itself knew they were coming for its secrets.

The basement archives were accessed through a narrow stairwell behind the clerk's office, the kind of cramped, descending passage that appeared in nightmares. Sarah led the way with her phone's flashlight, the beam catching on walls covered in portraits of Hollow's End's founding families. Men with hard eyes and harder mouths. Women with pinched faces and hands folded over their laps as if in prayer—or hiding something.

Every face seemed to watch them descend.

"God, it smells like a tomb down here," Melissa muttered, pulling her jacket tighter. The temperature dropped with each step, their breath now visible in thick plumes. Sarah's flashlight found the bottom: a stone floor worn smooth by centuries of footsteps, leading to a heavy oak door reinforced with iron bands.

No lock. It swung open at her touch, hinges shrieking.

The archive room stretched impossibly far back, far deeper than the building's footprint should allow. Floor-to-ceiling shelves held leather-bound volumes, wooden filing cabinets lined the walls, and in the center sat a long table covered in dust thick as velvet. The air tasted of mildew, old paper, and something else—something organic and wrong, like meat left to rot in a forgotten cellar.

"Jesus Christ," Melissa breathed. "How far back does this go?"

Sarah's flashlight beam disappeared into the darkness at the room's far end, swallowed completely. "I don't think it matters. We're looking for 1890 to 1963. Halloween Street's history."

They started with the filing cabinets, drawers that hadn't been opened in decades releasing sighs of fetid air when pulled. Sarah found it in the third cabinet: a folder labeled simply **HALLOWEEN STREET - COVENANT RECORDS - RESTRICTED.**

Her hands shook as she carried it to the table, Melissa clearing a space in the dust. The folder was thick, stuffed with documents spanning over a century. The first page was a property deed dated March 15, 1890, signed by seven family names: **Kane, Ashton, Wu, Winters, Cross, Grant, Donovan.**

"Grant?" Melissa's voice cracked. "That's our maiden name. Our family—"

"Keep reading," Sarah said, though her stomach had turned to ice.

The second document was a surveyor's report, and its clinical language couldn't disguise the horror:

"The proposed site for Halloween Street development consists of 2.4 acres formerly designated as HANGING GROUND (1692-1847) and POTTER'S FIELD (1847-1889). Ground-penetrating survey indicates mass burial site containing estimated 200-300 interments. Soil composition shows abnormal pH levels consistent with extensive decomposition. Recommend alternate location for residential development."

Melissa's fingernail traced the next line, circled in red ink by some long-dead hand: *"Recommendation overruled by town council vote 7-0. Development to proceed as planned."*

"They built houses on top of a mass grave," Melissa whispered. "They knew. They fucking *knew*, and they built there anyway."

Sarah turned to the next document, a newspaper clipping from the *Hollow's End Gazette*, October 1897:

MYSTERIOUS CHILD DEATHS PLAGUE HALLOWEEN STREET
Seven Children of Founding Families Succumb to Unknown Illness

In a tragedy that has shaken our community to its core, seven children ranging in ages from 4 to 12 have died in the past month, all residing on Halloween Street. Medical examiner Dr. Josiah Blackwood reports symptoms inconsistent with any known disease: sudden onset of violent nightmares, claims of "visitations" by deceased persons, progressive wasting, and in final hours, desperate attempts to claw through floors "to get to the singing below."

The deceased: Margaret Kane (7), Thomas Ashton (9), Li Wu (4), Caroline Winters (12), Joseph Cross (6), Abigail Grant (8), and Michael Donovan (11). Funeral services...

"One from each family," Sarah said, the pattern emerging like a corpse rising from deep water. "The same seven families who built Halloween Street."

"Retribution," Melissa said. "The dead don't like being built on."

But the next document revealed something far worse.

It was handwritten, dated November 15, 1897, on letterhead from a "Madame Esmeralda Corvus, Medium & Spiritual Consultant." The ink had faded to the color of rust, the script elaborate and looping:

To the Families of Halloween Street,

Your children's deaths are but the beginning. The dead you disturbed demand recompense for the violation of their rest. They will take and take until Halloween Street is empty of the living, and the houses themselves sink into the hungry earth.

However, there exists a method of appeasement, learned from practices older than this young nation. Every seventh year, on All Hallows' Eve when the veil grows thin, the debt must be paid. Each family line must offer unto the ground what was taken from it: **blood of your blood, bone of your bone, given willingly to the earth's keeping.**

The sacrifice must be genuine. The offering must be kin. And the ritual must be completed before the stroke of midnight, when October becomes November and the veil seals once more.

Refuse, and you condemn your entire line. Comply, and prosperity shall be yours, for the dead, once fed, are generous with their favor.

The choice is yours, but choose quickly. The singing has already begun.

Sarah's vision blurred. She had to read it twice, three times, before the full horror crystallized. "They were instructed to murder their own children. To feed them to the ground. And they—"

"Look at the next page," Melissa said, her voice hollow.

It was a contract, signed in seven different hands, dated November 20, 1897:

We, the undersigned, do hereby enter into COVENANT with the dead of Halloween Street. Every seven years, on the night of All Hallows' Eve, one member of our bloodline shall be offered to the earth as appeasement and recompense. This COVENANT shall bind our families in perpetuity, unto all generations, until such time as the debt is fully paid or the street itself returns to the ground.

Signed in blood and witnessed by the dead:

Seven signatures. Seven families promising to murder their own descendants, forever.

"1897," Sarah calculated frantically. "Then 1904, 1911, 1918... every seven years. The ritual would have come due in 1960—" Her breath caught. "No. 1963. Victor Kane's year."

She tore through the folder, searching for records from 1963. Found them: newspaper clippings, police reports, and at the bottom, a letter written in

Victor Kane's shaking hand, dated October 29, 1963:

To the remaining Covenant families,

I will not do it. I CANNOT do it. You ask me to take my son, my Benjamin, my beautiful boy, and throw him down a well to satisfy some ancient bargain made by men who chose murder over relocating a street?

Eleanor tried to run. I stopped her—God forgive me, I stopped her because I thought I could find another way. But there is no other way. The others performed their sacrifices. I received the confirmation letters. Seven families, and six have paid their blood price.

Only the Kanes remain in violation.

Tomorrow night, they will come knocking. Madame Corvus's instructions are clear: refuse the covenant, and the debt falls upon the violator's house alone. The curse, distributed among seven families, will focus entirely upon the Kane line. Every seven years, the dead will demand their due from us, and only us, until a Kane child is finally offered.

I will not murder my son. But I cannot let him live in this house, knowing what waits. Eleanor was right—we should have run. Instead, I have damned us all.

May God forgive me for what I'm about to do.

Victor Kane

The next document was the police report from November 1, 1963: Victor found dead from a self-inflicted gunshot wound. Eleanor missing, presumed fled. Benjamin discovered drowned in the basement well, cause of death ruled accidental.

Except it wasn't accidental. Victor had completed the sacrifice after all, unable to live with what he'd done, and then taken his own life. But Eleanor— Eleanor had tried to stop him. That's why he'd killed her first, buried her in the yard, sewn her mouth shut so she couldn't scream the truth.

"The ritual resets every seven years," Melissa said, her voice shaking. "1963, then 1970, '77, '84, '91, '98, 2005, 2012, 2019... and now. 2026. It's been seven years since the last family."

Sarah's blood turned to slush. "The family before us. The mother and two daughters who died three years ago."

"Three years ago would be 2023," Melissa calculated. "Three years *after* the

2020 ritual date. They lasted three years in that house before—" She stopped, understanding flooding her face. "Oh God. Sarah, they moved in after the ritual date passed. They moved into a house where the covenant had already been broken, where the curse was already active and waiting."

"And they died." Sarah's voice came from somewhere far away. "Eyes and mouths sewn shut. Punished for not completing a ritual they didn't even know about."

"But why didn't the curse take them on Halloween? Why three years later?"

Sarah turned back to Madame Corvus's original letter, reading more carefully. "It says the ritual must be completed before midnight on All Hallows' Eve. But it doesn't say what happens if you miss the deadline. Maybe… maybe the curse gives you time. Three years to figure it out, to attempt the ritual, to—"

"To choose." Melissa's face had gone gray. "Three years of haunting, three years of escalating terror, three years of watching your children slowly marked and claimed. And then, if you still refuse, if you still haven't offered the sacrifice…"

Sarah found another document, this one from 2023, a coroner's report. She read it aloud, her voice mechanical:

"Jennifer Morris, age 34. Daughters Sophia Morris, age 12, and Emma Morris, age 8. Time of death estimated between 11:47 PM and 12:03 AM on October 31, 2023. Cause of death: exsanguination from wounds to wrists and throat, manner consistent with ritual sacrifice. Ligature marks suggest the victims were bound. Black thread found in oral and orbital cavities, sewn post-mortem. Scene evidence indicates…"

Sarah couldn't continue. The words swam on the page.

Jennifer Morris had tried to complete the ritual. She'd tried to sacrifice her daughters to save them from something worse. But she'd been too late— eleven forty-seven was too close to midnight. The curse had rejected her offering and taken all three as punishment for hesitation.

"We moved in July," Sarah whispered. "It's October 20th. We've been in that house for three months. We have eleven days."

Melissa grabbed her arm. "Then we leave. Right now. Tonight. We get Lily and Max, and we drive until we're in another state, another—"

"The house won't let us." Sarah's laugh was broken glass. "The doors seal. The windows won't break. We tried to leave four days ago. We can't get out, Mel. The curse has already focused on us. On Lily."

She returned to the folder, desperate for something, anything that might help. Near the bottom, she found a final letter from Madame Corvus, dated 1904:

To those who inquire about breaking the Covenant,

There is no breaking. There is only completion or consumption. The debt will be paid in blood—either the blood you offer, or the blood taken from you.

However, know this: the curse requires willing sacrifice. Coercion, force, or murder masquerading as offering will be rejected. The victim must walk to the well of their own accord, understanding what they do, accepting their fate.

This is why the ritual fails so often. Who can convince a child to embrace death? What parent can ask this without madness?

The dead are patient. They will wait. And waiting, they grow hungrier.

Sarah's vision darkened at the edges. Lily had to willingly walk to the well. Had to choose to die. Had to accept being sacrificed. And if she refused—if Sarah couldn't convince her own daughter to embrace death—they would all be taken. Lily, Max, Sarah herself. Just like the Morris family.

"There has to be another way," Melissa said, but her voice carried no conviction.

Sarah kept searching, pulling out record after record. Seven families, fourteen decades, countless sacrifices. She found photographs: children standing by the well, faces resigned. She found letters from parents justifying what they'd done. She found asylum records for those who'd refused and gone mad from the guilt. She found death certificates for those who'd completed the ritual and taken their own lives afterward, unable to live with what they'd done.

She found Victor Kane's face in a photograph from 1962, holding Benjamin on his lap, both smiling. The handwriting on the back read: *"My son. My whole heart. I would burn the world for him."*

And then she found the most recent entry, dated three weeks ago—a letter from Robert Ashton to the remaining Covenant families:

The house is occupied. Single mother, two children, daughter age 10. Three months should be sufficient for the curse to establish claim. Recommend standard procedure: isolation, escalation, and education. By October 31st, she'll be desperate enough to consider any option.

The Kane line must be satisfied. We've delayed too long. The other families are experiencing breakthrough hauntings—the curse is spreading beyond Halloween Street. If we don't complete this ritual, by 2033 the entire town will be affected.

Payment upon successful completion.

R. Ashton

Sarah's hands crushed the paper. "They sold us. They deliberately sold us a cursed house knowing we'd either sacrifice Lily or die trying. This whole town—the remaining Covenant families—they're all complicit."

"Grant," Melissa repeated, her voice breaking. "Our maiden name is Grant. Our family was part of the original Covenant." She looked at Sarah with horror dawning. "You married out. You became a Brennan. But I'm still— Sarah, I'm still a Grant. My bloodline is one of the seven."

The implications crashed over them both. If the Covenant bound families through blood, then Melissa was as trapped as Sarah. And if the curse was spreading to other Covenant families because Victor's ritual had never been completed...

"Mom," Sarah breathed. "Does Mom know? Did she know about this when we were growing up?"

Melissa's face answered before her words did. "Why do you think she moved to Florida when we turned eighteen? Why do you think she never talks about Hollow's End, never visits, never—" Her voice cracked. "She got out. She married Dad and moved away and *got out* before her year came due."

"And she never warned us."

"How do you warn someone about this?" Melissa's laugh was hysteria dressed as humor. "Hey girls, by the way, our family has a multi-generational murder pact with a mass grave, so maybe don't move back to Hollow's End?"

Sarah's phone buzzed. A text from Hannah Winters—no, from Julia Kane: *You found the archives. Good. Now you understand. Eleven days, Sarah. Make the right choice. Your daughter's life for your son's. One for one. It's always been one for one.*

Another text followed immediately:

Eleanor tried to save Benjamin. Look what happened to her. She's STILL in the ground, STILL screaming, STILL suffering. Don't make Lily suffer for eternity because you were too proud to do what's necessary.

A third text, this one an image: Lily's bedroom, photographed from inside. Lily asleep in her bed, and standing over her, the translucent figure of a woman in a white Victorian dress. Eleanor Kane, reaching down with skeletal hands toward Lily's throat.

The timestamp on the photo: three minutes ago.

"We have to go," Sarah gasped. "We have to go NOW."

They ran for the stairs, Sarah's phone flashlight beam wild against the walls. Behind them, she heard it—or thought she heard it. A sound like hundreds of voices singing together, rising from the archive room's depths:

"Ring around the rosie, Pocket full of posies, Ashes, ashes, We all fall DOWN."

The door at the top of the stairs slammed shut before they reached it. Sarah hit it at full speed, shoulder screaming with impact. It wouldn't budge.

"No no no no—" She pounded on the wood, Melissa adding her weight, both of them throwing themselves against the door. It held firm, as if locked from the outside, as if sealed by hands they couldn't see.

The singing grew louder. The temperature plummeted. Sarah's breath came out as ice crystals. The lights of their phones began to flicker.

"Melissa, on three—" Sarah counted down, and they hit the door together with everything they had.

It opened so suddenly they tumbled through, sprawling onto the clerk's office floor. The door slammed behind them, and from the basement below came a sound like thunder, like the earth splitting open, like three hundred bodies trying to climb stairs at once.

They ran. Through the dark office, out the side entrance, into the October night that felt tropical compared to the archive's frozen air. Sarah didn't stop until they reached Melissa's car, didn't feel safe until they were pulling away from the town hall's looming shadow.

"Eleven days," Melissa said, driving too fast through empty streets. "What are we going to do in eleven days?"

Sarah looked at her phone. The image of Eleanor standing over Lily was still there, but now there was text overlaid on the photo, words that hadn't been there before:

ONE FOR ONE BLOOD FOR BLOOD
MOTHER FOR DAUGHTER CHOOSE

And beneath that, in a child's handwriting:

mommy please dont let her take me
i dont want to go in the water
it hurts down there mommy it hurts so bad

Sarah's hands shook so violently she dropped the phone. Melissa caught it, looked at the screen, and went white.

"Benjamin," she whispered. "That's Benjamin Kane. He's still in the well. He's been there for sixty-three years, and he's still—"

"Suffering," Sarah finished. "They don't die. The ritual doesn't kill them. It traps them. Forever. Conscious. Aware. In the dark and the water and the earth."

She thought of Lily's bright laugh, her careful drawings, her fierce protectiveness of Max. She thought of asking that beautiful, brilliant child to walk to a well and let herself be drowned, to let herself be trapped in eternal drowning for the rest of time.

She thought of Eleanor, sewn silent, buried screaming.

She thought of Jennifer Morris, who'd tried to save her daughters by killing them, and failed.

"There has to be another way," Sarah said, but the words felt like lies.

As they drove through Hollow's End toward Halloween Street, toward the house that waited with its basement door open and its well grate pulled aside, Sarah saw them: children standing at the edges of yards, watching. Children in old-fashioned clothes. Children who cast no shadows in the moonlight. Children who'd been sacrificed, decade after decade, century after century, to feed a curse that would never be satisfied.

Fourteen decades of children. Seven families. Generations of blood.

And in eleven days, Lily would either join them, or something worse would happen. Something the archives hadn't contained records for, because no one had survived to document it.

The house came into view, every window dark except one: the basement window, glowing with a faint, sickly green light that pulsed like a heartbeat.

Like something down there was waking up.

Like something down there was getting ready.

"Drive past it," Sarah said. "Don't stop. Just... drive past."

But as they passed the house, both front doors—the main entrance and the basement's exterior entrance—swung open in perfect synchronization. And from the darkness within came that sound again, clear as a bell across the October night:

Three knocks.

Three knocks.

Three knocks.

The dead were calling.

And they would not be denied much longer.

Twenty

Chapter 20: Officer Beck's Warning

Sarah pov

The knock came at 2:47 AM.

Three soft taps on the kitchen window.

I was already awake. I hadn't slept in days. Couldn't sleep. Not in this house. Not with what I knew now.

I'd been sitting at the kitchen table with Eleanor's diary open in front of me, reading the same page over and over. The words didn't make sense anymore. Nothing made sense.

The knock came again.

Tap. Tap. Tap.

My heart stopped.

"Don't answer it," Melissa whispered from the doorway. She'd been sleeping on the couch. Or trying to. "Sarah, don't."

But this was different. The knocking at night—the *other* knocking—that came from inside the house. From the walls. From the basement. That was them.

This was the kitchen window.

I stood slowly. My legs shook.

"It could be Julia," Melissa said. "Or worse."

I moved to the window anyway. Pulled back the curtain just an inch.

Officer Ryan Beck stood outside in the darkness, his face pale in the moonlight. He wasn't in uniform. Jeans and a jacket. His eyes kept darting to the street behind him like he expected someone to follow.

He pressed his finger to his lips.

I unlocked the window. Slid it open.

"Don't turn on any lights," he said. His voice was barely a whisper. "They're watching."

"Who's watching?"

"Everyone." He glanced over his shoulder again. "Let me in. Please. I need to tell you something and I don't have much time."

Melissa grabbed my arm. "Sarah, no. We don't know who to trust."

"He's a cop."

"So is Murphy, and look where that got us."

Beck leaned closer to the window. "Murphy was told to stand down. That's what I came to tell you. They shut down the investigation yesterday. Said there wasn't enough evidence to support your claims."

The words hit me like cold water.

"What?"

"Let me in," Beck said again. "Please. I'm risking my job coming here. I'm risking a lot more than that."

I looked at Melissa. She shook her head but stepped back.

I opened the back door.

Beck slipped inside quickly, closing it behind him with barely a sound. He didn't take off his jacket. Didn't sit down. Just stood there in my kitchen, breathing hard like he'd been running.

"You came here in the middle of the night to tell me Murphy quit?" I said.

"He didn't quit. He was told to stand down. There's a difference."

"By who?"

Beck pulled out his phone. The screen glow made his face look skeletal. "I shouldn't be showing you this. If anyone finds out I was here—"

"Just show me."

He turned the phone toward me. An email chain. Official police department letterhead.

Subject: Case #2024-1847 - Brennan Residence, 1313 Halloween Street

Detective Murphy,

After review with town counsel, this case is to be closed effective immediately. No further investigation warranted. The family has been advised to seek private assistance for what appears to be mental health concerns related to divorce trauma and relocation stress.

Do not respond to further calls from this address unless there is evidence of immediate physical danger.

Chief Ronald Cromwell

I read it twice.

"Cromwell," I said. "Any relation to the Mayor Cromwell from the 1800s records?"

Beck's expression told me everything.

"His great-great-grandson," Beck said. "Police Chief Ronald Cromwell. Mayor Dennis Cromwell's cousin. The Cromwells have run this town for five generations."

My hands went numb.

"They're part of it," I said. "The Collectors."

"I don't know what The Collectors are," Beck said. "But I know the Cromwells, the Ashtons, the Winters, the Kanes—all the old families—they protect each other. Always have. And they really don't like people asking questions about Halloween Street."

Melissa moved closer. "What do you mean they don't like it?"

Beck looked at her. Then at me.

"Seven people," he said quietly. "Seven people in the last twenty years have inquired about this house's history. Asked questions at town hall. Filed information requests. Tried to research property records."

"And?"

"They're all missing."

The kitchen suddenly felt smaller. Colder.

"Missing," I repeated.

"Vanished. No bodies. No evidence. Just... gone." Beck scrolled through his phone again. Showed me a list of names. "This is off the record. This doesn't officially exist. But I've been keeping track. Because something's wrong in this town and everyone pretends they don't see it."

I stared at the names.

Thomas Chen - Last seen March 2006 Angela Roberts - Last seen October 2009 David and Marie Halstead - Last seen July 2012 Jessica Farmer - Last seen October 2015 Marcus Webb - Last seen April 2018 Christina Vale - Last seen October 2021

Seven names. Seven people.

"Christina Vale was the woman who lived here before you," Beck said. "Her and her two daughters. They moved in July 2021. By October, all three were dead. The case was ruled murder-suicide. Christina supposedly killed her daughters and then herself."

"But you don't believe that."

"I was first on scene." Beck's voice went flat. Empty. "I've seen suicides. I've seen murders. What I saw in this house that night wasn't either of those things."

"What was it?"

He didn't answer for a long moment.

"Their eyes were sewn shut," he finally said. "Their mouths too. Black thread. And they were arranged in the basement around the well like they were kneeling. Praying. But their hands weren't folded. Their hands were reaching down into the well like they were trying to grab something."

I felt sick.

"Who did that?" Melissa asked. "Who could do that?"

"I don't know. The Medical Examiner's report said Christina did it to her daughters first, then herself somehow. But that's impossible. You can't sew your own eyes and mouth shut. You can't."

"Someone helped her," I said.

"Or someone made it look like she did it."

The house creaked above us. We all froze.

Just the house settling. Just the wood adjusting to temperature. Just normal sounds.

Except nothing about this house was normal.

"Why are you telling us this?" I asked Beck. "Why now?"

"Because October 31st is in five days," he said. "And the last three families that lived here all died in October. Right before Halloween. And because I saw you at town hall yesterday going through the archives. Which means you know about The Collectors. Which means you're asking the kind of questions that get people disappeared."

He put his phone away. Looked at me directly.

"I'm telling you this because you seem like a good person. Because your kids don't deserve whatever's happening here. And because I think you're in serious danger, but nobody's going to help you. Not Murphy. Not the Chief. Not anyone in this town."

"The doors won't open," Melissa said suddenly. "We've tried. Multiple times. They seal shut. The windows won't break. We're trapped."

Beck stared at her.

"What?"

"The house won't let us leave," I said. "Not since October 15th. We get maybe five or ten minutes every few days where the doors will open. Then they seal again. Like the house is breathing. Like it's deciding when we can go."

"That's not possible."

"Tell that to the ghosts."

Beck backed up a step. His hand went to his belt where his gun would normally be. But he wasn't armed. He'd come here as a civilian.

"I'm not crazy," I said. "I know how it sounds. But this house is haunted. Really haunted. And whatever happened to the people who lived here before— it's going to happen to us unless we get out."

"Then leave now. Right now."

"We can't. The doors—"

"I have a pry bar in my truck. We'll force them open."

"They won't open," Melissa said. "We've tried. We've tried everything."

Beck looked between us like he was deciding whether to believe us or call for a psychiatric evaluation.

Then his radio crackled.

All three of us jumped.

The radio was clipped to his belt. Police radio. It shouldn't have been on. He wasn't on duty.

But it crackled again. Static. White noise.

"I turned that off," Beck said. He grabbed it. Thumbed the power button. "It's off. It shouldn't be—"

A child's voice came through the static.

High and sweet and completely wrong.

"Tell her she can't leave."

Beck dropped the radio like it burned him.

It clattered onto the kitchen floor. Still making noise. Still broadcasting.

"Tell her Lily belongs to us."

My vision went white at the edges.

That voice.

I knew that voice.

"Ben?" I whispered.

"Tell her the doors will never open. Tell her it's almost time. Tell her we're hungry."

Beck stumbled backward. Hit the kitchen counter.

"What the fuck," he breathed. "What the fuck is that."

"It's Benjamin Kane," I said. "He's the boy who drowned in the basement. He's been talking to my son. He's been—"

"She can hear me," the voice said through the radio. Delighted. Playful. A child playing a game. "Hi, Sarah. Hi, Melissa. The Man says hello too. He wants you to know he forgives you for hiding his diary."

The radio screamed.

Not static. A human scream. High and desperate and full of pain.

Eleanor.

Eleanor Kane screaming.

Beck grabbed his radio and threw it across the kitchen. It shattered against the wall. Plastic and circuits and batteries scattering.

But the screaming didn't stop.

It was coming from the walls now.

From upstairs.

From the basement.

"I have to go," Beck said. His voice shook. "I have to get out of here. I shouldn't have come. I shouldn't have—"

"Wait," I said. "Please. You have to help us. You're a cop. You can—"

"I can't do anything." He was already moving to the back door. "Nobody can. You need to leave. When the doors open next time, you run. You take your kids and you run and you don't come back to this town ever."

"What about the other families?" Melissa said. "The Cromwells. The Winters. The people watching us. If they made those seven people disappear—"

"Then you don't let them see you leave."

Beck grabbed the door handle.

It turned easily.

The door opened.

For the first time in days, the door opened without resistance.

Beck stared at it. Then at me.

"It's letting me leave," he said.

"Because you're not family," I realized. "You're not part of it. The house doesn't care about you."

"Jesus Christ."

He stepped outside. Cool October air rushed in. I could smell leaves and earth and freedom.

"Go," Beck said from the doorway. "Next time the doors open, go. Don't wait. Don't pack. Just run."

"Where?"

"Anywhere but here."

He started to leave. Stopped. Turned back.

"The records you found at town hall," he said. "About The Collectors. Did you make copies?"

"Yes."

"Give them to someone outside Hollow's End. Someone who'll believe you. Because if something happens to you—if you disappear like the others—

somebody needs to know the truth."

"Beck—"

"I can't help you. I wish I could. But I have a daughter. I have a wife. And if the Cromwells find out I came here, that I showed you those files..." He shook his head. "I can't help you."

"You already did," I said.

He looked at me for a long moment. Then nodded.

"Lock the door behind me. Don't open it again unless you're leaving for good."

He walked away into the darkness.

I watched him go. Watched him get in his truck parked three houses down. Watched the taillights disappear around the corner.

Then I closed the door.

Locked it.

The moment the deadbolt clicked, I felt it.

The house settled.

A long, satisfied groan like an old man easing into a chair.

The temperature dropped ten degrees in seconds.

"It knew," Melissa whispered. "It knew he was here the whole time. It let him in so he could warn us. So we'd know we're trapped."

"Why would it do that?"

"Because it wants us to be scared."

She was right.

The house fed on fear. I knew that now. Every time we panicked, every time we screamed, every time we cried—it got stronger.

A door slammed upstairs.

Then another.

Then all of them at once. Every door in the house slamming in sequence like dominoes falling.

"The kids," I said.

We ran.

Up the stairs. Down the hallway. Lily's room first.

I threw open the door.

She was sitting up in bed, wide awake, staring at the wall.

"Lily? Baby?"

She turned to look at me. Her eyes were wrong. Distant. Glassy.

"He's here," she said. "The Man. He says it's almost time. He says you can't fight it anymore. He says Mommy tried to fight and look what happened to her."

"Lily, it's me. It's Mom. Look at me."

"She's in the water," Lily continued in that flat, dreamy voice. "She's been in the water for so long. She wants to come up but the rocks are holding her down. He put rocks in her pockets so she'd stay under. So she couldn't tell."

My throat closed up.

Eleanor.

She was describing Eleanor.

"Lily, listen to me—"

"He's standing behind you."

I spun around.

Nothing there.

Just the hallway. Just shadows.

But I felt it.

Cold breath on the back of my neck.

The smell of earth and rot and standing water.

"Get away from my daughter," I said to the empty air.

Lily laughed. It wasn't her laugh. Too deep. Too old.

"She's not your daughter anymore," she said in that wrong voice. "She's his. She always was. You just borrowed her for a little while."

Then she collapsed back onto the bed, unconscious.

I ran to her. Shook her.

"Lily. Lily!"

Her eyes fluttered open. Normal again. Scared.

"Mom?"

"I'm here, baby. I'm here."

"I had a nightmare. There was a man in Victorian clothes and he was smiling but his smile was wrong and he said—"

"Don't tell me what he said."

"But Mom—"

"Don't."

Because I knew. I knew if she said it out loud, if she repeated Victor Kane's words, it would make them more real. Would give them power.

Melissa appeared in the doorway with Max. He was half-asleep, rubbing his eyes.

"Everything okay?" she asked.

"No," I said. "Nothing's okay."

Max yawned. "Ben says the police can't help us. He says nobody can. He says we should just accept it and it'll be easier."

"Max, we talked about this. Ben isn't your friend. He's—"

"I know." Max looked at me with eyes too old for a seven-year-old. "He's dead. He's been dead for a long time. But he's still here. And he's still my friend even if he's trying to hurt us. He doesn't want to. But the Man makes him."

"The Man," I repeated. "Victor Kane."

"Ben calls him Father. But he's scared of him. He's really scared."

"Max—"

"Father says at midnight on Halloween, the doors to the underneath will open. And everyone who lives here will go down. And they'll stay down forever. Just like Ben. Just like his Mommy."

The house groaned around us.

Not settling this time.

Agreeing.

I looked at Melissa. She looked back at me.

Five days.

We had five days to figure out how to escape a house that didn't want to let us go.

Five days before Halloween.

Five days before midnight.

I carried Max back to his room. Tucked him in. He grabbed my hand before I could leave.

211

"Mom?"

"Yeah, baby?"

"Officer Beck is going to have an accident."

"What?"

"Tomorrow morning. On his way to work. Ben says the Man is angry he came here. So he's going to have an accident."

"Max, that's not—"

"Ben's never wrong about the accidents."

He rolled over. Closed his eyes.

I stood there in the darkness of my son's room, listening to him breathe, feeling the house breathe around us.

When I finally went back downstairs, Melissa was at the kitchen table with Eleanor's diary and all the documents we'd taken from town hall.

"We need to call someone," she said. "Police. FBI. Someone."

"Beck said—"

"I don't care what Beck said. We're not waiting here to die."

I picked up my phone. No signal. There hadn't been a signal since October 15th.

"Landline?" Melissa suggested.

I tried it. Dead.

Of course.

The house didn't want us calling for help.

"Then we write it down," Melissa said. "Everything we know. Everything we've found. We document it and we find a way to get it out of this house."

"How?"

"Mail?"

"The mailbox is outside. We can't reach it when the doors are sealed."

"Then we throw it. We throw it out the window when the doors open next time. Someone will find it."

It was a desperate plan.

But desperation was all we had left.

I sat down with her. Started writing.

My name is Sarah Brennan. I live at 1313 Halloween Street in Hollow's End,

Massachusetts. This house is going to kill me and my children. This is what I know:

I wrote for an hour.

Everything about The Collectors. The rituals. The disappearances. Victor Kane. Eleanor. Benjamin. The well. The mass grave. The town's complicity.

Beck's warning.

All of it.

When I finished, my hand was cramping. But I had twenty pages. Twenty pages of evidence.

"If something happens to us," I said to Melissa, "this will tell people why."

"Nothing's going to happen to us."

"You don't believe that."

She didn't answer.

The clock on the microwave clicked over to 4:44 AM.

The lights flickered.

Once.

Twice.

Then steady again.

"We should sleep," Melissa said. "We need our strength."

"I can't sleep."

"Try."

I went upstairs. Checked on both kids. They were sleeping. Really sleeping, not possessed-sleeping.

I locked their doors from the inside. Wedged chairs under the handles.

It wouldn't stop ghosts.

But it made me feel like I was doing something.

In my room, I lay down fully clothed. Shoes still on.

Ready to run.

Ready for anything.

I closed my eyes.

Immediately saw Victor Kane standing at the foot of my bed.

My eyes snapped open.

Nothing there.

Just shadows.

Just my imagination.

Just fear.

I tried again.

This time I saw Eleanor underwater, eyes sewn shut, mouth sewn shut, reaching up through black water toward a light she'd never reach.

I sat up. Heart pounding.

Sleep wasn't happening.

I went to the window. Looked out at Halloween Street.

Every house was dark.

Every window empty.

But I had the distinct feeling people were watching anyway. Behind those dark windows. Waiting. Monitoring.

Making sure we didn't leave.

My phone buzzed.

I jumped.

Grabbed it.

One bar of signal. Flickering. Barely there.

A text message was coming through. Loading.

From an unknown number.

I watched the screen as the message appeared letter by letter, fighting through whatever interference the house was throwing at it.

Don't trust Beck.

My blood went cold.

Another message.

He's Cromwell's nephew. He was supposed to keep you calm. Keep you here. Make you think help was coming.

Another.

Nobody's coming. The town wants you dead. Just like the others. I'm sorry. I tried to warn you. - M.W.

Margaret Wu.

The librarian.

She was trying to reach me.

I started typing a response but the signal died. One bar became no bars.

The message thread vanished.

Like it had never existed.

I stood there in the darkness of my bedroom, holding my phone, understanding.

Beck's visit wasn't mercy.

It was manipulation.

Give us hope. Make us think we had five days. Make us think we had a chance.

When really, we'd never had a chance at all.

The house had been toying with us from the beginning.

And we'd played right into its hands.

A child giggled somewhere in the walls.

Not Max.

Not Lily.

Benjamin.

And he was laughing.

Twenty-One

Chapter 21: Lily's Awareness

Sarah pov

Lily stopped drawing three days ago.

That's what I noticed first. Not the way she watched me from doorways. Not how she moved through the house like she was memorizing it. Not even how she whispered to empty corners when she thought I wasn't looking.

It was the drawings.

My ten-year-old daughter who couldn't stop sketching drowning families and skeletal hands and women with their mouths sewn shut—she just stopped. Her colored pencils sat untouched on her nightstand. Her sketchbook lay closed.

I should've been relieved.

Instead, my hands shook as I stood outside her bedroom door on the morning of October 25th. Six days until Halloween. Six days until midnight. Six days until I had to choose between my daughter's life and forty-seven strangers who lived on this cursed street.

The house groaned around me. The wallpaper in the hallway had started peeling in strips overnight, revealing older wallpaper beneath. And beneath that, older still. Like the house was shedding skin.

I knocked on Lily's door.

"Come in, Mom."

Her voice sounded different. Older. Calmer than any child's voice should be in a haunted house where ghosts knocked at 3:33 AM and wells tried to swallow seven-year-old boys.

I opened the door.

Lily sat cross-legged on her bed, still in her pajamas. Her hair needed brushing. Dark circles shadowed her eyes—she hadn't been sleeping either. None of us had. But her expression was... composed. Like she'd made a decision and found peace in it.

That terrified me more than any ghost.

"We need to talk," she said.

"About what, sweetheart?"

"Don't." She shook her head. "Don't call me sweetheart and use that voice. I'm not five. I know what's happening."

My throat tightened. "Lily—"

"I know everything, Mom." She pulled something from under her pillow. An iPad. The one I thought I'd hidden in the car three weeks ago. "I've been reading."

"Where did you get that?"

"The house gave it to me." She said it so matter-of-factly. "It was on my nightstand one morning. Unlocked. With all the browser history already open."

Ice flooded my veins. "What browser history?"

"Eleanor Kane's diary. Margaret Wu uploaded it to the historical society website last year. The town took it down, but it's still cached." Lily's fingers moved across the screen. "There are forums too. People who lived here before us. People who tried to figure out the curse."

"Lily, those websites—they're not—"

"They're real, Mom. I cross-referenced everything. Newspaper archives, property records, death certificates." She looked up at me with eyes that belonged to someone much older. "Did you know seventeen families have lived in this house since 1963? Seventeen families in sixty-two years. And fourteen of them had children who died here."

My legs gave out. I sat heavily on the edge of her bed.

"How long have you known?"

"Since the first week." Her voice cracked slightly. Just a little. Proof she was still my little girl under this horrible calm. "Since Max started talking to Ben. Since I saw that woman in the backyard. Since I found the well."

"Why didn't you tell me?"

"Because you're already dying inside trying to protect us." Tears welled in her eyes now. "I see it, Mom. Every time you look at Max and me. You're breaking. And I can't—I won't—let you break trying to save me when there might be another way."

"What other way?"

She set the iPad aside and reached under her pillow again. This time she pulled out a leather-bound book. Eleanor Kane's diary. The real one. The one Margaret Wu had given me weeks ago.

"You hid this in your closet," Lily said. "Behind the shoe boxes. I read it. All of it."

"Lily—"

"Victor Kane was going to sacrifice Benjamin to keep the ritual going. Eleanor tried to run. She packed bags and planned to take Ben to her sister's house in Vermont. But Victor found out. He killed her first. Shot her in the rose garden and buried her while Ben watched from the window."

"You shouldn't know these things," I whispered.

"Then Ben tried to run. Alone. Seven years old, just like Max. He made it to the basement. He thought he could hide in the well. But Victor followed him down. Victor held him under the water until he stopped moving. Then Victor went upstairs and shot himself."

"Stop."

"The ritual wasn't completed. Victor broke the covenant. And every seven years since then, the house tries to finish what Victor started. It needs a child's blood. A child who lives here. A child who—"

"Stop!" My voice came out too loud, too sharp. "I don't want to hear this!"

"But I need you to hear it!" Lily stood up on her bed, the diary clutched to her chest. "Because I've been talking to Benjamin. The real Benjamin. Not the thing in the well. Not the ghost that took Max. The actual boy who died here."

The room temperature dropped. My breath fogged.

"What did he tell you?"

"He's been trying to warn us. All this time. The singing, the whispers, leading Max places—he's not trying to hurt us. He's trying to show us things." Lily's hands trembled around the diary. "He showed me where Eleanor's body is. He showed me the black thread. He showed me the names carved in the basement walls—all the children who died here."

"And what else did he show you?"

Lily bit her lip. Fresh tears spilled down her cheeks.

"He showed me the loophole."

My heart stopped.

"What loophole?"

"The ritual needs a willing sacrifice. A child who agrees. Who walks into the well knowing what will happen. That's why it never works when people try to force it. That's why your sister and Tucker's plan to blow up the well might kill us all." She climbed down from the bed, holding the diary out to me. "Read page forty-seven. The entry from October 15th, 1963."

I took the diary with shaking hands. The leather was cold. Too cold. I flipped to page forty-seven.

Eleanor's handwriting was jagged, desperate:

The medium came today. Victor paid her $500 to explain the ritual properly. She told us the truth he didn't want to hear: the sacrifice must be willing. The child must agree. Must walk to the well themselves. Must say the words: "I give myself freely to balance what was taken."

Victor laughed. He said, "What child would agree to die?"

The medium looked at Benjamin playing with his trains. She said, "A child who loves their family more than they fear death. That's why the ritual is so rare. That's why it almost never works."

Victor sent her away. But I heard what she didn't say out loud. I heard it in the silence after she left.

219

He's going to make Benjamin agree.

The diary fell from my hands.

"Lily," I said carefully, each word costing me. "What are you planning?"

"Benjamin agreed because Victor threatened to kill Eleanor in front of him. He said yes to save his mother. But then Victor killed Eleanor anyway. The ritual was corrupted. The agreement was broken." Lily picked up the diary from where I'd dropped it. "But if I agree—really agree, with no threats, no forcing—and if I don't die…"

"No."

"Mom, listen—"

"No." I grabbed her shoulders. "Absolutely not. We are not discussing this. We're not even thinking about this."

"We have to!"

"I will blow up that well. I will burn down this entire house. I will drag you and Max out of here even if every door is sealed and every window is brick." My fingers dug into her arms. "But I will not let you walk into that basement and offer yourself to those things."

"Forty-seven people, Mom." Her voice broke. "Forty-seven people will die if we don't complete the ritual. I read about them. I looked them up. There's a baby on this street. Eight months old. There's an old woman who can't walk. There's a boy Max's age who has cancer and just finished chemo."

"I don't care."

"You're lying."

She was right. God help me, she was right.

"I do care," I admitted, my voice barely above a whisper. "I care about those people. But I care about you more. I will always care about you more. And I will not sacrifice my daughter to save strangers."

"Even if one of those strangers is me in a different house?" Lily pulled away from me. "What if someone else's mom makes the same choice you're making? What if she refuses the ritual and we all die anyway? Is that better? Is that less horrible?"

"Yes," I said flatly. "Yes, it's better. Because you'll be alive."

"Until the house falls into the ground at midnight!" Her voice rose to a shout. "Until the earth opens up and swallows all of us! Until Max dies because you were too afraid to let me try!"

"That's not fair—"

"None of this is fair!" She threw the diary across the room. It hit the wall and pages scattered. "I'm ten years old and I'm being haunted by a dead boy who drowned in a well and I'm supposed to just sit here and wait to die? I'm supposed to watch you fall apart? I'm supposed to let Max get pulled down into that water again?"

"We'll find another way."

"There is no other way! I've read everything! I've researched for weeks!" She gestured wildly at the iPad. "Every family that lived here tried something different. They tried exorcisms and cleansings and running away and ignoring it and fighting it and feeding it and nothing worked. Nothing works except the ritual. And the ritual needs me to agree."

"So you'll die instead."

"I'll *try* instead." She crossed her arms. Stubborn. Just like her father. Just like me. "Benjamin said there's a chance. If I say the words and go to the well but someone pulls me back before… before it finishes… the house might accept it as completion. The agreement would be made. The ritual would be satisfied."

"That's insane."

"It's a plan."

"It's suicide."

"It's hope!" Lily's face flushed red. "Which is more than you've given me! You've been walking around this house like you're already at my funeral! You look at me like I'm a ghost!"

Her words hit like a physical blow.

"That's not true," I whispered.

"It is true. You stopped hugging me. You stopped tucking me in. You barely even talk to me anymore because you're so afraid of… of loving me too much before I'm gone." Her voice broke completely. "But I'm still here, Mom. I'm still here and I'm fighting and I need you to fight with me, not just cry over me."

221

I couldn't breathe. The room spun.

"I'm sorry," I managed. "I'm so sorry, baby. I didn't realize—"

"I know you didn't." She wiped her eyes roughly. "But I need you to realize now. I need you to trust me. I've been preparing. I know what to say. I know how the well works. Benjamin's been teaching me."

"Teaching you how to die."

"Teaching me how to survive." She pulled out something else from under her pillow. A rope. Thirty feet of climbing rope I'd never seen before. "Tucker left this in the basement. I took it. And I've been practicing knots. The kind that won't slip even when they're wet."

My hands covered my mouth.

"You tie this around my waist," Lily continued, her voice eerily calm. "I go down into the well. I say the words. The house accepts it. Then you pull me back up before… before the water takes me all the way."

"And if it doesn't work?"

"Then I die. But we all die anyway if we do nothing."

"No." I stood up, backing toward the door. "No, we're not discussing this anymore. We're not planning this. We're not—"

The door slammed shut behind me.

I spun around. The lock clicked from the inside. The outside. Both at once.

"Mom?" Lily's voice was small now. Scared. "Mom, I didn't do that."

The temperature plummeted. Ice crystals formed on the windows.

Three knocks echoed through the room.

Then three more.

Then three more.

Not from the door. From inside the walls.

"It knows," Lily whispered. "It knows we're talking about it."

The knocking grew louder. Faster. A drumbeat of demand.

I tried the door handle. Locked solid.

"Lily, stay calm. Stay with me."

"I am with you." But her voice shook. "Mom, look at the walls."

I turned slowly.

The peeling wallpaper was curling back faster now. Revealing layer after layer. And underneath the oldest layer, carved directly into the plaster:

WILLING WILLING WILLING WILLING

The word repeated hundreds of times. In different handwritings. Different decades. Different desperate parents who'd carved it before their children were taken.

"It's been listening," I breathed. "This whole time."

"We need to get out of this room." Lily grabbed my hand. "Now."

I threw my shoulder against the door. Once. Twice. Three times.

It didn't budge.

The knocking stopped.

Silence pressed down like a weight.

Then Lily's iPad lit up on its own. The screen showed a video feed. The basement. The well.

And standing at the edge of the well, soaking wet, was Benjamin Kane's ghost.

He looked at the camera. Directly at us.

His mouth moved, forming words without sound:

Tonight. She comes tonight. Or he goes tomorrow.

The feed switched.

Now it showed Max's room.

Max asleep in his bed.

And standing over him, water dripping from her sewn-shut mouth, was Eleanor Kane.

Her skeletal hand reached toward Max's face.

"NO!" Lily screamed.

The door flew open.

I ran. Down the hallway, Lily right behind me. Into Max's room.

He was alone. Sleeping peacefully. No ghost. No water. No danger.

But his pillow was soaking wet.

And written in the moisture, in handwriting I recognized from the diary:

Tonight.

Lily grabbed my arm. "We don't have until Halloween. We have until tonight."

"How do you know?"

"Because Eleanor just told us. She's not waiting anymore. If I don't do the ritual tonight, she's taking Max to do it instead." Lily's fingernails dug into my skin. "She'll make him agree. She'll force him. And it won't work because he'll be too scared, so it'll just kill him for nothing."

"We'll protect him. We'll barricade—"

"Mom." Lily's voice was steel. "It's me or him. That's the choice. That's what it's always been."

Max stirred in his sleep. He mumbled something. A name.

"Ben says it's time to swim."

My blood turned to ice.

"When did you hear that before?" Lily asked.

"The night I caught him sleepwalking to the basement. A week ago."

"So she's been preparing him. Talking to him in his dreams. Getting him ready." Lily's face was chalk white. "If we don't act tonight, she'll take him tonight. While he's asleep. While he won't fight. While he'll go willingly because he thinks it's a game."

I looked at my son. Seven years old. Blond hair messy on the pillow. Face peaceful. Innocent.

Then at my daughter. Ten years old. Dark circles under her eyes. Face set with terrible determination. Already grieving herself.

"There has to be another way."

"There isn't. You know there isn't." Lily squeezed my hand. "I love you, Mom. And I'm ready. I've been ready since I figured it out. I just needed you to know why."

"Lily—"

"Promise me something."

"Anything."

"If it doesn't work. If I go down and don't come back up." Her voice wavered. "Promise me you'll take Max and run. Don't stay to get my body. Don't wait. Just run and don't look back and get him somewhere safe."

"I can't promise that."

"You have to."

"I can't leave you."

"You have to save him." Tears streamed down her face now. "Promise me, Mom. Please. Promise me one of us gets out."

The house groaned. The floor tilted slightly. Just a degree. Just enough to feel wrong.

In the hallway, water began seeping up through the floorboards. Black water. Well water.

It was starting early.

"Okay," I whispered. "I promise."

"Thank you." She hugged me. Hard. Desperately. "I love you so much."

"I love you too, baby girl."

We stood like that, holding each other, while the house creaked and settled around us. While water spread across the hallway floor. While Max slept on, unaware of the decision his sister had made.

"We should get Tucker," Lily said finally. "And Aunt Melissa. And the rope. We don't have much time."

She was right.

We didn't have much time.

But I held her for ten more seconds anyway. Ten more seconds of my daughter alive and in my arms. Ten more seconds before she walked down into that basement and offered herself to the dark.

Then I let her go.

"Get dressed," I said. "Warm clothes. And your sneakers."

"Okay."

She walked to her room. Calm. Composed. Like she was getting ready for school instead of death.

I went to wake Melissa.

The day passed in a blur. Preparation. Arguments. Melissa screaming that we couldn't let Lily do this. Tucker white-faced and shaking as he tested the rope. Father Gabriel arriving unannounced, saying he'd been "summoned" by a feeling he couldn't explain.

Isaac Stone showed up too. With Claire Donovan, recovered from her possession but haunted-looking.

"The house called us," Isaac said simply. "It wants witnesses."

Max stayed asleep all day. Unnaturally asleep. We couldn't wake him. Eleanor was keeping him under.

By eight PM, we were ready. As ready as we could be.

The basement door stood open. Waiting.

Lily wore jeans, a hoodie, sneakers. The rope was tied around her waist in a harness Tucker had rigged. He'd tested it seventeen times. It wouldn't slip. It wouldn't fail.

"Last chance to change your mind," I told her.

"I'm not changing my mind."

"Lily—"

"I'm saving my brother. That's what big sisters do."

She walked to the basement door.

The house held its breath.

Everything went silent. No knocking. No groaning. No creaking. Just silence.

Lily looked back at me once. Smiled. A real smile.

"Pull me back fast, okay?"

"As fast as I can."

"I know you will."

She descended the stairs.

We followed. Melissa, Tucker, Father Gabriel, Isaac, Claire. All of us. Witnesses to the impossible.

The basement was flooded. Six inches of black water covering the floor. The well in the center, grate removed, waiting.

Benjamin's ghost stood beside it. Visible now. Solid-looking. A seven-year-old boy with wet hair and sad eyes.

He looked at Lily.

She looked back.

"Hi, Ben."

"Hi, Lily."

His voice was clear. Real. Not a whisper or a groan. A child's voice.

"Are you scared?" he asked.

"Yes."

"Me too. I was scared when I went down."

"I know."

"But it doesn't hurt as much as you think. The water's cold. Then it's not cold. Then it's just quiet."

"Will you help pull me back?"

Benjamin's ghost smiled sadly. "I'll try. But I'm not strong anymore."

"That's okay. My mom's strong."

"Yeah." He looked at me. "Your mom loves you a lot."

"I know."

Lily took the first step toward the well.

The water rose to her ankles.

Another step. To her knees.

The rope uncoiled behind her. Tucker held it tight, wrapped around his waist. Melissa gripped it too. And Father Gabriel. And me.

We would pull her back.

We had to pull her back.

Lily reached the well's edge. Looked down into the darkness below.

"I give myself freely," she said clearly, "to balance what was taken."

The house shuddered.

The water in the basement began to swirl, spiraling toward the well.

Lily climbed onto the edge.

"I offer this willingly. I choose this. I—"

"Wait!" Max's voice, high and panicked, from the top of the stairs.

We all turned.

Max stood in the doorway, awake now, Eleanor's ghost visible behind him. Her hand on his shoulder.

"Don't do it, Lily," Max said. But his voice was wrong. The cadence was wrong.

Eleanor was speaking through him.

"She won't come back," Max/Eleanor said. "The rope won't hold. The well is too hungry. She'll drown like I drowned. Like Benjamin drowned. Like all the children drowned."

227

"Let go of my brother," Lily said.

"Come up here instead. Trade yourself willingly. Walk up here and let me take you."

"That's not how the ritual works."

"How do you know?" Max/Eleanor's smile was terrible on my son's face. "You're ten years old. You don't know anything about death."

"I know you're scared." Lily's voice was gentle. "I know you died trying to save Benjamin and it didn't work. I know you're trapped here with your mouth sewn shut and you can't scream. But this isn't the way to stop hurting."

Max/Eleanor's face crumpled.

"It hurts so much," she whispered. "It hurts all the time. The thread pulls. The water burns. I just want it to stop."

"Then let go. Let me finish this. Let me do what you couldn't do."

"You'll die."

"Maybe. But maybe I won't. And maybe that's enough to break everything. The ritual. The curse. The pain."

For a long moment, Eleanor stared at Lily through Max's eyes.

Then Max collapsed.

Eleanor's ghost stepped out of him, no longer possessing, just present. Her hands covered her sewn mouth. Water streamed down her dress.

She nodded once.

Lily turned back to the well.

"I give myself freely," she repeated. "I offer this willingly. I choose this to save those I love."

She stepped off the edge.

The rope snapped tight.

We pulled.

God, we pulled.

But the well pulled too.

The rope burned through our hands as Lily disappeared into the dark water below.

Ten feet.

Twenty feet.

228

Thirty feet.

The rope went slack.

"No!" I screamed. "No, pull! PULL!"

We hauled on the rope with everything we had.

It came up slowly. So slowly.

Too slowly.

And when we finally pulled Lily's body out of the well, she wasn't breathing.

Her lips were blue.

Her eyes were closed.

And carved into her forehead, fresh and bleeding, was a single word:

ACCEPTED

"No," I whispered. "No, no, no—"

Lily's eyes opened.

She gasped once.

Then started coughing up well water. Black and filthy.

"Mom?" she croaked.

"I'm here. I'm right here."

"Did it work?"

Before I could answer, the well began to glow.

Bright white light poured from its depths.

And rising from that light, no longer trapped, no longer suffering—

Benjamin Kane and Eleanor Kane, whole and healed.

They smiled.

"Thank you," Eleanor whispered.

Then they dissolved into light and were gone.

The well's glow faded.

The water in the basement drained away into nothing.

The house groaned one final time.

And at 9:47 PM on October 25th, something fundamental broke.

The curse cracked.

Not healed. Not gone.

But cracked.

Lily was alive. The ritual was complete. The willing sacrifice had been made and survived.

That should have been the end.

We should have been safe.

But as we carried Lily upstairs, as Melissa wrapped her in blankets, as Max cried and hugged his sister—

I saw it.

In Lily's wet hair, tangled and dripping.

Black thread.

Just one piece. Thin and strong.

And stitched through her skin.

Lily caught me staring.

Her hand went to her forehead, touched the carved word, came away with blood.

She looked at the blood.

Then at me.

"Mom?" Her voice was small. Terrified. "I can feel it. Something's still inside me. Something from down there. It came back with me."

The lights flickered.

All through the house, every door slammed shut at once.

And from deep below, from the well we'd just pulled her from, came a sound like laughter.

Child's laughter.

But not Benjamin's.

Something older.

Something that had been waiting in that well for much, much longer than sixty-two years.

Lily started to cry.

"Mom, I think I let something out."

Twenty-Two

Chapter 22: The Moral Calculus

⁓ᘛᘚ⁓

Sarah pov

The numbers wouldn't stop running through my head.

One child. Forty-seven people.

I sat on the parlor floor with my back against the wall. The house was freezing. My breath came out in white clouds. Outside, Halloween Street looked normal. Porch lights on. Jack-o'-lanterns glowing. Kids would be trick-or-treating tomorrow night while I—

While I what?

While I held my daughter's head under water in a cursed well?

My hands were shaking. They hadn't stopped shaking since The Woman in White showed me the vision two hours ago. I'd watched Halloween Street collapse into the earth. Houses crumbling. People screaming. The ground opening like a mouth and swallowing everything. Forty-seven people. I'd counted them in my head. The Johnsons with their twin boys. The elderly couple three houses down. The pregnant woman who'd just moved in.

All of them dead because I refused to kill my daughter.

"Sarah."

Melissa stood in the doorway. Her face was pale. She had a bleeding cut on her forehead from when the house threw her against the wall an hour ago.

"You can't seriously be considering this."

I didn't answer. Couldn't.

"Sarah. Look at me."

I looked up. My sister's eyes were red from crying.

"We're leaving," Melissa said. "Right now. We're taking the kids and we're getting out of this house."

"The doors won't open."

"Then we break through the goddamn walls. We—"

"We tried that," I said. My voice sounded dead. Hollow. "You saw what happened. The house won't let us leave."

"Then we wait. We hide. We survive until—"

"Until midnight tomorrow?" I stood up. My legs felt weak. "And then what? The street collapses and we all die anyway? Along with forty-seven other people?"

Melissa grabbed my shoulders. Her fingers dug in hard enough to hurt.

"Listen to me. Those people are not your responsibility. Your daughter is. That's it. That's the only choice."

"Forty-seven people, Mel."

"I don't care if it's four hundred. You are not killing your child to save strangers."

"Mom?"

We both turned. Max stood in the hallway. His pajamas were still damp from the well water. He looked so small. So young.

"Max, go back upstairs," Melissa said.

"No." Max walked into the room. His jaw was set in a way I recognized. Stubborn. Like his father. "I want to talk."

"Sweetie, the adults need to—"

"I'm not a baby." Max's voice cracked. "Ben showed me things. Down in the well. I saw what happens if we don't do the ritual."

My throat tightened. "Max—"

"Everyone dies, Mom. Not just people on the street. The curse spreads. It takes the whole town. Maybe more. Ben said the dead are so hungry. They've been waiting so long. If we don't feed them, they'll take everything."

Silence.

Then Melissa: "That's bullshit. The ghosts are lying to scare you."

"Aunt Mel—"

"They're manipulating you. All of you. Can't you see that?" Melissa's voice rose. "This is what they do. They make you think there's no choice. They make you think you have to sacrifice—"

"But what if they're not lying?" Max's eyes filled with tears. "What if it's true? What if we let everyone die because we were too scared to—"

"To murder your sister?" Melissa's face flushed red. "Is that what you're saying? We should kill Lily to save other people?"

"I didn't say that!"

"That's exactly what you're saying!"

"Stop it!" I shouted. "Both of you, stop!"

My voice echoed in the cold room. For a moment, no one spoke.

Then footsteps on the stairs.

Lily appeared in the doorway. She'd changed into clean clothes. Jeans and a sweater. Her hair was pulled back. She looked calm. Too calm.

"I'll do it," Lily said.

"No." The word came out before I could think. "Absolutely not."

"Mom, listen—"

"No. I am not discussing this."

"You don't have to discuss it." Lily walked into the room. Her voice was steady. Adult. "It's my choice."

"You're ten years old. You don't get to make this choice."

"Someone has to."

Melissa moved between us. "Lily, sweetheart, you don't understand what you're saying. You're scared and confused and—"

"I'm not confused." Lily looked at me. Her eyes were dry. Clear. "I've been thinking about this for days. Since I read Eleanor's diary. Since I understood what this house wants."

"What it wants is wrong," I said. My voice shook. "What it wants is evil. And we don't negotiate with evil."

"Even if not negotiating means people die?"

The question hung in the air like smoke.

I wanted to answer. Wanted to have something to say that would make this okay. That would give us a way out.

But I had nothing.

The temperature in the room dropped another ten degrees. Ice formed on the windows. The walls groaned.

"It's listening," Max whispered.

He was right. The house was always listening.

A knock on the front door made us all jump.

"Don't answer it," Melissa said.

Another knock. Then another. Three total.

"That's not the dead," I said. "It's not time yet. Not until—"

"Sarah? It's Dr. Rhodes. Please, I need to come in."

I ran to the door. Pressed my hands against the wood. "Amelia?"

"Open the door. I have information. About the ritual."

I grabbed the handle. Pulled. Nothing happened.

"It won't open," I shouted through the wood.

"Yes it will. The house wants you to hear this. It's allowing me entry for ten minutes. Then I'm out. Try again."

I pulled. This time, the door swung open.

Dr. Amelia Rhodes stood on the porch. She held a leather bag in one hand and an old book in the other. Her face was drawn. Exhausted.

"Inside," she said. "Quickly."

She crossed the threshold. The door slammed shut behind her.

"Ten minutes," Dr. Rhodes said. "That's all I have. The house made that very clear when it unlocked to let me approach."

She set the book on the coffee table. It was ancient. The cover was burned at the edges.

"I've been researching non-stop since the séance," Dr. Rhodes said. "I knew something was wrong. The pattern didn't make sense. So I contacted colleagues. Tracked down other cases. Other cursed houses. Other blood rituals."

"And?" Melissa's voice was sharp.

234

"And they all have one thing in common." Dr. Rhodes opened the book. The pages were yellow with age. "The rituals never work."

Silence.

"What?" I said.

"Look." Dr. Rhodes pointed to a handwritten account dated 1823. "A family in Salem. They were told to sacrifice their youngest daughter to appease spirits on their land. They did it. Slit her throat in the cellar. And you know what happened?"

We waited.

"Seven years later, the spirits demanded another sacrifice. Then another. The ritual doesn't end the curse. It feeds it. It postpones the inevitable while making the curse stronger."

My mind raced. "But The Collectors—"

"Were murderers hiding behind superstition." Dr. Rhodes flipped pages. "Every case I found follows the same pattern. Someone starts a blood ritual claiming it's the only way to stop a curse. But the curse never stops. It just demands more blood. More often. Until it consumes everything."

"So the ritual is fake?" Max asked.

"Not fake. Worse. It's real magic, but the wrong kind. Every sacrifice doesn't appease the dead. It binds them tighter to this world. Makes them hungrier. More desperate." Dr. Rhodes looked at me. "Eleanor Kane figured this out. That's why she tried to run. She knew Victor was going to make it worse."

"Then what do we do?" Lily's voice was small now. Young.

Dr. Rhodes closed the book. "You destroy the source."

"The well," I said.

"Yes. The well is the anchor point. It's where the burial ground's energy focuses. Where the dead gather. If you destroy it—sever the connection—the spirits lose their hold on this world."

Hope flickered in my chest. Small. Fragile.

"But?" I said. Because there was always a but.

Dr. Rhodes hesitated. "But releasing that much spiritual energy at once is dangerous. Maybe catastrophic. Three hundred and thirty years of trapped souls. Their rage. Their suffering. Their hunger. All released simultaneously."

"What would that do?" Melissa asked.

"I don't know. Maybe nothing. Maybe they dissipate peacefully. Or maybe..." Dr. Rhodes trailed off.

"Maybe what?"

"Maybe they lash out. One final violent release. Everyone in the immediate area could be killed. Or possessed. Or driven mad. I've read accounts of similar events. They're... not encouraging."

The hope died.

"So our choices are," Melissa said slowly, "kill Lily and postpone the curse. Don't kill Lily and let the street collapse. Or destroy the well and maybe kill everyone anyway."

"That's not entirely accurate," Dr. Rhodes said. "If you time it right—if you destroy the well at exactly the right moment—you might be able to channel the energy release. Direct it away from the living."

"How?" I asked.

"The ritual has specific timing. Midnight on Halloween. When the veil is thinnest. That's when the dead are most vulnerable to banishment. If you destroy the well then—at the exact moment they're expecting the sacrifice— you might catch them off-guard. Send them through the veil before they can retaliate."

"Might?"

"It's theoretical. I've never seen it attempted."

"Jesus Christ," Melissa muttered.

A door slammed upstairs. We all flinched.

"Eight minutes," Dr. Rhodes said, checking her watch. "I need to tell you the rest."

"There's more?" My voice came out strangled.

"The destruction has to be complete. Total. You can't just collapse the well. You have to obliterate it. Shatter the stone. Break the connection at a molecular level."

"How?"

"Explosives. Military grade if possible. And you need someone who knows what they're doing."

"Tucker," I said. "Tucker Davis. He's former military. He already saw the well. He was too scared to go back but maybe—"

"You have to convince him. Tonight. And you need materials. C-4 if you can get it. Otherwise high-grade commercial explosives."

"How the hell are we supposed to get that?" Melissa demanded.

"I don't know. But you have until midnight tomorrow to figure it out." Dr. Rhodes picked up her bag. "And you need protection. The house will fight you. The spirits will try to stop you."

She pulled out items. Salt. Iron filings. Rowan wood branches. Blessed silver.

"Create barriers. Salt lines around the basement. Iron in your pockets. Stay together. Don't let anyone get isolated. And whatever you do, don't answer when they knock."

Another slam. Closer this time.

"Six minutes," Dr. Rhodes said. Her voice was tense now. "Listen carefully. If you do this—if you destroy the well—you need to protect the children. The energy release will be strongest in the basement. You need to get Lily and Max as far away as possible. Upper floor. Locked room. Iron barriers."

"But we need to be in the basement to set the explosives," I said.

"Yes. Which means some of you will be in direct danger."

"How much danger?"

Dr. Rhodes met my eyes. "Potentially fatal."

The room tilted. I grabbed the back of the couch.

"But it's the only way to end this," Dr. Rhodes continued. "Really end it. Not postpone it. Not feed it. End it."

"At the cost of how many lives?"

"I don't know. Maybe none. Maybe all of you. But I do know this: if you do the ritual and sacrifice Lily, the curse continues. Seven years from now, it'll demand another child. And another. And another. Forever."

Footsteps on the stairs. Heavy. Deliberate.

"Four minutes," Dr. Rhodes said. "I'm running out of time. Is there anything else you need to know?"

"Yes," Lily said. Her voice was quiet. "If we do the ritual. If I go to the well willingly. If I let them take me. Would that really save everyone?"

"Lily, no—" I started.

"Would it?" Lily stared at Dr. Rhodes.

Dr. Rhodes looked away. "Short term? Probably yes. The house would be satisfied. The street wouldn't collapse. People would live."

"Then—"

"But you'd be dead, Lily. And in seven years, this happens again to another child. And again. And again. Your sacrifice wouldn't end anything. It would just feed the cycle."

"But people would live."

"Different people would die later."

"Later is better than now."

"Lily—" My voice broke.

"I'm just saying." Lily looked at me. Her eyes were red now. Tears finally coming. "I'm just saying maybe we can't let forty-seven people die. Even if it means..."

She couldn't finish.

I pulled her into my arms. She was shaking. Small. My baby.

"We're not killing you," I whispered into her hair. "I don't care what the house wants. I don't care what the curse demands. We're finding another way."

"But what if there isn't another way?"

"Then we die fighting. Together. But we don't give them what they want."

The footsteps reached the bottom of the stairs.

"Two minutes," Dr. Rhodes said. "I have to go. The house is forcing me out."

"Wait," Melissa said. "The explosives. Where do we even start looking?"

"Tucker Davis will know. Or try the old mining company outside town. They use explosives for demolition. Break in if you have to."

"Break in?"

"You're running out of time. And Sarah?" Dr. Rhodes looked at me. "Whatever you decide, decide fast. The house knows you're considering alternatives. It'll escalate to force your hand."

The parlor door swung open on its own.

Dr. Rhodes walked toward it. Then stopped. Turned back.

"One more thing. The Woman in White. She's the strongest spirit. The oldest. If you destroy the well, she'll try to stop you. She might try to possess one of you."

"How do we fight that?" Melissa asked.

"You can't. Not directly. But if someone gets possessed, iron will hurt them. Make them vulnerable. Use it if you have to."

"You want us to stab each other with iron?"

"I want you to survive."

Dr. Rhodes stepped through the doorway. The front door was already open. Waiting.

"Good luck," she said. "You're going to need it."

She left. The door slammed shut.

The lock clicked.

We stood in silence.

Then Max said, "So we're going to blow up the well?"

"I don't know," I said.

"We have to," Lily said. "It's the only way that doesn't involve me dying."

"It might involve all of us dying," Melissa pointed out.

"But at least we'd be trying to actually end this. Not just feeding it."

She was right. Of course she was right.

But the thought of setting off explosives in the basement while supernatural forces tried to kill us—while potentially unleashing three centuries of vengeful spirits—made my stomach turn.

"Mom?" Max tugged my sleeve. "There's someone in the hallway."

We all looked.

A shadow stood in the corridor. Tall. Male.

Victor Kane.

"You heard the doctor," Victor's ghost said. His voice came from everywhere and nowhere. "You have choices. All of them end in death. The question is: whose?"

"Get away from us," I said.

"I'm trying to help you understand. The ritual is mercy. Quick. Painless. Over in moments. But if you destroy the well? If you release us all at once?" Victor's shadow moved closer. "We will tear you apart. Every soul buried beneath this house will have their moment of freedom. And they'll use it to make you suffer as we've suffered."

"You're lying," Lily said.

"Am I? Ask Eleanor. Ask Benjamin. Ask the Woman in White. We've been trapped here for centuries. Do you think we'll go quietly?"

"We'll take that chance," I said.

Victor's laugh was like breaking glass. "Will you? Will you really risk your children's lives on a theory? On hope? When I'm offering you certainty?"

"Certainty that my daughter dies."

"Certainty that everyone else lives. Forty-seven people, Sarah. Their blood will be on your hands if you choose wrong."

"Get out of my house."

"Your house?" Victor's shadow filled the hallway. "This has never been your house. You were always just food. Another sacrifice. Another mother too weak to do what's necessary."

Something in me snapped.

"I am not weak," I said. My voice didn't shake anymore. "And I am not sacrificing my child to fix your mistakes. You broke this curse. You murdered your wife and son. You created this nightmare. Not me."

"I was trying to save him!"

"You were trying to save yourself! You didn't want to face what you'd helped create. The Collectors. The rituals. The murders. So you killed Eleanor to keep her quiet and then you killed yourself rather than face consequences."

Victor's shadow swelled. The walls cracked.

"You know nothing—"

"I know you're a coward. I know you're a murderer. And I know I'm not listening to anything you say."

Silence.

Then Victor screamed.

The lights went out.

The temperature dropped so fast I could feel ice forming on my skin.

"Mom!" Lily grabbed my arm.

"I'm here. I've got you."

"Sarah?" Melissa's voice in the dark.

"I'm here. Max?"

"I'm okay."

The lights flickered back on.

Victor was gone.

But the hallway was full of ghosts now. Dozens of them. Pale figures in old clothes. Colonial dress. Victorian gowns. 1960s suits.

All staring at us.

"They're all here," Max whispered. "Everyone who's ever died on Halloween Street."

He was right. I could see them now. The weight of three centuries of death pressing close. Their faces were hungry. Desperate.

Waiting.

"We need to call Tucker," I said. "Right now."

"The phones don't work," Melissa said.

"Then we go to him. We find a way out of this house and—"

"The doors won't open," Lily said.

"They will. They have to. Dr. Rhodes got in. That means they can open."

I ran to the front door. Grabbed the handle. Pulled.

Nothing.

Pulled harder.

Still nothing.

"Let us out!" I screamed at the house. At the ghosts. At whatever was listening. "Let us out or I swear to God I'll destroy this entire place!"

The door trembled.

Then slowly, slowly, it opened.

Just an inch.

Just enough to see outside.

Halloween Street looked normal. Quiet. Empty.

But standing on our front lawn was Tucker Davis.

He held a duffel bag.

Our eyes met through the crack in the door.

Tucker raised his hand. Knocked three times.

"Sarah," he called. "I brought what you need. Let me in."

Twenty-Three

Chapter 23: The Moral Calculus

S arah pov

I can't breathe.

The kitchen table is covered in papers. Town records. Death certificates. Eleanor's diary open to that final page where her handwriting goes shaky. The journal Margaret gave me with all those names. All those children. All those mothers who had to choose.

Forty-seven people live on Halloween Street. I counted them. Twice.

The Rodriguez family in the blue house. Five kids. Mrs. Chen who waves at us every morning. The Pattersons with their new baby. Old Mr. Kovac who can barely walk. Forty-seven lives.

Or Lily.

My daughter sits across from me. Ten years old. Her hair needs brushing. She's wearing her favorite Halloween pajamas even though it's four in the afternoon. She looks so small.

"Mom." Her voice is steady. Too steady. "We have to talk about this."

"No." My throat feels like I swallowed glass. "We don't."

Melissa slams her coffee mug on the counter. "Sarah, listen to me. We have less than seven hours. The house keeps opening the doors for minutes at a time. Next time they unlock, we run. All of us. We drive until—"

"Until what?" I snap. "Until the entire street collapses into the ground at midnight? Until forty-seven people die because we ran?"

"They're not your responsibility!"

"They're human beings!"

Max sits on the floor in the corner, building something with blocks. He's been quiet since we pulled him from that bathtub. Since he tried to drown himself. He looks up now, his seven-year-old face too serious.

"We should fight," he says. "Like in my games. When the monsters come, you fight them."

Lily shakes her head. "It's not that kind of monster, Max."

"Then what kind is it?"

She looks at me when she answers. "The kind that needs something. The kind that won't stop until it gets what it wants."

My hands are shaking. I press them flat against the table. "Don't. Don't even think about—"

"Someone has to say it." Lily stands up. She's so small but her voice doesn't waver. "I've been reading. I found other stories online before the internet stopped working. Other houses like this. Other curses. The only way to break them is—"

"No."

"—is sacrifice. Real sacrifice. Willing sacrifice."

Melissa crosses the room in three steps. "Lily, honey, you're ten years old. You don't understand what you're—"

"I understand perfectly." Lily's chin comes up. "I understand that if we do nothing, everyone dies. I understand that if we run, everyone dies. I understand that Mom has to choose between me and forty-seven other people, and that's not fair to her."

The words hit me like a fist. "Stop. Stop talking."

"Why? Because it's true?" Lily's eyes are filling with tears but her voice stays level. "Benjamin told me everything. He told me what his mom tried to do. She tried to run and his dad killed her and then killed him and then the curse got worse. He told me that every family that's lived here has tried to fight or run or make deals and it never works. The curse just gets hungrier."

"Benjamin is a ghost whispering in your ear." I'm on my feet now. "He's not a reliable source."

"He's been dead for sixty years because his father wouldn't let him go! He knows what he's talking about!"

"You are not dying. End of discussion."

"It's not your decision!"

The slap of her words stuns me silent. We stare at each other. My daughter. My baby girl who used to climb into bed with me during thunderstorms. Who brings me dandelions because she thinks they're beautiful. Who has her whole life ahead of her.

Max's blocks crash to the floor. "Stop yelling."

We both turn. He's standing now, hands in fists. "Just stop. You're both being stupid."

"Max—" Melissa starts.

"No." He glares at all of us. "You're arguing about dying or running or fighting but nobody's listening. Lily doesn't want to die. Mom doesn't want her to. And running won't work because the house won't let us. So we fight. We figure out how to kill the curse."

"You can't kill a curse," I say quietly.

"Why not? It's not a person. It's like… like a spell or something. Spells can be broken."

Lily wipes her eyes. "That's not how it works."

"How do you know? Have you ever broken a curse before?"

"No, but—"

"Then you don't know what works and what doesn't." Max crosses his arms. "I think we should blow up the house. Like in movies. Blow up the bad place and the bad thing dies."

"This isn't a movie." Melissa's voice is gentle but firm. "Real life doesn't work that way."

"This isn't real life!" Max shouts. "Real life doesn't have ghosts and wells that open from the inside and knocking that never stops! This is already like a movie! So why can't we blow it up?"

The front door rattles.

We all freeze.

Three knocks. Slow. Deliberate.

Then silence.

"It's only four-thirty," Melissa whispers. "The sun's still up."

Another three knocks. These ones from the kitchen wall right behind me.

I step away from it. My skin is crawling. "It's getting stronger. The closer we get to midnight, the more power it has."

Three knocks from upstairs.

From the basement.

From the windows.

All at once. A symphony of knocking that makes my teeth ache.

Then it stops.

The doorbell rings.

"Don't answer it," Lily says immediately. "That's how it gets permission to come in fully. If you invite someone in on Halloween—"

"I know." I'm already moving toward the door, looking through the peephole.

Dr. Rhodes stands on the porch. Her car is in the driveway. She's holding a briefcase and looks exhausted.

"How did she get past the locks?" Melissa hisses.

"The house let her in." I'm already opening the door. "Dr. Rhodes—"

"I know. I know I shouldn't be here." She pushes past me, breathing hard. "The doors opened five minutes ago. I drove like hell. We probably have ten minutes before they seal again."

"You should leave," I tell her. "Get out while you can."

"Not until you hear what I found." She sets her briefcase on the kitchen table, clicking it open. Papers spill out. Old maps. Photocopies of handwritten documents. Photographs. "I've been researching this house, this curse, for seven years. Ever since the Patterson family died here."

"Patterson?" Melissa picks up one of the photos. "The people with the new baby are named Patterson."

"Different Pattersons. The ones who died were Marcus, Jennifer, and their daughter Katie. Katie was eight." Dr. Rhodes pulls out a police report.

"Official cause of death was murder-suicide. Marcus allegedly killed his wife and daughter, then himself. But the evidence never added up. No fingerprints on the weapon. No motive. And their mouths were sewn shut with black thread."

My stomach turns. "Like Eleanor Kane."

"Exactly like Eleanor Kane. Like every sacrifice victim in this house for the last sixty years." She spreads out more papers. "I tracked down twelve families who've lived here since 1963. All of them had children. All of them faced the same choice you're facing now. And Sarah—" She looks at me. "Every single one who attempted the ritual died anyway."

The room goes silent except for the ticking of the broken grandfather clock that still somehow ticks.

"What?" Lily's voice is small.

"The ritual doesn't work." Dr. Rhodes pulls out a leather journal, the pages yellow and crumbling. "This belonged to one of The Collectors. A man named Edward Marsh. He documented every ritual from 1897 to 1954. The year he killed himself. In his final entry, he wrote: 'We were wrong. The ritual doesn't appease the dead. It feeds them. Every sacrifice makes them hungrier. God forgive us. God forgive what we've done.'"

Melissa sinks into a chair. "Then why did The Collectors keep doing it?"

"Because admitting the ritual was a lie meant admitting they'd murdered their own children for nothing." Dr. Rhodes's voice is flat. "It meant facing prosecution. Prison. Execution. So they kept going. They convinced themselves the next time would work. That they just had to do it right. They kept feeding the curse because the alternative was accepting they'd created it."

I can't process this. Can't think. "So the ritual never worked? Victor Kane refusing to sacrifice Benjamin didn't break anything?"

"Victor Kane's refusal exposed the truth. That's why the curse focused on this house. Because this is where someone finally said no." Dr. Rhodes meets my eyes. "Eleanor tried to run with Benjamin. Victor caught her. Killed her. Then killed Benjamin and himself. But the curse recorded what happened. It knows Victor tried to sacrifice his son and failed. It knows Eleanor tried to save him and failed. It knows Benjamin died screaming. All that anguish, all that trauma—it soaked into the land. Into the foundation. Into the well."

"The well." Max says it like a revelation. "That's where it comes from. That's where all the bad stuff is."

Dr. Rhodes nods slowly. "The well connects to the mass grave beneath Halloween Street. It's the physical anchor point for everything. The rituals were performed there. The bodies were thrown there. Generations of pain channeled into one location."

"Then we destroy it." I'm already moving, already thinking. "We collapse the well. Sever the connection. End the curse."

"It's not that simple." Dr. Rhodes holds up a hand. "If you destroy the well, you destroy the anchor. But all that energy has to go somewhere. Three hundred and thirty years of death and suffering and rage—it'll all be released at once."

"Released how?" Melissa asks.

"I don't know. Maybe it dissipates harmlessly. Maybe every spirit trapped here goes free and moves on."

"Or?"

Dr. Rhodes's face is grim. "Or it explodes outward like a bomb. Spiritual shrapnel. It could kill everyone in a three-block radius. It could level the entire town. I've never seen a curse this old, this concentrated. The risk is enormous."

"But it's a risk," Lily says quietly. "It's not certain death."

"No. It's not certain."

"Unlike the ritual. Which definitely kills whoever goes in the well."

"Yes."

Lily looks at me. "So we have a choice that might work but might kill everyone. Or a choice that definitely kills me but might not work and might kill everyone anyway."

"That's... accurate." Dr. Rhodes closes her briefcase. "I'm sorry. I wish I had better options."

The knocking starts again. Louder this time. More insistent.

From everywhere.

Dr. Rhodes flinches. "I need to go. My ten minutes are almost up."

"Wait." I grab her arm. "If we destroy the well—how do we do it?"

"Explosives. Enough to collapse the entire basement. You'd need someone with experience. Military background, maybe." She's backing toward the door. "And you'd need to do it at 11:59. One minute before midnight. Right before the ritual deadline. That's when the curse is most vulnerable."

"How do you know that?"

"Edward Marsh's journal. He wrote that the curse can only be broken when it's actively reaching for you. When it's exposed. Vulnerable." She's at the door now. "I'm sorry, Sarah. I wish I had better answers."

She's gone before I can respond. The door clicks shut behind her.

Three seconds later, every lock in the house slides into place.

We're sealed in again.

Melissa breaks the silence. "Tucker. Tucker Davis was military. He might—"

"He won't come back." I'm pacing now, trying to think. "He barely survived the basement the first time."

"Then we figure it out ourselves. How hard can it be? We buy explosives, we set them up, we—"

"We can't buy anything. We're locked in." I run my hands through my hair. "And we don't have time. It's almost five. We have seven hours to figure this out."

"Mom." Max is staring at the basement door. "It's open."

He's right. The iron door to the basement stands wide open. I know I locked it. I watched the deadbolt slide home.

Cold air flows up from below. It smells like wet earth and rust and something rotting.

Three knocks echo from the basement.

Then a voice. Child's voice. Benjamin.

"Come down. Come down and see. Come down and choose."

Lily takes a step toward the stairs.

"No." I block her. "Absolutely not."

"He's calling to me."

"I don't care."

"Mom, maybe he can tell us something. Maybe—"

"No." My voice is sharp. Final. "Nobody goes down there. Nobody."

The basement door slams shut so hard the whole house shakes. Pictures fall off walls. A window cracks.

Then the whispers start.

From the walls. From the floors. From the ceiling. Hundreds of voices all talking at once. I can't make out words but I can hear the tone. Angry. Demanding. Hungry.

Max covers his ears. "Make it stop."

"I can't."

The lights flicker. Once. Twice. They die completely.

We're standing in darkness except for the last rays of sun through the windows. Outside, the street is empty. No cars. No people. Just that unnatural fog rolling in.

Melissa finds a flashlight in the kitchen drawer. The beam cuts through the dark. "Okay. Okay. Let's think about this logically."

"There's nothing logical about this!" I want to scream but I keep my voice steady for the kids. "We're trapped in a house with a curse that wants my daughter dead. Logic left the building weeks ago."

"Then let's think about it strategically." Melissa's using her lawyer voice. The one she uses in court. "We have three options. One: we do nothing and everyone dies at midnight. Two: we attempt the ritual and Lily dies but maybe saves everyone else—except the ritual probably doesn't work so everyone might die anyway. Three: we destroy the well and maybe break the curse but maybe kill everyone in the blast radius."

"Those are all terrible options," Max says.

"They're the only options we have."

Lily sits on the floor, pulling her knees to her chest. "I vote for destroying the well."

"Of course you do," I say. "Because that's the option where you might not die."

"No. Because that's the option where we're doing something instead of just feeding the curse what it wants." She looks up at me. "Dr. Rhodes said the ritual makes it hungrier. Every sacrifice for a hundred and thirty years has made it stronger. So if I go into that well, even if it saves everyone this time, what about seven years from now? What about the next family? We'd just be passing the curse along."

"That's not your responsibility."

"Maybe not. But it's the right thing to do."

"The right thing?" My voice cracks. "The right thing is not blowing up a basement and hoping the curse doesn't kill us all!"

"The right thing is trying to stop this forever instead of just surviving tonight!"

We're shouting at each other again. I can see the fear in her eyes even though she's trying to be brave. She's terrified. My baby is terrified and trying to pretend she's not.

Melissa steps between us. "Both of you, stop. Fighting won't help."

"Then what will?" I'm shaking. My whole body is shaking. "Tell me, Melissa. Tell me what to do. Tell me how to save my daughter and not get everyone else killed. Tell me how to make a choice I can live with."

She doesn't answer. Because there is no answer.

The sun is setting. I can see it through the window. The sky is turning that deep orange-red that happens right before dark. In the distance, I hear children laughing. Trick-or-treaters already out on other streets. Happy. Safe. Normal.

We're not normal anymore.

We haven't been normal since we moved into this house.

Max speaks quietly. "I think we should call Tucker."

"He won't come back."

"We should try. Maybe if we explain everything. Maybe if he knows about Dr. Rhodes's research."

"The phones don't work."

"The landline in the kitchen worked yesterday."

I'd forgotten about that. The old rotary phone mounted on the wall. I try it now. The dial tone buzzes in my ear.

My hands shake as I dial Tucker's number from the business card he left. It rings. Once. Twice. Three times.

"Davis." His voice is gruff.

"Tucker, it's Sarah Brennan. I need—"

"No." The word is immediate. Final. "No. I told you. I'm not going back in that house."

"Please. Just listen. We have new information. Dr. Rhodes found—"

"I don't care what she found. I don't care about research or curses or any of it. I went into that basement and I heard things no living person should hear. I'm done."

"Tucker, there are forty-seven people on this street. If we don't stop this, they all die."

Silence on the line.

Then: "That's not my problem."

"It is if you have any shred of human decency." My voice is hard now. "You were a Marine. You took an oath. To protect people."

"I also took an oath to stay sane. That house isn't right. What's in that basement isn't right. I'm sorry about those people but I can't help you."

"You can. You're the only one who can." I'm begging now. "We need someone who knows explosives. We need to destroy the well. End this. But we can't do it alone."

Another long silence.

"You want to blow up the basement."

"Yes."

"You understand what you're asking? The amount of explosives you'd need? The risk?"

"Yes."

"And you're sure this is the only way?"

I look at Lily. At Max. At Melissa standing there with her flashlight. At this kitchen that should be normal and safe but reeks of death and cold.

"I'm not sure of anything. But it's the best chance we have."

Tucker breathes out slowly. "I need to think about it."

"We don't have time. It's five-thirty. We need to move by eleven."

"Jesus Christ." He's quiet for so long I think he hung up. Then: "I'll call you back. Give me thirty minutes."

The line goes dead.

I hang up and turn to my family. "He's thinking about it."

"That's not a yes," Melissa says.

"It's not a no."

The knocking starts again. But this time it's not random. It's rhythmic. Deliberate. Like a heartbeat.

Boom-boom. Boom-boom. Boom-boom.

It's coming from the basement.

Max moves closer to me. "What's it doing?"

"Counting down." Lily's voice is hollow. "It's counting the hours. The heartbeats. Until midnight."

The lights flicker back on. But they're wrong. Dimmer than before. And they're pulsing with that same rhythm.

Boom-boom. Boom-boom.

In the living room, the grandfather clock starts ticking again. But backwards. The hands are moving counterclockwise.

"It's playing with us," Melissa whispers.

I gather my children close. Max on one side. Lily on the other. Melissa stands with us. A family. Broken but together.

"Listen to me," I say quietly. "Whatever happens tonight, whatever we decide, we're doing it together. Nobody makes this choice alone. Nobody sacrifices themselves without all of us agreeing. Understood?"

Lily nods. Max nods. Melissa squeezes my shoulder.

The knocking continues. That steady, horrible heartbeat.

Boom-boom. Boom-boom.

Outside, the street lights flicker on. But the fog is so thick now I can barely see them. Halloween Street is disappearing into white mist.

The phone rings.

I snatch it up. "Tucker?"

"Against every instinct I have—I'm in." His voice is tight. "I'll be there in forty-five minutes with what we need. But Sarah, I need you to understand something."

"What?"

"This is a Hail Mary. A long shot. If we destroy that well and the curse doesn't break—if it explodes outward like Dr. Rhodes thinks it might—people will die. A lot of people. And their blood will be on our hands."

"I know."

"Do you? Do you really? Because I've seen what explosives do. I've seen collateral damage. And if we're wrong about this—"

"We're not wrong."

"You don't know that."

He's right. I don't.

But I know that doing nothing means Lily dies. I know that attempting the ritual means Lily dies and probably everyone else too. I know that we're out of options and out of time.

"Forty-five minutes," I tell him. "Don't be late."

I hang up before he can change his mind.

Lily looks at me. "We're really doing this?"

"We're really doing this."

"What if it doesn't work?"

I kneel down so we're eye to eye. "Then at least we tried. At least we fought. At least we didn't just hand you over to something evil and hope it kept its word."

She hugs me. Her small arms tight around my neck. "I'm scared, Mom."

"Me too, baby. Me too."

Max joins the hug. Then Melissa. The four of us standing in the kitchen while the house pulses around us and the knocking continues and the clock ticks backwards.

Boom-boom. Boom-boom.

Six hours until midnight.

Six hours to set up explosives in a basement that doesn't want us there.

Six hours to destroy a curse that's had three hundred and thirty years to grow strong.

The basement door rattles. Not like it's trying to open. Like something inside is trying to get out.

I pull my family closer and make a promise. To myself. To them. To whatever's listening.

We're not going quietly. We're not giving up. And we're sure as hell not following anyone else's rules.

If this curse wants a fight, we'll give it one.

The door stops rattling.

The knocking stops.

For one perfect moment, the house is completely silent.

Then every door in the house slams open at once.

Twenty-Four

Chapter 24: Preparation for Halloween

arah pov

S I make the decision at 4:17 AM on October 30th.

We're going to destroy the well.

My hands shake as I write it down. The pen barely works. The ink keeps disappearing off the page. Reappearing. The house doesn't want me planning this.

I don't care what the house wants anymore.

Melissa finds me in the kitchen. Her eyes are red. Neither of us has slept.

"You're serious about this?" she asks.

"We blow the well at 11:59 PM tomorrow night. One minute before midnight. One minute before the ritual is supposed to happen."

"And if it doesn't work?"

I look at her. "Then we die trying instead of giving them Lily."

She nods slowly. "Okay. What do we need?"

"Explosives. Someone who knows how to use them. And maybe a miracle."

"I know where to get two of those things."

The sun rises like it's struggling. The light through the windows is gray. Wrong. Outside, Halloween Street is covered in fog so thick I can't see Hannah's house across the road.

The fog moves like it's breathing.

Lily sits at the table drawing. She won't look at me.

"Baby, where's your brother?"

"In his room. He wouldn't stop crying. Ben kept telling him something."

My stomach drops. "What was Ben telling him?"

"That he's sorry. That he has to do what Father says. That it'll be over soon."

I take the stairs two at a time. Max's door is locked from the inside.

"Max! Open this door!"

Silence.

"Max!"

The lock clicks. The door swings open by itself.

Max sits on his bed. His eyes are wrong. Too dark. Too old.

"Mom, Ben says you're making a mistake."

"Ben isn't real, baby."

"Yes he is." Max's voice drops lower. Not his voice. "I've been real this whole time, Mrs. Brennan. And I've been trying to help. But you won't listen. None of you will listen."

I grab Max's shoulders. His skin is ice cold. "Get out of my son."

"The well has to be fed. That's the rule. If you destroy it, everything comes up. All of us. Not just me and Mother and Father. All of us. Three hundred years of us."

"Max, fight him. I know you're in there."

Max blinks. His eyes clear for just a second. "Mom, I'm scared."

Then they go dark again. "Tomorrow night, Mrs. Brennan. One way or another, it ends."

I pull Max into my arms. He's shaking. Or I'm shaking. I can't tell anymore.

Downstairs, someone pounds on the front door.

Three times. Hard.

Melissa screams.

I carry Max down the stairs. He's limp against me. Breathing. Still alive. Still mine.

Through the front door window, I see Tucker Davis standing on the porch. He looks like he hasn't slept either. His truck is in the driveway. The fog curls around it like fingers.

I open the door. "You came back."

"Yeah, well. I'm an idiot." He won't meet my eyes. "But I was at my sister's place last night. Her kid's birthday. Four years old. And I kept thinking about your boy. About what you said. About how no one should have to sacrifice their kid to save themselves."

"I need explosives, Tucker. Military grade. Enough to collapse a well and everything under it."

He finally looks at me. "You want to blow up your basement."

"I want to blow up what's underneath my basement."

"Lady, you know that's insane, right?"

"I know that my son is possessed by a dead child who drowned in 1963. I know that if I don't destroy that well by midnight tomorrow, something is going to take my daughter into it. I know that this entire street is built on a mass grave and that corpses have been knocking on my walls for three weeks. So yes. I want to blow up my basement."

Tucker stares at me. Then he laughs. It sounds broken. "Okay. Okay. I got C-4 left over from my demo days. Kept it. Wasn't supposed to. But I kept it."

"Can you get it here by tonight?"

"Already in the truck."

Melissa appears behind me. "You brought military-grade explosives to a residential street?"

"Lady, this street stopped being residential about three hundred years ago." He's not wrong.

Tucker carries two black cases into the house. The house groans when he crosses the threshold. Every lightbulb shatters at once.

"It knows," Lily whispers. "The house knows what you're planning."

Glass rains down around us. Tucker doesn't flinch. Just sets the cases on the floor. Opens them.

"C-4. Detonators. Remote trigger. We'll need to set charges in a specific pattern to bring down the well without collapsing the entire foundation. Maybe."

"Maybe?"

"I'm a handyman, not a structural engineer. I'm doing my best here."

The temperature drops fifteen degrees in five seconds.

Max lifts his head from my shoulder. "Father is angry."

"I don't care what Father is."

"He says you can't stop what's already started."

Someone knocks on the door again. Three times.

We all freeze.

Tucker's hand goes to his belt. He's carrying. I can see the gun.

"Don't answer it," Melissa says.

The knocking continues. Three knocks. Pause. Three knocks. Pause.

"It's not sunset yet," I say. "We're allowed to answer before sunset."

"Are we?" Tucker asks. "Because I'm pretty sure the rules stopped applying to this house a long time ago."

I look through the window.

Isaac Stone stands on the porch. Behind him, an old man in priest's clothes leans on a cane.

Father Gabriel.

I open the door.

Isaac carries a leather bag that clinks when he moves. "We heard you're planning something stupid and suicidal tomorrow night. Thought you might need help."

Father Gabriel limps past me without asking permission. His leg is still in a brace from when the house threw him down the stairs. "I told myself I'd never enter this house again. I told the Lord I'd done my duty and failed. But then I dreamed about a little boy drowning. Every night for a week. Same dream. Same boy."

"Benjamin," I say.

"He showed me what your son looks like, Mrs. Brennan. They could be brothers."

Max stares at Father Gabriel. "You fell down the stairs. That was funny."

"Max, stop it."

"That wasn't Max talking," Gabriel says quietly. "Was it?"

"Not always. Not anymore."

259

Isaac sets his bag on the coffee table. Pulls out containers. "Salt blessed by three different faiths. Iron filings from a church bell. Rowan wood from a tree that's never been touched by death. Silver coins minted before 1900. And this."

He holds up a small cloth bundle. Unwraps it.

A knife. Old. The blade is black.

"Obsidian," Isaac says. "Used by the indigenous people who lived here before the colonists came. Before the hanging ground. Before any of this. It's the oldest thing connected to this land. And it doesn't belong to the curse."

"What do we do with it?" Melissa asks.

"If things go wrong tomorrow night, if the spirits manifest physically, this can cut them. It's one of the only things that can."

Tucker snorts. "You want us to knife-fight ghosts."

"I want you to have a chance."

The house shudders. A sound like grinding teeth comes from the walls.

Father Gabriel crosses himself. "It's listening. It's always listening."

"Good," I say. "Let it listen. We're destroying the well tomorrow night at 11:59 PM. We're ending this."

"You can't end it," Max says. Not his voice again. Benjamin's. "You can only change who it takes."

I set Max down. Kneel in front of him. "If you're really trying to help, Benjamin, then help. Tell me how to save my son. Tell me how to save all of us."

Max's eyes flicker. Benjamin's voice comes out softer. "I don't know. I'm seven. I've been seven for sixty-two years. I don't know anything except drowning and being cold and waiting. I don't want to wait anymore, Mrs. Brennan. I'm so tired of waiting."

Tears run down Max's face. I can't tell if they're his or Benjamin's.

"Then let him go," I whisper. "Let Max go, and we'll help you. I promise."

"You can't help me. No one can. Father made sure of that."

The lights flicker. Come back on. Half of them stay dark.

Isaac starts pulling things from his bag. Setting them on the floor. "We need to create barriers. Protection circles. We fortify the basement first. Make it as hard as possible for them to interfere while Tucker sets the charges."

"They'll fight us," Gabriel says. "The moment we go down there, they'll know."

"Yeah, they will." Tucker checks his gun. Checks it again. "So we do it fast. We do it right. And we don't stop no matter what we see or hear."

Melissa grabs my arm. "Sarah, are you sure about this? Really sure? Because once we start, we can't undo it."

"I'm not sacrificing my daughter to a three-hundred-year-old lie."

"But what if it's not a lie? What if the curse is real? What if destroying the well really does release everything underneath?"

"Then we fight everything underneath."

She doesn't look convinced. But she nods.

We spend the next six hours preparing.

Isaac draws symbols on the floor in salt and iron filings. Protection circles. Binding marks. Things he says are older than the house. Older than the colonists. Older than the curse.

The house fights him every step. The salt blows away even though there's no wind. The iron filings rust in seconds. The marks fade as fast as he draws them.

"It's getting stronger," Isaac mutters. "The closer we get to Halloween, the more power it has."

Tucker maps out the basement. Measures the walls. Calculates blast radius. He won't let any of us go down there with him.

"Too dangerous. I see something, I'm shooting first. Can't have civilians in the way."

He goes down alone. We hear him moving around. Talking to himself. Praying maybe.

He comes back up twenty minutes later. His face is gray.

"What did you see?" I ask.

"The well isn't sealed anymore. The grate's completely gone. And there's something down there. In the water. Moving."

"What kind of something?"

"The kind I'm not going back down there without a bigger gun."

Lily draws in her notebook. Won't show me what.

Max sits in the corner. Sometimes he's Max. Sometimes he's Benjamin. I can tell by the eyes.

Father Gabriel blesses the explosives. Tucker looks at him like he's crazy.

"Can't hurt," Gabriel says. "Might help."

"It's C-4, not holy water."

"Son, at this point, I'll bless your shoelaces if it makes you feel safer."

Melissa makes coffee. Burns it. Makes it again. Her hands won't stop shaking.

"I keep thinking about Mom and Dad," she says. "How they'd handle this. What they'd say."

"They'd say we're out of our minds."

"Yeah. Probably." She laughs. Sounds like crying. "But they'd also say protect the kids no matter what. That's what parents do."

"That's what we're doing."

"By blowing up a basement."

"By refusing to give up."

The sun starts to set. We all feel it. The air gets heavier. Colder.

The knocking starts early.

Three knocks on the walls. The ceiling. The floor.

"They're excited," Isaac says. "Tomorrow's Halloween. Tomorrow's the night. They think they've already won."

"Let them think that," Tucker says. "Overconfident enemies make mistakes."

"These aren't enemies. They're victims who became predators."

"Same thing in my book."

Father Gabriel finishes his blessing. Sits down hard. He's exhausted. The house has been draining him since he walked in.

"I need to tell you something," he says. "Something the church knows. Something we've hidden."

We all stop. Look at him.

"The Collectors weren't just a secret society. They were sanctioned. By the church. By the town. By the people who were supposed to protect the innocent. They knew what was happening. They knew families were being pressured to sacrifice children. And they allowed it because Hollow's End was wealthy. Because the church got donations. Because turning a blind eye was easier than stopping it."

Silence.

"You're saying the church let children die for money," Melissa says.

"I'm saying evil is rarely one monster. It's usually many people choosing comfort over courage." Gabriel looks at me. "I failed you once, Mrs. Brennan. When I tried to exorcise this house. But I won't fail you tomorrow. Whatever happens, I'll be here."

"Even if it kills you?"

"Especially if it kills me. Some debts can only be paid in blood."

The knocking gets louder. Faster.

Max stands up. Walks to the basement door.

"Max, stop."

He doesn't stop. His hand reaches for the doorknob.

I run across the room. Grab him.

He turns around. His eyes are completely black.

"Father says it's time to practice," Benjamin's voice says through Max's mouth. "He wants to show you what happens tomorrow. He wants you to see."

The basement door swings open.

Cold air rushes out. It smells like rot and old water and something else. Something wrong.

From the darkness below, we hear singing.

A child's voice. Singing a nursery rhyme.

"Ring around the rosie, pocket full of posies, ashes, ashes, we all fall down."

Then another voice joins. A woman's. Eleanor.

"Ring around the rosie."

Then a man's. Victor. Deep. Angry.

"Pocket full of posies."

More voices. Dozens of them. Children and adults. The dead below the house. The mass grave. All singing together.

"Ashes, ashes, we all fall down."

263

Max goes limp in my arms. His eyes clear. He starts crying.

"Mom, I'm sorry. I'm sorry. I can't stop him. He's too strong."

"It's okay, baby. It's okay."

It's not okay.

The singing stops. All at once.

Tucker slams the basement door shut. Locks it. "We're not going down there tonight. We wait until tomorrow. We do this in daylight. Or as close to it as we can get."

"The ritual is at midnight," Isaac says. "We have to set the charges before then. We have to be ready."

"Then we go down at noon. We have twelve hours to plant the explosives and get out before Halloween night starts."

Melissa looks at me. "Can we last that long? Can the kids?"

I don't know. Max is getting worse every hour. And Lily—

Where's Lily?

"Lily?"

No answer.

"LILY!"

I hear her voice from upstairs. "I'm in my room, Mom!"

I run up the stairs. The others follow.

Lily's room is freezing. Her breath comes out in clouds. She's standing at the window. Looking out at Halloween Street.

"Baby, what are you doing?"

"Watching them gather."

I look out the window.

The fog has cleared enough to see.

There are people standing in the street. Dozens of them. Just standing. Staring at the house.

But they're not people.

They're transparent. Flickering. Ghosts.

Colonial-era clothing. Nooses around their necks. Some with crushed skulls. Some with twisted limbs. The hanged. The executed. The buried beneath the street.

They're all waiting.

"They're here for tomorrow," Lily says. "They're here for me."

"No. No, they're not getting you."

She turns around. Her eyes are full of tears. "What if I want to go? What if it stops all of this? What if it saves Max? What if—"

"Stop. Stop talking like that."

"But Mom—"

"No. You are ten years old. You are not sacrificing yourself for anyone. Do you understand me?"

She nods. But she doesn't believe me. I can see it.

Downstairs, something crashes. Glass breaking. Lots of it.

We run back down.

The living room windows are shattered. The protection circles Isaac drew are destroyed. Salt and iron everywhere. And standing in the middle of the room—

Hannah. Julia. Whatever she is.

She's covered in blood. It runs from her eyes. Her mouth. Her hands.

"You can't stop it," she says. "I tried to stop it in 1963. My mother tried to stop it in 1934. Every generation tries to stop it. And every generation fails. The Collectors won. They always win. Because the curse is real. Because the debt must be paid. Because—"

Tucker shoots her.

The gun is deafening in the small room.

Julia doesn't fall. The bullet passes through her. Hits the wall behind.

She's not alive. She hasn't been alive. Maybe for days. Maybe since she revealed herself.

The Woman in White is wearing Julia's corpse like a costume.

"Tomorrow night," the thing wearing Julia says. "Midnight. The girl goes into the well. Or all of you go into the ground. Those are the only choices. Those have always been the only choices."

She smiles. Her teeth are black. Rotted.

Then she collapses. Julia's body hits the floor. Empty. Used up.

Father Gabriel moves forward. Checks her pulse. Shakes his head.

"She's been dead for hours. Maybe longer. The entity was animating her."

"They can do that?" Melissa's voice is high. Panicked. "They can walk around in dead bodies?"

"Tomorrow night they'll be strong enough to do anything," Isaac says. "That's what Halloween means here. That's what the thinning of the veil means. They'll be as solid as we are. As dangerous as we are. Maybe more."

The house laughs. I swear it laughs. A sound like wind through a broken chimney.

Max pulls away from me. Walks to the basement door again.

"Max, no."

"Ben says I have to see. He says I have to know what's coming."

"You're not going down there."

He looks at me. His eyes are Max's eyes again. "Mom, I have to. I have to see. Please. I'm so scared. I need to know what's going to happen to me."

"Nothing is going to happen to you. I won't let it."

"But what if you can't stop it? What if nobody can?"

The basement door rattles. The lock strains.

"We need to secure this house," Tucker says. "Now. Before night really falls. We need every window boarded. Every door reinforced. We make this place a fortress."

We work fast. Tucker has plywood in his truck. We board up every broken window. Nail them in place. Isaac redraws the protection circles. Uses three times as much salt. Three times as much iron. Father Gabriel blesses every entrance. Every threshold.

Melissa takes the kids upstairs. Locks them in Lily's room. The only room that still feels relatively safe.

By 9 PM, we're done. The house is sealed. Dark. All the lights are off except candles. Electricity isn't reliable anymore.

We sit in the living room. Julia's body is covered with a sheet in the corner. We can't get it outside. The doors won't open anymore. The house is keeping us in.

"We're trapped," Melissa says. "We're already trapped."

"We have until tomorrow noon," Tucker says. "We go down, we set the charges, we blow the well. Simple plan."

"Nothing about this is simple."

"Simple doesn't mean easy."

Father Gabriel prays quietly. His hands shake. He's terrified. We all are.

Isaac sharpens the obsidian knife. "If they manifest physically tomorrow night, aim for the chest. Center mass. Don't hesitate. They're already dead. You're not killing them. You're just sending them back."

"And if that doesn't work?" I ask.

"Then we run. And we pray."

The candles flicker. All of them. At the same time.

The temperature drops.

And from upstairs, Melissa screams.

We all run. Take the stairs as fast as we can. Lily's door is open. Melissa stands in the doorway. Not moving. Staring.

I push past her.

The room is empty.

Lily sits on the bed. Alone.

"Where's Max?" I ask. "Where's your brother?"

She points at the closet. Her hand shakes.

I open the closet door.

Empty. Except for a single wet footprint. Child-sized. Leading from the back of the closet to where the floor drops away into darkness.

A hole. In the floor of the closet. Freshly opened. Going straight down. Into the basement. Into the well.

And from below, I hear Max's voice. Singing.

"Ring around the rosie, pocket full of posies, ashes, ashes, we all fall down."

He's in the well.

Benjamin took him into the well.

Twenty-Five

Chapter 25: All Hallows' Eve Begins

Sarah pov

The clock in the hallway chimed six times.

October thirty-first. Six PM.

Halloween had officially begun.

I stood in the parlor with my hand pressed against the cold window, watching the sun sink behind the skeletal trees. The Harvest Moon was rising. Blood-red. Swollen. Like something infected pushing through the skin of the sky.

"Sarah." Melissa touched my shoulder. "We need to finish the barricade."

I turned. Tucker Davis was nailing boards across the parlor door. Isaac Stone drew symbols on the floor with salt and iron filings. Father Gabriel sat in the corner, hands clasped, lips moving in silent prayer. His leg was still in a cast from when the house threw him down the stairs.

Lily sat on the couch. Too calm. Too still.

"Where's Max?" My voice cracked.

"Still upstairs," Melissa said. "I checked on him five minutes ago. He's sleeping."

"He shouldn't be sleeping." My hands were shaking. "Not in this house. Not today."

"Sarah, he's exhausted. He needs—"

The temperature dropped.

Not gradually. All at once.

My breath came out in white clouds. The windows frosted over in seconds. Patterns spread across the glass like veins. Like something alive was growing.

"It's starting," Isaac said. He didn't look up from his salt circle. "Right on schedule."

Tucker finished the last nail and stepped back. "That should hold."

"Should?" I stared at him. "We need better than should."

"Lady, I don't know what you want me to tell you." Tucker wiped sweat from his forehead despite the cold. "I've reinforced every entrance. If something gets through, it ain't gonna be physical."

A sound came from the walls.

Dripping.

Wet. Thick. Wrong.

I turned. The wallpaper was bleeding. Dark red stains spread from the seams, running down in rivulets. The floral pattern twisted. Changed. Became faces. Screaming mouths. Empty eyes.

"Oh God." Melissa backed away. "Oh God, oh God—"

"Don't look at it." Isaac grabbed her arm. "Don't give it your attention. That's what it wants."

"What *is* it?"

"The house is waking up." Isaac's voice was steady but his hands weren't. "Everything that's been sleeping. Every death. Every moment of suffering. It's all surfacing."

The portraits on the walls started moving.

Not like paintings coming to life in a fairy tale. Like something was trapped behind the canvas. Pushing. Bulging. The painted faces stretched and distorted. Their mouths opened too wide. Their eyes rolled back.

Then they screamed.

All of them. At once.

The sound was inhuman. Glass shattered. The chandelier swayed. I clapped my hands over my ears but it didn't help. The screaming was inside my skull.

Inside my bones.

Lily didn't move. She sat perfectly still, eyes closed, lips moving. Counting.

"Lily!" I ran to her. Grabbed her shoulders. "Lily, look at me!"

Her eyes opened. For a second—just a second—they weren't her eyes. They were black. Completely black. No iris. No white.

Then she blinked and they were normal again.

"It's okay, Mom." Her voice was too calm. "They're just afraid."

"Who's afraid?"

"Everyone who died here." She looked past me at the bleeding walls. "They've been trapped for so long. They don't know how to be quiet anymore."

Tucker crossed himself. "Jesus Christ."

"Won't help." Father Gabriel stood up, leaning on his cane. "I already tried. This house rejected God a long time ago."

"Then what do we do?" Melissa's voice was rising. "We just sit here and wait to die?"

"We wait for the right moment." Isaac finished the salt circle and stood. "Eleven fifty-nine. When we detonate the well. That's our window."

"That's six hours from now." I looked at each of them. "We have to survive six hours in here."

"Five hours and fifty-four minutes," Lily said quietly.

The lights went out.

Not all at once. One by one. Starting from the back of the house and moving forward. I heard each bulb burst. Pop. Pop. Pop. Glass raining down.

Then darkness.

Complete. Total. The kind of darkness that presses against your eyes.

"Flashlights!" Tucker's voice came from somewhere to my left. "I put flashlights in the—"

Something moved in the dark.

Not walked. Moved. Like water. Like smoke. I felt it pass by me. Cold. Wrong. Smelling like dirt and old coins.

A flashlight clicked on. Tucker's face appeared, ghostly and harsh in the beam. He swung it around the room.

The parlor wasn't empty anymore.

They stood around us. Dozens of them. Translucent. Flickering. Like candle flames about to go out.

Colonial women in long dresses, nooses around their necks. Their heads hung at wrong angles. Children in Victorian clothes, skin blue and bloated. Men in work clothes, missing limbs, covered in dried blood.

And more. So many more.

They stood perfectly still. Just watching.

"Don't move," Isaac whispered. "Stay inside the salt circle."

"We're not in the circle," Melissa said. "Sarah and Lily are by the couch. Tucker's by the door. You're the only one in the circle."

"Then get in. Now. Slowly."

I reached for Lily's hand. Her fingers were ice-cold.

"Can you walk?" I whispered.

She nodded.

We moved. One step. Two steps. The ghosts tracked us with their eyes. Empty. Hungry. Dead.

Tucker stayed frozen by the door. "I can't move."

"Yes, you can." Isaac held out his hand. "Walk toward me. Don't look at them."

"I can't feel my legs."

"That's the fear. Push through it."

Tucker took a shaking step. Then another. One of the ghosts moved with him. Matching his pace. A woman with a crushed skull. She opened her mouth. Black water poured out.

"Faster," Isaac said.

Tucker broke into a stumbling run. We all did. Converging on the salt circle. I pulled Lily in first. Then Melissa. Tucker crashed in after us. Father Gabriel was already there, cane raised like a weapon.

We huddled together. Six living people in a circle of salt, surrounded by the dead.

The ghosts pressed closer. Not crossing the line. But testing it. Reaching out with translucent fingers. Pulling back at the last second.

"How long will the salt hold?" Melissa asked.

"As long as they believe it will," Isaac said. "Salt doesn't have power on its own. It's symbolic. Protective. But if they stop believing—"

One of the ghosts stepped over the line.

A child. Maybe seven years old. Same age as Max. Same curly hair. Same gap in his front teeth.

Benjamin Kane.

"Hello, Sarah." His voice was wet. Like he was speaking underwater. "You have something that belongs to us."

I put Lily behind me. "Stay back."

"We don't want to hurt her." Benjamin tilted his head. "We just want what was promised."

"No one promised you anything."

"Father did." Benjamin looked sad. So impossibly sad. "He promised. Then he lied. Mother tried to save me. He hurt her. He hurt me. And now we're all stuck."

"I'm sorry that happened to you." My voice shook. "But Lily isn't part of this. She doesn't owe you anything."

"Everyone owes." More ghosts stepped over the salt line. The woman with the crushed skull. A man with a bullet hole in his forehead. A girl with her mouth sewn shut. "This house is built on debt. On blood. On broken promises."

Tucker pulled a gun from his jacket. "Back off."

"Bullets won't work," Isaac said.

"Yeah? Watch me." Tucker aimed at Benjamin and pulled the trigger.

The sound was deafening in the small room.

The bullet passed through Benjamin like he was made of smoke. It hit the wall behind him. The wall bled more. Dark. Thick. Spreading.

Benjamin smiled. "See? You can't hurt us. We're already dead."

"But you can hurt us," I said. "That's the point, isn't it?"

"We don't want to." Benjamin looked at Lily. "We want her to choose. Come to the well. Finish what Father started. End this."

"No." I grabbed Lily tighter. "Never."

The temperature dropped lower. My fingers were going numb. My lips felt like ice.

"Then you'll all die," Benjamin said simply. "At midnight. The house will fall. Everyone on Halloween Street will fall with it. Forty-seven people. Because of you."

"Because of your father." I spit the words. "Not me. Victor Kane broke the covenant. Victor Kane murdered your mother. This is his fault. Not ours."

"Father is here." Benjamin pointed to the doorway. "He wants to talk to you."

The air in the parlor changed.

Thickened. Pressed down. Like the house was holding its breath.

A figure appeared in the doorway. Tall. Broad-shouldered. Wearing a suit from the 1960s. His face was handsome except for the hole where his right temple should be. Brain matter still clung to the edges. Fresh. Wrong.

Victor Kane.

He looked at me with eyes that reflected nothing. "Hello, Sarah. I'm sorry we're meeting under these circumstances."

His voice was normal. Polite. Like we were at a dinner party.

That made it worse.

"Stay away from my daughter."

"I don't want to hurt her." Victor stepped into the room. The ghosts parted for him. "I want to help her. Help all of us. This has gone on long enough."

"You killed your wife." The words came out hard. Angry. "You murdered your son. You don't get to talk about helping anyone."

"I made a mistake." Victor looked at Benjamin. Something that might have been regret crossed his face. "I thought I could save him. I thought refusing the ritual would end the curse. I was wrong."

"So you killed him anyway."

"I gave him peace." Victor's voice didn't change. Still calm. Still polite. "He was terrified. Eleanor was hysterical. They were going to run. The Collectors would have hunted them down. Made it worse. I ended it quickly. Mercifully."

"Mercy." I laughed. It sounded insane even to me. "You call that mercy?"

"What would you call it?" Victor looked at me. Through me. "What will you do when midnight comes? When you have to choose between Lily and forty-seven innocent people? Will you sacrifice the many to save the one? Or will you be practical?"

"Don't listen to him," Father Gabriel said. "He's trying to justify his sin. Make you complicit."

"I'm trying to give her a choice." Victor spread his hands. "Something Eleanor never got. Something my son never got. I'm being generous."

"Where's Max?" The question burst out of me. "Where is he?"

Victor smiled. "Safe. For now."

"What did you do?"

"Exactly what I said. He's safe. Comfortable. Not afraid." Victor took another step closer. "I can keep him that way. Or I can let him go. It depends on you."

My heart was slamming against my ribs. "Let me see him."

"After we make our arrangement."

"No arrangement. Give me my son back."

"Give me your daughter first."

The room went silent except for the sound of blood dripping from the walls. Drip. Drip. Drip.

"You're insane," Melissa said. "You're asking her to kill her own child."

"I'm asking her to make an exchange." Victor looked at Lily. "One child for another. One sacrifice for forty-seven lives. It's simple math."

"It's evil," Father Gabriel said.

"It's necessary." Victor's voice finally changed. Harder. Colder. "Do you think I wanted this? Do you think I enjoyed putting a gun to my head after drowning my son? I did what had to be done. Now it's her turn."

"No." I moved between Victor and Lily. "You don't touch her."

"Then Max stays where he is."

"Where? Tell me where!"

"The well." Victor smiled. "Where else? Where all the children go eventually. He's at the bottom. In the water. With Benjamin. They're playing together. Becoming friends."

My vision went red. I lunged at him. My hands passed through smoke and cold air. I stumbled. Nearly fell.

Tucker caught me. "Sarah, don't. He's baiting you."

"He has Max." I was screaming now. Couldn't stop. "He has my son in that well!"

"Not yet," Victor said. "Max is still alive. Still breathing. But the water is rising. Slowly. Inch by inch. At midnight, it'll reach his mouth. Then his nose. Then..."

He didn't finish. Didn't need to.

"You bring him up right now." My voice broke. "Please. Please, he's seven years old."

"So was Benjamin." Victor's face was stone. "Bring me Lily. I bring you Max. Simple trade."

"Why?" Tears were running down my face. "Why do you need her?"

"Because she looks like Eleanor." Victor's eyes went distant. "Same eyes. Same spirit. I see my wife in her. The ritual requires it. A mother's blood or a mother's reflection. Lily is close enough."

"This is insane."

"This is survival." Victor leaned closer. "You have until midnight. Six hours. Decide which child you love more."

"I love them both!"

"Then both die." Victor started to fade. Becoming translucent. "Choose, Sarah. The well is waiting. Max is waiting. Every second you waste, the water rises higher."

"Wait!" I screamed. "Wait, don't go!"

But he was already gone. Just smoke. Just cold air.

The other ghosts faded with him. One by one. Until we were alone in the parlor again. Just the six of us.

The walls stopped bleeding. The portraits went still. The temperature rose a few degrees.

Like the house was giving us a moment to breathe. To think. To decide.

Lily grabbed my hand. "Mom."

I looked at her. Really looked. Her eyes were red. She'd been crying silently while I screamed at Victor.

"I'll go," she whispered. "If it saves Max, I'll go."

"No."

"Mom—"

"No." I pulled her against my chest. Held her so tight. "No. Never. Do you understand me? Never."

"But Max—"

"We'll get Max." I looked at the others. "We're getting him out of that well right now."

"Sarah, it's a trap," Isaac said. "Victor wants you panicking. Making emotional decisions."

"My son is drowning."

"Maybe. Maybe not. We can't trust anything Victor says."

"We can't risk it." I pulled away from Lily. "Tucker, how much explosive did you bring?"

"Enough to blow the well. Not enough to blow it and fight off an army of ghosts."

"Then we make a choice." I looked at each of them. "We go now. We get Max. We blow the well before midnight."

"What about the plan?" Melissa grabbed my arm. "We need to wait until eleven fifty-nine. That's when the veil is thinnest. That's when the explosion will actually work."

"My son will be dead by eleven fifty-nine."

"You don't know that. Victor could be lying."

"And if he's not?" I pulled my arm free. "If Max is really down there? If the water is really rising? You want me to wait six hours?"

Melissa opened her mouth. Closed it. She didn't have an answer.

"I'll go with you," Tucker said quietly. "I can move fast. Set the charges. Get the boy. Get out."

"It's suicide," Isaac said. "The house won't let you. Not yet. It's too early."

"Then I die trying." I looked at him. "What would you do? If it was your child?"

Isaac was quiet for a long moment. Then: "I'd go."

"So we go." I turned to Father Gabriel. "Can you keep Lily safe? Here in

276

the circle?"

"I'll die before I let them take her."

"That's what I'm afraid of." I knelt in front of Lily. Took her face in my hands. "Stay here. Stay in the circle. Don't leave no matter what you hear. Understand?"

"Mom, you can't go down there alone."

"I'm not alone. Tucker's with me."

"Tucker can't fight ghosts."

"I'll fight." I kissed her forehead. "I'll fight the dead if I have to. Just stay here. Stay safe."

"Promise you'll come back."

I looked into her eyes. Wanted to promise. Wanted to lie. But I couldn't.

"I promise I'll try."

That was the best I could do.

Tucker moved to the barricaded door. Started pulling nails. The boards came away one by one. He was moving too fast. Hands shaking. Making noise.

The house heard.

The knocking started.

Not from the door. From everywhere. The walls. The ceiling. The floor. Even the furniture. Everything knocked. Three beats. Pause. Three beats. Pause.

Knock. Knock. Knock.

Knock. Knock. Knock.

Over and over. Endless. Deafening.

"They know we're leaving the circle," Isaac shouted over the noise. "They're coming back."

The temperature plummeted again. My breath fogged. The windows frosted completely opaque.

Shadows moved behind the ice. Dozens of them. Hundreds. All the dead of Halloween Street. All the victims. All the angry ghosts.

They pressed against the windows. Against the walls. The house groaned under their weight.

Tucker ripped the last board away. "Door's open. We go now or never."

I looked back at Lily one more time. She was crying. Silent tears running down her face.

"I love you," I said.

"I love you too."

Then I turned and ran.

Tucker ran with me. Out of the parlor. Into the hallway. The knocking followed. The walls knocked. The floor knocked. Pictures jumped on their hooks.

The basement door stood open at the end of the hall.

Dark. Waiting. Like a mouth.

"Subtle," Tucker muttered.

We ran toward it. Thirty feet. Twenty feet. Ten.

The door slammed shut.

Tucker didn't slow down. He hit it with his shoulder. It didn't budge. He tried again. Nothing.

"Locked."

"Locked or held?"

"Does it matter?" He stepped back. Raised his boot. Kicked hard. The door shuddered but held.

Behind us, ghosts materialized. Filling the hallway. Blocking the path back to the parlor. They didn't speak. Just stood there. Watching. Waiting.

Judging.

Tucker kicked again. The wood splintered. One more kick and it would give.

The lights in the hallway went out.

Darkness. Complete. Total.

Then sounds.

Wet breathing. Close. Right behind my ear.

Small hands touched my back. My arms. My hair. Children's hands. Cold. Wrong.

"Sarah." Benjamin's voice in the dark. "Father is angry. You left the circle. You broke the rules."

"There are no rules," I said. My voice shook. "This isn't a game."

"Everything is a game." Benjamin giggled. It sounded like drowning. "And you're losing."

Tucker kicked the door one final time. It exploded inward. Fresh darkness beyond. Basement darkness.

"Go!" Tucker shoved me forward.

I stumbled through. He came after me. The door slammed behind us.

We were in the basement.

Alone with the well.

And something was already climbing out of it.

Something that looked like Max but moved wrong. Climbed wrong. Bent wrong.

It smiled at me with Max's face. "Mommy. You came."

But the voice wasn't Max's voice.

And I knew—God help me, I knew—this was what Victor had meant.

I'd made my choice.

And I'd chosen wrong.

Twenty-Six

Chapter 26: Into the Well

⦵⦵⦵

Sarah pov

"No."

The word came out harder than I meant it. Victor Kane's ghost stood in the center of the parlor, his face half-shadow, half-rot. Behind him, the walls bled. The portraits screamed. And somewhere below us, Max was drowning.

"Give me the girl," Victor said again. His voice sounded like it was coming from underwater. "I'll return the boy. That's the deal, Sarah. That's always been the deal."

"I said no." My hands were shaking. I gripped the iron poker Tucker had given me. "You're not getting either of them."

Victor's smile stretched too wide. "Then you lose both."

"Sarah." That was Melissa, her voice thin with fear. She stood pressed against the wall, as far from the ghosts as she could get. "Maybe we should—"

"No." I didn't look at her. Couldn't. "We're going down there. We're getting Max. And then we're ending this."

"The basement is sealed," Isaac said. He had chalk dust on his hands from the protective circles. His eyes were too wide. "The door won't—"

"Then we break the door." I turned to Tucker. "You have the explosives?"

"Yeah, but—"

"Can you blow the basement door?"

Tucker's jaw worked. He was scared. We were all scared. But he nodded. "Small charge. Enough to crack the lock mechanism."

"Do it."

"Sarah, wait." Father Gabriel leaned heavy on his cane. The fall down the stairs had broken more than his leg. "If we go down there, into the well itself... we might not come back up."

"Max is down there."

"Max might already be—"

"Don't." The word came out like a slap. "Don't say it. Don't even think it."

Lily grabbed my hand. Her fingers were ice cold. "Mom. I can hear him. He's singing."

We all stopped. Listened.

And then I heard it too. Faint. Distant. A child's voice drifting up through the floorboards.

"Ring around the rosie, pocket full of posies..."

Max's voice.

"Move." I pushed past Isaac, past the chalk circles, past Father Gabriel. "Tucker. The door. Now."

We ran. All of us except Father Gabriel, who couldn't keep up. Down the hallway toward the kitchen, where the basement door stood like a mouth. It was different now. Covered in symbols I didn't recognize. Black marks that looked like they were burned into the wood.

And it was cold. So cold I could see my breath.

"Back up," Tucker said. He was already pulling something from his pack. Something that looked like clay wrapped in wire. "I mean way back. This is gonna be loud."

We pressed ourselves against the far wall. Tucker worked fast, his hands steady despite everything. He pressed the explosive against the lock, ran a wire back to where we stood.

"Cover your ears," he said.

Then he twisted something. Sparked something.

The explosion wasn't loud. It was a crack, sharp and clean. The door shuddered. The lock mechanism shattered. And the door swung open.

The smell hit first. Rot and wet earth and something else. Something like old meat left in the sun.

"Jesus," Melissa whispered.

"It's okay." I didn't know who I was trying to convince. "It's okay. We go down, we get Max, we come right back up."

"And set the charges," Tucker said. "Don't forget. We blow the well at eleven fifty-nine."

I checked my phone. Dead. Had been for hours.

"What time is it?"

Isaac looked at his watch. It was an old wind-up, the only kind that still worked in the house. "Eleven thirty-two."

Twenty-seven minutes.

"Then we move fast." I grabbed the flashlight from Tucker's pack. "Melissa, you stay with Lily. Don't let her—"

"I'm coming." Lily's voice was small but firm. "Max is my brother."

"Lily—"

"He went down there because of me. Because I'm the one they want. I'm coming."

I looked at her. Really looked. She was ten years old. She should've been trick-or-treating. Should've been laughing with friends, eating too much candy, scared of nothing worse than Halloween decorations.

Instead she was standing in a cursed house, offering to walk into a well full of ghosts.

"Stay behind me," I said. "Don't let go of my hand. If I say run, you run. Understand?"

She nodded.

"Tucker, you're with me. We need those charges set. Isaac, you do… whatever it is you do. Protective circles or whatever. Melissa, Father Gabriel—"

"We'll guard the door," Melissa said. She pulled Lily close, kissed her forehead. "You bring Max back."

"I will."

The basement stairs were steep. Narrow. And they shouldn't have been this dark. Even with the flashlight, the darkness seemed to swallow the beam. Like the light couldn't quite reach.

"There's something wrong with the air," Tucker said behind me. "It's too thick."

He was right. Breathing felt like drowning.

We reached the bottom. The basement was bigger than I remembered. The ceiling stretched up impossibly high. And at the center, the well.

The grate was completely gone now. Just a circular opening in the floor, maybe three feet across. And from inside—

"Ring around the rosie..."

"Max!" I ran to the edge, dropped to my knees. "Max, baby, I'm here!"

"Mom?"

His voice echoed up from below. Sounded so far away.

"I'm coming down! Just hold on!"

I shone the flashlight into the well. The beam caught water maybe twenty feet down. Black water. Still as glass. And in the center, a small shape.

Max.

He was standing in the water, neck-deep. His face was pale. Too pale. And he wasn't alone.

Standing next to him, hand on his shoulder, was a boy in old-fashioned clothes. Benjamin Kane.

"Mom, I can't move," Max said. "My feet are stuck."

"We're coming!" I turned to Tucker. "Do you have rope?"

"Yeah, but—" He was staring into the well. "Sarah. That water. It's not right."

"What do you mean?"

"The well was sealed. Been sealed for years. There shouldn't be water."

"I don't care what should or shouldn't be. My son is—"

"Sarah." Isaac's voice was sharp. He was setting up symbols around the well's edge, working fast. "That's not water."

I looked again. The flashlight beam caught the surface. It wasn't reflecting right. It was too dark. Too thick.

And then I saw them.

Beneath Max. Beneath the surface. Faces. Dozens of faces, pressed up against the underside of the water like it was glass. Mouths open. Eyes empty.

The mass grave.

"Oh God," I whispered.

"The well connects to it." Isaac's hands were shaking as he drew symbols. "It always has. That's how they performed the ritual. They lowered the sacrifices down, and the dead... they pulled them under."

"Then we pull him up."

"It won't let go easily."

"I don't care."

Tucker was already tying rope around my waist. "You're not going down there alone."

"Yes, I am."

"Sarah—"

"You need to set the charges. Isaac needs to finish his circles. I need to get Max. That's how this works."

"Mom." Lily was next to me suddenly. I hadn't heard her come down the stairs. "Let me help."

"No. Absolutely not."

"Benjamin is down there. He'll listen to me."

"Lily, no—"

"Please." Her eyes were huge. Terrified but determined. "He's my brother."

I pulled her close. Kissed her hair. She smelled like home. Like safety. Like everything I was trying to protect.

"You stay here," I said. "You call down to Benjamin. Tell him to let Max go. Can you do that?"

She nodded.

Tucker checked the rope twice. Three times. "You feel three tugs, we pull you up. No matter what. Understand?"

"Understand."

"Sarah." Melissa was at the bottom of the stairs, her face pale. "Please be careful."

"I will."

I gripped the rope. Sat on the edge of the well. My legs dangled into darkness.

"I'm coming, Max!"

Then I pushed off.

The descent felt wrong immediately. The walls of the well were stone, slick with something that wasn't water. The air grew colder with every foot. My flashlight flickered.

"Mom!" Max's voice. Closer now.

"Almost there, baby!"

Twenty feet shouldn't have taken this long. But the well kept going. The rope kept playing out. And the darkness kept pressing in.

Finally, my feet hit water.

Except it wasn't water.

It was cold. Thick. It grabbed at my legs like hands. I gasped, nearly dropped the flashlight.

"Max?"

"Here!"

I swung the light. There. Three feet away. Max was standing in the black liquid, eyes wide with terror. Benjamin's ghost stood next to him, transparent in the flashlight beam.

I waded toward them. Each step was agony. The liquid pulled at me, tried to drag me down. Beneath the surface, those faces pressed closer. Mouths opening and closing. Silent screams.

"Max, grab my hand!"

He reached out. Our fingers touched.

And then something pulled him under.

"MAX!"

He vanished beneath the surface. Completely gone.

I didn't think. Didn't hesitate. I dove.

The liquid closed over my head. It wasn't like drowning in water. It was like drowning in memories. In pain. In centuries of death.

I saw Eleanor Kane running through the house, Victor chasing her with a gun.

I saw Benjamin screaming as his father held him under in a bathtub.

I saw the mass grave, bodies piled on bodies, hanged and forgotten.

I saw every sacrifice the Collectors ever made, every child they threw down this well, every scream that never reached the surface.

But I also saw Max.

He was sinking. Hands pulling him down. Dead hands. Dozens of them.

I kicked hard, swam deeper than should have been possible. My lungs burned. My vision darkened.

I grabbed Max's arm.

The hands pulled harder.

No.

I pulled harder.

Something in the darkness shifted. The pressure increased. It felt like the well was collapsing, like we'd be crushed.

Then Benjamin's ghost appeared. He was glowing faintly, the only light in the darkness. He touched the hands pulling Max.

And they let go.

I yanked Max up, kicked toward the surface. My chest was screaming. Black spots crowded my vision.

We broke the surface gasping.

"Mom!"

"I've got you! I've got you!"

Tucker was already pulling on the rope. We rose fast, water streaming off us. Except it wasn't water. It was black and thick and it evaporated like smoke.

Hands grabbed me, pulled me over the edge. I collapsed on the basement floor, Max in my arms.

"He's freezing!" Melissa threw a blanket over us. "Sarah, he's not breathing right!"

Max coughed. Black liquid spilled from his mouth. Then he sucked in air, huge gasping breaths.

"It's okay," I said, holding him so tight it probably hurt. "You're okay. You're safe."

"Charges are set." Tucker was working fast, placing clay-like lumps around the well's edge. "Timer's armed. We have fifteen minutes."

Isaac finished his protective circle. "This should contain the blast. Should keep the spirits from escaping when the well ruptures."

"Should?" Melissa's voice rose. "What do you mean should?"

"I mean I've never blown up a cursed well before!"

"Everyone stop!" Father Gabriel shouted from the stairs. "Something's wrong!"

We all froze.

"What?" I asked.

"Melissa. Come here."

Melissa frowned. "Why?"

"Just come here. Into the light."

She walked toward the stairs. Into the glow from the flashlights.

And I saw it.

Her shadow was wrong.

It didn't match her movements. When she stepped forward, it moved sideways. When she raised her hand, the shadow reached down.

"Oh no," Isaac whispered. "Oh no no no—"

"What?" Melissa looked confused. "What's wrong?"

"How long?" Father Gabriel's voice was shaking. "How long have you been down here?"

"I just came down. I wanted to make sure Sarah—"

"No." I stood slowly, keeping Max behind me. "You didn't come down. You stayed upstairs. With Father Gabriel."

Melissa's face went blank. Then she smiled.

It wasn't her smile.

"Clever," she said. But the voice was wrong. Layered. Multiple voices speaking at once.

"When?" I asked. My heart was hammering. "When did you take her?"

"When you weren't looking." The thing wearing Melissa's face tilted its head. "When you were so focused on the boy. When the sister thought she was safe upstairs. Just for a moment. That's all I needed."

The Woman in White. She'd possessed Melissa.

"Where is she?" I took a step forward. "Where's my sister?"

"Oh, she's here. Watching. Screaming. But I'm in control now."

Tucker raised something. I realized it was a gun. "Let her go."

"Or what? You'll shoot? This is her body. You kill me, you kill her."

"Sarah." Isaac's voice was urgent. "The circle. Get everyone inside the protective circle. Now."

I grabbed Max, pushed him toward Isaac. "Lily, go!"

But Lily wasn't moving. She was staring at possessed-Melissa with wide eyes.

"Lily, run!"

"There you are." The Woman in White's smile widened. "The one they chose. The one who looks like Eleanor. Do you know why you look like her, child?"

"Don't listen!" I shouted.

"Because you're hers. Reborn. Same soul. Same sacrifice."

"That's not true," Lily said, but her voice shook.

"It is. And you know what that means?" Possessed-Melissa took a step forward. "It means you belong in the well. Just like she did."

She lunged.

Not at me. At Lily.

I threw myself between them, but possessed-Melissa was fast. Impossibly fast. She grabbed Lily by the arms, lifted her like she weighed nothing.

"No!" I grabbed Melissa's wrist. Her skin was ice cold.

"The ritual completes tonight!" The Woman in White's voice boomed from Melissa's mouth. "With or without your permission!"

She threw me aside. I hit the wall hard, vision exploding into stars.

When I could see again, possessed-Melissa was carrying Lily toward the well.

Lily was screaming.

Tucker fired. The bullet went wide. Isaac was chanting something, but possessed-Melissa walked right through his protective circle like it wasn't there.

"Tucker!" I gasped. "The detonator!"

"We have twelve minutes!"

"Blow it now!"

"We're too close! We'll die!"

"BLOW IT!"

Tucker's face went white. Then he reached for the detonator.

And possessed-Melissa smiled.

She dangled Lily over the well's edge. One hand gripping my daughter's wrist. Lily's feet kicked at empty air.

"Do it," the Woman in White said. "Blow the well. But I'll drop her first. She falls, she dies. She dies, the curse spreads. Everyone on this street. Everyone in this town. All dead by dawn."

"Mom!" Lily was crying. "Mom, please!"

I couldn't move. Couldn't breathe.

Tucker's hand hovered over the detonator.

Max was screaming.

And possessed-Melissa's grip on Lily started to loosen.

"Choose," the Woman in White whispered. "Save her and doom the town. Or blow the well and watch your daughter die."

"There has to be another way," I said. "Please. Please, there has to be—"

"There isn't. There never was. The curse always wins."

Lily's wrist slipped an inch in possessed-Melissa's grip.

"I'm sorry, Sarah," Tucker said.

And he pressed the button.

Twenty-Seven

Chapter 27: Betrayal and Sacrifice

Sarah pov

Melissa's hand closed around Lily's wrist.

"No—"

I lunged forward but Tucker grabbed my shoulder. His grip was iron. His voice cut through the chaos.

"Sarah, wait. Look at her eyes."

I looked.

Melissa's eyes were wrong. Clouded white. Milky. Like cataracts had grown over them in seconds. Her mouth stretched too wide. Her neck bent at an angle that should have hurt.

"That's not your sister anymore," Tucker said.

"Melissa—" My voice cracked. "Mel, I know you're in there—"

The thing wearing my sister's face laughed. The sound came from somewhere deep. Somewhere that wasn't her throat.

"Little Sarah," it said. Melissa's voice but layered with something else. Something ancient and bitter. "Always the stubborn one. Always questioning. That's why Eleanor liked you."

"Julia." Father Gabriel stepped forward. His leg brace scraped against concrete. "Julia Kane, I command you in the name of—"

"Save your breath, priest." Possessed-Melissa dragged Lily toward the well. My daughter fought but Julia was stronger. "Your God has no power here. This ground rejected Him three centuries ago."

The basement had become a war zone. Ghosts pressed against Isaac's salt circle. The air was so cold my breath came out in clouds. The knocking came from everywhere. Walls. Ceiling. Inside my own skull.

Max was still in the well. Neck-deep in that black water. Singing.

"Ring around the rosie, pocket full of posies, ashes, ashes, we all fall down." His voice was small. Distant. Wrong.

"Tucker." I grabbed his arm. "Get Melissa away from Lily. I don't care how."

"She's possessed by—"

"I know what she is. Stop her."

Tucker moved. He was fast for a man his size. Former military. He closed the distance in three strides and wrapped his arms around Melissa from behind.

She snarled. Actually snarled. Her head whipped back and connected with Tucker's nose. Blood sprayed. He didn't let go.

"Father!" Tucker shouted. "Now would be good!"

Gabriel limped forward. His hands shook as he pulled out his Bible. The pages were scorched from the last exorcism attempt. Half the words were burned away.

"In the name of the Father—"

"Your father abandoned you," Julia said through Melissa's mouth. "Just like Victor abandoned his son. Just like every man in this town abandoned their children to the earth."

"—and of the Son—"

Melissa's body convulsed. Her spine arched backward. Bones cracked. Tucker held on but I could see the strain in his face.

"—and of the Holy Spirit—"

"There is no spirit here!" Julia shrieked. "Only debt! Only payment! Only the collection that must be made!"

Lily broke free. She stumbled away from the well. I caught her. Pulled her behind me.

"Mom." Her voice was so small. "Mom, Aunt Melissa is—"

"I know, baby. I know."

Isaac was at the well's edge. Setting up the explosives. His hands moved fast. Professional. But I could see the fear in every movement.

"How long?" I asked.

"Five minutes to set the charges. Then we have thirty seconds to clear the blast zone."

"We don't have five minutes."

"Then we'll have four."

The ghosts pressed closer. The salt circle was holding but barely. I could see cracks forming in the lines. Victor Kane stood at the front of the dead crowd. His face was a ruin. Half his skull missing from the gunshot. He smiled with broken teeth.

"Sarah Brennan," he said. "You look so much like her. Did you know that? Eleanor had your eyes."

"Fuck you."

"Such language. And in front of your daughter." He tilted his head. "But I understand. You're frightened. Eleanor was frightened too. Right up until the end."

I wanted to run at him. Wanted to tear him apart. But he was already dead. Had been dead for sixty-two years.

Tucker slammed Melissa against the wall. She laughed. Blood ran from her nose from the impact but she just laughed and laughed.

"You can't stop this," Julia said. "The ritual must complete. The girl goes into the well. The debt is paid. The cycle continues."

"The cycle ends tonight," Gabriel said. He pressed the Bible against Melissa's forehead.

She screamed.

The sound split the air. Every ghost in the basement recoiled. Even Victor stepped back. The scream wasn't human. It was the sound of metal scraping bone. Of ice cracking. Of something ancient and furious being denied.

"I will not leave this vessel!" Julia shrieked. "I will not return to the dark! I will not—"

"Julia Kane, I cast you out!"

Black smoke poured from Melissa's mouth. It hung in the air. Writhing. Taking shape. For a moment I saw her. Julia. An old woman with hate-filled eyes and a mouth full of accusations.

"You don't understand," Julia's smoke-form said. "I'm trying to save you. The ritual is the only way. Without it, the street falls. Everyone dies. I've seen it happen. I've watched it almost happen. You think you're being brave but you're condemning forty-seven people to—"

The smoke dispersed.

Melissa collapsed. Tucker caught her before she hit the ground.

"Mel?" I dropped beside her. Touched her face. "Melissa, can you hear me?"

Her eyes were normal. Brown. Clear. Terrified.

"Sarah?" She grabbed my arm. "What—what happened? Why am I—"

"Later. Right now we need to—"

Max's singing stopped.

The silence was worse than the sound.

I spun toward the well. Max was gone. The black water was still. Empty. Like he'd never been there at all.

"No. No no no—"

I ran for the well. Isaac grabbed me.

"Sarah, don't! The charges are set. If you go down there—"

"My son is down there!"

"And you'll die if you jump!"

"Then I die!"

I shoved him off. Ran to the well's edge. The rope Tucker had secured earlier still hung there. Disappearing into the black.

Lily screamed behind me. "Mom, don't! Please don't leave me!"

I looked back. My daughter. Ten years old. Eyes huge with terror. Melissa was barely conscious. Tucker's nose was broken. Gabriel could barely stand. Isaac was surrounded by equipment that might explode.

And Max was in the well.

"Lily." I made my voice steady. "I'm coming back. I promise."

"You can't promise that."

"I'm your mother. I can promise anything."

I grabbed the rope. It was slick. Cold. Wet with something that wasn't water. I wrapped it around my wrist. Once. Twice. Tight enough to hurt.

"Sarah, wait—" Tucker started forward.

"Keep them safe," I said. "If I'm not back in three minutes, blow the charges."

"We'll wait."

"No. You won't." I met his eyes. "Three minutes. Then end this."

I dropped over the edge.

The fall was immediate and wrong. Gravity pulled but the air resisted. Like falling through syrup. Through gelatin. Through something thick and alive that didn't want me passing through.

The rope burned my hands. I held on.

Descended.

The walls of the well were stone. Ancient stone. Carved with symbols that hurt to look at. They moved. Shifted. Reformed themselves into words. Names. Dates. All the people who'd died here. All the children who'd been thrown into the dark.

Mary Whitmore, 1897. Age 12.

Thomas Ashton, 1904. Age 9.

Catherine Morrison, 1911. Age 14.

Samuel Wu, 1918. Age 8.

On and on. Dozens of names. Generations of sacrifice. Carved into stone by hands that wanted the truth remembered even if throats couldn't speak it.

The temperature dropped. My breath frosted. The rope was so cold it stuck to my palms. I kept descending.

Above me, voices. Muffled. Distant.

Lily screaming my name.

Tucker shouting orders.

Gabriel praying.

I descended.

The walls began to change. Stone became dirt. Dirt became something else. Something organic. Soft. Almost like flesh. I didn't look too close. Didn't let myself think about what I was touching.

The rope ended.

I hung there. Feet dangling in open air. Below me was black. Complete black. The kind of dark that felt intentional. Hungry.

"Max!" My voice echoed. "Max, baby, where are you!"

Nothing.

Then—

"Mommy?"

His voice came from below. From the dark. Small and scared and so very far away.

I let go of the rope.

Fell.

Fell forever.

Fell through time.

Fell through memory.

I hit water. Except it wasn't water. It was cold and thick and it burned my skin. I went under. Opened my eyes even though every instinct screamed not to.

I saw them.

Bodies. Dozens of bodies. Floating. Suspended. Children in old-fashioned clothes. Their eyes were open. Their mouths were open. Screaming silently in the dark.

I kicked for the surface. Broke through. Gasped.

I was in a chamber. Underground. Vast. The walls were dirt and roots and bone. The ceiling was lost in shadow. And in the center of it all was a pile of stones. An altar. And on the altar—

Max.

He sat there. Cross-legged. Calm. His clothes were soaked. His lips were blue. But he was smiling.

"Mommy came," he said. "I told Ben you would. I told him you always come."

"Max, baby, we need to go—"

"Not yet. You have to see first. You have to understand."

The air rippled.

The chamber changed.

Suddenly I was somewhere else. Same place but different time. The chamber was lit with lanterns. The altar was clean. And standing around it were men in suits. Old suits. 1890s suits. Seven men. Seven families.

The Collectors.

I watched them bring in a girl. She couldn't have been more than thirteen. Crying. Begging. They tied her to the altar. One of the men stepped forward with a knife.

"No—" I tried to scream but no sound came out.

I wasn't really there. This was memory. The land's memory. Showing me.

The man with the knife spoke. "For the prosperity of our families. For the security of our town. For the continuation of the covenant. We offer this sacrifice."

He cut her throat.

The girl stopped moving.

The men waited.

Nothing happened.

One of them checked for a pulse. Shook his head.

"It didn't work," another said. "She was supposed to be the seventh. Seven families. Seven children. The medium said—"

"The medium lied."

They stared at the dead girl. At what they'd done.

Finally, the eldest spoke. "We can't tell anyone. If word gets out we murdered—"

"Then we don't tell anyone. We bury her. We say she ran away. We continue the ritual every seven years and tell everyone it's working. Make them believe the curse is real."

"But there's no curse."

"There will be. After tonight." The eldest man smiled. It was a horrible smile. "We've created our own curse. We've soaked this ground in innocent blood. That has power. We'll convince the town it was necessary. We'll make them complicit. And anyone who questions it—"

He didn't finish. Didn't need to.

They'd killed one child and decided to kill more to cover up the first murder.

The ritual had never been about appeasing spirits. It had been about maintaining power through fear and shared guilt.

The vision dissolved.

The chamber returned to darkness. To the present. To my son sitting on that altar surrounded by the bones of lies.

"Do you see now?" A woman's voice. Gentle. Sad.

Eleanor Kane stepped out of the shadows.

She looked different from the ghost I'd seen before. More solid. More human. Her dress was torn. Dirty. Her hair hung in wet tangles. But her face was kind.

"They lied to us all," Eleanor said. "For over a century. There was no ancient curse. No covenant with the dead. Just men who killed a child and built an empire of terror to hide their crime."

"Then why—" My voice shook. "Why the hauntings? Why the ghosts? Why did Benjamin drown?"

"Because the land remembers." Eleanor moved closer. I could see the marks on her throat. Where Victor's hands had been. "So much innocent blood spilled here. So much pain. It soaked into the earth. Made the ground sick. Made it hungry. The curse they pretended to appease became real through their own cruelty."

"Victor knew?"

"Victor's grandfather was one of the seven original men. Victor grew up knowing the ritual was a lie. But he also grew up knowing what happened to people who tried to stop it. He watched his own father murdered when he tried to confess. Made to look like suicide." Eleanor's ghost knelt beside Max. Touched his hair with transparent fingers. "When our turn came, Victor said we had to do it. Had to kill Benjamin. To keep the family safe. To maintain the lie."

"But you tried to run."

"I tried to save my boy." Tears ran down Eleanor's ghost face. "I packed our bags. Made it as far as the car. Victor caught us. Dragged us back inside. He held Benjamin under the well water until he stopped struggling. Then he came for me."

I felt sick. "The sewing of mouths—"

"So I couldn't scream the truth. Even in death." Eleanor looked at me. "But Benjamin found a way. He's been trying to warn every family that moved in. Trying to show them it was all a lie. That if they just refused to participate, the cycle would break."

"But the Woman in White—"

"Is real. She's the accumulated rage of every child murdered here. Every lie told. Every truth silenced. She doesn't want sacrifice. She wants acknowledgment. She wants someone to say it out loud. To name the sin."

Max stirred on the altar. His eyes focused on me.

"Mommy, Eleanor showed me everything. The Collectors made it all up. They're the monsters. Not the ghosts."

I climbed onto the altar. Pulled Max into my arms. He was so cold. Too cold.

"We're leaving, baby. Right now."

"You have to tell people," Eleanor said. "You have to make them believe. The only way to end this is to expose the truth. Let the light in."

"How? Who's going to believe—"

"Isaac's explosives will destroy the well. But they'll also expose the chamber. The bodies. The evidence. Everything the Collectors tried to hide for 127 years." Eleanor smiled. It was heartbreaking. "Truth is the only weapon against a lie."

A rumble above us. The rope was being pulled up. Fast.

Tucker's voice echoed down. Distant. Urgent.

"Sarah! Time's up! Thirty seconds!"

The explosives.

Eleanor's ghost began to fade. "Go. Save your children. End this."

"Wait—" I grabbed for her but my hand passed through. "Will you—will you find peace?"

"When the truth comes out, yes. When Benjamin and I are finally laid to rest in honest ground." She was almost gone. Just a shimmer. "Tell them we're not monsters. Tell them we're just the ones who said no."

She vanished.

The chamber shook. Dust rained from the ceiling. Roots burst through the walls. The altar cracked beneath us.

"Max, hold on to me!"

He wrapped his arms around my neck. His legs around my waist. He weighed nothing. Was he even really here? Was he already—

No. I felt his heartbeat against my chest. Faint but there.

The rope was gone. The well shaft above was collapsing. We were trapped in an underground chamber with thirty seconds before it exploded.

"Mommy, I'm scared."

"Me too, baby. Me too."

The walls split open. Black water poured through. The same water from the well. Rising fast. Already at my ankles. My knees. My waist.

I looked up. The ceiling was falling. Stone and dirt and the bones of murdered children raining down.

"Close your eyes, Max!"

He buried his face in my neck.

The water rose to my chest. My shoulders. My chin.

I took a breath. The last breath.

The water closed over our heads.

And everything went dark.

Then—light. Blinding white light. Someone grabbed my arm. Pulled. Hard. I held Max tighter. We were moving. Flying. Being dragged upward through collapsing earth and impossible space.

I opened my eyes.

Lily's face. Inches from mine. Her hand locked around my wrist. She was screaming. Pulling with strength that shouldn't exist in a ten-year-old.

"I WON'T LET YOU GO!" she shrieked. "MOM, I WON'T LET YOU DIE!"

Behind her, Tucker and Melissa grabbed Lily. Used her as an anchor. Pulled all three of us up. Up through the well shaft. Up past the collapsing walls. Up toward the basement.

We broke the surface just as the explosives detonated.

The blast threw us backward. The well imploded. The floor cracked. The entire basement caved in on itself. Stone and earth and 330 years of lies folding inward like a mouth closing.

Tucker covered us with his body as debris rained down.

Then silence.

I opened my eyes.

We were in the parlor. I didn't remember getting there. Tucker must have carried us. Lily was crying. Max wasn't moving in my arms.

"Max? Baby?" I shook him. "Max, wake up—"

Gabriel pushed me aside. Put his ear to Max's chest. Checked his pulse.

"He's breathing. Faint. But breathing."

Melissa wrapped a blanket around Max. Around me. I was soaking wet. Freezing. Shaking so hard my teeth rattled.

"Did we—" I couldn't form words. "Is it—"

"The well's destroyed," Isaac said. He was covered in dust. Bleeding from a cut on his forehead. "The chamber beneath collapsed. Nothing could survive that."

"The ghosts?"

"Gone."

I looked around the parlor. Empty. No more spectral figures. No more knocking. No more cold spots. The house felt... normal. Dead. Just a building.

"We did it," Tucker said. "We actually fucking did it."

Melissa hugged me. Lily pressed against my side. Max stirred in my arms. His eyes opened.

"Mommy?"

"I'm here, baby."

"Did Eleanor—did she—"

"She's free now. They all are."

Max smiled. Closed his eyes. Went to sleep. Real sleep. Not possession. Not influence. Just exhaustion.

I held him and cried.

We'd survived.

Then I heard it.

A car. Outside. Multiple cars. Doors slamming.

Voices.

Angry voices.

I stood. Walked to the window. Looked out at Halloween Street.

Forty-seven people stood in the road. Every resident of the street. Led by Hannah—no, Julia Kane. But Julia was supposed to be dead. We'd seen her ghost. She'd been exorcised.

Unless that had been a lie too.

Julia's face twisted with rage. Behind her, people held torches. Actually held torches like we were in some Victorian nightmare.

"They destroyed the well!" Julia shouted. "They've doomed us all! The curse will take the entire street now! We have to complete the ritual before midnight or—"

"Or nothing," a new voice said.

Detective Murphy pushed through the crowd. Behind him, state police. A lot of state police.

"Julia Kane, you're under arrest for conspiracy to commit murder. For your role in the deaths of—"

Julia laughed. "You can't arrest me. I'm saving this town. You don't understand what you've done. Without the ritual—"

"Without the ritual, this town might finally start healing."

Margaret Wu stepped forward. She held a box. Old. Leather. Cracked with age.

"I found these in the town hall archives," Margaret said. "The original Collectors' meeting notes. Confessions. Proof that the curse was fabricated. Proof of every murder. Every coverup." She opened the box. "This ends tonight."

Julia's face drained of color. "You can't—those are supposed to be destroyed—"

"They were hidden. But I found them." Margaret looked at the crowd. At the people who'd lived their whole lives in fear of a lie. "There is no curse. There never was. Just men who killed a child and built an empire of terror to hide it."

The crowd wavered. Uncertain. Afraid. Angry.

Then someone started crying. A woman in the back.

"My daughter," she sobbed. "My daughter was taken in '04. They said it was the ritual. They said it was necessary. She was twelve."

Another voice. A man. "My nephew in '97."

"My sister in '83."

"My son—"

"My baby—"

The crowd fell apart. Some ran. Some collapsed. Some just stood there as decades of lies crashed down on them.

Julia backed away. "No. No, you don't understand. The ritual has to continue or—"

"Or what?" Murphy grabbed her arm. "Or the truth comes out? That's already happening."

Julia looked at the house. At me standing in the window.

"You've killed us all," she said.

Then the ground opened beneath her feet and swallowed her whole.

Twenty-Eight

Chapter 28: The Truth of the Curse

S arah pov

My hands burned on the rope.

Max's fingers were ice when they locked around my wrist.

"Mom—"

"I've got you. I've got you."

I pulled. My shoulders screamed. The rope bit into my palms through the leather gloves Tucker had given me. Below us, the well went down forever. Black water. Reaching hands made of bone and rage. Voices screaming in languages I didn't know.

"Pull!" Melissa shouted from above.

I pulled.

Max came up inch by inch. His lips were blue. His eyes were unfocused. But he was breathing. He was alive.

"Almost there," I gasped. "Almost—"

His weight suddenly lightened. Tucker was hauling on the rope, his face purple with effort. Father Gabriel gripped my waist. Together, we dragged Max over the well's crumbling stone edge.

I collapsed on the basement floor with my son in my arms.

He was so cold.

"Blankets," I said. "Now."

Melissa was already stripping off her jacket, wrapping it around Max's shaking body. Isaac threw me the emergency blanket from his pack. I cocooned Max in it, rubbing his arms, his legs, trying to force warmth back into him.

"Max. Max, look at me."

His eyes found mine. Slowly.

"M-Mom?"

"I'm here."

"Ben tried to—he said I had to—"

"Shh. It's over. You're safe."

But even as I said it, I knew it wasn't true.

The basement shook.

Dust rained from the ceiling. The single bulb Tucker had rigged swung wildly, throwing shadows across the stone walls. All around us, the dead were manifesting. Dozens of them. Colonial dresses and rope burns. Victorian suits and gunshot wounds. Children in nightgowns with blue lips.

They formed a circle around our group.

Behind them, the well pulsed with dark light.

"We're out of time," Father Gabriel said. His face was gray. Blood still stained his collar from where Julia—possessing Melissa—had clawed him. "Eleven thirty-five. Twenty-five minutes until midnight."

"The explosives are set," Tucker said. He had his phone out, the detonator app glowing on the screen. "Say the word and I blow this thing to hell."

"Not yet." Isaac's voice was sharp. "The spirits are too agitated. If we destroy the well now, we might release them all at once. The psychic backlash could—"

"Could what?" Melissa snapped. "We're already trapped in a basement with fifty ghosts and a possessed well. How much worse can it get?"

The Woman in White stepped forward.

The other spirits parted for her like she was royalty.

She looked different now. More solid. More real. Her dress wasn't white anymore—it was red at the hem, like she'd been walking through blood. Her face was beautiful and terrible. Eyes that had seen three hundred years of suffering.

"You cannot destroy what you do not understand," she said.

Her voice echoed wrong. Like it was coming from the walls. From beneath our feet.

"Then help us understand," I said.

I stood slowly, keeping Max behind me. My legs shook. My hands were still numb from the cold of the well. But I made myself meet her eyes.

"You wanted me to sacrifice my daughter. You said Lily was chosen. You said the ritual had to be completed or the street would be consumed. Why?"

The Woman in White tilted her head.

"You ask the wrong question, Sarah Brennan."

"Then what's the right question?"

"Not why. Who."

Behind her, Victor Kane's ghost materialized. He looked more decayed than before. His face was a mask of rot. His suit was stained with old blood—his own, from the gunshot that killed him.

"The ritual must be completed," Victor said. His voice rattled like bones in a bag. "I failed in 1963. But you can succeed. Give us the girl. Save your son. Save yourself. Save the street."

"No," I said.

"Sarah—" Melissa's hand was on my arm. "Maybe we should—"

"No."

I pulled away from her. Stepped closer to Victor's ghost. Close enough to smell the death coming off him.

"You murdered your wife," I said. "You drowned your son. You want me to believe you care about saving anyone?"

Victor's rotting face twisted into something like a smile.

"I was protecting my family line. The ritual requires sacrifice, but it ensures prosperity for those who remain. The Collectors understood this. Survival requires hard choices."

"Bullshit."

The word came out harder than I expected. Louder. It echoed in the basement, and several of the spirits flinched.

Victor's smile vanished.

"You dare—"

"I dare. Because I know what you did. I read Eleanor's diary. I found her body in the backyard with her mouth sewn shut. I know the truth."

"You know nothing."

"I know you killed her because she tried to run. Because she wouldn't let you murder Benjamin for your ritual. Because she discovered something that terrified her more than you did."

I was shaking now. Not from fear. From rage.

"What did Eleanor find out, Victor? What secret was so dangerous you had to silence her permanently?"

Victor's ghost flickered.

Behind him, other spirits began to murmur. Their voices created a sound like wind through dead trees.

"Tell her," Eleanor's ghost said.

She appeared next to Victor. But she didn't look at him. She looked at me. Her throat was still torn where the rope had been. Her lips were still stitched with black thread.

Somehow, she spoke anyway.

"Tell her the truth you made me die for."

Victor's ghost lunged at Eleanor, but he passed through her like smoke through smoke.

"You will be silent!" he roared.

"I've been silent for sixty-two years," Eleanor said. "I'm done."

She turned to me. And even though her mouth couldn't move, I heard her words crystal clear.

"There is no curse, Sarah. There never was."

The basement went silent.

Even the other ghosts stopped moving.

"What?" I whispered.

Eleanor drifted closer. Her presence was cold but not malevolent. Sad. So unbearably sad.

"The Collectors created the ritual in 1897," she said. "Not to appease ancient spirits. Not to balance books with the dead. They created it to justify murder."

"That's not—" Victor started.

"It's true," Eleanor said. "I found their original meeting notes in Victor's safe. I read them the week before he killed me. The Collectors needed a way to eliminate weak links in their families. Children with disabilities. Wives who knew too much. Heirs who asked too many questions. So they invented a curse. They built this house on the hanging ground deliberately. They brought in a medium who taught them just enough occult practice to make it seem real."

My stomach turned.

"They murdered people," I said. "For money. For power."

"For control," Eleanor said. "Every seven years, they eliminated someone inconvenient and called it sacrifice. They used fear and superstition to make their families comply. Anyone who refused was ostracized. Ruined. Sometimes killed and made to look like accidents."

"That's a lie!" Victor's ghost was coming apart at the edges. Literally. Pieces of him were flaking away like ash. "The curse is real! The dead demand payment!"

"The dead demand nothing," The Woman in White said.

Everyone turned to her.

She stood perfectly still. Her red-hemmed dress pooling on the floor like blood.

"I was the first to die on this ground," she said. "1692. I was hanged for refusing to reveal where I hid my daughter. The colonists thought I was a witch. I was just a mother who wouldn't let them hang a child."

Her voice cracked.

"After I died, I stayed. I watched them bury the condemned in unhallowed ground. I watched the earth soak up their fear and pain. I watched the land... remember."

"What does that mean?" Isaac asked. He was scribbling notes frantically, his occult training fighting with the reality in front of us.

"Trauma saturates places," The Woman in White said. "Violent death. Anguish. Terror. It seeps into the soil like poison into water. This ground has held three hundred years of suffering. It became… aware. Hungry. Not cursed. Just scarred."

She looked at me.

"When the Collectors began their murders here in 1897, they fed the land's hunger. Each sacrifice added to the weight. Each death increased the psychic pressure. The spirits didn't demand the ritual. The ritual created spirits that believed they should demand it."

"A self-fulfilling prophecy," Father Gabriel breathed. "Dear God."

"Not God," The Woman in White said. "Just humans. Doing what humans do best. Creating suffering and calling it necessity."

Victor's ghost was barely visible now.

"You're lying," he said. But his voice was weak. "The Collectors saved this town. The prosperity—"

"Came from stolen land and insider trading and criminal enterprise," Eleanor said. "Not from rituals. Not from magic. From the same corruption that's always made powerful men rich."

"Benjamin." I looked around the basement, searching for the small ghost who'd been haunting my son. "Where's Benjamin?"

The child ghost appeared beside the well. He looked… different. Less decayed. Almost peaceful.

"I'm here," he said. His voice was high and clear. A little boy's voice.

"Did your father really drown you for a ritual?" I asked. "Or did he murder you to keep you quiet about what he'd done to your mother?"

Benjamin looked at Victor's ghost.

"He drowned me because I saw him kill Mama," Benjamin said. "I was hiding in the closet. I saw everything. He told me we were playing a game. That I had to go swimming in the well. That I'd come back up if I loved him enough."

My hands clenched into fists.

"He murdered you to silence you. Then he killed himself and made it look like a ritual gone wrong. He hid behind the curse to cover up domestic violence and child murder."

"You understand nothing!" Victor's ghost was nearly gone now. Just a voice and a flicker of shadow. "I did what was necessary! The ritual required—"

"The ritual required nothing," I said. "Because there was no ritual. Just a convenient excuse for weak men to kill their families."

I turned to The Woman in White.

"You said you're not the curse. You said you're the consequence. What does that mean?"

Her red-hemmed dress began to glow.

"For three hundred years, I have been the witness," she said. "I have carried the weight of every soul buried in this ground. Every hanged witch. Every murdered child. Every sacrificed wife. Their anguish became my anguish. Their rage became my rage."

"So you are the curse," Melissa said.

"No. I am what their curse created. A guardian made of grief. I did not demand sacrifice. But when the Collectors began killing here, I... responded. I reached out to their victims. I showed them the truth. I helped their spirits manifest. I gave voice to the voiceless."

"You traumatized families," Father Gabriel said quietly. "You made them see ghosts. Hear knocking. Experience the terror their ancestors inflicted."

"Yes," The Woman in White said. "Because someone had to. Someone had to make the cost visible. Someone had to force the truth into the light."

"But you threatened my daughter," I said. "You told me Lily had to die or the street would be consumed."

"I told you what the Collectors' spirits believe. What generations of ritualistic murder has conditioned the land to expect. The psychic pattern is real, Sarah. Even if the original curse was not. At midnight on Halloween, the weight of three hundred years will reach critical mass. This ground will convulse. And yes—the street will collapse. The houses will sink. People will die."

"Unless we complete the ritual," Melissa said.

"Unless you break the pattern," The Woman in White said.

The basement shook again.

Harder this time.

Cracks appeared in the walls. Dust poured from the ceiling. The well's stone rim crumbled, pieces falling into the black water below.

"Eleven forty-two," Tucker said. His finger hovered over the detonator. "Whatever we're doing, we need to do it now."

"How do we break the pattern?" I asked.

The Woman in White looked at me.

Really looked at me.

And for the first time, I saw past the ghost. Past the three hundred years of pain. I saw the woman she'd been. The mother who'd hidden her daughter. Who'd died to protect her child.

Just like Eleanor.

Just like every mother who'd been murdered here because they refused to sacrifice their children.

"Tell the truth," The Woman in White said. "Refuse the ritual. Speak it out loud. Break the lie that has fed this ground for one hundred and twenty-seven years."

"That's it?" Isaac asked. "That's all it takes?"

"Truth is never simple," she said. "And this truth has been buried under a century of blood. But yes. Speak it. Believe it. Make it real."

I looked around the basement.

At Melissa, bleeding and exhausted. At Tucker, finger on the trigger. At Father Gabriel, clutching his rosary with shaking hands. At Isaac, his scientific mind trying to reconcile the impossible.

At Max, wrapped in blankets, alive because I'd refused to leave him behind.

At Lily, standing at the top of the basement stairs. I hadn't seen her come down. But there she was. My daughter. Watching. Waiting.

"I need everyone to hear this," I said.

My voice was steady.

I stepped into the center of the spirit circle.

"I am Sarah Brennan. I bought this house with my children. I was told there was a curse. I was told a ritual was necessary. I was told my daughter had to die to save others."

The spirits pressed closer.

"I'm telling you all—spirits, Collectors, whatever you are—the curse is a lie. The ritual is a lie. The Collectors murdered their families for money and power and dressed it up as necessity. There is no ancient debt. There is no balance to maintain. There is only trauma pretending to be destiny."

Victor's ghost screamed.

It was the sound of something breaking.

"I refuse the ritual," I said louder. "I refuse the sacrifice. I refuse to participate in a cycle of violence created by men who were too weak to admit they were just murderers."

"Sarah—" Melissa's voice was tight with fear.

"I refuse," I said again. "And I'm calling out every member of the Collectors, living and dead, who benefited from this lie. You are not protectors. You are not martyrs. You are murderers who hid behind superstition because you were too cowardly to face what you'd done."

The basement exploded with sound.

Fifty ghosts began speaking at once. Screaming. Arguing. Some were shouting at me. Some were shouting at each other. Some were crying.

The well erupted.

Black water geysered up, hitting the ceiling. But it wasn't water anymore. It was memory. It was pain made visible. I saw flashes of every death that had happened here. Every sacrifice. Every murder dressed up as ritual.

I saw a young woman thrown into the well in 1904.

I saw a teenage boy shot in the basement in 1918.

I saw a little girl drowned in the bathtub upstairs in 1939.

I saw them all.

"You see?" The Woman in White's voice cut through the chaos. "You see what they did. Generation after generation. All of them claiming necessity. All of them lying."

"I see," I said.

Tears were streaming down my face.

"I see. And I'm sorry. I'm so sorry for what was done to you. But it ends now. No more sacrifices. No more lies. No more children murdered because adults were too selfish to stop themselves."

The water from the well began to recede.

The spirits grew quieter.

Victor's ghost was gone completely now. Just gone. Like he'd never been there.

Other Collectors' spirits were fading too. Their forms coming apart. Their voices disappearing.

But the victims' spirits—the ones who'd been sacrificed—they grew stronger.

Brighter.

The Woman in White walked to me.

She reached out her hand.

I took it.

Her skin was cold. But not painful. Just... present.

"You broke the pattern," she said. "No ritual. No sacrifice. Just truth."

"Will it be enough?" I asked.

"I don't know," she admitted. "The land has been scarred for so long. The psychic weight is enormous. But you've stopped feeding it. You've stopped giving it permission to demand blood. That's a start."

The basement shook again.

"Eleven fifty-six," Tucker said. "Four minutes."

"Set off the explosives," I said.

"What?"

"The well is the anchor point. The physical manifestation of the lie. We destroy it, we destroy the last piece of the ritual's power."

Isaac was nodding frantically.

"She's right. The well is where the sacrifices happened. Where the bodies were hidden. It's the focal point for the psychic energy. If we collapse it—"

"We might release all that energy at once," Father Gabriel warned. "It could be catastrophic."

"Or it could finally let these spirits go," I said.

I looked at The Woman in White.

"What do you think?"

She smiled. It was a sad smile. But genuine.

"I think I'm tired," she said. "I think we're all tired. Three hundred years is long enough."

"Do it," I said to Tucker.

"Everyone upstairs. Now!" Tucker started herding people toward the stairs. "Move! Move!"

I grabbed Max. Melissa grabbed Lily. Father Gabriel and Isaac scrambled up the stairs ahead of us.

The spirits parted to let us through.

As I reached the stairs, I looked back.

The Woman in White stood beside the well. Other victim spirits gathered around her. Benjamin's ghost held her hand. Eleanor's ghost stood on her other side.

They were all fading.

But they were smiling.

"Thank you," The Woman in White said. "For breaking the chain."

"I'm sorry it took so long," I said.

"So are we."

Then we were running.

Up the basement stairs. Through the kitchen. Into the hallway. Tucker was shouting at everyone to get outside, to get clear of the house.

But the front door wouldn't open.

"It's locked!" Melissa yanked on the handle. "It's still locked!"

"Windows!" I ran to the parlor. The window was sealed shut. So was the one in the dining room. Every exit was still blocked.

"We're trapped," Lily said.

She didn't sound scared. Just... resigned.

"Eleven fifty-eight," Tucker said. "I'm detonating in ninety seconds whether we're clear or not. If that well explodes while we're all in the basement—"

"The house won't let us out," Isaac said. He was checking every window, every door, his movements frantic. "It's still operating under the old rules. It thinks the ritual needs to be completed."

"Then we convince it otherwise," I said.

313

I walked to the center of the parlor.

"House," I said. "I know you can hear me. I know you're aware. You've been traumatized. You've absorbed three hundred years of death and pain. But it's over. The ritual is ended. The lie is exposed. Let us go."

Nothing happened.

"Please," Lily said. She walked up beside me. Put her small hand in mine. "Please. We're not going to hurt you anymore. No more blood. No more sacrifice. You can rest now."

The house groaned.

Every window rattled. Every door shuddered.

And then—

The front door swung open.

"Go!" Tucker shouted. "Go now!"

We ran.

Out the front door. Across the porch. Down the steps. Into the front yard. As far from the house as we could get.

Tucker pulled out his phone.

"Eleven fifty-nine," he said. "Detonating."

He pressed the button.

For three seconds, nothing happened.

Then the house shook.

The basement exploded.

The sound was like the earth splitting open. Fire and smoke and dust erupted from every window. The house shuddered. Cracked. Began to collapse in on itself.

And then—midnight.

Every clock in Hollow's End chimed twelve.

The ground beneath Halloween Street convulsed.

I grabbed my children and held on.

Twenty-Nine

Chapter 29: midnight approaches

Sarah pov

The basement is chaos.

Max is in my arms. He's shaking. His skin is ice cold and his lips are blue but he's breathing. He's alive. That's all that matters.

"Tucker, set the charges!" Isaac is shouting. His voice cracks. "We have ten minutes!"

"I'm trying!" Tucker's hands are shaking as he presses C4 against the well's stone base. "The stone won't—it keeps moving—"

The well is breathing. I can see it. The stones expand and contract like lungs. Black water bubbles up from below, spilling over the collapsed grate. It doesn't flow like water should. It crawls.

Melissa stumbles toward me. Her face is white. There's blood on her temple where Julia threw her against the wall before I pulled Max out.

"Sarah." Her voice is raw. "We need to leave. Now."

"We can't leave." Father Gabriel is on his knees by the protective circle Isaac drew. Salt and iron filings. Rowan wood branches. His hands are clasped in prayer but I can see them shaking. "If we run, it follows. You saw what happened to Beck."

Officer Beck. He tried to run three hours ago when the spirits first manifested. We heard him screaming from outside. Then nothing.

The house won't let us leave anyway. Every door sealed at sunset. Every window. We're trapped until midnight.

I look at the watch Tucker set on the floor. 11:51 PM.

Nine minutes.

"Mom." Lily's voice is small. She's standing at the edge of Isaac's circle, staring at the well. "Do you hear that?"

I hear everything. The house is screaming. Floorboards above us groan and crack. Walls split open. The temperature dropped to freezing the moment the Harvest Moon hit its peak. Our breath comes out in clouds.

And the knocking. God, the knocking. It's everywhere now. Not just three knocks. Hundreds. Thousands. Every surface. Every wall. The dead demanding entry.

"Lily, stay in the circle." My voice doesn't sound like mine. "Don't move."

She doesn't listen. She never listens.

She takes a step toward the well.

"Lily!" I try to get up but Max won't let go. His fingers dig into my coat. He's not speaking. Hasn't spoken since I pulled him out. His eyes are open but unfocused. Shock.

"I hear him," Lily says. "Benjamin. He's calling me."

"No." Melissa moves fast. She grabs Lily's arm. "You're not going near that thing."

"He's scared." Lily's eyes are wet. "Aunt Melissa, he's so scared. He doesn't understand why his father did this. He doesn't understand why he's still here."

The well erupts.

Water shoots up like a geyser. Black and thick and wrong. It hits the ceiling and splashes down around us. Where it touches skin it burns. Melissa screams. Lily screams. I cover Max's face and feel drops hit my back.

It's not water. It's cold and oily and it smells like rot. Like three hundred years of death.

"The charges!" Isaac is pulling Tucker back. "Set them now!"

"They won't stick!" Tucker's face is desperate. "The stone is too wet—too cold—the adhesive won't—"

The basement door flies open.

Julia Kane stands at the top of the stairs.

But it's not just Julia. There are others behind her. Shapes in the darkness. People but not people. They're dressed in old clothes. Victorian. Colonial. Their faces are gray. Their eyes are holes.

"You can't destroy the well." Julia's voice echoes. Layered. Multiple voices speaking through her mouth. "The ritual must be completed. Our families require it."

She starts down the stairs. The others follow.

I count six. Eight. Ten. They keep coming.

"Sarah Brennan." Julia stops three steps from the bottom. "Your daughter carries the blood. Eleanor's blood. The ritual was interrupted in 1963. It must be finished."

"There is no ritual." My voice shakes but I force the words out. "You murdered your own children. For money. For power. You called it a curse but it was just murder."

"It was survival." Another voice. A man in a suit from the 1920s. His throat is cut. "The land demands payment. It always has. Since 1692."

"We didn't create the curse." A woman in a colonial dress. Her wrists are tied with rope. Ligature marks. "We simply learned to feed it. To control it. To profit from it."

"Seventeen families." Julia's smile is wrong. Too wide. "Seventeen sacrifices over 127 years. Seventeen inheritances preserved. Seventeen scandals buried. Seventeen futures secured."

"You're murderers." Father Gabriel struggles to stand. "You killed children."

"We saved the town." Julia takes another step. "Without the ritual, the dead rise. Hollow's End burns. Everyone dies. Our sacrifice protects thousands."

"Liar." Isaac's voice is cold. "I've studied this. There is no mass rising. The curse is focused. Contained. It only affects this house because you keep feeding it. You keep bringing victims here."

"Because if we stop—" Julia's face twists. "If we stop, the truth comes out. Our families fall. We face justice for what our ancestors did."

"So you keep killing." Melissa's voice breaks. "You keep murdering to cover up the murders."

"Yes." Julia's voice is simple. Honest. Horrible. "We do."

11:53 PM.

Seven minutes.

The spirits move closer. They form a half-circle around us. Blocking the stairs. Blocking escape.

"Give us the girl," Julia says. "Or we take all of you."

"No." I hold Max tighter. "You're not touching her."

"Then you condemn forty-seven people to death." The man with the cut throat gestures up. "Everyone on Halloween Street. The well collapses, the barrier breaks, and the mass grave opens. Three hundred years of angry dead. They'll tear this street apart."

"You're lying." But my voice wavers.

"Am I?" Julia smiles. "Eleanor thought we were lying too. Victor told her the truth in the end. Right before he shot her. Right before he drowned their son. He knew. He understood. One child or an entire community. One sacrifice or mass death."

"He murdered them!" I'm shouting now. "He murdered his wife and son!"

"He did what had to be done." Julia's voice is soft. Pitying. "And so must you."

Lily pulls away from Melissa. Before anyone can stop her, she walks toward Julia.

"Lily, no!" I try to stand but my legs won't work. Max's weight. The cold. Fear.

"I'll do it." Lily's voice is steady. Too steady for a ten-year-old. "I'll go to the well. Just let my mom and Max and Aunt Melissa leave first."

"No!" I'm screaming. "Lily, get back here!"

"Lily, don't." Melissa is crying. "Please don't."

"A wise choice." Julia reaches for Lily's hand. "The blood knows. Eleanor's blood calls to—"

"But I have a question first." Lily stops just out of reach. "If the curse is real, if the ritual works, why are you dead?"

Julia freezes.

"You said you were Victor's niece. You said you survived because your mother completed the ritual in 1963. But you're a ghost. You're one of them." Lily points at the spirits behind Julia. "So the ritual didn't save you. You died anyway."

"I—" Julia's form flickers. "I lived until—"

"Until when?" Lily's voice gets stronger. "How old were you when you died? Twenty? Thirty? Did the ritual protect you? Or did the other Collectors kill you when you knew too much?"

The spirits behind Julia shift. Whisper. Their forms blur and merge.

"She's right." A woman's voice from the mass of dead. "Julia died in 1989. Car accident. Except it wasn't an accident."

"Shut up." Julia's voice splits. One voice desperate. One cold. "The girl must—"

"You were going to expose them." The same woman pushes forward. I recognize her. Margaret Wu's grandmother. The Kane's housekeeper. "You tried to tell the truth about Victor. About Eleanor. About Benjamin. So they killed you too."

"No." Julia's shaking. Her form is splitting apart. "I believed. I kept the secret. I protected the families."

"You tried to save Eleanor." The housekeeper's ghost is sad. "You helped her pack. You were going to drive her and Benjamin to Boston. But Victor found out. And after he killed them, the other Collectors couldn't trust you. You were a loose end."

"Stop." Julia's voice is breaking. Human now. Not layered anymore. "Stop, please."

"They ran you off the road." The housekeeper moves closer. "Made it look like drunk driving. You were twenty-six years old. You had a daughter. They killed you and they took your daughter and they raised her in the lie."

Julia collapses. She's on her knees. Her form is flickering between solid and transparent.

"My daughter." Her voice is small. "Where is my daughter?"

"She had a daughter too." The housekeeper kneels beside Julia. "And that daughter had a daughter. Your bloodline continued. But they never knew

319

about you. The Collectors erased you from the family tree."

"No." Julia's crying. Gray tears. "No, I sacrificed everything. I kept the secret. I protected them."

"And they murdered you for it." Lily's voice is gentle now. "Just like they murdered everyone who tried to tell the truth."

The other spirits are shifting. Changing. Their faces clear. They're not all Collectors. Some are. But most are victims. Children. Wives. Husbands. People who refused. People who resisted.

"You're not the curse." Lily looks at all of them. "You're prisoners. They trapped you here. They used you to scare people. To justify more killing."

"Yes." The housekeeper stands. "We're not demons. We're not evil. We're just people who died badly and couldn't move on because this place is poison."

"The land isn't cursed." Isaac's voice is shaking. "The well isn't magic. It's just a well."

"The Collectors made you believe you had to stay." Lily takes another step toward Julia. "They made you think you were the curse. But you're just victims. Like Benjamin. Like Eleanor. Like me."

11:55 PM.

Five minutes.

Julia looks up at Lily. Her face is breaking apart. Reforming. She's not possessed anymore. She's just herself. A woman who died forty-three years ago. A woman who tried to save a life and paid with her own.

"I'm sorry." Julia's voice is clear now. Human. "I'm so sorry. I believed them. I thought—I thought if I helped complete the ritual, if I brought more families here, I could finally rest. But they lied. They've always lied."

"It's okay." Lily reaches out. Takes Julia's ghostly hand. "You can rest now. You don't have to help them anymore."

"But the well—" Julia's eyes go wide. "If Tucker destroys it, the mass grave—"

"There is no mass grave." Isaac moves forward. His voice is certain. "I found the town records. The bodies were moved in 1895. Reburied in the cemetery. The Collectors lied about that too. They needed people to believe the land was cursed. But it's just land."

"So the ritual—"

"Never did anything." Isaac's hands are shaking but his voice is steady. "The prosperity. The luck. The wealth. It all came from murdering heirs and consolidating inheritance. Simple greed. They used occult theater to hide common crime."

The spirits are dissolving. Not violently. Gently. Like fog in sunlight. They're letting go. One by one. They're leaving.

But not all of them.

Three remain. Solid. Dark. Angry.

I recognize them from the portraits. The town founders. The original Collectors.

"Clever child." The tallest one speaks. His voice is rust and smoke. "You've freed the sheep. But the wolves remain."

"We created this." Another steps forward. A woman with a rope burn on her neck. "In 1692. We came to this land to escape persecution. But we brought our persecution with us. We hanged the innocent. We took their land. We built our wealth on their bodies."

"And when their ghosts rose—" The third founder smiles. "We learned to profit from that too."

"You're not ghosts." Father Gabriel's voice is hoarse. "You're something else."

"We're the first." The tall one spreads his arms. "The first to kill in this place. The first to make murder profitable. The first to feed the land with innocent blood. We are the curse. We always have been."

"Then you're just men." Melissa's voice is cold. "Evil men who died and refused to leave."

"We are this house now." The woman laughs. "We are the walls. The foundation. The well. Destroy us and you destroy the house."

"Good." Tucker's voice is grim. He's standing by the well. The charges are set. Wired. Ready. "This house should burn."

"But the girl must stay." The tall founder points at Lily. "She carries Eleanor's blood. That blood belongs to us. We let Victor keep Eleanor for twenty years. Let her bear him a son. But she was always ours. Marked from birth. Her grandmother was a Collector's daughter. The bloodline is ours."

"Lily." I finally find my voice. "Come here. Now."

She doesn't move. She's staring at the well.

"Benjamin?" Her voice is soft. "Are you still there?"

Silence.

Then. From the well. A small voice. A child's voice.

"Lily?"

"I'm here." She moves closer. Too close. "Benjamin, can you hear me?"

"I'm cold." The child's voice is fading. "I've been cold for so long. I want my mother."

"Your mother is gone." Lily's crying now. "She died a long time ago. Your father hurt her. He hurt you. But that's over now."

"He said I had to stay. He said I had to wait. He said the ritual needed me."

"Your father lied." Lily kneels at the well's edge. "There is no ritual. There never was. He just didn't want to admit he murdered you."

"But I'm still here." Benjamin's voice is small. Confused. "Why am I still here?"

"Because you're scared to leave." Lily reaches into the well. Her hand disappears into the black water. "Because you don't know where to go."

"Lily, don't!" I'm moving now. Max slips from my arms. Melissa catches him. I'm running toward my daughter.

"It's okay, Mom." Lily doesn't look at me. "Benjamin won't hurt me. He's not like them."

"I didn't want to stay." Benjamin's voice is clearer now. "But Father said I had to. He said I was keeping Mother safe. He said if I left, Mother would be alone forever."

"Your mother's not alone." Lily's voice is gentle. "She's with my mom's friend. The housekeeper. They're together. They're free. They're waiting for you."

"Really?"

"Really." Lily's hand goes deeper into the well. "But you have to let go first. You have to stop holding onto this place. You have to stop believing your father."

"He said I was bad." Benjamin's voice breaks. "He said I made Mother want to leave. He said it was my fault."

"No." Lily's crying harder now. "No, Benjamin, you weren't bad. You were just a little boy. Your father was sick. He was evil. What he did wasn't your fault."

11:57 PM.

Three minutes.

The three founder spirits move forward. They're solid now. Corporeal. Their hands reach for Lily.

"The child must stay," they say in unison. "The well requires him. We require him. He is our anchor."

"No." A new voice. Strong. Female. Familiar.

Eleanor Kane materializes between Lily and the founders. She's not gray anymore. She's full color. Real. Her dress is wet. Her hair hangs in dark ropes. But her face is fierce.

"You will not touch my son again."

"Eleanor." The tall founder smiles. "You have no power here. You died without fighting. You let Victor silence you."

"I fought." Eleanor's voice is ice. "I fought and I lost. But I've been fighting ever since. For sixty-two years I've been fighting. Every family you brought here. Every child you tried to take. I fought. I whispered warnings. I left signs. I tried to save them."

"And failed." The woman founder laughs. "Every ritual completed. Every sacrifice made. You failed, Eleanor."

"Not every ritual." Eleanor looks at me. "Some families escaped. Some children lived. And now this mother—" She points at me. "—she solved it. She found the truth. She broke the lie."

"One family." The third founder waves dismissively. "In 127 years. One family. We still win."

"No." Eleanor's form blazes brighter. "Because she's going to tell. She's going to expose you. And everything you built will fall."

"She'll die first." The tall founder's hand shoots out. Not toward Lily. Toward me.

His fingers close around my throat. They're solid. Cold. Crushing.

323

I can't breathe. Can't scream. Can't—

"Let her go!" Lily's shouting. "Benjamin, help! Please!"

The well erupts again. But this time it's not black water. It's light. Pale blue light. Cold and clean.

Benjamin rises from the well.

He's seven years old. Blond hair. Blue eyes. He's wearing pajamas. He's soaking wet. But he's smiling.

"Let go of Lily's mom," he says. His voice is clear. Strong. "Let go or I'll leave."

The founder's grip loosens. Just slightly.

"You can't leave," the tall one says. "You're bound here. We bound you."

"You lied to me." Benjamin floats higher. He's standing on air now. "You told me I had to stay to protect Mother. But Mother doesn't need me to stay. Mother needs me to go."

"Benjamin, no—" The founder releases me. Reaches for Benjamin instead. "You don't understand. Without you, we lose our anchor. Without an anchor, we fade. We cease."

"Good." Benjamin's smile widens. "You should cease. You're bad men. You hurt people. You hurt me."

"We made you eternal!" The woman founder's voice rises. "We gave you power!"

"You gave me pain." Benjamin looks at Lily. "Thank you for telling me the truth. Thank you for helping me understand."

"You're welcome." Lily's smiling through tears. "Your mom's waiting. Over there. Can you see her?"

Benjamin turns. His face lights up. "Mother!"

I don't see Eleanor. But Benjamin does. He's looking at something behind me. Beyond me. Somewhere I can't perceive.

"Mother, I'm sorry." His voice is small. "I'm sorry I couldn't save you."

A pressure builds in the room. Warm. Gentle. Like arms wrapping around us all.

Eleanor's voice, though she's fading: "You have nothing to be sorry for, my love. Nothing. You were perfect. You are perfect. I love you."

"I love you too." Benjamin's form starts to dissolve. Not violently. Gently. Like morning mist. "Goodbye, Lily. Goodbye, everyone. Thank you for letting me go."

"No!" The three founders lunge. But they pass through him like smoke. "No! Come back! You can't—"

"I can." Benjamin's voice is distant now. "I'm free."

He's gone.

The well goes dark. Silent. Still.

11:58 PM.

Two minutes.

The founders scream. It's not human sound. It's rage and loss and the sound of power dying. They turn on us.

"If we fall, we take you with us!" The tall one's face splits open. Something dark and ancient writhes behind his features. "This house is us! We are this house! Destroy the well and the house falls!"

"I know." Tucker's hand is on the detonator. "Sarah, get Lily. Get out. Now."

"The doors—"

"Benjamin's gone. The anchor's gone. The doors will open." Tucker's voice is calm. "Isaac, get them upstairs. I'll give you thirty seconds."

"Tucker, no." I'm moving toward him. "You can't—"

"I'm old." He smiles. Sad. "Sick. Lung cancer. Six months, maybe. This is a better death. Now go."

"Tucker—" Father Gabriel starts forward.

"Go!" Tucker shouts. "I'm not asking!"

The founders are collapsing in on themselves. Their forms twist. Merge. Become something massive. Something dark. Something ancient that wears human shapes like masks but is so much older. So much worse.

"Twenty-nine seconds," Tucker says calmly. "Twenty-eight. Twenty-seven."

Isaac grabs my arm. Melissa has Max. Father Gabriel pulls Lily. We run for the stairs.

Behind us, the thing that was three founders roars. It lunges for Tucker.

"Twenty seconds," Tucker says. His voice is steady. "Nineteen. Eighteen."

We hit the stairs. The basement door is open. Light spills through. Cold

325

night air.

"Fifteen. Fourteen."

We're in the hallway. Running for the front door. It's open. Wide open. The first time since sunset.

"Ten. Nine."

We hit the front porch. Halloween Street is empty. Fog everywhere. The Harvest Moon is blood-red overhead.

"Five. Four."

We're on the lawn. Running. Fifty feet from the house. Seventy-five.

"Two."

I look back.

Tucker is standing in the basement doorway. Behind him, the darkness surges. Reaching for him with a thousand hands. But he's smiling.

"One."

The explosion is light and sound and fury.

The well collapses. The basement implodes. The entire foundation of the house cracks like an egg. The Victorian manor—three stories, wraparound porch, widow's walk—it all folds in on itself.

The sound is thunder. The light is blinding. I cover Lily and Max with my body. Melissa covers us. Father Gabriel shields us all.

The house is screaming. The founders are screaming. Three hundred years of lies and murder and darkness—all of it collapsing.

And then. Silence.

11:59 PM.

I look up.

The Last House on Halloween Street is gone. Just rubble. Just broken stone and splintered wood and settling dust.

The fog is clearing. The moon's light is normal now. Silver, not red.

The street is quiet.

"Is it over?" Lily's voice is muffled against my chest.

"I think—" I start to say yes.

Then the rubble shifts.

Something crawls out from beneath the wreckage.

It's not Tucker.

It's tall. Dark. Its limbs are too long. Its face is wrong. It's everything the founders were hiding beneath their human masks.

And it's looking right at us.

"Run," Father Gabriel whispers.

The thing smiles.

And midnight strikes.

Thirty

Chapter 30: The House After Halloween

Sarah pov

The explosion threw me backwards.

My ears rang. Dust choked my lungs. I couldn't see anything through the smoke and debris.

"Max!" I screamed. "Lily!"

"Mom!" Lily's voice cut through the ringing. "Mom, I'm here!"

I crawled forward. My hands scraped against broken floorboards. Something wet soaked through my jeans—water from the collapsed well, or blood, I couldn't tell.

"Sarah!" Melissa coughed somewhere to my left. "Sarah, answer me!"

"I'm okay." My throat burned. "Where's Max?"

"I've got him." Tucker's voice, rough and strained. "He's breathing. He's alive."

The smoke began to clear. Gray dawn light filtered through the destroyed basement ceiling. Half the floor above had collapsed. I could see straight up into the kitchen.

The house was dying. Finally.

I found Lily pressed against the far wall, covered in dust but uninjured. I pulled her into my arms.

"It's over," I whispered. "It's over."

But even as I said it, I felt them.

The cold came first. Not the brutal, bone-deep freeze of the past month. This was gentler. Softer. Like winter morning air.

"Mom." Lily's grip tightened on my arm. "Look."

Three figures stood in the ruins of the basement.

Eleanor Kane. Benjamin. And the Woman in White.

But they weren't the twisted, vengeful things from Halloween night. Eleanor looked young, peaceful. Benjamin held her hand, smiling. Even the Woman in White—the thing that had terrorized us—seemed lighter. Transparent.

"Sarah." Eleanor's voice was barely a whisper. "Thank you."

I couldn't speak. My throat closed.

"You broke it," Benjamin said. His voice was a child's voice. Sweet. Normal. "The lie. You told the truth."

The Woman in White moved closer. I flinched, but Lily stayed still.

"For three hundred and thirty years," the Woman said, "I have been bound here by their cruelty. By the lies they told about curses and rituals. By the blood they spilled and called it necessary."

"I'm sorry," I managed. "I'm so sorry for what they did to you."

She almost smiled. "You freed us all. The ones buried beneath this street. The ones silenced. The children taken. We can leave now."

"Where will you go?" Lily asked.

Eleanor knelt beside her. For a moment, I saw the mother she'd been. Desperate. Protective. Willing to die to save her son.

"Somewhere without pain," Eleanor said. "Somewhere we can rest."

Benjamin waved at Max, who stared back with wide eyes.

"Goodbye, Max," Benjamin said. "You were a good friend."

"Bye, Ben," Max whispered.

The three spirits turned toward the collapsed well. Toward the morning light streaming through the broken ceiling.

They walked into the light.

And dissolved like mist.

The temperature returned to normal. The pressure that had squeezed the house for a month—that crushing, suffocating weight—lifted.

I could breathe.

"Jesus Christ." Tucker stood, limping. Blood ran down his temple. "Did that just—did they just—"

"They're gone," Father Gabriel said from the stairs. He'd stayed above ground during the explosion, too injured to descend. "The dead have finally been released."

Melissa pulled herself upright, wincing. "Is anyone hurt? Max, baby, are you okay?"

"I'm cold," Max said. "And wet. But I'm okay."

Sirens wailed in the distance.

"That'll be Murphy," Tucker said. "I called him before we blew the well. Figured we'd need cops if we survived."

"If we survived," I repeated. "God."

I looked at my children. At my sister. At the people who'd helped us fight. We'd survived.

We'd actually survived.

Detective Murphy arrived with six state police cars and an ambulance.

He took one look at the destroyed house and his face went pale.

"What the hell happened here?" he demanded.

"Gas leak," Tucker said smoothly. "Old pipes. The whole system went up."

"Gas leak." Murphy's eyes narrowed. "Right. And the supernatural activity you reported all month?"

"Mass hallucination from carbon monoxide poisoning," I said. "That's what it was, wasn't it?"

Murphy stared at me. Then at the house. Then back at me.

"You're telling me there's a rational explanation for all of this."

"Isn't there?" I asked.

He opened his mouth. Closed it. Looked at the ruined Victorian, at the collapsed basement, at the four of us standing there covered in dust and blood.

"I'll need statements," he finally said. "From all of you."

"Of course," I said. "But first—Detective, there's something in the basement you need to see."

The chamber beneath the well had been exposed by the explosion.

It was older than the house. Older than the street. Stone walls carved with symbols that made my skin crawl even now, with the spirits gone.

And inside—

"Don't touch anything," Murphy ordered the state police. "This is a crime scene."

Crime scene didn't begin to cover it.

Seventeen stone tablets lined the walls. Each one carved with a name, a date, and a family crest.

Sarah Mitchell - 1897 - Age 9

Thomas Ashton - 1904 - Age 12

Grace Winters - 1911 - Age 8

On and on. Seventeen names. Seventeen children. Seventeen sacrifices spread across 127 years.

"My God," one of the state troopers whispered. "This is a mass murder evidence room."

But it wasn't just the tablets.

Ritual tools lay arranged on a stone altar. Knives. Bowls. Candles burned down to stumps. And books—leather-bound journals dating back to 1897, filled with meeting minutes from something called "The Collectors' Society."

Murphy picked up one of the journals with gloved hands. He read silently for a long moment.

"This is…" He looked sick. "This is a record of organized child murder spanning over a century."

"They called it a ritual," I said quietly. "An appeasement to a curse. But it was just murder. Powerful families killing their own children and calling it necessary."

"The Collectors," Murphy read. "Founding members: Thomas Cromwell, Jonathan Wright, Robert Ashton Senior, Victor Kane, Samuel Winters." He looked up. "These are the oldest families in Hollow's End. The wealthiest families."

"And their descendants have been covering it up ever since," Melissa said. "Selling this house to vulnerable families every seven years. Pretending it was haunted to hide the real crime."

Murphy's radio crackled.

"Detective?" a voice said. "We've got a situation at 47 Maple Street. You need to come see this."

Murphy's jaw tightened. "What kind of situation?"

"A body, sir. Julia Kane. She's been dead for hours."

Julia's house was three blocks from Halloween Street.

They found her in her living room, seated in an armchair, hands folded in her lap. Like she'd just sat down and died.

The medical examiner said it was a massive stroke. Estimated time of death: 9:30 PM on Halloween night.

"That's impossible," I said. "She was at the house after that. She was—"

I stopped. Because how could I explain that Julia had been possessing my sister? That her spirit had attacked us while her body died alone in her living room?

Murphy watched me carefully. "She was what?"

"Nothing," I said. "I'm confused. The last few days have been…"

"Traumatic," he finished. "I understand. But Ms. Brennan, I need you to be straight with me. When was the last time you saw Julia Kane alive?"

I thought about the rules. About what I could say without sounding insane.

"She came to the house yesterday afternoon," I said. It wasn't quite a lie. Her body hadn't been there, but her spirit had. "She was trying to convince me to… to stay. She said the house was important. That Halloween Street had a purpose."

"A purpose." Murphy wrote that down. "And what purpose would that be?"

"Maintaining the lie," Father Gabriel said from behind us. "Julia Kane was Victor's niece. She survived the 1963 ritual because her mother completed it—sacrificed Julia's younger brother. Julia spent her entire life protecting the secret."

Murphy turned to him. "You're telling me this woman was complicit in child murder?"

"I'm telling you she was a victim who became an accomplice," Father Gabriel said. "Trauma does terrible things to people. Makes them believe the unbelievable. Julia convinced herself the ritual was necessary. That the curse was real. Because accepting the truth—that her brother was murdered for nothing—would have destroyed her."

Murphy was quiet for a long time.

"I'm going to need more than folklore to build a case," he finally said.

"You have the chamber," I said. "You have the journals. You have seventeen documented victims and the names of the families responsible."

"I have evidence of historical crimes," Murphy corrected. "But most of the perpetrators are dead. And the living descendants will lawyer up and claim they had no knowledge of their ancestors' actions."

"So they get away with it?" Melissa's voice shook with anger. "They murder children for over a century and just walk away?"

"I didn't say that." Murphy's expression hardened. "I said building the case will be difficult. But I've got seventeen dead children and a conspiracy of silence that needs breaking. The state police are already contacting the FBI. This is going to be the biggest investigation Hollow's End has ever seen."

He looked at the house where Julia had died.

"And if any of those families try to run or destroy evidence, we'll know they're guilty."

One week later, we moved out.

The house was condemned. The entire foundation was unstable after the explosion. The town council voted to demolish it immediately.

I watched from Melissa's car as the wrecking ball swung.

The first impact shattered the turret windows. The second collapsed the wraparound porch. The third brought down the entire front wall.

Lily sat beside me, her hand in mine.

"Are you sad?" she asked.

"No," I said. And I meant it. "That house was never our home. It was a trap.

A lie. I'm glad it's gone."

"Me too." She leaned against my shoulder. "Will they ever find all the people who knew? About the murders?"

"I don't know, baby. Maybe. Probably not all of them."

The house collapsed completely. A cloud of dust rose into the November sky.

Max pressed his face against the window on the other side. "Ben would be happy," he said. "He hated that house."

"Yeah," I said softly. "I think he would be."

Melissa started the car. "Ready to go home? Real home?"

"Yes," I said. "God, yes."

We drove away from Halloween Street. From Hollow's End. From the town that had tried to feed my children to its guilt and lies.

Behind us, I heard the wrecking ball swing again.

And again.

And again.

Until there was nothing left.

The investigation exploded across national news within three days.

FBI agents descended on Hollow's End. They excavated the chamber beneath the house. They seized records from the town hall. They interviewed hundreds of residents.

Margaret Wu's historical exposé hit shelves two weeks later: "The Collectors: How a Murder Cult Hid Behind Halloween for Over a Century."

I read it in Melissa's living room in Boston, curled up on her couch while the kids played upstairs.

Margaret had done her research. Every victim was named. Every family was exposed. The descendants of The Collectors fought back with lawyers and PR firms, but the evidence was overwhelming.

Robert Ashton was arrested for conspiracy and fraud. He'd known about the murders and had been paid to recruit vulnerable families.

Mayor Dennis Cromwell Junior—descendant of one of the founding Collectors—resigned in disgrace.

Reverend Samuel Wright's church was investigated for covering up historical crimes.

But Margaret saved the worst revelation for the epilogue.

"In the 127 years of The Collectors' operation," she wrote, "seventeen children were ritually murdered by their own families. But excavation of Halloween Street revealed twenty-three sets of remains beneath the houses."

Twenty-three.

Six victims no one had recorded. Six children whose murders hadn't even been documented in the Collectors' meticulous journals.

Six families who'd killed and never confessed, even to their fellow conspirators.

I closed the book and stared at the wall.

How many more were there? How many victims across how many towns? How many other cursed houses hiding organized murder behind ghost stories?

My phone buzzed.

Detective Murphy: *Thought you should know - Father Gabriel performed a burial service for Eleanor and Benjamin Kane today. Hallowed ground. Full honors. Thought it might give you some peace.*

I typed back: *Thank you. It does.*

Another message came through, this time from Hannah Winters' number. But Hannah—Julia—was dead.

I opened it anyway.

This is Hannah's daughter. Found your number in her phone. Mom wanted me to tell you something if anything happened to her. She said: "Tell Sarah Brennan I'm sorry. Tell her Julia died in 1963 with her brother. The thing that lived in my mother's body after that wasn't her anymore. Tell her the curse was real—not supernatural, but real. The curse of guilt and complicity. Tell her she broke it."

I stared at the message for a long time.

Then I deleted it.

Three months later, I woke at 3:33 AM.

My bedroom was dark. Melissa's house was silent. Outside, Boston winter wind rattled the windows.

And someone knocked on my door.

Three times.

Gentle. Soft. Nothing like the thunderous pounding from Halloween Street.

My heart stopped.

No. It's over. It's finished.

But I'd learned not to ignore things that woke me at 3:33 AM.

I got up. Crossed the room. My hand shook as I reached for the doorknob.

The hallway was empty.

But on the floor, directly in front of my door, lay a single white rose.

I picked it up. It was real. Fresh. The petals were soft and perfect. It smelled like Eleanor's garden—like the roses that had grown behind the house before they all died.

"Mom?"

I spun around.

Lily stood in her doorway, rubbing her eyes. Her hair was tangled from sleep. She looked so small in her oversized pajamas.

"Baby, what are you doing up?"

"I had a dream," she said. "Mrs. Kane was there. And Ben. They were in a garden. A big garden with white roses everywhere. They looked happy."

My throat tightened.

"Mrs. Kane wanted to say thank you," Lily continued. "She said you saved them. She said they can finally rest now."

I looked down at the rose in my hand.

"She said to give you that," Lily added, nodding at the flower. "So you'd know it was real. So you'd know she's okay."

"Come here, sweetheart."

Lily walked over and I pulled her into a hug. She was warm and solid and alive. My daughter. Safe.

"Are you scared?" she asked into my shoulder.

"No," I said. And I realized it was true. "I'm not scared anymore."

"Me neither. It feels different now. Like something heavy is gone."

"It is gone," I said. "The weight. The guilt. All of it. They're free now."

Lily pulled back and looked at the rose. "What are you going to do with it?"

I held it up to the dim hallway light. The petals seemed to glow faintly. Or maybe that was just my imagination.

"I think…" I paused. "I think I'm going to let it go."

I opened my hand.

The rose petals began to fall. One by one. Drifting down like snow.

But they didn't hit the floor.

They dissolved into light. Soft, warm light. Like sunrise. Like hope.

Like forgiveness.

Lily and I watched until the last petal vanished.

The hallway was empty again. Just us. Just the normal darkness of a house at night.

"Mom," Lily whispered. "Do you think we'll ever see them again? Ben and Mrs. Kane?"

"No, baby," I said. "I think they've moved on. To somewhere better. Somewhere they don't need to come back from."

"Good," she said. "They deserve that."

"Yeah. They do."

We stood there for a moment longer. Then Lily yawned.

"I'm tired."

"Me too. Let's go back to bed."

I walked her to her room and tucked her in. She was asleep before I even closed the door.

Back in my own bedroom, I checked the time. 3:47 AM. The witching hour had passed.

I climbed into bed and closed my eyes.

And for the first time in three months—for the first time since we'd moved into that house on Halloween Street—I slept without nightmares.

No knocking at 3:33 AM.

No cold spots or phantom voices.

No ghosts demanding impossible choices.

Just sleep.

Just peace.

Just us.

Morning came soft and gray through the curtains.

I woke to the smell of coffee and the sound of Melissa making breakfast downstairs. Max's laughter echoed from the kitchen. Lily was singing in the shower.

Normal sounds. Safe sounds.

I lay there for a moment, listening.

Then I got up and went to join my family.

The nightmare was over.

We'd survived.

And that—that simple, beautiful fact—was more than enough.

Six months later

The last house on Halloween Street existed now only in photographs and news articles.

The lot where it stood remained empty. The town council debated what to do with it. Memorial park. Community garden. Something to acknowledge the victims.

But for now, it was just empty land.

I never went back to Hollow's End. Never wanted to. That chapter was closed.

But sometimes, on quiet nights when the wind rattled the windows and the old house sounds of Melissa's place settled around us, I thought about Eleanor and Benjamin.

I thought about Julia Kane, dead in her armchair, her soul split between victim and accomplice.

I thought about The Woman in White and the centuries of pain that had finally been released.

And I thought about the choice I'd made. The choice to refuse. To fight. To expose the truth instead of accepting the comfortable lie.

That's what broke the curse in the end. Not sacrifice. Not ritual. Not appeasement.

Just the truth.

The simple, terrible, liberating truth.

Some curses are real—but they're made by living hands, not supernatural forces. They're made by people who choose cruelty and call it necessity. Who choose violence and call it tradition.

And they can be broken by people who choose differently.

By mothers who refuse to sacrifice their children.

By journalists who expose secrets.

By priests who offer grace instead of damnation.

By communities that finally say: enough.

The dead don't need our blood.

They need our honesty.

They need us to remember them, acknowledge them, and refuse to repeat the sins that created them.

That's what Eleanor taught me.

That's what Halloween Street taught me.

And that's what I'd teach my children—not through ghost stories, but through the simple act of living differently. Living honestly. Living without the weight of inherited guilt.

The rose was long gone.

But its message remained:

Thank you. We can rest now. And so can you.

I carried that with me.

Every day.

Every night.

Every moment I held my children and knew they were safe.

The last house on Halloween Street was gone.

But we were still here.

Still breathing.

Still fighting.

Still free.

And that was the greatest victory of all.